GHOST

ELLE ANDREWS PATT

AN ANDREA KELLEY MYSTERY

THE ARCHIVIST BOOK 1

Blue Beech Press

Knoxville, Tennessee USA

Front cover design by Lacey Patt (laceypattphotography.com)
Back cover design by Charles A. Cornell
Cover Imagery Sources: iStockphoto.com

ISBN (PB): 978-1-7347544-1-4
ISBN (EBK): 978-1-7347544-0-7

Published by BLUE BEECH PRESS
5923 Kingston Pike
Knoxville, TN 37919

Ghost/An Andrea Kelley Mystery/The Archivist Book 1 -- 1st ed. MARCH 2020

ACKNOWLEDGEMENTS

Thank you to all the City Island Fiction Writers for initial critique and edits, but especially Veronica H. Hart, Dr. Robert Hart, Joan King, Lois Gerber, Jeff Boyle, Trish Ruffino, Matthew Hudson, the late Bob Kamholtz, and M. J. Carlson, who also beta read. Much thanks to my Time Turners, especially my First Reader, Kelley Walters and Copy Editor, Claire Wilkins (unmistakable.co.nz). Thanks also to Bruce Woodworth for the many, many Sunday writing meet-ups, Ashley Schairer for the fast read and her enthusiasm for this book, and Keith Short for taking me ghost-hunting. A huge thank you to Paul Stevens for the great suggestions and thoughtful edits that shaped the final version of this book. Much thanks also to the many people with expert knowledge in ghost hunting, law enforcement, and the other million little things that I asked about on my way to completing this work. Even the smallest tidbit carries weight when every word counts. Any mistakes or taking of authorial license to bend or break how things "really work" is on me. My fifteen years spent living in North Carolina and visiting West Virginia informed the development of my characters and story. The people of Charleston, West Virginia gamely fielded my questions, gave me tours, and generally let me be nosy about how they live. There again, I have strayed here and there for fictional purposes and security. I have a great love for the region and her peoples. Thank you to my enduring husband and family for giving me the space and time and patience that allows me to write.

—EAP

GHOST

PART I

"I DROWNDED."

Andrea eased her eyes open in the dark to squint at Billie Mae Robbins.

All of six, with flaxen hair, Billie Mae had the bluest eyes south of a sunny sky. And she glowed, just a bit, as she stood next to the bed. As usual, she wore a white cotton nightgown, the kind that only went to the knees. Today, a vivid purple bruise crossed the midpoint of her throat, thin as wire, staining the skin below it in a lighter hue until it faded above her collarbone. And today, she was drenched. Andrea's heart dropped.

"I don't think you drowned," Andrea murmured. Water dripped from the ends of Billie Mae's hair, the drops vanishing as they fell. It might not mean anything. She didn't want to wake Taka. The man lay sprawled over more than half her bed, but since he'd tracked and nailed a killer in a little over thirty-nine hours without sleep, she was letting him have more than his fair share. Plus he was big and pretty and threw a lot of body heat, a total plus during October in West Virginia.

"I drownded."

She had this conversation with Billie Mae three or four times a week with a dry Billie Mae.

"I drownded all by myself," the little girl insisted.

Andrea rolled onto her side to face her. There was another conversation they had sometimes when Andrea made bacon, which she made more now than ever simply because it was fun to see Billie Mae laugh. But this particular conversation was solemn and grave and almost always took place just before dawn broke and filled the master bedroom with muted brightness. Keeping it normal, Andrea whispered back, "I don't think you did."

"I did," Billie Mae shouted, stomping her bare foot, little fists clinched tight. Andrea flinched, even though she expected it and knew Taka couldn't hear her.

"Where?"

She pointed out the window. Fed by a branch of the Elk River, manmade Lake Vickers lay a good half-mile away. After sunrise, Andrea knew, the lake might be visible through that window as a flat grey smudge beyond the fog-wreathed reds and yellows of the trees growing across all the yards downslope from her.

"Your mother strangled you in the bathtub, Billie Mae," Andrea whispered. She made an effort to say it as a statement of fact, to not be mean, but it had been weeks upon weeks of this dialogue already. She'd move, but she loved both the house and the fifteen-minute commute south to downtown Charleston. The steep West Virginia hills above the flat river valley city demanded narrow switch-backing roads that often slowed rush hour traffic to a crawl, but her location off Greenbrier let her bypass the worst of it. The discounted rent she negotiated after the first time Billie Mae had woken her didn't hurt either.

Billie Mae's face crumpled, tears welled and then spilled onto her baby cheeks. She shook her head, her long, wet hair swinging. Andrea couldn't ignore her. She lifted the covers, letting the cool air rush in, and got up. The hardwood floor was cold beneath her bare feet. She shivered. Taka grunted and grabbed at the blankets, pulling them back in close. There were still things she needed for the house. Throw rugs and a sleeper sofa were two of them.

Andrea padded out of the room. Sniffling, Billie Mae trailed her down the hall to the bathroom and climbed into the tub to pout while Andrea went about her morning routine for her near daily run. The claw-footed tub was not the one she died in. The landlord, Kenny, tore that one out years ago. Watching Billie Mae in the mirror as Billie Mae watched her brush her teeth, Andrea saw the exact moment she blipped out of existence, leaving behind a faint whiff of earthy damp and, Andrea already knew, a small puddle in the tub. She supposed she should be grateful that the miserable little spirit didn't leave wet footprints on the hardwood floors. She'd make bacon later and see if that drew Billie Mae out in a better mood.

ANDREA WARMED UP on her driveway, jumping jacks and walking lunges. Frost covered the lawns lining the narrow, rural cul-de-sac, one of three lying back to back across the shallow, rising flatland above Two Mile Creek. Her stalwart little house, covered in cedar siding, looked sturdy, the white shutters bright. Taka's Yukon sat like a black monster behind her FX, snugged up in the carport. The little blue Infinity SUV was getting old, but she didn't like the newer ones as much and it suited her work just fine.

Yellow leaves from the maple beyond the carport covered her car and drive, some drifting out to join up forces with the huge leaves from the ancient oak in the front yard. Maybe Taka would rake for her while she mulched the scraggly beds around the azaleas along the front of the house.

She jogged down her street, but instead of crossing Timber Way, she opted for her longer route and turned right at the stop sign. Within a quarter mile, a cruiser whooshed past her, no sirens, but lights flashing. She slowed, hearing another coming behind and moved onto the grass of the nearest yard. Both turned left down Cooper, the twisting gravel track that ended at the public boat ramp for Lake Vickers. Could it really be happening again?

Picking up her pace Andrea crossed the street and ran down Cooper. The Charleston Medical Examiner's van blew past her in a cloud of dust. Close to the ramp a couple of people stood in their yards, newspapers in hand as they watched the activity. Walking again, Andrea wiped the sweat from her upper lip and then her temple. The van joined the Charleston Police Department cruisers and a Kanawha County Sheriff's Bronco parked to the left of the ramp, while a yellow Hummer and a black pick-up truck, both hitched to boat trailers, crowded the right side of the small lot at the end of the road.

A cluster of officers and three civilians, two men and one woman, who kept wiping tears from her face, stood in front of the center of attention, a late-model bass boat cocked sideways to the ramp in the shallow mud. She recognized a CPD patrolman, Eric, tying yellow crime-scene tape to a tree and waved to him.

He sauntered over, tape unspooling from one hand while he slid the other over his wind-blown hair to smooth it. "Hey, Andrea, you live near here?"

"Yeah, on Double Branch. What's happened?"

The lake rippled in the light breeze, the water grey and foreboding. She'd swum across it once, on a dare, but it gave her a chill thinking of it now. The lowered sky said they'd be getting icy rain later in the day. In the distance, three boats bobbed in and out of sight on the rough chop.

Following her gaze Eric said, "State stocked a good portion of the larger streams with trout a couple of weeks ago. Bass are still biting, too."

Andrea lifted her chin towards the group by the ramp as the ME van's stout red-faced driver joined them, clipboard in hand.

"Another kid. A lot fresher."

"Damn," Andrea muttered.

"Yeah," Eric said to the ground. He glanced up as he started walking again. "Heard Taka was interested."

"He is," Andrea said, walking alongside him. Just days ago, Andrea had called Taka, amazed that Billie Mae had appeared that morning literally dripping what smelled like pond water, something she had never done before, and fixated on the view downslope. Later that day, a child, nearly skeletal, had been pulled from the lake, the case assigned to another detective. "I'm sure he can't do anything now until he's cleared though."

"That was a hell of a takedown last night," Eric said. Taka hadn't said much when he showed up at her door, but she'd gotten some of the details from social media and the news. Taka had shot a suspect. It wasn't the first time. "Dave was there. Said Taka was a damn bear."

He'd be a damn growly bear this morning, too, and as mopey about this poor kid as Billie Mae... who had been soaking wet again this morning.

"Thanks, Eric," she said and left him to finish setting his perimeter. She retraced her steps home, forcing herself to run, even though she didn't feel like it anymore.

THE AROMA OF fresh coffee soaked the air. Andrea found Taka in the kitchen, scrambling eggs, and listening to the little TV tucked into the corner near the stove, still wearing the shorts and ratty Army tee he'd slept in. She hovered in the kitchen doorway as the reporters talked about the murder of a junior at the University of Charleston.

Although drug-related murders were becoming all too common in this part of West Virginia, they didn't normally happen to pretty, young co-eds. Add in the shooting of the suspect by unnamed cops and Saturday morning viewers with no place to go. The Charleston news anchors were almost giddy.

Taka wasn't much of a morning person at the best of times. The coverage of the murder, murky video of the shoot-out, and footage of the suspect's arrival at the hospital wouldn't help today. She knew better than to congratulate him on not killing the guy.

"I'm okay," he said without turning away from the stove. She was struck anew by the breadth of his shoulders. At six feet, Taka was not much taller than her, but built on a wide frame. A result, he said, of the Cherokee blood contributed by his grandmother to a long linage of Scots-Irish-English stock. Since she could claim that heritage herself, Andrea thought it more likely the mix of Maori and African blood laid over the Asian on his father's side. He'd recently taken up the term "person of color" and seemed a lot happier when white people like her invariably asked about his heritage. Without mercy, he'd teased her about crushing on his dominant genes ever since they'd been paired up in science at Andrew Jackson Middle, up the road in Cross Lanes.

William Taka was Andrea's best and oldest friend.

"Smells good in here," she said, even as she was suddenly overwhelmed with sadness. "Was Tracy with you?" Detective Tracy Manners was Taka's most frequent partner and workout buddy. Despite being constantly harassed for his name, he was one of the most affable, gentle men Andrea had ever met.

"Yeah. Got hit in the vest. He's bruised, but fine."

She slipped her arms around him, laying her head on his mid-back.

He patted her hands and finished cooking the eggs. When he turned off the stove and set the pan to one side, he turned and hugged her back hard. "What's up?"

"Kid in the lake."

Gripping her upper arms, he stepped back and held her away from him. "Another one?"

"Yeah, more recent."

"Did Billie Mae show this morning?"

Andrea nodded. "Soaked, just like last time."

"Eat up," he said, letting go of her.

"Taka," she said, but he was already down the hall, on the way to get dressed.

She pulled plates down, divided the eggs and dropped shredded cheese onto her portion. She poured coffee for both of them and then took her mug and her eggs to the kitchen table. Motion in the back yard beyond the large picture window caught her eye.

Billie Mae stood outside, still dripping wet.

Shocked, Andrea jumped. Her plate fell with a thunk onto the table. It overbalanced and crashed to the floor. Her coffee sloshed onto the table as she set it down. Ripping the back door open, she hurdled down the two low steps onto the concrete patio. Billie Mae walked through the maples, threading between the rhododendrons. Deep red leaves dropped from the dogwoods to the ground as she passed under their spreading branches.

"What is it," Taka hissed from the door. Andrea glanced back. Barefoot and shirtless, he held his raised Glock steady in both hands, the muzzle pointed towards the trees. He turned on one heel, smooth as ice, tracking Billie Mae's progress.

"Can you see her?"

"No. Who?"

Andrea pointed. "Billie Mae."

Taka lowered his gun. "No, the trees are moving in the breeze, though."

They were. They swayed in Billie Mae's wake.

Andrea stepped onto the brittle, brown fall grass.

"Wait," Taka said. "I need shoes."

While Andrea waited on him, Billie Mae faded at the rear property line, a long, wooded ditch that divided Andrea's yard from her downslope neighbor. He came back out in boots and his Charleston PD windbreaker. They crunched to the back of the yard, ducking between the trees. Andrea tracked right while Taka tracked left.

A darker spot of blue under a settle of leaves at the foot of a maple near her next-door neighbor's four-board fence drew Andrea's attention. She squatted and plucked the leaves back. The tiny blue Keds tennis shoe lay on its side. A streak of dirt stood out on its nearly new fabric. The white laces were untied, tangled with each other. She had no idea how it came to be there.

"Don't touch it," Taka said from over her shoulder, his shadow falling across her and drawing down the dread of gloom tickling her.

"Maybe it's not—"

"Ever seen Billie Mae outside before?"

Andrea shook her head no. "She was soaking wet."

Kneeling, Taka dropped a hand on her back. "I can't call it in, not until I talk to the guys at the lake. Can't tell them your ghost gave us evidence."

"You don't even believe—"

"I believe in you."

A churning ball of angst formed in Andrea's chest. She never thought it mattered to her if Taka didn't believe, but now she found the careful way he always spoke and the shuttered look he watched her with when she talked about Billie Mae did bother her. Would he rather believe she was psychic?

"Sorry," he said, not for the first time these last few months.

"I don't want to stay here by myself."

He took her elbow as they stood. "It might be nothing. If it is related, there's no reason to think anyone would know where it is and come get it, especially not during the day with the cops around the corner."

She must not have looked convinced.

"But you don't have to stay," he added.

They went back through the kitchen. Taka zipped up his windbreaker, swiped his keys from the counter, and they walked straight out to his Yukon.

SPECTATORS HAD GATHERED at Eric's line of yellow tape, eyeing the emergency vehicles and the grey lake beyond them. The ME's van was gone, but two detectives, standing out in their khakis, dark shirts, and hip holsters, had shown up. Andrea stayed in the car while Taka took point and strode right into the scene without hesitation. The resulting intense huddle made Andrea nervous, with several glances being directed her way.

And then Taka was shaking his head and shaking hands and trudging back through the muddy gravel past the grim boaters who'd found the body. One of them reached out his hand and touched Taka's arm. Taka turned, listened with a small frown creasing his brows, and then trotted back to the detectives. Andrea got out of the Yukon.

The CPD dive team arrived, a WCHS news van in its wake. Eric moved to intercept the van while Taka and one of the detectives, Dan Cozner, pulled the tape for the dive team and then re-secured the perimeter. A reporter Andrea recognized from the Charleston Gazette-Mail crept along the gravel in her brown Honda and then wedged it out of the way behind the news van. Through the trees, Andrea could see half the neighborhood drive by on winding Timber Way above, but only one or two more walkers stopped to gawk.

She made her way over to the crime tape, her belly squirreling

"Kid didn't have shoes, but boater man over there said he saw one fall from the body when they hooked and reeled it in," Taka told her when she reached him. "It sank, but he knows where. Marked the GPS for the investigation."

"You know," Dan Cozner said. "Even though TV shows get most of it wrong, they're good for teaching that kind of shit. Did you forget your shirt?"

Taka glanced over at him, the corner of his lip quirking up. "It was dark blue or black," he continued saying to Andrea. "Tony'll be over when he's done," he said, pushing his thumb at a tall, dark haired CSI tech Andrea had seen floating around at department functions.

"Okay," she said. "Should I go back now?"

"We're gonna wait until they launch. Make sure Eric doesn't need help with crowd control until most of the vehicles are gone."

They stood around talking about nothing while watching Cozner and his partner work. Eric poked fun at Taka for running out of the house without a shirt. Andrea wrapped her arms around herself, her sweatshirt not quite enough in the moist chill.

When the techs were done processing the boat for anything that might have contaminated or compromised the body, the fishermen loaded it up on the Hummer's trailer. Eric let them through the tape as the dive master backed his CPD Tahoe down the ramp to float the team's sleek, flat, motor boat into the water. It took twenty minutes or so for them to launch. The GPS coordinates put them quickly out of sight and the little crowd of neighbors wandered off in twos and threes. Moving over to allow the cameraman to better frame the ramp, the WCHS reporter started yet another take. Taka nodded over at Andrea. She ducked under the tape and turned, waiting for him to catch up.

"Detective Taka, a word?" the Gazette reporter called out.

He shook his head and kept walking.

"Sir, Detective Taka, about the shooting," she persisted, trotting over.

"No comment," Taka growled.

"Did you know the suspect was Councilman Miller's nephew?"

"No comment."

The reporter stared hard at Andrea, trying to place her. Andrea looked down, letting her hair fall over her face, hoping she wouldn't remember Andrea contributed research to a cold case article she wrote the previous year. Getting in the Yukon's passenger side, Andrea slammed her door at the same time Taka slammed his. He started it up and backed away, the reporter following for several strides until he gunned forward again in a three-point turn.

"Our names weren't released," he bitched.

"You aren't hard to recognize, Taka. Did you know he was Miller's nephew?"

"Not until afterwards."

Which begged another question. Taka lived with his girlfriend, Melinda. She was tall like Andrea, but built on a tiny bird's frame topped with a luxurious mane of fake red hair. Also unlike Andrea, she was frilly and girly and had a viper's tongue installed in place of her absent compassion. Apparently there were other compensating factors, but hopefully Taka would tire of them sooner rather than later.

"Why'd you come to my place last night?"

"I lost my keys," he mumbled.

No wonder he'd woken her up last night to let him in. She'd thought he was just afraid she'd shoot him for an intruder since she wasn't expecting him. Rolling her eyes, Andrea said, "Her highness wouldn't let you in if you knocked?"

"She sleeps with ear plugs and a white noise machine. I didn't even try."

Taka was a light sleeper and while he didn't tuck his gun under his pillow, because he wasn't an idiot, he always kept it close. Each of his three stints in inter-agency undercover had changed him, made him a darker, edgier, older version of the Taka he used to be.

"How can you sleep with all that loud shush-shush going on?"

"I don't," he said, glancing over at her.

That explained a lot, actually, including the heavy shadows under his eyes that eight hours of unusual-for-him deep sleep hadn't even touched.

Charleston cops drew their weapons regularly, but most retired without ever discharging one outside the range, let alone to shoot someone. In eleven years with the department, Taka already had three shoots on his record, no deaths. Although they'd all been justified, the department would be worrying about his liability at this point. If anyone else noticed, if they thought fatigue had played a factor in escalating the pursuit, the CPD's internal Professional Standards Division or PSD, Charleston's version of Internal Affairs, would use it against him.

"Does this make four?" she asked.

He turned onto her drive. "Yeah. Second highest now. Ronnie Horton has seven," he said, staring into Andrea's carport as he shut the truck off. "Must've been windy here."

Andrea craned her neck to see what he was looking at. A dented and paint spattered aluminum bucket stood upside down next to her overturned trash can. "That's not mine."

"Stay here," he said and got out, easing his door shut. He drew the concealed Glock he always carried off-duty, and crept into the carport, turning his head left, right, and up. Andrea looked up, too, but the carport roof was flat—there wasn't much to see. The yards to either side were empty of people.

The can shifted. Taka leapt back, bringing his gun to bear.

CHAPTER TWO

ANDREA THREW HER door open and vaulted out without thinking.

"Snake," a voice on the driver's side of the Yukon barked.

Taka spun with his gun raised in both fists, knees bending in defense mode.

Andrea skidded to a stop in her headlong rush, hand on the Yukon's hood to steady herself.

Mr. Huntley raised his hands. They were as withered and ancient as the rest of him. "Your little girl trapped it in there." He was her across the street neighbor. And she only knew his name because it was written on his mailbox. He misunderstood their blank stares. "I was raking. Watched her do it. You gonna shoot me for it?"

Lowering his arms, so the gun pointed down, Taka tilted his head and drew himself up in that way that Andrea associated with the start of many, many, arguments. A high school girlfriend had coined it "confused puppy". "What?"

"Gonna shoot me?" he repeated, eyebrows lifted.

"No, sorry," Taka said, raising his left hand, fingers spread, holstering his weapon with his right at the same time. "What'd you say?"

"It's that snake she plays with on the front stoop. She's trapped it in my paint bucket."

The can scraped against the concrete. They all looked at it.

Taka lifted his leg and knocked the can over with the tip of his boot.

A sleek black snake struck at his leg, missing, then drew back, holding its ground. They stood still. The snake flicked its tongue out over and over, tasting the air. Within seconds, it lowered itself and made a run for it, rapidly S-curving its way out of the carport and into the grass.

"Black racer," Andrea said.

"Can I have my bucket back?"

Taka grabbed it up and handed it to the old guy.

"Tell your girl not to go rummaging about in my shed without coming to ask me first."

"Huh," Andrea said.

"I find that snake in my yard," Mr. Huntley said as he about faced and headed back across the street, "I'm going to kill it."

"It eats mice," Andrea said.

"Don't got mice," he called back over his shoulder. "But I like my song birds. Had three nests this year in my bird houses."

Taka waved. "Yes, sir," he said, shoving Andrea towards the carport door.

Andrea fumbled with the door lock and they fell inside.

Slamming the door shut so hard the frame shook, Taka put a hand over his heart. "Damn. Almost shot the old guy." He stood up and held his hand out. It was shaking. "Crazy old man. I'll go make nice later and see if he saw anything this morning. Maybe he saw snake girl head into your back yard."

She'd seen Billie Mae in her back yard, not a wandering neighbor girl. "Let's go out back and make sure the shoe's still there."

"Why wouldn't it be?"

Andrea shrugged.

They went through the house and out the back. The shoe remained where they'd left it. Andrea huffed out a big breath

"Let's canvass the yard," Taka suggested. "I'll start by the carport and work back and forth through this half. You start at the fence and walk the other half. Just go back and forth like a lawn mower, see if there's anything else unusual."

"Okay."

The back yard was partially fenced by default. There was a bit of white three-foot-high picket tying the corner of the outside wall of her house to the row of overgrown nandina shrubs that had threaded themselves through a series of chain link panels installed along the west line. The wild thicket of nandina effectively blocked her view of that neighbor's yard. The back line was unfenced, but wooded with brushy undergrowth filling the steep ditch. Andrea couldn't see the house back there at all. A waist-high brick wall, painted white, backed her carport, with a walkthrough into the carport alongside the mudroom wall. The four-board fence along the east side—closest to the shoe—boasted full wire mesh top to bottom.

The lush yard beyond it, deep with trees and beautifully maintained beds containing hostas, butterfly bushes, and daylilies, lay between her and her end of the cul-de-sac neighbor, Susan something-that-started-with-a-P.

Zig-zagging back and forth, Andrea found nothing. Taka found a broken branch and what might be half an adult-sized footprint in the dried grass. Whether or not it was important remained a huge question mark.

"You got a real camera?" Taka teased.

He knew she did. He'd been with her when she found it at the Best Buy in Barboursville.

She simply nodded and went to get it. After she checked the light settings and dialed up auto everything, she handed the camera to Taka. He took about twenty establishing shots of the surrounding yard while she trailed along behind him.

The Nikon D3s had cost her all the room on her credit card, but for some of the sites she worked at, it was invaluable. Technically, she archived historical files at the Waltham-Young Community Library, a private institute for public use, but her job as a trained archivist entailed so much more than that. She worked on lots of different projects at Waltham-Young Community Library, including research for the local Charleston Police and the State Police, headquartered across the river from each other. But her true passion lay in the locations of significant historical events in West Virginia and how those specific locations affected the events that made them famous. The Nikon could not only document physical properties—the trees, the houses, the lay of the land—it also documented how day and night looked upon the site, how the weather moved over it.

Where did the dawn hit first? Where did the runoff of a storm collect? She went repeatedly to the same sites to collect reams of images to study when piecing together verification of historical fact for a client. Commonsense told her a lot, but so did documenting the site and how the passage of time affected it.

Trying to avoid his own shadow, Taka shot the shoe and its immediate location from several different angles and views, along with the possible partial footprint, in hopes the computer techs could map the highs and low by contrast and figure out the brand of the print. Of course, the CSI would document as well, but Taka was afraid the grass was springing back into place as they waited for her arrival, obscuring what they'd seen earlier. The clouds continued to build and a gustier wind kicked up.

They made their way to the tiny patio. Andrea sat on the top step of the back door while Taka went in to refresh the coffee and put on an actual shirt. Neither smoked, though at just this second Andrea understood the urge to do so, wishing she had something to keep her fingers busy. Unable to just sit and wait, she went in and cleaned up the uneaten breakfast while the coffee perked.

ANDREA PARKED HERSELF on the top step of her back patio as Taka directed the Crime Scene Investigator who had come knocking, a woman Andrea had never met before to the location of the little Keds. They joined the dark-haired tech from the lake in walking off the yard again. Afterward, Taka lingered near the carport, where he could keep an eye on any neighbors who might venture over for a better look. Fat raindrops began to drop onto the parched yard. The CSI hurried to collect the little Keds. Andrea retreated to her kitchen table to watch through the big picture window.

Still measuring distances as the tech took official photographs in the light rain, the CSI answered her cell. Her face hardened and body language sharpened. When she finished, she sent the tech on his way. The rain started to fall in earnest. In her mudroom off the kitchen, Andrea grabbed towels off the sack on her dryer, and opened the carport door.

Taking a towel, Taka said, "The divers recovered a size 1 Keds in blue. There's a couple of uniforms canvassing the area. Maybe one of your neighbors got something on camera."

"I'm going out to the lake," the CSI said, waving off the second towel. "See if the shoes are a match."

Everyone hated murder, but to kill a kid... It seemed to Andrea that given the opportunity, most of the CPD officers she knew would readily see the perpetrator off with one bullet to the head and an unmarked burial, no problem. Training helped keep that from being standard operating procedure, and it was the only reason the kid Taka shot was still breathing. You could take the cop out of the rural backwoods, but you couldn't take the backwoods out of the cop. And most every West Virginia native in law enforcement was from the backwoods to some degree.

After Taka changed, they hustled up some sandwiches and split the only dill pickle Andrea had left evenly between them.

"What are you going to do about Melinda?"

He sobered. "Can I sleep on your couch for a few days?"

Andrea opened her mouth. Closed it. Started again. "Coward."

He ducked his head.

"You're just gonna stay with me until she takes the hint and removes herself from your condo?"

He shrugged.

"It's your condo. Tell her to leave."

He swallowed the huge bite of his sandwich he'd taken. "No, really," he said, before popping the bite of pickle in his mouth.

"I should've known. You only stay over when you're single."

Taka stuffed more sandwich into his mouth while giving her a practiced side-eye with his brows raised.

"Okay," Andrea said. "But you're on the couch."

They cleaned up and then Taka stripped his boots off, padded into her tiny living room, and turned the TV on. A football game erupted in full roar. It appeared he was staying awhile. Andrea had expected him to head over to CPD. Apparently, his administrative leave was more hobbling than she'd thought it would be. She pulled down her big blue pitcher, dropped ten tea bags in, and filled the pitcher with filtered water from the tap for sun tea before remembering the rain, despite the grey wavering light filling the kitchen and roaring beat of it against the window and roof.

She thought about the frantic search that must be going on for the child pulled from the lake and the news his or her parents would soon be receiving on this stormy cold day. They'd never warm up again, just like their child. Just like Billie Mae. Cold to her bones, Andrea retreated to Taka's warm protection on the couch, settling under his outstretched arm. He snorted at something one of the commentators said, casually dropped his arm around her, and tugged her up against his side.

TAKA'S PHONE, WEDGED into the side cushion of the couch from where it'd slid off his thigh, buzzed. Shoulder aching from the takedown the night before, he fished it out while watching the replay of a questionable touchdown. A fumble. He knew it.

Carson Lazar, CPD's go-to lawyer. *Good time to call? It's important.* Taka's breath caught, his skin flushing cold. It could only be about the kid he shot. And he had been just a kid, twenty-one years old.

He extricated himself from under Andrea, who only murmured and wriggled into a more comfortable position, her dark hair spread out over her shoulder and arms. She'd never been much for naps until her accident. This Billie Mae thing disconcerted him. Although he'd never seen her and had told Andrea repeatedly that all she was hearing were the sounds of an old house, he had dreamed about her once.

He'd seen her sitting at the end of the bed when he woke sweating from a nightmare, his breath harsh in his ears. She patted his foot and blinked back at his owlish stare until his dream faded and then he'd closed his eyes and drifted back into sleep, to then lurch awake, actually awake, his heart thumping.

Then a couple of weeks ago he heard Andrea talking in the can. Andrea had said, your mother didn't drown you, and a second voice, a little girl's, with a hollow echo in the core of her words, said with conviction, I drowned. The childish lisp lifted the hair on his arms and the back of his neck and he'd bolted past, stumbled down the stairs. Standing here now, in the wan grey light, with the noise of the game filling the room, a drop of cold sweat trickled down his ribs.

He suppressed a shiver. That little girl's voice hadn't sounded anything like Andrea, though it must have been, had to have been, her. Maybe he could stay with his friend Scott instead. He had issues with that option, but fear wasn't one of them. Andrea's insistence that Billie Mae was present in the house, that she'd been in the yard this morning, scared him a little.

The shoe in the yard scared him more.

He didn't want to focus more of CPD's attention on Andrea by demanding she see a therapist anytime soon.

His phone buzzed again, a missed text reminder.

Taka beelined from the hall into the kitchen. The rain had slackened, but continued to fall. Hitting buttons on his phone, he went through the mudroom, eased the door open and stepped down into the carport in his socks.

Carson picked up immediately, souring Taka's stomach even more if that was possible. "Taka."

"Did he die?"

"No. At least not yet."

"That doesn't sound good." He eyed the wet edge of the concrete pad, tamping the urge to pace. Instead, he wrapped his free arm over his chest and tucked his hand into his pit against the cold.

"It's not. He's diabetic on top of it all. You know he's Councilman Miller's nephew?"

And a white boy? Yeah. "He was shooting at us, Carson. He beat Deborah Watkins to death. Slammed her head into a wall. And then shot an officer. Tracy took a bullet in the vest and so did I." Shooting a suspect, even after he had murdered someone and fired on police, required reams of forms, a Professional Standards Division review, and a Shooting Board investigation before reinstatement to duty. Taka would be doing paperwork for days, but it was a justified shoot, no one could deny that. "Greg Stack is good at his job, he'll make sure PSD pushes it through the shooting board."

"Allegedly murdered," Carson corrected. "And I don't think Greg's going to be able to it push through Pro Standards. There's more."

"What more?"

"The gun he used. It was a gift from someone who was maybe taking things a little too seriously with him."

Taka frowned. "I'm not following."

"He was playing both sides of the fence, Taka. Had a society girlfriend, a Holbrook no less, but word is he was also playing sub to an older guy. A very influential older guy."

Taka's heart double-thumped. "Who?"

"Dewey Sanderson."

"Fuck," Taka breathed.

"Yeah."

CHAPTER THREE

TRAPPED BY THE rain, Taka spun a full circle on his heel before he took the phone from his ear and bent over, both hands on his knees. Dewey Sanderson had come up four years ahead of Taka at Nitro High, and was a new graduate of Colgate University when Taka first met him at a gun club near Cross Lanes. Later, he'd learned Dewey's habit was to have a pretty girl on his arm up front, but a boy in the background, always a few years younger. He'd started in high school, luring middle graders in with promises of pot and stashes of porn. It was always consensual and he stayed under the radar.

The local New York cops serving Colgate turned a blind eye when he moved onto the high school crowd while in college. It was technically statutory rape by then, but if you weren't nailing hetero couples, it wasn't going to play right when you went after the other side. And he was Dewey Sanderson, son of six-time senator and former speaker of the house, Dante Sanderson, so no one was looking to pick him up and slap him on the wrist. Since then, he'd graduated to consenting adults in the form of naïve college kids.

Carson's faint voice drifted up to him. "Taka? Taka!"

He straightened up and took another deep breath before answering. "I'm here."

"Dewey's pissed. He had a real soft spot for the boy."

Sanderson's money sat in a lot of tills in Charleston and his family practically owned Taka's hometown of Cross Lanes. Having Dewey pissed at him again would make it hard for him to live here. Last time he'd joined the Army to get away.

"Nothing you could've done different, Tak, but ..."

"I know. It's gonna take time to sort this out, feed it to the media so they get it right."

"Right," Carson said. "And believe me, they want to know, but we're keeping it tight. No one needs to know where that gun came from. It won't go national unless the Sanderson name comes up and Dewey doesn't want either the publicity or his dad involved. What he does want is your hide."

"Carson. That boy killed someone. He was shooting at us."

"You want back out there, I know."

"I'm a cop, Carson. Yeah."

Carson took a sharp breath and blew it out again. "I'll do my best."

And Taka knew he would. Carson had been repping Charleston's boys in blue for twelve years. He couldn't wave a wand big enough to disappear Dewey Sanderson, but he could make some of the cascading complications a little smaller by confusing the issue and throwing lots of paperwork in the way. Taka could wave his truce with Dewey goodbye. It had allowed them to co-exist at a room's length distance in tiny Charleston. And domino-like, there went his budding friendship with Scott, who worked for Dewey. It'd been nice to have a non-cop buddy who got the vagaries of his job and still returned his calls when Taka was a no-show.

"Stay off social media. That goes for Melinda, too. And Andrea."

"Not a problem." He had a stagnant Instagram account, Melinda had quit posting anything about him weeks ago, and Andrea would understand when he asked, but he doubted she ever posted anything not related to books, her job, or Waltham-Young anyway.

Shit. Dewey Sanderson's gun in the hand of a diabetic boy and love interest. Yeah, Taka was fucked.

WHEN SHE WOKE up, it was to delicious odors wafting from the kitchen. Taka's famous take-care-of-anything meat sauce for ladling over his couldn't-be-beat, boiled in beer, al dente spaghetti. Andrea kept the ingredients on hand. She figured most everyone did, they were so common, but he combined them in an out-of-the-box way that she had never been able to duplicate. She got up, went to the bathroom, and tried to put her thick, tangled hair in order before she splashed water on her face. She knew Taka only made his sauce when he needed to focus and let his emotional intensity settle on simmer.

She wandered back to the kitchen. He was stirring the sauce in her biggest pot, which meant plenty for the freezer, and he didn't turn when she came in. Thinking of the freezer, she pulled it open to see if she still had a frozen baguette for garlic bread. She found it cozied up to the ice maker. Andrea glanced over at the stove clock. It was only four. "Now or later?" she asked.

"Later," he said. "Let's go shooting."

Her plans for the weekend had been scrapped the second Billie Mae showed up wet, so she figured she might as well humor Taka. When he got like this there just wasn't really a choice in the matter anyway. He'd taught her to shoot on his Colt 1911 semi-automatic, one of two handguns, three rifles, and a shotgun he'd received as gifts or inheritances from his father and uncles. They spent a lot of weekend afternoons blasting away at the range. After all these years, he still wore her dorky pink ear protectors because the scarred black ones he owned fit her better.

Her mom had always wrinkled her nose when they came back in from firing, but had never asked about the cordite or why her daughter smelled as strongly of it as Taka did. She'd been in the advanced stages of cancer by then and knew Andrea, unable to count on her brother, would soon be on her own. She wanted her to be able to take care of herself but refused to consider guns as protection for her little girl. They had a "don't ask, don't tell" policy in effect.

All her mom would say when they came in was, been shooting, Taka? She always pronounced his name funny, for all that she obviously loved him. She always said "Toekah" with a long "o."

She'd say, Toekah, you're not handing my girl that gun, are you? And he'd say, no, never, ma'am, with a smirk, to which her mom always nodded in reply, because they both knew they were lying and that in itself was a sort of truth.

The day after his eighteenth birthday he bought Andrea a pistol, a used Smith and Wesson 39, as her first gun. Her second was the Sig Sauer P229 he gave her as a college graduation present. When she ditched her roommate for the single life in an industrial-type warehouse studio, he brought her a shotgun, a Remington 12-gauge. When she moved in with Billie Mae, she'd needed a distraction at first. One night Taka helped her saw off the barrel of that same gun to just over legal length. The evening hours spent sanding it by hand relaxed her way more than latch hooking or knitting. It was surprisingly meditative, like humming "om," but with purpose. Deadly purpose, but still.

Staying prepared for self-defense and short-term survival interested them both. They kept go-bags in their cars. Andrea didn't know if it was from growing up poor in West Virginia, or simply their personalities. Taka almost always had a partner or help on call, but Andrea rarely did, and there were times she drove deep into backcountry for Waltham-Young assignments. While her car was mostly reliable, you just never knew when you might need emergency supplies. Or a gun. And the ability to use it.

She shut the freezer door and peered down into the sauce pot. Taka scooped up a bit in a long wooden spoon and offered it to her for tasting. "Mmmm," she said, her eyes closing. "It's heaven in a red sauce." She grinned. "Should be perfect when we get back."

Taka smiled, but his eyes were shuttered. Intense, that was Taka. His brain would be on overdrive between the shooting, the kids in the lake, and Billie Mae. "Go get dressed," he said, "I'll turn this down."

In her room, she put on jeans and a tee shirt and grabbed a heavy flannel shirt to shoot in. A rugged plastic case on the floor of her closet, which was securely locked with a six-digit code, held her goggles, cleaning kit, and two of her pistols. She slung a small canvas rip bag over her shoulder. It held her ear protectors and ten boxes of ammo— always. She refilled it every time she came home from the range.

She'd never drawn her gun in public, let alone pointed it at a person, but Taka had taken her hunting at least four times a year for the last three years, teaching her what his Uncle James had taught him. They'd taken rabbits, turkey, and deer, sharing the extra meat with Taka's fellow officers and some of the Waltham-Young staff.

"Good choice," Taka said, his voice firm, as he watched her clear her carry gun and swap it from her purse to her bag. He'd already have his own Glock on him and CPD officers carried the same Smith and Wessons as they were trained on at the State Police Academy.

A gun fired by an officer in the line of duty would be confiscated by CSI, though, and, in West Virginia anyhow, sent to the State Police for test firing to compare the spent bullets to those recovered from the crime scene. "Your duty weapon already at the ballistics lab?"

"I'm assuming. They issued me another, though," he said, patting the backpack she knew held extra mags and the Glock when he was on-duty.

His old Colt was stored in the Yukon, along with a .22 and his tactical rifle. "My truck."

The gun club was out Martin Hollow Road, about a twenty-minute drive northeast from her place, in the boonies between Milliken and Rutledge. They didn't talk on the way over.

TAKA LOADED UP faster than Andrea did. She hadn't fired her carry, a Sig 239, in a month. She slipped a loaded magazine into it, racked the slide and de-cocked it before laying it on the bench alongside Taka's Glock. While she situated her paper target at ten yards, he laid the other guns and ammo he wanted to shoot on the table. After putting on her goggles and ear protectors, she waited for Taka to give her a thumbs up before she took her stance, pulled through the Sig's double action, and fired through the mag, five rounds in the chest and five rounds in the head.

As she slipped her empty magazine, checked the chamber, and re-loaded, Taka ran the target in. He grinned at the tight placements and then slapped another target up. "You doing another or spinners?"

"Spinners." She chose five, shooting from about ten yards to two, hitting each with two rounds.

Taka's eyebrows shot up. "Damn, you been cheating on me?"

"No, just thinking about that shoe."

He nodded in agreement. She cleared the gun and stepped back. He came forward, raised his Glock and ran through the same spinners as she had, but then jettisoned the mag and reloaded in seconds, gracefully brought his gun to bear, and fired back down the range in reverse, hitting only the gongs, plink, plink, plink, out to the 20 mark. Grim and silent, he again ejected the empty mag, which bounced off the ground as he plucked another full one off his utility belt, slapped it home and fired back up the line. The last one, at about five yards, clanked with the center trajectory force of his bullet and jumped off its swinger arm.

He stood still, weapon still raised, but then slowly relaxed and eased the Glock down as a cease fire order echoed from the intercoms all down the range under the muffled pops of small ordinance coming from another alley.

He cleared his throat and glanced over his shoulder at Andrea. Andrea shrugged, her chest a little hollow from the boom, boom, boom of the big gun in rapid fire succession and from the sheepish expression on Taka's face. He hated murder involving kids, but they'd only just started this case and had none of the details. The shoe might not even be related. The kid in the lake may not have been murdered. Something else was… Oh.

"Wow. She really got to you, huh? Did you talk to her today?"

Taka hung his head, a little chagrined, she thought, that she had figured out it was the woman in his life that topped his list of stressors at the moment.

"She texted me."

"Cuss you out?"

He shook his head. "Nope. Just said bye. Key in kitchen. Nothing about...nothing. I wish she'd been really pissed."

"Meh. Don't think it's over, big boy."

But he just stood there with his feet planted, staring at the wet gravel between his boots.

"That's not the real problem."

He lifted his head to meet her eyes. "Carson called. Turns out that kid I shot is Dewey's current boy."

Everything in her stopped for a moment and then surged forward. "Fuck!"

Taka shrugged. "Exactly what I said."

"Need a bigger gun?"

He smiled, even if it was more of a grimace.

They took turns shooting, firing each of the weapons they'd brought twice, and then swapping. They ran different drills with each. After clearing everything and counting the empty mags to be reloaded, they shouldered their bags and signed out.

SOMEWHERE SOUTH OF Milliken on the return home, Taka broke Andrea's reverie as she watched the sunlight flicker through the passing trees. "It is, y'know, over."

"With Melinda?"

"Yeah. I kinda met someone. It's nothing yet, but it might be something. Maybe."

"Did you tell her?"

"No. She's maybe been seeing someone else herself."

"Taka—"

Taka's phone rang just as they hit Greenbrier Street. "Taka," he said. "Yeah, so what?" He glanced at Andrea. "Okay. Yeah, first thing Monday."

He thumbed his phone to end the call and looked over at her. "I pulled Billie Mae's digital file last week."

"I requested that file six months ago. You showed no interest in it." Andrea said.

"Her mother was convicted of her murder," he said in a flat tone she couldn't quite decipher. It wasn't exasperated. It wasn't wary or angry, but it was close. "I didn't want you getting obsessed with a solved case."

"But now?"

He concentrated on the empty curving road ahead, his fingers tight on the steering wheel. Bright flashes of color on the wooded hillsides whipped by. "You knew about that first kid at the lake before the first responders arrived. Did you dump that kid in the lake?"

Andrea slid down in her seat, crossing her arms. Seriously?

"Did you kill this one?"

Andrea turned her glare on him only to find him looking at her. He held her gaze for a moment too long. "Road, Taka."

He went back to driving. "You knew because of Billie Mae, you said. So, yeah. I decided to look up Billie Mae. There was a lot missing, so I requested the physical records. I haven't had a chance to look at them yet, but Billie Mae came up on a case search and now Ronnie Horton wants them back."

Lieutenant Ronnie Horton, the only other investigator with more shoots than Taka now and riding an admin desk as Chief of Detectives for the rest of his career because of it. Despite Taka's pissiness at having to try and crow bar Billie Mae into his reality, she couldn't resist asking. "Why would that come up on a search?"

"They did a violent crimes search within a five-mile radius of the lake. I'm sure some geek in analysis wants to compare them all around Lake Vickers, make sure our bases are covered."

Months ago, she'd read through the scanty police file that was all she was given in answer to her Freedom of Information request, looking for inconsistencies. She should be happy more eyes were on the supposedly solved case, but she wasn't.

She was scared.

CHAPTER FOUR

PULLING INTO THE drive, Andrea sat up, wondering what the items scattered across her carport could be.

"Shoes?" Taka said.

His lips pursed as once again he shoved the truck into gear while confused about what he might be facing. They got out and considered the random arrangement. Taka picked up an orange tennis shoe.

"This is yours, right?" he asked, frowning up at Andrea.

"Yes."

One of the yellow wedge heels she'd bought at Macy's last summer in New York lay next to the rear tire of her FX, a black flat she often wore to work next to it. There was one of her silver-striped trail running shoes from the time she became obsessed with running on the mountain biking trails in Kanawha State Forest. She hadn't worn those in at least two years. They were still in an unpacked box. A chill swept her spine and the hair on her arms and nape rose.

They were all single shoes. Hers. Heels, and boots, and sandals, and tennis shoes.

"What the fuck," Taka said, and strode to the far side of the carport, at the edge of the concrete.

Except one.

It was another kid's Keds, this one dirty white with a yellowed and soil-encrusted rubber toe. The tough canvas was torn, and stained deep brown in uneven patches. Dirt filled the eyelets. The dangling laces were ragged at their ends and badly frayed.

Andrea shook her head. "That's Billie Mae's," she whispered.

Taka looked sharply at her, the shoe trembling in his shaking hand. "What?"

"That's Billie Mae's."

"How do you know?"

"She wears those sometimes, when I make bacon. With jean shorts and a yellow, long-sleeved tee shirt."

"This isn't possible, Andrea."

"Taka. You're..." Andrea's tongue stuck to the roof of her dry mouth. She tried again. "You're holding it in your hand. Does it feel real?"

He examined the shoe in his hand like he'd not seen it before that very second.

"Where are the files?"

"In the Yukon," he said, his voice coming from far and away. "What..."

. . . should he do with the Keds, Andrea finished in her head. "I'll get a Ziploc," she said and squeezed by him when he didn't move.

She unlocked the mudroom door off the carport, which held her washer and dryer, jackets on wall hooks, boots and shoes under a little bench—one boot, she noted in passing, one orange tennis shoe. Inhaling the sublime, familiar smell of Taka's simmering sauce, she walked through the kitchen, snatched the correct drawer open, and plucked out a quart-sized Ziploc baggie.

She kept three different sizes on hand. She used a lot of Ziploc baggies when she went into the field for work, bagging everything from fabric and landscape samples to crumbling old books to water samples from lakes and rivers. She took another deep breath, focused on the slide of the baggie's thin plastic between her fingers, and willed herself to calmness. This wasn't any different. Just another clue to research.

Back outside, Taka lowered the ratty shoe into the Ziploc, his eyes blank. It had really rattled him. Andrea wasn't used to seeing Taka nervous. Her building anxiety notched up a level. She zipped the bag closed. They zigzagged around the garage, picking up the shoes and then she followed him into the mudroom where they dumped them on the bench.

"Was the door locked?"

Andrea nodded.

"I set the alarm."

"It wasn't on when I came in."

She set the Ziploc and her gun case on the kitchen table and followed Taka into the entry hall, where he stacked the duffle bags and his own cases on the long table along the wall. Without consultation, they went straight up to her bedroom. Taka slid the walk-in closet's pocket door open.

Chaos reigned. Her shoes were everywhere. The boxes she had stacked against the wall and never unpacked were torn open. "Uff," Taka said.

Andrea's gaze locked on small eyes peering out from between her dresses at the back of the small space. Billie Mae burst through them, her arms opening, and sent a writhing black snake flying at Andrea's face.

"Andrea!" Taka yelled.

Pain spiked through her back and a horrendous pressure detonated in her chest, her breath exploding outwards. Lying on the hard floor, she gasped, but couldn't get any air. Her lungs burned. She rocked on her back, helpless, lifted her knees. A long groan grated up her throat. She opened her mouth wide, but still she couldn't draw a breath. Taka landed on his knees beside her, hands drawing her up to lean against him. The smallest amount of air possible reached her aching lungs.

"That's it, small breaths, tiny ones. You knocked the wind out of yourself."

She was too focused on breathing to hit him, but she wanted to. And where was the damn snake?

DOWNSTAIRS, THE CLOSET door firmly shut upstairs, Taka said, "Has Billie Mae done this before?" She thought he meant purposely scare her, but then he continued. "Moved things? Ghosts move things, don't they?"

Like she was the expert on anything ghostly. She'd done a little research at Waltham-Young, in the big drawers of paranormal files they'd collected from many, many sources over the years. Her favorites were the ones collected from Appalachian storytellers, but the tales were long on atmosphere and short on detail. She latched onto his second question, the sane one. "I don't know," she said defensively, but of course, she did know.

Ghosts did all sorts of creepy things. They levitated objects, put missing items in the middle of floors, threw cans and jars and hairbrushes, broke vases, even started cars. Had Billie Mae ever done any of that sort of thing? Not in her experience. "She's never moved anything—" But wait, that wasn't true, was it?

Andrea had lost her little diamond earring and found it three days later sitting on the rim of the bathtub. Billie Mae hadn't shown that morning, but Andrea remembered whispering thank you into the empty air. "Except once," Andrea corrected herself. "She found my earring."

"From the pair Chuck gave you?"

"Yes. How'd you know?"

"They're the only earrings you have that would be important to you, right?"

"Right."

Chuck had been her only serious boyfriend. She thought he might want to marry her one day and she could honestly say that the thought that she might want to marry him back had crossed her mind as well. But he was Air National Guard, one of the first to deploy to Iraq after the regular military had started coming home. En route, transferring through Wiesbaden, Germany, he and three other airmen were killed in a car wreck on an icy road. She'd had boyfriends since then, and a couple of short-term affairs, but nobody like Chuck. The only other man to hold the same kind of strings to her heart was looking more than a little freaked out as he checked the living room for the missing snake he claimed he never saw.

"Are you sure it's not still upstairs?" she asked for the third time.

He shoved the couch back against the wall. "Certain."

She stood in the little foyer, watching for movement in the dining room, which she'd made her home office. Her chest still aching with the memory of her momentary suffocation. "Did she move it to my yard? That blue shoe this morning? Could she do that?"

"Can we just..." Wearing an uncharacteristic lost look, Taka waved a hand in the air. "Leave this till later?"

Andrea nodded.

They ended up at the kitchen table, staring at the small, lonely, dirty, shoe in the middle of the table.

The furnace kicked on, filling the room with its comforting hush.

Dropping into a chair, Taka reached out and snagged her gun case, spurring Andrea into action. While she started noodles, pulled the baguette from the freezer, and got it into the oven, he stripped the guns and began to clean them. The familiar scents of the cleaner and his sauce intensified in the close air of the kitchen. Her tension seeped away in tiny increments.

How many times had they done this over the years? If she and Taka were still doing this sort of thing ten years from now, would she be happy? Would she be happy if there was a woman beside him? Or another guy pulling out the butter, sprinkling the garlic powder onto the bread?

She knew she never wanted Taka out of her life, but did she want to let other people into their life together? Was there really room for someone else when her best friend, William Taka, was still in full bore, too?

By the time Taka set the second gun down, cleaned and ready to go, the noodles were cooked, the bread toasty, and Andrea was pulling plates off her open shelving. He re-packed her gun case and stood up.

"You going back in the closet alone?"

He laughed. "No fucking way. Just setting it by the front door. We'll do your closet together." When he came back in, he moved the shoe and gathered silverware and paper towels while she ladled sauce onto the hot noodles. Together, they put everything on the cleared table and sat down to eat.

"Parmesan," she said, leaping up again. They both liberally coated their spaghetti with the canned cheese and dug in.

Thankfully nothing and no one interrupted them. Andrea sat back, replete.

"So, Taka," she said, soaking up sauce with a last chunk of garlic bread. "Any ideas on how to go about checking on that shoe?"

His eyebrows lowered when he concentrated, making him look fierce. Her brain conjured a sudden image of him in the used canoe he bought when he was sixteen. That summer had been glorious. Andrea remembered showing off their well-practiced move while her friend Jenny sat in the stern. She and Taka dove out opposite sides of the canoe into Beech Fork Lake and then swum like otters underneath the canoe, switching places. They'd popped up with their backs to the canoe, grasped the sides and reverse somersaulted up into the middle of it, flinging water as they slung their heads up to grin at each other. Jenny had actually squealed out loud.

Andrea knew all the reasons why that boy rarely surfaced in this complete grown-up here with her now, this cop, Taka the fierce, but his sharp adultness still caught her attention sometimes. It seemed ridiculous that she was asking this Taka what to do with a shoe some ghost had left in her carport.

"Go through the files tonight and tomorrow?" He pushed his chair away from the table. "There might be photos."

"There weren't any in the file I requested in the spring."

"No. That one was pretty fucking thin," he said, picking up both their plates as he stood. Headed for the sink, he glanced at the shoe, sitting across the kitchen on the sideboard. "And I have no idea what we've got now or what's readable. There was a roof leak at the annex last year. The original box was ruined."

"Do you remember if the file says where her mother was committed?"

He shook his head, watching the sink fill. "It didn't. She was probably evaluated at South Central, but after that, I don't know. She plead guilty."

"I read through the news articles online. Her initial confession was supported by circumstantial evidence, she was sentenced, and then sent to an appropriate mental facility for women. I remember that, 'appropriate mental facility for women.'"

They made short work of the kitchen and Taka went out to the Yukon for the files and his iPad. Keeping an eye out for the apparently non-existent snake, Andrea sidled into her office to disconnect her laptop from the large monitor on her desk.

As usual, her screensaver, a quote by Zora Neale Hurston, scrolled across a blue background: **Research is formalized curiosity. It is poking and prying with a purpose.** But as Andrea crossed the room, a tag followed: *I waz drownd* scrolled across the screen in big purple letters. Andrea's pulse leapt.

"Billie Mae," she said out loud. "You are scaring me."

A certain hyperaware electric tingle often lived in her skin when Billie Mae was present and that was absent now. Andrea still felt spooked. "You weren't drowned, Billie Mae," she whispered, sounding harsh to her own ears. "You're just tapped into those kids who were." Hearing the words crystallized what she'd been thinking.

Billie Mae was giving them clues.

CHAPTER FIVE

ANDREA UNDOCKED AND closed her laptop, already trying to sort what Billie Mae was trying to give them. Maybe Andrea had just remembered wrong, what Billie Mae had been wearing when she died. The ruined Keds might be another kid's, maybe the skeleton from the lake. And what did snakes have to do with shoes?

Taka joined her in the hall, letting a fresh, cold breath of October in with him.

"That's a big box," she exclaimed.

They spread out at the kitchen table. Andrea skimmed the original summary report sitting atop the other files in the musty cardboard box while Taka broke down the tactical rifle to clean it. The same report as she'd seen before, it must've been the only document loaded into the database when the system was upgraded in 2010. Billie Mae Robbins was six in 2003 when she was found in a dry tub, soaking wet. Her mother, Etta Robbins, was distraught and hardly able to communicate. The bruising and long thin tear across Billie Mae's neck matched her Mom's halting murder confession though, and she was later remanded to the custody of the state for lifelong incarceration. No other investigative work was ordered or completed aside from talking to the neighbors, who to a body, described the relationship as loving, but absently neglectful. No husband or father appeared to be in the picture.

The victim, Billie Mae Robbins, had been dressed in the exact outfit Andrea recalled: jean shorts, yellow long-sleeved tee, and white Keds tennis shoes. Only one had been found on the body. The other had been the subject of a search, since its location might establish a timeline and shed insight on the events leading up to her murder. It had never been found. Andrea got up and retrieved the shoe.

"It's the correct kind," she said. "It's the correct size and color and it's the left one, which was missing."

Taka snapped the last piece closed on the gun and set it down.

They both regarded the dirt-encrusted shoe.

"It didn't come out of my closet."

"It had to have been out in the yard, right? Overlooked and then buried over the years."

"We have it now, so why'd she—"

"Throw the snake at you? I don't know. Let's go walk it again, look for anything different from earlier, maybe freshly turned dirt."

Andrea glanced out the window. There was no moon and no lights shone through from the street, the only security light being down at the intersection. She really didn't want to egg Billie Mae on out in the dark.

"Flashlights?" Taka prompted.

"We should've thought of doing this before dark."

"We were in shock."

"Yeah," she said half-heartedly. "I'll get them."

She got up again to pull her big green Maglite from under her bed upstairs and then retrieved the smaller red Duralight from under the couch in the living room. Taka had the mudroom Mag in his hand when she came back, slapping it in his other palm and glaring at it.

"Batteries in the junk drawer," she said, tipping her chin at the end of the kitchen counter.

He fished them out while she checked the beams of the two flashlights she held before she set them down and slid her boots back on. She tied the knots tight, double bowing them.

Taka snorted at her stall tactic. "Ready?" he said.

"Windbreaker," she replied, and went and got it. She stuffed the small flashlight between her leather belt and the waistband of her jeans. He handed her big Mag back to her, holding onto it until she looked up at him.

"You okay?"

Not trusting her voice, she only nodded.

They walked the same pattern as earlier in the day through the damp grass. The steady, back and forth swing of Taka's light was reassuring. Andrea scanned the fence lines. The only fresh earth in the yard, a shallow scrape under the fence, appeared to be a opossum's escape route from the yard rather than a hole something the size of the Keds could be plucked from.

"Hey," Taka hissed. "Look here." He stood at the rear corner of the house, at the far side of the carport. She trotted over, her light careening over bushes and trees, and then pointed it down in trepidation. There wasn't much to see. A dark hole as wide as her fist. It sloped down under the concrete foundation of the carport. Dirt flared from it onto the grass.

"Um, snake?" she ventured.

"Like a black racer?"

Could it be that Billie Mae had been advertising the location of her missing tennis shoe for however long Mr. Huntley had been seeing her? He said "your little girl" so had he never seen her before Andrea moved in? Didn't he think it odd that Andrea never took her anywhere? Suddenly Andrea had more questions for Mr. Huntley than a kindergartner at the county fair.

Taka grunted. "We can't question him without tipping him off that no little girl lives here," he said, his thought processes running along the same lines as hers.

"I'm not sticking my hand down there," she said.

Taka disappeared and came back with her old rake. Although grey and weathered, the wooden handle was perfect for poking. He handed her his light, saying, "Hold this." Andrea rolled her eyes.

Edging the rake handle into the hole, Taka probed it with gentle pokes. A good foot or so of handle disappeared.

"I'm just hitting dirt. Might be nothing. Let's check the rest of the foundation along the house and kind of non-suspiciously check the front yard. We can look at this better in the morning."

Andrea nodded. How weird had this day turned out anyway? "Non-suspiciously?" she said.

"Swing your light wide. If anyone happens by, just say we're looking for my keys."

She nodded again, starting to feel numb.

They separated and walked the perimeter of the house. Andrea stopped and pulled her phone from her pocket. Yes, black racers do use old burrows as dens. Interesting. She went through the gate on the far side of the yard, flashlight centered along the concrete block of the house's foundation. A line of dried mud sat several inches up the block from rainfall erosion. She'd have to ask Kenny about installing gutters someday.

Around front, Taka was making a show of checking the ground around the Yukon. Moving faster, she scanned the grass and swept across the yard, looking for uneven spots or dirt mounds. She found an ant hill, but that was all. Lifting her head, she threw a furtive glance across the street. She thought Mr. Huntley might be watching them from his front window, though she couldn't tell for sure. Her other neighbors wouldn't alert without a very loud commotion.

The beagle that lived in the backyard next to Mr. Huntley's bayed, sharp and low. Andrea jumped, her hand flying to her pounding heart. Taka's light swung up, pointed across the street. The beagle let loose again with a long deep hunting howl. Spotlights on the corner of the house came on. Taka opened his truck door and Andrea walked over, eyes still downcast to check the last of the yard, but nothing seemed remiss out front. Taka held his hand out. She took it and tilted her head up, giving him a wide fake smile that made him laugh. He slammed the door shut, beeped the alarm, and they walked back to the front door. Andrea patted her pockets.

No keys.

"I found mine in my tactical bag this afternoon," Taka said and tugged them from his jeans pocket. He opened the door and held it for her.

She flicked the porch light on as they entered and then shut the door firmly behind him and turned the lock. She leaned against it, her forehead against the cool wood. "What are we doing?"

"Looking for wherever that shoe's been hidden all these years."

"Seriously, are we seriously doing that?"

"You mean are we seriously thinking a ghost knows what happened to her or these other kids and do we believe her?"

Andrea turned to face him. "I looked it up. That could be a black racer den."

Drawing a deep breath, he straightened himself, tipping his head back to study the ceiling, thinking before he spoke. "The facts are clear. A girl in this house was murdered. At the time of her death, she was wearing her right shoe. We—"

"Found the left shoe." Andrea.

Taka's focus shifted to her. "Someone found a left shoe. Correct color, correct size."

"But we have it now. Why does it matter where it was buried?"

He considered her for a long moment, that shuttered look back in his eye. "She threw the snake at you *after* we had the shoe. It must matter."

"Do we try to dig up tonight?"

"No, I think if we did that after the police presence today, all your neighbors would call it in at the same time and we'd be having to try to explain all this to both Ronnie Horton and Captain Cahill before we can even explain it to ourselves. We'll wait until tomorrow. And to cover ourselves, we'll head to Lowe's first thing and buy a flat of discounted pansies or a bush, something that can be planted this time of year."

"Blueberries."

"Okay," he said, in a tone of voice that really meant "that was fast." "Blueberries it is."

"Why do we have to cover ourselves?"

"Well, ghost info. I really don't think I can take the teasing, can you?"

She opened her mouth.

"Wait, don't answer that. I just remembered you have an entire department devoted to the paranormal at your job."

She smirked. "It was more fun when you didn't believe in ghosts."

"Too late now," he said. "But I want the plausible excuse of planting something—"

"Blueberries."

"—if we dig up anything we can actually run by the department. And I want to go through that box, see what Detective Ford's investigation found to support Etta Robbins confession."

THEY SPLIT A beer and sorted the paperwork as they emptied the case box of a dozen damaged files, and a pile of water stained floppy discs. "I have a USB floppy drive," Taka said, doubt lacing his voice.

"Not getting anything off these," Andrea said, turning them over in her hand.

Taka took one only to squint at the smudged and indecipherable label, before waving a hand at the files. "I'm sure all this paper is the hard copy, anyway. Can't do that anymore."

The last file contained eight by tens of scene photos. Andrea glanced at the top one— Billie Mae in her shorts and yellow tee, lying crumpled and wet in the tub, face turned away from the camera, the ligatures

Andrea saw several times a week clearly visible on her neck. She pinched the file closed and offered it to Taka, who placed it to one side for later. Two wrinkled folders containing thirty pages or so each were spotted with mold and stuck together. Andrea pulled them apart and laid the pages on the floor, one by one. Another held duplicates of all the case's request forms. She shuffled those together and put them back in the box. The other files were a mix of handwritten and typed pages. Taka sneezed explosively.

"Gesundheit."

He sneezed again. "Wow," he said, his eyes watering. And then he sneezed again and yet again, convulsing each time. He stood, sneezing again, and again. "Can you..." He waved his hand in the direction of the moldy papers on the floor. She scraped them up. Reaching for the last, which had slid under his chair, she sneezed, too, and again and again.

Fighting for breath between sneezes, she brought her hands up, letting go of the papers. They scattered like leaves on a wind gust, floating sideways through the air. One landed on the kitchen table, the others back on the floor. Both of them breathed hard, waiting for the next round. Taka's face was red, his cheeks wet. He leaned over to catch his breath. Andrea's lungs hurt. She sniffed and wiped her eyes.

"Hey," Taka breathed.

Practicing caution, Andrea knelt to re-gather the papers, keeping them as far from her face as she could.

"This is a witness statement," Taka continued. "Oliver Fitch."

"A witness statement? There weren't any witnesses. When police arrived, Etta Robbins was alone, except for Billie Mae's little brother, who was only four."

"Ford canvassed after the murder. Mr. Oliver Fitch said he'd seen Billie Mae down on Cooper—" The road that ran down to the boat ramp.

"He saw her that day?"

"Saw her..." He considered the report, squinting at the handwriting. "Saw her just before dark the night before, running back to her house from down the street. Said she had a firecracker lit to her tail."

Andrea made a grab at the paper. "Let me see that."

He kept it out of her reach. "That's what it says." Taka laid it down, keeping a proprietary hand on it and ran his index finger under the line for her to read. It did indeed say that the girl ran like she had a lit firecracker tied to her tail.

"She was six. He didn't stop her?"

"One, not his child. Two, he did stop, but she didn't turn when he called after her. He didn't know her name, just called out..." He consulted the report and read out loud. "'Girl, hey girl.' Said he knew her name now and he was awfully sorry he didn't offer her a ride, but she was running towards home."

"Where does Mr. Fitch live?"

"Baltimore."

"Baltimore?"

"Yeah. He was, let's see, visiting his sister at the time."

"Hmmm," Andrea said.

"Yeah," Taka agreed, nodding. "Big hmmm." His gaze rolled over the rest of the photocopy. And then his eyes widened, his lips opening. They were chapped, Andrea noted, and then tamped down the voice in her head offering to moisten them for him. "The sister, her name's Pepper."

"First or... oh, now that is interesting."

"Isn't it? Last name. She lives next door."

Andrea saw her gardening sometimes. Fifties, thick-waisted with the profile of a Roman beauty, and shoulder-length blond hair.

Andrea once more rounded the moldy papers up from the floor, with nary a sneeze.

Taka's eyebrows rose. "I don't think we're in Kansas, anymore, Dorothy."

CHAPTER SIX

AT TEN FIFTEEN, Andrea stifled a huge yawn.

"Me, too," Taka said and slapped the courtroom file he was reading closed. "Mom was mum after her initial confession. Said she didn't know what happened. She was angry. Said it over and over until she got herself convicted. What happened to the brother?"

Andrea shrugged. "Went to health and human services first, then to a relative. That's all the report I found said." She waved a hand at the box. "If I'm remembering right."

"You have the memory of a spring hinge bear trap, darlin'," Taka drawled. "Mind if I…"

Share my bed? Andrea thought, but didn't say out loud. "Stay? No, of course not."

"I'm just a cuddle toy to you, aren't I?" he asked with suspicion.

She tilted her head, lifting her lip in the patented half smile she'd perfected the year she fell in love with a boy in school who liked to emulate James Dean. It took her months to discover she'd never score a date with him, but the smile had proved useful for years. She always pulled it out when being coy. No harm, no foul, and she hoped Tommy Duker was blissfully happy, but she was still of the opinion that they'd have had beautiful children.

Taka assessed her calculated expression. "You're thinking about Tommy Duker, aren't you," he said, and let loose a grin that lit his whole face up.

She failed to stop the bubble of giggle that burst up out of the anxiety of the day.

"You are! You do know he's a married actuary in Tulsa now, don't you?"

"An actuary," she squeaked, surprised at how the info that he married flushed heat into her cheeks.

Taka laughed. Put his head back and laughed like that was the funniest two words he'd ever heard.

"I thought he was—"

"So did he. But now he's happily married to some chick named Anna and they have four kids. Still surprises the hell outta him."

"When did you talk to him?"

"When his dad died last year. He came by the station for something to do with the estate. Want I should get him to send pics of the beautiful kids you didn't have for him?"

"No," she said primly. She could still think of him in rainbow-land if she wanted. "Damn, you ruined him for me. Now all I can picture are his kids."

"Sorry, porn queen. Why don't you go read some of that fanfic stuff online so you can sleep tonight? I'll clean this up."

She handed him the moldy stack of papers and he waved them under his nose. Nothing. Andrea wiped her nose at the reflexive tingling she felt waiting for him to sneeze. She still needed to set the closet to rights. She'd never sleep if she left it trashed. In the mudroom, she bagged all the single shoes that belonged upstairs. As she passed Taka, she said, "I'll jump in the shower before I attempt the closet. Then the bathroom's all yours.

TAKA STRAIGHTENED THE case box, separating the documents they'd looked at from those they hadn't, and put the top back on. He picked up the Ziploc containing the shoe, turning the bag in his hands. The scene photos of the right shoe showed the same distinctive zigzagging line of stitching along the worn rubber edge. While not unique in itself, the stitching had been traced with a wavering hand in blue marker. The left Keds was stained and the blue marker faded, but there, along with a little blue flower drawn on the canvas above the instep.

He put the kettle on to boil, checked the football scores on ESPN in the living room, and then carried Andrea's laptop and a cup of chamomile tea upstairs for her. A bedroom lay at either end of the short hall with a bathroom sitting between them. He paused at the top of the stairs to listen to that comforting sound of non-loneliness, the shower running. He imagined opening the door, the warmth of the steam filling the tiny room. He could hardly turn in that shower without pulling the curtain down by accident. Definitely not a place for two. Even as his blood stirred in anticipation of the slide of wet skin on his own, his heart lurched.

Never. Never would he risk whatever it was he and Andrea were to each other. Not friends; best friends. Not lovers; soul-mates. He'd read once, in a book he thumbed through to better understand a witness statement, about the concept of souls which were divided for incarnation into two separate bodies. He and Andrea could be that. It sometimes made sense at three in the morning when he couldn't sleep. One soul, living as two.

Tearing himself from his thoughtful drift, he set the laptop on Andrea's king-sized bed. It ate up the little room with its massive size. The frame was a mahogany four-poster she'd gotten at a fire sale in Hickory, NC, and wedged into the hatchback of her FX in little disassembled pieces for the drive home. As payment for bed assembly he'd demanded sleeping privileges and after a token argument against, she'd surprised him and honored his demand. He'd never intended to take her up on it, but then one night after a nightmare he had tiptoed in, laid down beside her, and lost himself to the habit forever when she spread her heat against his side and sighed.

God, he was a fool.

She had the best taste in sheets. Some blah blah Egyptian high thread count that was cotton or bamboo or something, but felt like silk. He refused to buy the same for himself, because he would only ruin them with spilled beer and bread-crumbs while he watched TV. Andrea said bedrooms were for sleeping and sex and not TV watching.

Top-of-the-line plantation shutters in black dominated the window, which she had chosen as the focal point of the room. She told him she only closed them during the full moon. An antique wardrobe, darkened by age, and three narrow floor-to-ceiling bookcases complemented the four-poster and hardwood floor. Taupe walls, dark sheets, and a duvet covered in deep blue and green peacock swirls as finishing touches made her bedroom the ultimate retreat, for all that he could cross it in three short strides.

He contemplated the closet door. After wiping his sweaty palms on the thighs of his jeans, he slid the door open. The interior remained trashed, he was disappointed to see. "Billie Mae, the least you could do is clean up after yourself," Taka muttered, feeling stupid even as the words slipped out. Did he really believe in ghosts now?

Setting his mind on the task in front of him, he plucked a green canvas woody thing from the shoe bag that he thought he remembered being called an espadrille, and hunted up the other, lying beside a stack of tax forms and underneath a knit hoodie. He looked at the pair and then threw them out into the bedroom. Andrea so did not need those shoes. He threw out a ratty pair of black heels and a florescent red dress, which was hanging neatly, but didn't deserve the space, and then tossed a khaki wedge with a collapsed heel.

"Ow," Andrea yelped. "Hey, what are you doing?"

She had on the blue terrycloth robe she bought the summer they went white-water rafting on the Gauley over in Oak Hill and her spare clothes had gotten soaked.

"What are you doing," she said again, in a sterner voice.

"Gathering daises," he said. He looked around at the almost fully committed neatness surrounding him. "Cleaning your closet?"

"What's this stuff out here?"

"The burn pile."

"Really?"

"Really," he said gravely. He tugged a wine-colored pair of bell bottom jeans off the shelf at his eye level, where he was kneeling on the floor sorting shoes. "What's with these?"

She stalked in and snatched them from him. "Mine." She looked down at them and frowned, then smiled all crooked. Not her fake smile, but a real one, the one where her chin wrinkled up as she tried to keep the smile off her face. She tossed the pants out the door. "I don't know what they are. Goodwill's now. I'll finish up. Why don't you grab a shower? I put fresh sheets on the couch."

"Okay," he agreed. They both knew that despite his earlier remark, she was his cuddle toy, not vice versa. They liked to pretend he'd stay where he started at the beginning of the night. He groaned as he stood. His feet were asleep.

Andrea smirked. "There's always the guest room, old man."

Not only did the guest room have the smallest double bed ever made, it gave him the creeps. "Never again."

"And yet you'll sleep in here, after Billie Mae scared us silly," Andrea said, spreading her arms out to indicate the whole room.

"Safety in numbers."

She laughed and waved him away. Taka stomped the pins and needles out of his feet as he trudged down the hall.

SEARING ORANGE FLAME *races along the black lines of ink that curl around his wrist and up his forearm. He screams. Thinly corded stiff rope abrades the skin of his wrist as he tugs, trying to escape the flames. His back lights up and then his hair catches. He shakes his head, his long hair fanning out in a blaze of flame that tears, rips, sears into his ears, his scalp, his eyes. Inhaling burning, heated breath, inhaling fire—*

Taka sat straight up, gasping, reaching for the Glock beside him.

His hand landed on nothing. He opened his eyes. Sweat trickled over his brow from his forehead and down his ribs from his pits. He blinked and rubbed his hand across his eyes to clear the sting of salt from them. He was sitting on Andrea's couch, a tangle of bed sheets around his waist. The ceiling fan ticked steady as a metronome above his head. He shivered in its cool breeze, goosebumps rising on his wet skin. Jerking the sheets away, he swung his legs over to put his feet flat on the floor. The soft carpet gave under his toes.

He reached down beneath the couch and fingered his gun for reassurance. The house was quiet. The night was quiet. Generally, there was little traffic noise here and only the occasional volley of barks from the beagle across the street. No other dogs lived on the surrounding streets, at least no outside alarm kind of dogs.

Taka's family had always had outside dogs. They guarded not only their own seven acres, but the neighbors, too. They knew their job. They curled up on the front and back doorsteps at night. His mother's tap on the window could silence them. Sometimes she would wade out among them in the dark and quell whatever beast they barked at—chase it off or help them tree it—and then they'd all settle without complaint back into the purpose of their lives, watching and waiting for the next intrusion.

Taka had ventured the dog discussion with Andrea once, but she said no, in a voice like his mother's, which brooked no argument, and that was the end of it. She didn't want the guilt of not meeting its needs and knowing she was failing. She didn't mention her own mother and the years she spent dying, but Taka knew that's where her resistance lay. He wanted a dog, but shit, he couldn't even keep his girlfriend occupied and happy.

He hadn't told Andrea the whole of Melinda's text that, combined with Carson's call, had him whipping up a batch of comfort sauce. *Calld u'r wrk. U'r at hers? A Scott came lkng 4 u? U're nvr home. Key n kit.*

U're nvr home. Both she and Andrea were right. He kept odd hours and might be gone for days, sometimes with no notice. His heart no longer jumping, he took a real breath. He stretched. The night light above the kitchen stove flickered, startling him. Silence. After a moment he got up and went into the kitchen. The light burned steady. He opened the refrigerator door, and pulled out the water pitcher. Sitting at the table to drink a glass, he let the sweat dry on his skin. His shirt was damp, but it was the last tee he had packed, so he'd just sit until it dried a bit. The trees swayed outside. Darker than burnt. He needed to arrange a load of cordwood for Andrea. He had a fireplace too, but it was gas.

The thought of flames leaping up the gas jets brought his recurring dream back to him, and the memories it was rooted in. Tooling around off base one day in the backend of nowhere, just driving with all the windows down, no one in his face, or ordering him around, he'd stopped for gas. A black 4Runner pulled up behind him as he climbed back into the junker Sunbird he owned at the time, but he didn't really look at it. Pulling away from the pump, he glanced in the rearview and there the driver stood, white guy, white hair plastered to his head, shirt clinging to his skinny chest. The man raised his right hand in a fist. Gas sprayed from the pump handle in his left hand. He let it drop, his fingers stretched wide.

Riveted to the rearview mirror, he saw the man's mouth open as the lighter leapt into life in his raised hand. A tenth of a second. A breath. A lifetime.

Taka looked back to the road to find a big rig turning in off the road in his way to the right. He jerked a hard left onto the two lane. A sedan coming at him fishtailed, brakes smoking. Standing on the accelerator, Taka slipped the Sunbird between the two and then spun the wheel, the retreads screeching, and dropped the Sunbird into the deep ditch on the other side of the road. He flung himself out the far side, through the passenger door, to see what was happening over the top of the car.

The driver of the sedan bailed out, leaving it sitting on the road and ran for the cover of the Sunbird, his breath shrieking, spit on his chin, terrified. They watched the burning man flail on the ground in his self-created hellfire, arms and legs kicking until he laid still. The flames rose three or four feet high. The stench of burned flesh drifted over the road. They didn't notice the lady standing frozen, the pump nozzle she'd been removing from her ancient mini-van's tank gushing, until she moved, dropping it, to yank at the van's sliding door.

The van disappeared in a blinding flash, a deep whump of vacuum pressing on Taka's inner ear. A concussive wave of heat rolled over him. Taka couldn't look away. The entire back half of the van was engulfed in flame. The burning woman tumbled to a stop ten feet into the parking lot.

The truck driver swung down out of his cab with a big extinguisher in hand. An employee came running out of the store with the same, customers spilling out behind him. Next to Taka, the sedan driver sobbed. Legs weak, Taka jerked the Sunbird's rear door open and laid across his back seat to snag his extinguisher. He ran across the road. Someone crouched next to the burnt woman, patting at her smoldering clothes. The employee doused what was left of the man who started it all. Taka joined the truck driver in battling the mini-van fire, biting back the acid that filled his throat when he saw the kid-sized blackened corpse inside.

Taka had met his Maori grandfather exactly one time. He hadn't said much amid the loud crush of an impromptu family reunion, but just before Taka left, he'd pulled Taka close to him, leaned down, and said, "Try your best, that's all God wants from you."

He'd seemed sure and confident and Taka hoped someday he'd be able to say those words to a grandson in just such a way. With total certainty. But in the meantime, the burnt woman still haunted him. She'd stayed when she could have run and she'd tried her best, but it hadn't been good enough. His brother had done the same, years later, on an aircraft carrier. Although Taka had been thousands of miles away, he knew exactly how Andrew had flailed and burnt and fallen. Saw it in his head over and over.

Taka burned in his dream, a participant, not a spectator. Penance for all the things he'd been too dense to understand or too scared to make happen until too late, for all the times he didn't try his best. Maybe, like he'd absorbed the injustice of the burnt woman's death although she had tried her best, Andrea had absorbed the wrong done to Billie Mae, was somehow manifesting the seemingly ghostly disturbances through her empathy.

The melancholy of standing in the hall, his ear to the door, listening to Andrea's shower run, wanting the hot wet slide of her skin on his, washed over him. The kitchen closed around him. I'm not scared of it, Taka told himself. He pushed himself to his feet, breaking the spell. I'm scared of losing it.

Glancing at the sideboard, Taka decided yes, he would. Moving the fancier Eagle Rare out of the way, he lifted the Jack Daniels Black and helped himself to a finger, neat. It burned down his throat. He'd never sleep now. He fingered his phone, sitting on the table. Scott would be leaving work about now. He was just a bartender at Dewey's, but trying for more. He probably already knew that Taka wouldn't be dropping by the club any more. Deciding against, Taka went back into the living room and sat on the couch for a few minutes. Nope. He shuddered, imagining Billie Mae's presence right beside him.

He stalked upstairs and pushed Andrea's half-closed door open with his fingertips, slipped through the wan moonlight drifting through the window, and slid without a ripple into the lake of her dreams.

CHAPTER SEVEN

WAKING ON HER side, Andrea opened her eyes. Billie Mae stood in front of her. Looking at the floor. Andrea rolled over to see what she was doing. Her feet were bare. Billie Mae wiggled her toes. Andrea followed her long legs back up to her jean shorts and frowned at her yellow tee. Billie Mae had never greeted the morning dressed in her death day outfit before. Dawn always brought Billie Mae in her nightgown. Andrea opened her mouth to speak. Billie Mae winked out of existence.

Surprised, Andrea rose up on one elbow, but then stopped herself. Sunday. Pulling the covers up over her head, she rolled over and burrowed in against hot Taka. Her brain spun, showing her Billie Mae's bare toes wiggling over and over. Somehow, she fell back asleep.

When she woke up again she pinched Taka's bicep until he opened one eye.

"Bacon. Coffee. Lowe's."

He closed his eye and rolled over with attitude, bouncing her up and down on the mattress. But she knew he'd get up. She went down the hall to the bathroom, goosebumps rising across her shoulders and arms as she thought about Billie Mae. The bacon would lure her out. Wanting to be ready to go right after breakfast, Andrea wound through her whole bathroom routine before she opened the door again and ran into Taka, who had his fist raised to knock.

"About to send in the hounds," he grumbled.

She sneered at him and flounced down the hall to get dressed. She had the coffee rolling and was laying bacon in the pan when he appeared in the kitchen, dressed in jeans and nothing else.

"Hey," he said, hanging his head. He sweated through his tee shirts at night and if he thought she didn't know that well... whatever. She couldn't function, yet, waiting for the pan to heat. She pointed at the mudroom. Three of his shirts, a ragged-out pair of jeans, and five pairs of jockeys were sitting on her dryer. She kept burying them, but they were there.

"Underneath," she called, when he had been gone too long.

He shambled back in. "Thanks," he mumbled. "How come you have so much of my underwear?"

She shrugged. "Considering I never get to take them off you, I haven't the foggiest."

Silence.

Andrea looked over her shoulder. He was simply standing, a piqued look on his face. "What? Did I say that out loud?" she said.

He closed his eyes.

Not the reaction she expected. She focused on the sizzling bacon.

A flicker of shadow moved unnaturally in the corner of her eye.

"Hiding, Billie Mae?" she asked. "Come out, come out, wherever you are."

The shadow moved, not at all paired to the light behind whatever was throwing it. It made her kind of sick to her stomach.

"Billie Mae?" She said uncertainly, glancing around. She turned.

Taka's gaze followed the shadow. It moved nearly bare toe to bare toe with him. Billie Mae shimmered into being. Taka relaxed and walked through her to sit at the table. He raised a shaky hand to his eyes and rubbed them. "Shit," he said. "I think I saw her."

Andrea's jaw dropped. "You saw her?"

"I don't know. Maybe it was just the light."

Billie Mae stood watching Taka somewhat gleefully, like he was a chocolate bar. Andrea wondered if Billie Mae had picked that up from watching her watch Taka.

"Do you see her now?"

He glanced around the room. "No. I'm just tired. Probably just got her stuck in my head after yesterday."

Andrea laughed. Billie Mae's rich, little girl laugh echoed along.

Taka spooked, his body jerking.

"You heard that! You heard her!"

Billie Mae and her bare feet vanished. The bacon wasn't even done yet.

"That's weird," Andrea said, her excitement fading.

"I think I'm gonna faint," Taka stage-whispered.

Andrea dropped the tongs in her hand and ran over to him. Laying her hand against the back of his neck, she shoved his head down between his knees. "Breathe," she demanded. Taka was too big to be sprawled across her kitchen floor. She'd have to call for help or wait him out.

He gagged a little and then sat quietly under her hand, breathing in through his nose and out his mouth.

"She poofed already," Andrea reassured him. "But that was her. You saw her. You heard her laugh with me."

He shook his head and sat up, pushing her hand away. "I think I'll just sit here until the coffee's ready."

"You do that," she said, amused at his weak stomach. She'd never seen a ghost other than Billie Mae, but Billie Mae had never scared her. Until last night. Sure she had the willies after their first couple of encounters, but no, it didn't really bother her. Still, she was glad she'd never seen any others. Have one show up in the library and she'd probably faint dead away, but here, in this house she already loved, Billie Mae fit fine. Until now.

Andrea flipped the bacon and shut off the clucking coffee pot before pouring it into mugs.

"Thanks," Taka said when she set his mug down on the table. As she turned away, he caught her hand, eyes downcast. He reeled her in and hugged her. God, she loved him. She hugged him back and then patted his head and let go.

Reluctantly, it seemed to her, he unwound his arms from her waist. "Why haven't we ever..."

She knew exactly where he was going with those aborted words. They'd had this conversation at least four separate times, always during crises, in their long history together. She raised her brows. He took a sudden interest in his coffee.

Andrea rescued the eggs and scooped them out on a plate, stacking four pieces of bacon beside them. The leftover spaghetti sauce heating in the microwave went on top. Decorated in red, the fluffy, yellow eggs looked amazing. She set the sauce bowl on the counter, found shredded cheese in the refrigerator and sprinkled it on the meal. Grabbing two forks, she sat down, the plate between them.

When he took hold of his fork she held onto it until he looked up at her. "You're my best friend," she said. "Just say the word." Put the ball squarely in his court, that's what she'd done last time, too. "I won't wait on you, but I won't turn you down, either."

Taka nodded. They didn't speak through their shared breakfast, though he did get up and make toast, handing her a buttered slice as she took the last bite of eggs. They fought over the last of the sauce with their torn pieces of toast. He cleared and put the clean dishes away while she rinsed the pans and tidied the counter and then handed him the dirty plates and silverware, which he loaded in the washer. They always worked like this, she mused. Had been for years. Doing the couple dance without all the juicy parts. And not a lot of words passed between them.

HE WENT TO dress while she checked e-mail. She left her computer open on the kitchen table while she took the trash out, glancing into the back yard when she did, still wary. When she came back in, he was online.

"Hey," he said. "I'm looking up Etta Robbins. I want to find out where she's at."

Andrea washed her hands and then peered over his shoulder. "You couldn't call someone down at the station to look up her location?"

"I don't want to answer any questions right now, y'know? Inmate search is public, anyway."

"Yeah, I capeesh." She watched him scroll through the links to various articles on the case and the trial. "It never occurred to me before yesterday that I might want to know where she's been all this time. It's not like she could help me with Billie Mae."

He keyed in *West Virginia inmate search* as he said, "I want to talk to her."

Andrea shuffled over and sat in the empty chair beside him. "Taka, it could take weeks to file the paperwork for you to go talk to her officially about her case when she's already been convicted. We need to figure this out now. What if these kids from the lake are related to Billie Mae somehow?"

He stared at the screen, thinking. "You could talk to her," he said, looking up at her. "You're living in this house and you're an archivist. You document the past for a living. No one will think twice about your interest in Billie Mae's death. You could say you're writing a book."

He started typing again. Andrea didn't lie very well, that had been pretty well-established by the time she was six and she'd never caught on. Taka wouldn't lie. He could, and very, very well, but he would do so only on the job, and wouldn't risk his job for a lie. "How else would I keep catching bad guys?" he'd explained when Andrea's girlfriend Fran asked him to go in and tell Blockbuster that the movie he'd loaned her had been returned when really, she had run it over in her driveway, along with her coffee mug and the mail she'd set down to look at a fairy ring in the grass.

"Got her. She's at Lakin Correctional near Huntington."

She rolled her eyes. "Let me think about it. Can we copy Billie Mae's case file?"

"It's been prosecuted, so the file's a public record. There doesn't appear to be anything sensitive as far as procedure in it." He chewed his bottom lip. "But I wouldn't copy it at like, FedEx, or anywhere like that."

It was currently a solved case. The department already knew he had the file if things blew up. Andrea had requested and been granted access to it in the spring under the Freedom of Information Act. They could argue her subcontractor status. She reached into her jeans pocket and pulled out her keychain with the key to the Waltham-Young library. "We can copy it. For reference. We'll destroy it later."

Taka shook his head, eyes closing in resignation, and then opened them, saying, "Let's go to Lowe's."

THEY DROVE EAST on 64 through Charleston, the fog burning off faster with every mile. The parking lots of the numerous churches they passed were all full. Neither she nor Taka held much with organized religion, but Taka had a very strong faith in God and his purpose on Earth. Andrea, not so much. She wanted to, but she had trouble reconciling all the pieces that felt right to her. Like both reincarnation and an afterlife. Like both forgiveness and vengeance as justice. Like her conviction that if there was a God, He was smart enough to figure out different kinds of people would approach Him in different ways, ergo, different takes on belief in Him. And Hell? She couldn't fathom a place of pain for all eternity with no chance of learning a better way.

Sure, maybe short term torture or instruction and then boom try this lifetime on for learning and if you still don't get it, get dunked in flames again but for all time, one shot at getting it right? It didn't sit well with the beauty of the world to her. Then there was Billie Mae. No doubt a few devotees would burn Andrea at the stake and condemn her to hellfire and damnation for all eternity just for having seen Billie

Mae. On the flip side, some would call her only an echo, a reflection of a mirror darkly, to quote the bible badly.

How could Billie Mae interact with them? Answer questions? Apparently move physical objects? If she really was a spirit, is an afterlife on earth purgatory? Andrea had tried to apply research mode to religion, but always got bogged down by unanswerable questions within a few pages of any study guide. Keeping faith meant letting go of a lot of unanswered questions.

Taka seemed content with that. Even when he got caught up in traffic on the way to a crime scene, or had a flat tire or got hurt on the job, he would only say through clenched teeth that there's a reason for everything. Maybe they'd have been in a wreck if they sailed through on clear roads. If his leg hadn't stopped that bullet, the soldier beside him would have bought it. The water heater flooded his closet to bring the super's attention to the old lady downstairs who needed Health and Human Services.

Fifteen years after her mother died Andrea still questioned why. But when Taka's older brother Andrew, ground crew on an aircraft carrier, was involved in a fiery crash on deck and died two months later without ever leaving the burn unit, Taka came home on leave and refused to join in the general lament of "why." Instead he sat outside the open door, watching the kids run around his aunt's front yard, letting the conversation glide over him and away. When Andrea joined him, he leaned into her and said, "God has a plan. My brother was an important part of it. He's an important part of me and I'm still here."

What was the purpose in Billie Mae's death? In any young child's death. In what way did people learn anything from them? She'd pushed Taka once on that very point. He had sighed, and tipped the empty shot glass next to his beer at an angle, watching the dregs slide down to form one perfect, amber drop as he rocked the glass. "If even one person donated money in that kid's name or stopped to help a child who needed it or picked flowers and laid them on the grave of someone they used to know…. If even one person stopped and thought, what a terrible thing, then that death, that *life* affected another. What does it mean in God's greater plan?" He'd shrugged, downed the last of his beer, and taken her home.

In a book he'd have made tender love to her, but they weren't a book, so he had let her get her own car door and go up her front walk alone and let herself in before he drove away, immersed in thought. She could write a book describing the cumulonimbus formations Taka's thoughts produced. And she could write a book about Billie Mae. Maybe that was God's reason, to touch many. She cleared her throat.

"Yes?" Taka said, his gaze straying from the road.

"Nothing," she said. "Just thinking."

He sighed, settled his hands at ten and two, and drove, thinking, too, so hard, Andrea could actually see his thoughts gathering, forming like mist around him.

"What's that smell?" he said.

Smoke, her brain supplied. "Holy cow, it's smoke. We're smoking," she said out loud, waving her hand through the wisps of grey.

Taka glanced around, checking his mirrors for other vehicles. "Is it that blue wagon to the left?"

Andrea craned her head. "No."

The odor strengthened and then smoke belched out of the Yukon's front vents into their faces. Flame licked out from under her side of the hood.

"Shit," Taka yelped and steered them to the shoulder. A black car blew its horn as it hurtled by on their left, rocking the Yukon in its wake. Smoke filled the car. Holding her breath, eyes watering, Andrea covered her nose and mouth with both hands.

"Now what," Taka snarled, shifting the truck into park. He turned the ignition off and pulled the key out in a short, sharp movement as he jerked on the hood release. They both piled out, coughing. Although Andrea didn't know much about engines, she met Taka at the front of the Yukon. He felt for the catch, released it, and shoved the hood up. Thick, black smoke billowed out and the flames roared straight up, making them both jump back.

CHAPTER EIGHT

TAKA DARTED AWAY and brought back an impressive fire extinguisher to have in a car, though it still didn't look up to the job to her. He sprayed it onto the flames. Andrea backed up further, coughing. The fire died fast as Taka emptied the extinguisher. The thinning smoke trailed away on the breeze, as did the expended gas from the extinguisher.

"Hmmm," Taka grunted, extinguisher still held at the ready. Andrea inched forward, searching the engine compartment for any flickers of leftover flame. No fire. No soot. No scorching. No visible residue from the chemical.

"What kind of extinguisher is that?"

A patrol car pulled in behind them, lights flashing. The young officer sprung out and came to join them in their consternation. "Detective Taka, isn't it," he said, gaze roaming over the engine.

"Uh, yeah," Taka said. "I'm sorry…"

"Chris Mendel, sir. We haven't actually met, but you're kind of..." He leaned away, assessing Taka. And then lifted his eyes to Taka's, his brows rising with them. "Unforgettable?"

Taka grinned. "Is that what they're calling me these days?"

"When they aren't calling you heartless, sir."

"Heartless?" Taka said, raising his hand to his chest. "Me?"

"And relentless," the officer added, with a smile. He was tall and gawky, but had a little paunch going despite his youth.

"That I am, Patrolman Mendel." He turned, extending a hand out towards Andrea. "This is my friend, Andrea. Right now we're on a mission to hit Lowe's for gardening supplies and, uh, this happened." He waved his hand through the last of the dissipating chemical fog and smoke.

"Halguard, sir?"

Taka held up the red extinguisher. "Pretty impressive, isn't it."

"I guess they mean it when they say no residue," Mendel agreed. He leaned in under the hood. "I don't see any scorch marks, sir."

Taka did the same. "I don't see anything, either."

"Do you know where the fire originated, sir?"

"No. Call me Taka."

"Yes, sir," Patrolman Mendel said. "Had a fire just like this a couple of weeks ago. Right here, I think, or within a couple hundred of yards anyway." He stepped back. "Several witnesses, but no one had an extinguisher. Everyone said it just went out, sudden as it started. That engine turned right over, sir, when the fire department tried it."

"Really," Taka said. He tilted his head at Andrea, a crease forming between his brows, his lips tight.

"I don't recommend it," Mendel stuttered. "Guy just jumped in and cranked it up after we'd stood there scratching our heads awhile cause the engine looked fine."

Taka vacillated.

"Go ahead," Andrea said. "Can't hurt it any more than the fire should have."

He made a face and took the keys from his pocket. The engine started right up and purred along in the same tone it always did. Andrea and Mendel stepped to either side when Taka waved them out of the way and rolled it forward ten feet. It was fine. He dropped it into reverse and rolled back. He shook his head and left it running while he got out and peered into its guts again. "I don't get it," he said.

Mendel shrugged. "Weird," he said, in a happy, life's-odd-and-I-don't-really-care tone.

An interesting thought occurred to Andrea. Not one Taka would like. "Patrolman Mendel, could you put the report of the other incident on Detective Taka's desk at end of shift?"

Mendel narrowed his eyes at her, his thumbs tucked in his utility belt.

Surprising her, Taka nodded and said, "Please."

"Yes, sir," Mendel said. "You okay here, then?"

"Yes, I believe we are," Taka said, dropping the Yukon's hood. "Don't know how. You could send a note down to someone in DOT to get someone to drive this section and check for anything on the road that might be lighting up when it's driven over."

They all looked at the perfectly normal grey paving, no pot holes or staining, and the cars whizzing by without incident.

"Maybe you should wait on that," Taka said.

"Maybe I should, sir. Thank you."

"You could check for incident reports on any chemical spills on the roadway," Andrea suggested and then bit her lip. They both nodded, though.

"Good idea," Taka said.

"I can certainly do that without..." Mendel paused, looking twelve years old as he searched for the phrasing he wanted. "Looking silly," he finished sheepishly.

Taka clapped him on the back and Mendel rocked forwards with the blow, having to step over to catch his balance. He grinned at Taka. "Yes, sir," he said, nodding as if Taka had spoken.

"Company," Andrea said, pointing at the state trooper slowing down to pull in behind Mendel's patrol car.

"Have a better day, folks," Mendel said and trundled off to meet him.

Taka looked at her. "What the fuck was that? What made you ask for the other driver's file? Is it another clue? How much is that gho—Billie Mae capable of, anyway?"

Andrea shrugged. "I'll look stuff up tomorrow, at work."

"What stuff?"

"Paranormal stuff, I don't know."

"Does she know?"

"Know what?"

"Y'know, my thing with fire. About Andrew."

Andrea shrugged. "I don't know how."

"You know."

"I do. But I'm not Billie Mae."

He held her gaze, but she had no idea what he was thinking.

"Everything okay, Detective?" The State Trooper stood behind his open car door, one foot out on the asphalt and one foot in.

Taka waved at him.

When they were squared away again, Taka pulled back out into traffic. Mendel and the trooper followed for a short distance. The car ran fine all the way to Lowe's Hardware, on the far east side of town. They sat in silence. By the time they arrived, Taka seemed decided on letting whatever he'd been thinking go.

He drooled just a little over a chainsaw and then a gas-powered log splitter, envisioning for her a weekend in the woods with "the boys," chopping wood for the winter. "Then wood wouldn't cost you anything, Andrea," he said before amending it to, "not much of anything." She knew he knew that he'd be crashing at her place just to build fires, and while he pitched in for food, it still cost her something for him to take up space in her house. Not to mention the hot water. Not that she minded.

They picked out a stout shovel and then two blueberry bushes which, as Andrea had thought, were regularly planted in the fall, and according to the garden clerk would overwinter just fine, especially with the windbreak the carport wall provided. "Little green leaves all over it by March or April," he claimed, enthused. "Depending on the frost."

They were cheap, and that's really all Andrea cared about, although it would be nice if she could beat the birds to some of the berries when they ripened. Taka snared a clear plastic tarp and heavy duty Ziplocs on the way out. The truck started right up. They both took a deep breath, Taka muttering, "Thank you," on his exhale.

The day blossomed gorgeous on the ride through downtown to the Kanawha river and Waltham-Young, the sky brilliant and the sun cheery in the sixty-eight-degree day. Andrea stripped her jacket off, dug in her purse for sunscreen, and smeared it on her arms. Taka watched her with one eye and drove with the other. "You should go work out with me," he said.

Andrea looked at her arms. They didn't look bad. At thirty-three, she didn't have the saggy triceps her young mother friends were starting to carry. "I like my arms."

"I like your arms, too," he said, giving her on what any other man she might call a leer.

"Pfft"

"Pfft?"

"My arms are good and what does it matter if you like them?"

"It matters because they aren't always gonna look like that and if you want them to look like that when you're forty, you should come work out with me."

From the corner of her eye, as she searched now for her face block, she saw him twist his lips up at his own words. "Maybe I will," she said, calling his bluff. She was sure it was a bluff. He was still teetering on his earlier rumination about their relationship and the reminder that his brother would never have another. He hadn't stuffed all his feelings back in the Taka Box which held all personal relationships at arm's length and labeled them "friendships."

"Good. We set up a schedule as soon as this"—he circled his hand in the air—"is over."

"You're on," she said.

THE INTERIOR OF Waltham-Young felt desolate under the dimmed Sunday afternoon lighting. According to Connie on the front desk, the only people in the building were security and an assistant in the third-floor file room. After clearing them in she sat back down with her feet propped up, watching the building's camera feeds on nine screens and the Green Bay game on the tenth.

Stephen Young had a passion for research that the public library couldn't support. Henry Waltham had money. Motivated by a desire to create a legacy for himself, Waltham struck a deal with Young and made the community a gift that half a century later it still didn't quite understand, but Andrea did. If research were edible, Andrea would be very, very fat.

Through the lobby boasting soaring works of modern art, they climbed a set of open stairs, Taka lugging the case box, and turned left past the conference rooms into a hallway with a wall of windows. Outside lay a courtyard that was easily one of the prettiest spots in all of Charleston. One massive old oak with a trunk span of seven feet anchored the plantings of dogwood, butterfly bushes, fireweed, red tips, red buds, and white azaleas. Seasonal flowers balanced the colors and a stone path that wound around and around in a spiral to the wooden benches built around the oak. Waltham-Young had other gardens, including edibles and koi ponds, but this little place of peace was Andrea's favorite.

Her office was half way down the window wall. She swiped her secure ID card and they entered her work space through the sliding glass pocket door. To the right, the wall was covered in cork, to which everything, absolutely everything, she needed was thumbtacked.

Photos of her travels, her friends, and all her siblings, Christmas the year they all went skiing, Shep, her old dog who passed years ago. Photocopies of documents she'd located for clients, bills that needed paying. A folded map of the New River Gorge trails teased her from the very center of the display. A pendant found taped to the bottom of a dresser drawer at an estate sale graced the upper right-hand corner.

Glancing left, Andrea half expected Billie Mae to be sitting in her office chair, with a big grin on her face. Floor to ceiling cabinets held all her supplies. A long counter along the back wall allowed her to spread out files and documents, and below it, open shelves accommodated all the various sizes of books she used for reference.

Andrea and most of the other full staff archivists and librarians had desktop copiers in their offices for small batch work, but it would take too long to run Billie Mae's file that way. She snagged her copier key from its storage on a thumbtack on the cork wall. They walked on through the L-shaped hallway, around the courtyard garden, and into a large room that held several overhead projectors corralled in one corner and three printers that collated and stapled and double sided and might serve you tea as well if you punched just the right buttons.

In this room she could use just one printer at a time. She inserted her key for inventory control of paper and ink. Taka slid the papers in each file off their metal pins, Andrea stacked them in the feeder tray and kept track of the copies. They watched as the printer spit them out in short order and Taka replaced them as Andrea stacked the next. They did the loose pages last. Half an hour and they were done.

Back in Andrea's office, they slid the copied contents of each file into individual manila folders, and marked them according to the original files.

"That wasn't too long," Connie said when they left.

"Longer than a Kentuckian is tall," Andrea smarted back.

"Then that's one big catch," Connie said, waving.

Andrea backed through the double front doors, hugging the manila folders against her chest, Taka on her heels, lugging the case box. "I don't get it," he said.

"Moby Dick, Taka."

"Librarian humor sucks," he grumped.

AT THE HOUSE, everything appeared normal and quiet to Taka. The neighbor two doors down was mowing his lawn. They unloaded and carried everything around to the back of the carport. The hole looked the same in daylight as it had the night before.

God, he hoped the snake wasn't in there, even if it was harmless. And he hoped there wasn't worse evidence of a crime down there—if that's where the Keds had been hidden. Please let it be a chipmonk hole. "This is really stupid. There's no logical reason to be digging this hole up."

Crossing her arms over her chest as she stood next to him, Andrea nodded. "I'd totally agree if Billie Mae hadn't been sitting out front in full view of Mr. Huntley with a snake on her lap for long enough that he thinks she's my daughter."

Taka stuck the shovel in, cleared a little patch of grass and then drove the blade down. Andrea stood behind him, hands on her hips, though he knew he could hand her the shovel and she'd dig into the hard soil with passion, even if it took her longer. His phone vibrated in his back pocket. He ignored it, thinking it was a text, but it was a call. Pausing, he pulled it out with a glance at Andrea before he looked down. Carson.

He handed the shovel over to Andrea and thumbed the phone open as he walked deeper into the yard. "Taka."

"Hey, Tak, got a meeting with the County on this shooting. They're sending O'Malley."

"Well, shit." O'Malley was an investigator with the Kanawha County Prosecutor's Office, which meant... "Did he die?"

"No. Hanging in there."

"He was shooting at us, Carson." How many more times would he say that? A hundred? A thousand? "He beat a girl, slammed her head in a wall, and left her to die. We did nothing wrong, why's the County stepping in already?"

"Allegedly killed," Carson corrected him. "And the County's involved because he's related to a City Councilman. Conflict of interest for Charleston PD."

"That's bullshit."

"Actually, it'd be better for you normally, but I'm not going to lie. Having Dewey Sanderson on the rampage, with or without his dad's influence, is going to make this particular game a lot harder to play."

A thunk had him turning around. Andrea lifted the shovel again to drive the point down into the cold ground with another thunk. Off-duty and still digging up a case to work on, that was him in a nutshell.

"It's not a game, Carson. This is my life."

"I know. Tuesday. One o'clock, okay? Pro Standards' conference room."

Taka sighed. Carson wasn't the bad guy, and he'd become a close friend. "What about Tracy?"

"Detective Manners is clear of O'Malley and depending on PSD's report, off administrative leave after his Shooting Board hearing late next week. You were lead and both the bullets in Zach Taylor's chest were yours."

"That was fast."

"Not every day a Charleston cop shoots someone, Taka. PSD is pulling out all the stops, cashing in on all their favors. Tuesday. One o'clock. Upstairs, okay?"

"Yeah, Carson," Taka grouched, watching Andrea stomp on the shovel's back edge. "Tuesday. One o'clock. Got it."

"Did he die?" Andrea asked when he took the shovel back just as she was lifting it again.

"No, but the Kanawha PA's calling it a conflict of interest for the CPD because of Miller's involvement, so now the County's stepping in with their own investigation."

"But not the State Police."

He blanked for a second, not able to even imagine it. "No," he said, sharper than he intended. "It was a clean shoot." A total prick since the first time Taka met him seven years ago, O'Malley didn't act like the field training officer he'd once been for the State Police Academy, which trained every police officer in the state no matter what agency employed them. Someday Taka really, really, wanted to know what had happened to make the man so bitter towards cops, but O'Malley was also honest and detail-oriented and a good investigator. "I swear, Andrea, it was clean. I'll be back on duty in no time."

Andrea had dug quite the hole already, piling the dirt on the tarp they'd spread out just in case there was evidence and the dirt needed sifting later. Taka turned the shovel over and probed with the sharp edge. Then he picked it up and chunked it in, loosening the dirt, a rocky brown soil with streaks of clay. He evened the space out to about two feet square and deep.

Andrea left and came back dragging the hose. She watered the blueberry bushes, loosening them from the sides of their pots. Working now under the edge of the foundation, Taka started angling the hole back, but lost the little tunnel, which collapsed on itself as he dug.

"Hey," he said. "Get me a flashlight, will you?"

He took the light from her when she returned and lay down on his belly to peer into the hole and under the foundation. The carport was on a slab, and the hole fell away at an angle underneath it. "I wonder how long the carport's been here. Was it added or was it here when Billie Mae lived here?"

"I don't know. I can call my landlord."

"Not yet," he said. He stood up, handing her the light back and dug the entrance out wider and deeper before carefully hollowing the tunnel leading back under the slab. Sweat dampened his shirt and ran down his face and neck. He dropped down again after a while and held his hand up. Andrea slapped the light into it.

"Shit," he said.

"You know, I think you've said that more in the last twenty-four hours than you have in the past six months."

"Well, shit," he said again.

"What is it?"

"I think it's bone."

"What do you mean, bone?"

"It's a skull, I think."

CHAPTER NINE

ANDREA DROPPED DOWN onto her belly, too, wedging in beside Taka to get a not-very-good view into a small burrow.

He pointed the light at a cracked yellowed dome poking out of the back. "It's kind of small."

"Kids are kind of small."

"No, I mean animal small." He reached in.

"Wait!"

"What? I'm not calling a CSI out for a non-human skull."

"Okay, be careful."

Taka stretched all the way out, arm buried to his shoulder, toes wedged into the grass. Andrea scooched over and he wiggled in a bit tighter, his face scrunching up. "I got it, I think, wait." He shifted his arm, scrabbling around the curve of bone until he could wedge his fingers beneath a dulled edge.

"What are you doing?"

"Gotta dig a little," he said, prying dirt away until the skull loosened. He scooted back, drawing his arm out. It was larger than he'd thought it would be, and topped in something papery and grey. A snakeskin. Taka brushed it off the broken dome and scraped the snout clean of clay.

Andrea ran a finger over it. "Dog."

"Large dog," Taka said in agreement.

"Anything else in there?"

"The rest of it, I think. I could feel a jumble of something hard in the dirt."

"Let's dig a little more."

They took turns, carefully excavating under a good portion of the slab. He was right. The bones were there, along with a small ratty blanket, and a nearly disintegrated stuffed rabbit.

"Weird," Taka said. "It's a burial."

"Yeah, but nothing you could say wasn't just a regular pet grave. People put all sorts of stuff in, right? That bunny could be the dog's," Andrea reasoned.

"Maybe. At any rate, we can't prove Billie Mae's shoe came from there and it's nothing we can call the department in on. Probably has nothing to do with any of it."

"Maybe. Was the blue shoe in my yard a definite match to the one the divers found at the lake?"

"No one let me know for sure and I'm not calling in today. It's not my case. I'm already getting shut down on Billie Mae."

"Let's get some pictures."

When they finished, he bagged the blanket and bunny in separate large Ziplocs. After turning the dog skull to study the large fracture that traversed the dome and split into two branches above the right eye socket, he bagged it, too. "So it's impossible to say this is where Billie Mae's white Keds came from," he said, running his fingers over the plastic zipper to close the bag.

"Right," Andrea said, picking up on his tone.

"*And* it's pure supposition to think this is in any way connected to the blue Keds. *And* the blue Keds might not have anything to do with the boy in the lake."

"Let's just..." She didn't finish. She dragged the blueberries over. He groaned, but back filled most of the excavated dirt into the hole and helped her plant the bushes to either side of it along the edge of the concrete slab, giving them enough room to spread to all sides. He packed the extra dirt around them with the flat of the shovel and she watered them in.

"I'll have to get mulch or something," she said, staring at the freshly turned dirt.

Taka was pretty sure she was thinking of her mom's grave, though. Or Chuck's. Or maybe even his brother's. He was. And the child graves at the cemeteries. The balloons and stuffed bunnies.

Andrea bent down and picked up the Ziplocs.

"Now what do we do," Taka asked, because he really didn't know what to do about any of it. He'd take back those bullets from Zach Taylor's chest if he could. Believe in Billie Mae if he could. Leave the dog buried. If he only could.

"I guess I'm going to read those case files. Melinda's gone. Are you going—"

"No," he answered without waiting for her question. "I'm staying."

"All righty, then."

They went in and washed up and grabbed the box and got started.

TAKA SIGHED AND stretched. They'd eaten spaghetti in the living room and gone over their appropriated files again, taking the time to read the details, trying to begin committing them to memory, so that when the right piece fell into place, their brains would recognize the answer to the puzzle. Looking at his watch, Taka smirked.

"What," Andrea said, her voice sleepy.

"It's been eleven whole hours since anything overly weird has happened." He could see her doing the math.

"What about the dog skull?"

"Nah, that's not weird."

She cocked her head. After a long minute she said, "I believe you're right."

"I'll clean up," he offered and thought maybe she nodded, but he couldn't really tell. She was locked in the zone, absorbing the details, and he didn't want to bother her. He stacked their dirty plates and stuck his fingers down in their water glasses and carried everything into the kitchen. He liked her kitchen. It had a tile floor, continuous with the mudroom, and she'd laid a rag rug down in front of the sink. Another one anchored the kitchen table, which was square and matched the pine sideboard on the wall between the kitchen and the living room.

The light was good during the day through the huge window, and the old wooden cabinets and pitted butcher block counters spoke to him. The landlord had dropped a reclaimed white farm sink in. It was extra deep and wider than a regular sink. Taka had never seen one outside a magazine before, but this kitchen was made for it. He started the battered dishwasher, and wiped down the scarred white stove top, chasing down the red sauce that had simmered up out of the pot while heating, splattering all over the raised burner and into the tinfoil covered drip pan.

Opening the sideboard to retrieve the coffee beans, he got distracted by Billie Mae's bagged Keds once again. He picked it up and turned it in his hands, following the line of marker to the tiny blue flower. The insubstantial blond imp he thought he'd seen that morning was barefoot. He swallowed the roll of his yellow spot and tamped down the bloom of impossible in his gut until it lay deep and still.

Say his ninety-nine percent certain deductions were correct and it really was Billie Mae's missing shoe. So what? What did Billie Mae expect them to conclude? That the killer dropped a blue Keds belonging to his current victim in the yard of another murder victim, perhaps a former victim? He'd seen stupid before, but that would rank up there near the top.

Why draw their attention to the dog's grave? Was the fracture in the dog's skull peri- or post-mortem? If the Robbins owned the dog, maybe the killer defended himself. Did he—or she, Taka reminded himself, because Billie Mae's mother had, after all, been convicted of her murder—had she done the dog, too? Buried it before calling for help? Changed clothes? Mrs. Robbins wasn't wet like Billie Mae. Billie Mae had been soaking wet.

But she hadn't drowned. According to the coroner and the state's medical examiner, there wasn't any kind of water in her lungs. No chlorinated tap water. Definitely no lake water. It might have felt that way to her, though, like she was drowning. She was lying in a bathtub, after all, and died slow as her lungs filled with her own body's fluid and her throat swelled. She died from asphyxiation as a result of strangulation. The deep ligatures in her neck were undeniable. But her mother wasn't wet. And the tub Billie Mae was lying in was dry, an issue never addressed by the ME, only noted.

Oliver Fitch's witness statement said Billie Mae had been down on Cooper while "running away." Had she gone back to the lake that morning after her misadventure the evening before? She was almost seven, but would she have been that brave? If she had gone back, did she fall in? Mrs. Robbins confessed to being angry with Billie Mae for going outside that morning. He'd have been mad with Billie Mae too, if that was the case.

He sighed and laid the shoe on the table. Tomorrow when he returned the case file, he'd be better able to gauge his own level of crazy when his betters decided if they would run the shoe for trace evidence or just cubbyhole it away as a curiosity, along with Billie Mae's closed case files. There was nothing he could do with the dog. Maybe Billie Mae just wanted her blanket back.

Taka started the coffee brewing and then checked in on Andrea. She was sitting on the floor, one leg bent at the knee, and the other sticking straight out in front of her. Rolling her bottom lip, she had all her energy concentrated on the report she held in front of her. Her eyes moved back and forth at a rapid rate as she twirled her long hair around her index finger.

"What are you, five?" he said out loud.

"What," she said, when she looked up after a second's lag. She blinked her mental fog away and smiled at him. "What?"

"Nothing," he muttered and stuffed his hands in his pockets. She was beautiful and had never appreciated that fact, didn't even believe it, he was sure. She had a slightly wide face through the temples, but sharp cheekbones framed her deep brown eyes and played well with her strong jaw and curved lips. Her hair was down around her shoulders, which were broad and carried the heavy teardrops of her breasts just fine above her narrow waist and wide hips. Her legs were long, her thighs proportionate to her height. Everything about her reflected her mountain-bred genes and hands-on approach to life.

"There's a 'not right' to all of this, she said. "None of it quite fits together. Her mom's serving a life sentence."

"I know," he agreed, leaning his shoulder against the frame of the arched opening between the hall and the living room. "But, square one. Billie Mae's ma confessed, and there's no evidence to prove she's lying."

Andrea leaned over, searching through the papers on the floor and came up with her yellow legal pad. A similar search produced her pen. "Okay, I'll do it."

She scribbled in her pad.

After a minute, Taka gave up waiting for her to explain herself and went to stare at the coffee streaming out of the plastic funnel of the coffee maker into the glass carafe. His neck and shoulders were stiff from the hit his Crown Vic had taken before the foot chase and shooting on Friday. He didn't even want to try and see the bruise across his shoulder and back from the bullet he'd taken in his vest. He was going to pay double tomorrow for firing the rifles at the range and digging up the stupid dog.

He dug around in the cabinet for ibuprofen and then filled two mugs with coffee, laced both with honey and hers with milk, and took them out to the living room, exchanging her mug for the pad Andrea handed him.

He squinted at her tiny, looping cursive. *Born to Etta Anne James and David Robbins on November 10, 1996 in Terra Alta, West Virginia, high in the Allegheny Mountains, Billie Mae Robbins was looking forward to her seventh birthday. In a dry bathtub, her arms and legs bruised, her clothes and hair soaked with water and stained with the blood seeping from two deep ligatures across the front of her throat, she died days before her planned celebration. When police arrived, Etta Robbins confessed to the violent strangulation of her only daughter. She could not recall what the murder weapon may have been, nor what time the death occurred, or why she did it. To investigators, she never spoke more than ten words and expressed little emotion. But later, in follow-up interviews, she often rambled for long periods about the days preceding Billie Mae's death with tears streaming down her cheeks, which she did not seem to notice.*

"Uh," Taka said.

"It's my book."

"Your book?"

"You know I can't lie, Taka. So, I'm really going to write a book. Maybe just for me, and I might not actually follow through, but I want to. I intend to."

"And when you go to talk to Billie Mae's ma, you'll really mean it."

"I will. I'll even tell her it's my first book, but give her my credentials."

"Why don't you write?"

"I do. Frequently."

"No," Taka said and sat on the couch. "Not articles. Not for work. Books. Why don't you already write books? You read for hours, I've seen you. Don't you want to write books like that? Or short stories like you read online?"

"I have written stories. But then I delete them."

"You don't keep any of them?"

"Well, some are on discs, but—"

"I have a USB disc drive, too," he said, and sipped his coffee, thrilled he'd trapped her.

She stared at him.

"I want to read them," he said.

"Umm, no. My teenage ramblings are not for public view. But I'll write you one for your birthday, deal?"

"My birthday's not until April." Birthday cake would be good right about now, he thought. Something from that bakery on MacCorkle, or even a cupcake. Or a Twinkie. Maybe he did need to go home.

Her eyes crinkled with amusement as one side of her lips tilted up. "I have Oreos stashed in the produce drawer, under the lettuce."

Damn, I *do* love her. He skedaddled and pulled them out. They sat side by side on the couch and shared them with the last quarter of the Seahawks game on for noise while he flipped through the neighbors' statements and she continued making notes.

CHAPTER TEN

TURNING RIGHT FROM her street onto Timber Way the next morning, Andrea detoured down to Cooper and the lake, grateful there was nothing to see, before she doubled back. The drive into town on Greenbrier was slow. During the good years, buildings in Charleston had grown upward at a rapid pace, one historic building at a time being bulldozed to make way for multi-story towers, bringing congestion with them. Andrea really missed the quaint town she'd grown up visiting without much thought to the beauty and graciousness around her. The bright spot these days was the renovated Capitol Street area with thriving restaurants, bars, and enterprising shops offering something different from the indoor mall at Charleston Town Center.

The Charleston PD shared space with City Hall in a historic four-story limestone building with an imposing neoclassical facade. She drove between it and the even grander rock-faced Kanawha County Courthouse, wondering what Taka would be facing today at his meeting. Continuing west along the Kanawha River, she followed the red tail lights in front of her in the heavy morning fog on Kanawha

Boulevard. Three blocks from Waltham-Young, Taka's ringtone blasted from her phone. She thumbed the accept.

"Good morning, Taka."

"The way I move ain't fair, I know," he sang.

One of the blessings of ringtones was that people generally didn't know what song you'd chosen for them, but Taka rung her phone when she'd lost it in the house a few weeks ago and now he knew.

"Yeah, yeah," she muttered.

"You left early."

"A little. I want to research Billie Mae's mom and try to find her family before my morning meeting. Maybe call my landlord about the carport, see if he remembers which of his tenants had dogs."

"I'll look, too. I'll call you if anything interesting pops up. Billie Mae show up today?" he said.

"No. Good luck explaining her shoe."

"I'll tell Ronnie Horton you found it," he countered and hung up.

Andrea negotiated the funny little stiff right where Kanawha Boulevard hit a dead end at Patrick Street Bridge and made a quick left into the parking lot of the library. Grabbing her briefcase, she did a good imitation of a speed walker into the building. Sweeping through the big double doors, she heard Marji call, hey ya, from the reception desk and waved back.

With sixty full-time staffers, at any one time there were about ten of them traipsing through the halls, the common areas, and the inner sanctum of the various dedicated research rooms. She waved, nodded, and said hi, but didn't stop for conversation. A DAR meeting was taking shape in the main library, preparations being made for the arrival of fifteen or twenty older women later in the morning. They'd be all spiffed up for their southern lunch to follow. Andrea loved seeing them. For some of them, it was probably the highlight of their monthly social calendar.

In her office, she dumped her bag and purse, checked the time, and settled down in front of her computer for some concentrated research on some of the best database access in the world.

Normal visitation at Lakin Correctional didn't look likely anytime soon. The inmate had to send an application to visitors and the approval process took weeks. No tagalong guests even with an approved family member. As far as family went, Etta Robbins didn't have much. Her son was placed with a family member, a sister–in–law, Anna Hooper, but Andrea didn't know her age to narrow down the dozen possibilities. She added tracking down contact info for each possibility to her to-do list, but she really needed to find out if there was any reason to pursue any of this. She tapped her pen against her teeth. There was always more than one way to skin a coon, but you had to know the other ways, which meant web surfing until you found anything relevant.

The Lakin website didn't prove useful, but she eventually located an inmate handbook and then a policies manual. Counsel was granted both regular and after hours visits. A few minutes later she had Etta Robbin's defense info pulled up. Her public defender was now living in Wheeling. Glancing at the wall clock, Andrea called the woman's private practice number. Before she had time to get nervous, she was patched through to her office by a young man with a crisp, efficient cheeriness.

Andrea identified herself as an employee of Waltham-Young and Jessica Hiller immediately embraced her. They chatted for a moment about the library and then Andrea ventured out on the twiggy limb Billie Mae and her own damnable curiosity were herding her onto. "I'm calling today about an independent research project. I'm living in a house where a child died in 2003. You represented her mother, Etta Robbins?"

"Oh, Etta. She was so sad. I'd only been a public defender for a couple of months. She confessed, so I got handed the case to usher through the courts. She broke my heart."

"I've been looking at the case. The evidence is... scanty."

"I agree, but she confessed," Hiller said, her tone verging on defensive.

"She did," Andrea said, trying to think of how to explain a ghost, a couple of shoes, a random dog's skull, and two horrible murders as the reason she needed an interview with Etta Robbins. She should've thought this through better.

"But you noticed there was no explanation for the ligatures except for the wicket she said she used, which wasn't recovered. And that the child was wet, her clothes dirty, although the tub was dry and Etta pretty clean."

"Yes."

"If you're just looking to satisfy your curiosity, I can't help you, Ms. Kelley."

"Oh, no, Ms. Hiller," Andrea said, the word "book" already on her tongue, though being called out stung a little. Instead she heard herself say, "I intend to free her."

As soon as the words hit the air, Andrea knew that's what she really wanted. To free Billie Mae. To do that, maybe she needed to uncover the truth behind Etta's incomplete confession, why Billie Mae insisted she died by herself. And maybe that truth meant freeing Etta Robbins, too.

Hiller laughed, the sound distorted by the phone's microphone. "That's ballsy. What did you say you do?"

"I didn't. I'm an archivist."

"What does an archivist do?"

"We preserve the past, collect stories, and document history in a million different ways. We research," Andrea said, the definitions she memorized in school coming back to her. The profession was so varied that few people understood its full potential. She had almost forgotten her full potential. "Our work strengthens collective memory, that's what I do here at Waltham-Young. But archivists also protect the rights, property, and identity of everyday citizens. That's what I want to do for Etta Robbins. If I could only talk to her, I might be able to re-visit the investigation. Maybe she's guilty, I don't know, but neither does anyone else, as far as I can tell. Not for sure."

Silence on the other end of the line. Andrea had about a minute and a half to get downstairs to meet her client. "Are you still there?" she finally asked.

"I'm going to verify you. Mind if I run a background check?"

"No, not at all."

"I'll get back to you." Hiller said and hung up.

Andrea pocketed her phone, snatched up the folder with her meeting notes, and ran.

IT DEFINITELY FELT like a Monday. Taka was muscle sore. And Zach Taylor and the buried dog had gotten chummy in his fiery dreams during the small amount of time he'd slept. He worked through a stack of preliminary shooting board requests, Professional Standards Division review surveys, and CSI forms regarding the confiscation of his duty weapon. After reading through the transcripts of his initial statements to the PSD investigators when he was interviewed at the hospital, he signed off on them. He wrote and filed yet another statement and timeline of the events Thursday and Friday. And that left him with only his notes on the investigation into Deborah Watkins' homicide that lead him to suspect Zach Taylor, still recuperating in the hospital from the two bullets Taka had put in his chest.

Taka carefully went through them, checking all the details again and then formally transferred her case to the detective who'd taken it right after the shooting. Tracy Manners had come in the day before and done the same, he was informed. His supervisor, an Assistant Chief of Detectives, reminded him not to talk to Tracy until after their shooting boards met, to stay off social media, to not talk to reporters, and to set up his next interview for Tuesday morning with the investigator in PSD handling his after-action review. While he was there, Taka requested a meeting with Lieutenant Ronnie Horton, Chief of Detectives, to talk to him about Billie Mae's shoe, but he was out of office.

He returned to his desk, aware of the deeper ache in his upper back from the bullet hit, the familiar current of the officers coming and going, the phones ringing, the shouts from desk to desk here and there as he made an Excel spreadsheet of Billie Mae's investigation: all the cops involved, when they'd spoken to whom, and what evidence was collected, analyzed, filed, and when. He'd only just gotten started on the witness statements when Detective Chief Ronnie Horton himself tapped him on his shoulder.

"Hey, Taka, I know you been following the drownings. Coroner's report is back on the second one. I was wondering if you could eye it, see anything that might pull in the Robbins case."

Taka sat back in his chair. "Why?"

"Why? I thought you were interested." He waved the file over the papers scattered on Taka's desk. "Is this the Robbin's case?"

"Yeah. You need it right now?"

"If you're not interested in this file, yes."

"I want it, I want it," Taka said. "Geesh."

"Well, you want in and then you get all suspicious when I let you?"

"This case is weird, Lieutenant. I just... I don't know. I want to know who else is interested, I guess."

"Between you and me, Taka? The captain wants to know if they match up, she wants eyes on it without the paperwork."

Captain Rebecca Cahill was Bureau Chief for Investigative Services and sharp, with a gut better than anyone else in the room. If she was feeling something on this case, he felt better about his own instincts. "Okay. I can do that."

"Keep it low profile. And I want that case box in my office by end of day."

Taka leaned over to grab the Ziplocked shoe out of the box on the floor. "It matches the description for Billie Mae Robbin's missing shoe. Andrea found it planting blueberries."

Horton's face twisted up as he ran a hand over his balding head. "Christ. The timing. Document the circumstances, y'know, citizen turned it in, yada, yada, but just keep it with the files for now."

"Any chance I could interview Etta Robbins?"

"On a closed case? None. Plus, you're on your desk."

"Andrea?"

"Less than none. I want that box end of day."

"Yes, sir," Taka said, because his mother didn't raise him stupid.

Horton was halfway across the bull pen before he turned back. "Hey, Taka," he called and Taka looked up from the report he'd already opened. "Try not to shoot anyone else, they stick you upstairs eventually." Laughter broke out around the room. Taka mock-glared at everyone and waved the older man off.

The call that seven-year-old Adam Ward was missing had come in to CPD about the time the boaters found his body. The kid had not drowned. He'd been dead when he went into the water. Thin bruising and a long laceration across his throat, high up under the jaw, and more bruising on the inside sole of his right foot. No broken bones, no head injury. Probable COD was slow asphyxiation and resulting edema due to strangulation by garrote. Rope fibers were embedded in his skin. Blood work pending. Like Billie Mae, he'd probably felt like he was drowning.

.He lived a street over from Andrea, on a corner next to Timber Way. The skin on Taka's neck tightened. Dr. Robert Huntley had been walking to his home on Double Branch Lane from the U-Save on Oakley and talked to the kid's ma as she was searching her chain linked back yard for Adam, her toddler daughter in her arms. The kid had been camping in the back yard, excited about the new tent they'd bought. His dad had checked on him before leaving for third shift, but only from a window after seeing Adam's flashlight was still on. Huntley suggested she report Adam missing.

It took Taka a minute to place the name. The old guy who lived across the street from Andrea and took an interest in Andrea's "daughter" had suggested Adam's ma report him as missing. It'd been his paint bucket the snake had been trapped under. His gaze strayed to the Ziplocked shoe. Had Huntley lived there when Billie Mae died?

Taka sat back in his chair, wondering how far Captain Cahill would let him go beyond compiling data and into re-investigating to fill in the missing details in Billie Mae's files for a better comparison to the current cases. He woke up his laptop and added new columns to his spreadsheet: find out who'd been living in the surrounding neighborhood during the time of Billie Mae's death, and where they'd been during the recent deaths. He'd need to compile info on their backgrounds and careers, families, who they were, what they did.

He rubbed his head. His neck was tight and he knew that portended a banger of a headache by the late afternoon. He thought about calling Andrea, but then looked out across the room. Karl and Matt and Oscar were still at their desks, pounding on keyboards or scratching away at paper files. "Ding, ding," he called, letting his voice carry across the loud, crowded room. "Going to Sam's if anyone wants to come with." He stood up and strapped his holster back on and adjusted the badge clipped to his belt.

As he walked out, others joined him—Dan Cozner and Matt, Sheryl. Fields, a new transition from Special Enforcement, came, tucking his gun away. "Hey, Karl," Taka shouted. "You coming?"

"I am. I'll catch up."

AMONG THE VARIOUS citizens on trips to City Hall for whatever they needed, Taka spotted the Gazette reporter from the lake loitering in the lobby with a couple of other news types. But his group did, too, and closed ranks around him. She just shook her head at him as they passed, but the others gave it a try, following halfway down the block outside.

"Is my name out there, yet?" he asked no one in particular.

Walking beside him, Sheryl bumped his bicep with her shoulder. "Yeah. Twitter and Facebook. But no one really cares that a cop shot an armed white boy murderer. His uncle's getting more flack for defending him."

"Most of the coverage is on the girl he killed," Karl added. "Doesn't hurt that you're kinda black."

Good to know that wasn't an issue this one time ever. CPD was overwhelmingly white. Taka rolled his eyes and glanced back at Fields, the only black investigator at CPD, who only shook his head in response.

"Shut up, Karl," Cozner said.

"Just sayin'" Karl said, but shut up.

The five-minute walk was brisk and Taka felt a little better when they crowded into the sports bar. They ordered burgers, wings, and fries along with their waters and sodas, though Taka would've loved a beer and a shot of Jack to loosen himself up. Then he remembered he was technically on leave and waved down the table at the waitress. "Michelob."

"What's up, Taka, you look like you haven't slept in three days," Cozner said, leaning in so that the others couldn't hear. "Girlfriend troubles?"

"Well, I guess you could say that. Girl's in the wind, but it was my fault. I got O'Malley tomorrow."

"The County's pushing this shooting? Really?"

"Councilman Miller can't trust us city cops. Keep up, Cozner," Karl said, pulling up a chair at the end of the table.

"Kid was a damn druggie and he was shooting at us."

Karl held up his hands. "I got it, Taka, got your back, too. Sorry I wasn't there. You go in there growling, O'Malley's gonna take you apart. You know that, right?"

"Yeah. Got Advil?"

Cozner shook his head.

Karl dug around in his pants pocket and came up with a little foil Advil packet. He held it out between two fingers, and then opened his palm, revealing three round, yellow tablets. "Caffeine. Want them?"

Taka lifted his hand, hesitated. "No, man. I'll get a cup of coffee when we get back."

Karl shrugged and slipped them out of sight again.

Caffeine, guarana, Ritalin, Adderall, dexies, speed, base. Go pills were a pretty common habit in both the military and law enforcement, but it wasn't talked about. Taka had done his share, but more and more these days, he found they just ragged him out and put him on edge, and he was edgy enough all on his own, thank you very much.

The Advil didn't help much, though the greasy burger settled his stomach, and he felt better as they trekked back to the shop. In deference to his headache, Taka waved off his friends for a detour to the river. Letting the others move off, Fields pulled off his NY Yankees ball cap and handed it to him. "Be sure to come in through the garage, Tak. Call if there's trouble."

TAKA SLOUCHED PAST the pedestrians in front of City Hall and crossed Kanawha Boulevard to Haddad Riverfront Park's stage seating under huge white sails on steel beams. The concrete steps gave a magnificent view of the river and its south bank. He watched the water for a long while, tracking the slow slide of a coal barge downriver, thinking on the shoot and Adam Ward and Billie Mae. And Andrea. Did he really want to start something new when she'd so plainly spelled out an invitation to deepen their relationship?

His phone rang. Andrea.

"I got nothing," he answered.

"I got a meeting with Etta Robbins," she said. "I think."

"You think?"

"Her old defense lawyer's secretary says I do, but I guess I'll see when I get there."

"You got one for today? That's not even possible."

"Three o'clock. Wish me luck."

"Luck," he said. "Call me when you're done."

CHAPTER ELEVEN

ETTA ROBBINS HAD been moved from the West Virginia Department of Health and Human Resources' Forensic Evaluation Unit on the campus of the South Central Regional Jail in Charleston to the sprawling Lakin Correctional in West Columbia shortly after her trial. It was an all-women's campus focused on behavior-driven, gender-specific, and cognitive programs aimed at moving inmates into community facilities or successful release. Ninety percent of its occupants were incarcerated for drugs. Billie Mae's mother was among the few serving life sentences for other crimes.

Still disbelieving the information that Jessica Hiller's secretary relayed to her, Andrea arrived at the prison before three. As promised, Jessica Hiller, a short blonde, stood waiting for her near the security gate.

"We were lucky Etta Robbins still had me listed as her attorney of record," Hiller said as they shook hands. "You owe my admin friend an expensive bottle of wine."

"Thank you so much."

"Just make it worth the effort. There was always something wrong with that confession, but there was nothing I could do."

They presented their identification. Andrea's credentials as a new hire at Hiller and Associates, there to conduct a bi-annual follow-up interview to assess need for further counsel had been received earlier and a visitor's badge was waiting for her. Since she wasn't a lawyer, she was escorted to the regular visitation area where "special" visits were scheduled every weekday afternoon, while Hiller trundled off to her already scheduled meeting, the only reason a string was pulled to allow Andrea a visit on same day notice.

She used the restroom in the lobby and, after rinsing her face in cold water, gave herself a hard look in the mirror. She dusted her face with powder, glossed her lips, and straightened her ponytail. Tucking the shorter layers back behind her ears, she wished she had gel. Then she pulled her hairband out and shook her hair loose. She finger combed it and once again tucked the shorter sides behind her ears. She frowned into the mirror and forced herself out into the lobby again before she lost her nerve altogether. It wasn't the first time she'd visited a prisoner, but the other visits had been to her brother and cousin. The stupid idiots had both served time more than once for illegal BASE jumping, trespassing, and drug possession. She suspected her brother actually found living in general pop a kind of rush. His addictions would best him one day and she'd long ago put him at arm's length. They weren't close.

Only a few visitors sat waiting in the lobby, a couple of women with a toddler, a thin man with a visible chemo port jutting from his neck, and a soldier in camouflage holding a girl of about five. Andrea claimed a locker and placed her purse and satchel inside, regretting the fact that she wasn't allowed to take her notebook and pen with her. Minutes later the lobby guard whisked past her to the door into the visiting room, checked each visitor's badge, and frisked them again before directing them to separate tables and numbered chairs. A guard on the other side of the room allowed the inmates to enter.

Mrs. Robbins entered last, looking around uncertainly. The guard pointed in Andrea's direction. She hesitated until the guard walked her over.

"Ms. Kelley?"

"Yes," Andrea said. She directed her focus on Mrs. Robbins. "I'm here to speak to you, Mrs. Robbins." Andrea glanced up at the imposing female guard. "I'm with your lawyer's office, Jessica Hiller? I want to document your story."

"Oh." Mrs. Robbins hands fluttered at her chest. "Oh. All right."

"Sit down, Etta," the guard said, her voice soft.

She sat, sinking down with a wariness that seemed familiar to Andrea, but it took her a moment to place the action. Etta moved like a prey animal, slow and tentative, ready to bolt. She was shorter than Andrea, maybe five foot six, and wry. Her hair was braided back from her face and she wore loose beige cotton pants and a beige button down smock over a white long-sleeve top with streaks of different color paints spilled across it. The guard returned to her post.

"You paint," Andrea said.

"I do," she said. "I do."

"What do you paint?"

"Animals, always. A dog a day. The service dogs that live here, you know. The ones in training." Andrea did know, but only because she had researched the prison a little as she ate lunch. "Sometimes I draw horses. I tried a carriage horse once, but the cart was all wrong." She laughed, but sobered the next instant. "Now really, what is it you want? I have nothing."

"All I want is for you to consider speaking to me about Billie Mae."

Mrs. Robbins blanched, her fair skin losing its pale blush. Taka told her once that most people who have murdered, including kids, are so busy hiding their secret that they don't react viscerally to the request for more info. Verbally, some fall completely silent, many of them you can't shut up. Billie Mae's mom moved from one extreme to the other in her police interviews.

Andrea explained she was a specialized type of librarian, summarized Waltham-Young as a center for cultural studies, and said that she was familiar with Billie Mae because she lived in Mrs. Robbins' former place of residence. She and Taka had gone round and round over telling Mrs. Robbins about Billie Mae's ghost and decided not to share.

"It's been at least four years since someone's come to ask me about Billie Mae. I loved her, you know."

My mother loves me, Billie Mae had said, so yes, Andrea knew that already.

"I argued with Billie Mae, did you know that?" she asked, feeling Andrea out.

A thin, cold thread snaked down Andrea's spine. She didn't know how she should answer. "I read all the police reports available to me. I'm very curious about how you remember that day."

"Billie Mae," Mrs. Robbins said.

The windowless room smelled of ozone and Clorox and Mrs. Robbins' paints. Andrea watched the couple next to them lean as far over the table between them as possible to talk in a rumble of murmurs. Beyond them, an older inmate held the toddler on her lap, visiting with the two women who looked like her daughters. She sat huddled over the baby, rocking her as she sucked on a bottle of juice. Andrea smoothed her palm over the scarred wood of the table, waiting Etta out.

"She was mad at me," Etta started in a near whisper. Her voice built strength with each following word until it sounded normal. "She wanted fruit loops, which her father used to give her on Sunday mornings at his parents' house and I wouldn't buy them."

"You were divorced?"

She shook her head. "David died when Billie Mae was four, but she remembered those fruit loops. Every now and then she threw a temper tantrum over them. David and I lived in my in-law's cottage on Terra Alta, behind the main house. He died on that lake." She pressed her fingers against her eyes. "I'm sorry. So long ago and still..."

Andrea ducked her head. Mrs. Robbins had been in her mid-twenties when her husband passed, leaving her with two young children. At that age, Andrea had been living in a studio apartment, working nights as a fact checker and sleeping until midday.

"Billie Mae remembered. And I did buy those bitty boxes of Fruit Loops on his birthday and at Christmas, but she wanted them that day and I refused to go buy them. Such a simple thing. Not hard to put her in the car with her brother and go. I should've. She just wanted something of her father. I worked, so this was at the end of a long day for them in daycare. Sometimes we rubbed on each other like sandpaper. She was so like David in so many ways." She studied the tabletop between them and then looked past Andrea, her eyes roaming over what Andrea knew to be featureless grey wall. After a few seconds, her eyes settled on one spot.

"That day?" Andrea prompted after three minutes of avoiding Mrs. Robbins' thousand-yard stare in silence.

Mrs. Robbins startled, her hands bouncing on the table. She laced her fingers tightly together.

"That day?"

"Yes, we argued. Billie Mae ran down the street, her blanket and Fortune, her sleepy rabbit in her arms, determined to find her daddy to take care of her instead of mean old me. I ran out into the street after her, of course, but Dr. Huntley was in his yard—"

"Mr. Huntley? He saw Billie Mae?"

"Yes. Or maybe no. He knew I was up after her though and he suggested I let her walk down the street. He said, kids run away and wait to see if you come after them. If you do, they've proved something to themselves that will make them think they're in charge, if you don't, they come home chastened, and willing to accept your authority. I remember what he said on account of Billie Mae." Her voice dropped in volume. "Chastened, they come home chastened," she repeated. "I respected him. He wrote a book on child rearing and had five kids of his own."

"Did he now," Andrea said. She didn't remember seeing a witness statement in the files from Mr. Huntley. Her fingers itched for the pen and notebook in the lobby locker. "I didn't know Mr. Huntley wrote a book," she said

"Doctor. Doctor Huntley. It was good," Mrs. Robbins said. "I had a copy back then. I don't know where it ended up, after." She stared down at her hands for a long moment before lifting her gaze again. "He said to wait on her to come back. The neighborhood was safe enough. Things didn't happen to kids that they didn't get themselves into on their own. I worried a few minutes on the lake. What if she went that far? But I knew she wouldn't. Her boundary was the same as every other kid on the street, the stop sign.

"But when it was getting on dusk and Billie Mae wasn't back, I walked outside and up she pops, dirt all over her face and crying. She said, Mama, there was a man who talked to me. She said, I was scared. I took her straight home. She wasn't hurt or nothing. We went back inside and had dinner and the kids had baths and we all went to bed. When I woke up it was later than usual. Know how you can feel that in the air? It was later than usual, and Steven was in the kitchen, eating cheerios, kicking his feet. I remember that, on account of all the bruises I put on Billie Mae. I picture my feet swinging and swinging."

She wasn't being ingenious. Mrs. Robbins' voice had slowly lost color, becoming monotone at the end. She might not even know that Andrea was sitting there listening, her expression focused far away, her eyes fixed on nothing in this plane. Andrea wondered if Mrs. Robbins already knew about Billie Mae's un-death.

"I looked out the window. There was fog rising off the ground." She turned her haunted eyes on Andrea, her gaze sharpening. "You know how that back door got built, why there's a big picture window in the kitchen? Kenny Meyers did it, so I could watch the kids while I worked in the kitchen. He knew I didn't have help. I looked out and there was my baby, my Billie Mae. I stood for a long time before I could move." Mrs. Robbins swallowed, and then swallowed again, like a dog getting sick to its stomach. "I was so mad at her for going out before I was even awake, so mad because she wanted only her daddy. She wouldn't listen to me." Her breath hitched. She twisted her fingers tighter together. "I went out back and snatched up one of the croquet wickets and wrapped it around her ungrateful little neck."

Mrs. Robbins had brought the wicket up several different times during questioning. The ME's report stuck to the facts, stating Billie Mae had been strangled by garroting without offering conjecture on the actual weapon used. A wicket had never been found. "Did you mean to kill her?"

"I don't know." Mrs. Robbins lifted her hands to her face, seeming now to be in genuine distress. "I don't know. I was so mad at her for going out that early without me."

Andrea remained quiet. Mrs. Robbins sucked great drafts of breath in through her nose and blew them out through her mouth. She closed her eyes.

"They weren't allowed out that early. The kids." She shook her head. "She knew better."

"Was it raining?"

Mrs. Robbins shook her head, still lost in her story.

"Was she wet when you went into the yard?"

"I don't know, I just don't know. She was so cold. I took her upstairs. I thought." She looked away, seemed to take inventory of the inmates around them.

The little girl and her soldier daddy sat directly behind her, the girl singing to herself in a sweet tone, while her parents talked to each other. "Hold, hold, hold my hand, hold, hold, hold my hand..."

"The little girl behind you," Andrea offered, "is singing."

Mrs. Robbins nodded and let her breath out. "I thought, if I could just warm her up. She was so cold."

Not knowing where to go with that, not wanting to push Mrs. Robbins too far, Andrea changed tack. "Did Billie Mae have her blanket and rabbit in the yard with her that morning?"

Mrs. Robbins kept her eyes closed tight, but her lips pursed. She was thinking about it. About what to say, maybe? Or was she really trying to remember?

"Fortune, her sleepy rabbit. Never slept a day without him. I wanted to put him in the coffin but I didn't have no say by then, no say at all in how she was... No, she didn't have Fortune with her in the yard. No. No. All the men..." She swallowed hard. "All the men standing around and he was sitting on the table by Steven and that dog we had, Tuck, he was sleeping there at Steven's feet. That damn dog. He never barked when he should have and always barked when he shouldn't. Didn't bark at all those men in the house."

"What happened to him?"

"Disappeared one night. I come up to the jail by then, but that's what Dr. Huntley told me. He just up and disappeared. I think Dr. Huntley took him to the shelter, but was just too polite to say. Tuck was big. He took some time to care for and there wasn't anyone left for him then."

"What kind of dog was he?" Andrea had no idea if an analysis of the dog's bones from under the foundation could actually determine breed, but nothing ventured, nothing gained.

"He was a blue tick hound, loyal as the day is long to David, do anything for him. I saw that dog retrieve from 300 yards and beeline right back for Dave. I couldn't do that stuff with him, but he was a good dog for around the house. Stuck to the kids. I sure wish he'd gone out with Billie Mae. She was just lying there."

Without thinking, Andrea followed Mrs. Robbins' lead. "She was lying down outside? Not standing?"

"She was wet and cold."

"She was wet?"

"I don't know why you keep asking that!" Her raised voice attracted the guard's attention. Andrea smiled at her, hoping she wouldn't feel the need to check on them. No such luck.

The guard walked over and leaned down next to Mrs. Robbins. "Everything okay, Etta?"

Rigid in her chair, Mrs. Robbins leaned away from the guard. "Yes, of course. I don't know why you're asking."

After a long, searching look, the guard said, "Okay, Etta. Just call me over if you need anything."

Andrea waited until the guard resumed her post and then leaned forward and kept her voice low and calm. "You carried her in?"

"She wasn't allowed outside that early."

"There was grass noted on the police report, on Billie Mae's clothes, but not on yours."

"I couldn't say." Mrs. Robbins said, her voice cracking. She cleared her throat. "I couldn't say. It was all my fault. I got up late."

"What happened to Fortune, the sleepy rabbit? Do you still have him?"

"No, no, I don't know where he is. Maybe Steven knows. He's living with David's sister. At Terra Alta, where Dave died. That damn lake."

The words leapt to her tongue, but Andrea stopped herself from asking again about how Billie Mae got wet. Had she been down to Lake Vickers that morning after her attempt to get there the night before?

"What about her blanket?"

Mrs. Robbins shook her head, pressing her lips down tight. "She ran away the day before. She wanted fruit loops. And the day before that she danced with Steven in the kitchen, and the day before that she got an A on her art project at school. I loved her, I truly loved her."

They sat in silence for several minutes. It was plain Mrs. Robbins was through talking for the day. Her jaw clenched hard enough to raise the tendons in her thin, wrinkled neck, Mrs. Robbins stared down at her hands. Andrea caught the guard's eye, but then had another thought.

"You said you respected Dr. Huntley, did you like him?"

Mrs. Robbins tilted her head without looking over at Andrea, as if she were listening for thunder, or a distant train whistle, someone calling her name. The room fell silent just then and they could hear the little girl again, "Hold, hold, hold my hand..." A goose walked over Andrea's grave. In that way that small crowds have, everyone went back to their muted conversations at once.

"No," Mrs. Robbins said suddenly. Andrea had to think to remember what question she had asked. Did she like Dr. Huntley. "Not for any reason. He just didn't really fit in. Now, Jason Cobb, he was nice. Solid. A good man to have nearby after David was gone. He came to check on the house for me when I had a question and Kenny couldn't come. Made sure my locks worked and helped me shut off the water one time when the pipe under the bathroom sink burst."

Jason Cobb had lived across the street from Andrea, where the beagle lived now, according to the address on the statement he gave Detective Ford in Billie's Mae's file. But she thought someone named Brad lived there now.

"Thank you, Mrs. Robbins. May I come again sometime? I'm still gathering data. I'd like my research to be as thorough as possible."

"I killed her. It was my fault. You can write that down in your lawyer stuff."

"Yes, ma'am. May I come again?"

"Yes, yes, that'd be fine, lady, that'd be fine."

CHAPTER TWELVE

ANDREA WAVED THE guard over and collected her things from the lobby locker. Sitting in her FX in the parking lot, she wrote down their conversation verbatim, as close to it as she could remember, before heading out. Highway 62 followed the Ohio River south through thick stands of evergreens and hardwoods still clinging to their leaves, though most of the fall color was gone. She took her time, processing, thinking. Once she got back to work, she'd need to focus. She had at least three hours of research into draping fabric from the Civil War era ahead of her. On the outskirts of Charleston, she hit 1 on her speed dial and Taka picked up on the second ring.

"Talk to me."

She relayed Etta Robbins story, her lack of knowledge as to where the rabbit and blanket and even the hound, Tuck, ended up, about her conversation with Dr. Huntley.

"She said a man scared Billie Mae. I think that must have been Oliver Fitch."

"Your neighbor's brother."

"Yeah. Susan Pepper."

Andrea could hear him tapping something on his desk as he thought. "The second kid in the lake was Adam Ward. Garroted. He lived near you."

Had she seen him around? "What about the first one?" She knew Taka would understand her. The little near skeleton. Poor kid.

"Don't know yet. We need background on your neighbors," Taka said.

Andrea bit her tongue on the "you think?" that tried to jump off it. She took the ramp for the river road, glancing west at the brilliant hues of the sun setting over the hills.

"If their dog was still alive," Taka said suddenly, "that kills my theory it died defending Billie Mae. And my second one, too, that maybe she just wants her blankie back."

Andrea laughed. "Really? You had theories already?"

"Always, darlin'. Maybe Ma's lying and did the dog herself."

"How's this? Dr. Huntley did the dirty and disposed of the dog rather than taking it to Animal Control."

"And buried Billie Mae's blanket and rabbit with it?" Taka scoffed.

"He's the father of five kids, apparently, so yeah, he probably has a heart."

"You just said he had five kids *and* that he killed the dog, that's heartless."

"You're just jealous I have a theory, too."

"Hey, do you think Mrs. Robbins could identify them? The blanket and toy?"

Andrea chewed the inside of her lip. She cataloged the reactions she had seen as she recalled the disjointed conversation. "I think we'd be asking for a lawsuit if we tried that."

"She's not exactly stable?"

"Got it in one."

"Dogs are buried in towels and blankets and old tee shirts every day."

"Other families have lived there since Billie Mae died," Andrea agreed.

"That rabbit, though."

"Yeah, exactly." Traffic picked up near Waltham-Young and Andrea slowed the car, turning her thoughts to the remainder of her day and the waiting fabric samples. "What about the shoe?"

"One in the yard is a match with Adam Ward's from the lake. Detective Chief just gave me a look when I showed it to him, said to leave it with the case box."

She pulled into her space and cut her engine. "I gotta go, Taka. You still at mine?"

"Is that okay?"

"You're single again," she said, grinning even though he couldn't see her. "It's expected."

AT HOME THAT night, Taka poured wine, a deep Merlot, and made roast beef sandwiches with Hellmann's and cheddar and carried it all into the living room. Andrea had spread out the case reports on the coffee table, along with the pre-trial and trial documents Jessica Hiller's courier had unexpectedly delivered to Waltham-Young. For background noise, she grabbed the remote and flipped channels past the political pundits to Monday night football.

"Okay, shoot," Taka said, after he'd settled on the floor at the foot of the couch and taken a big bite of his sandwich, one eye on the game.

Andrea tore bite sized nibbles off and rehashed her conversation with Mrs. Robbins from the notes she'd written down, before turning the page to Dr. Huntley. "He's Dr. Robert Huntley, 72 years old, doctorate in Developmental Psychology. He's authored or co-authored nine child care books, two textbooks, and six picture books. Has five grown children he raised as a single father after his wife died in a car accident twenty-two years ago."

"Wikipedia rocks," snarked Taka. "Checked out on my end. Nothing irregular. But he did talk to Adam Ward's ma when she was looking for him. Told her to call the cops."

Her brain stuttered a little, but then she nodded, pressing her lip out as she thought. That wasn't so surprising, all things considered. "I checked online tax records. He bought the house in 2001, so he's been around a long time. I looked up the house between him and Susan Pepper, too. Jason Cobb sold it in 2004, a year after Billie Mae died. Moved to East End."

"So," Taka said, "As a writer who wants to get the story correct, you need to interview Susan Pepper, Dr. Huntley and Jason Cobb, right?"

Andrea narrowed her eyes at him. "I guess so. Is that all right?"

"What do you mean?"

"I'm practically investigating. Do I need to clear it with someone?"

"Criminal investigation's closed, Andrea. Ronnie Horton wanted the files to flip through since it was a funky case at the time, with everyone wondering if Billie Mae had been at the lake and both those kids being found in it. I think in the course of your research, you should maybe interview all the cops that worked the case. See what they remember. If you start digging things up that don't work, we can take it in then. Until then, the more we can do on our own, the better."

"For who?"

"For us. We're talking ghost here, Andrea. We're talking a murder case the cops maybe fucked up, even if it did seem an easy touchdown because the mother's insane."

"I thought they wanted to know if Billie Mae's case lined up? If they dropped the ball?"

Taka put the forgotten sandwich in his hand down. He closed his eyes and took a deep breath, never a good sign.

Her pulse sped up. "What?"

Opening his eyes, he said, "I mentioned Huntley to Ronnie when I left Billie Mae's case file with him tonight. Told him you got the info from Etta Robbins. He was, uh…"

"Taka," she said, tensing up, already on the defensive.

"Not happy. I didn't tell him we copied the files. If she ever mentioned Huntley, I don't remember, but we should double-check while we're absorbing the details. And keep in mind that she's an unreliable witness."

Andrea sighed. She was an archivist, not a cop, but she'd talked to a lot of unreliable witnesses and done a lot of cross-checking in her career. This wasn't that much different.

"After I finish a direct comparison of the cases," Taka continued, "I can work here, but I can't do anything else at HQ or be out asking around."

"We're gonna need stuff, Taka. Lab work and, and..." She looked down at her sandwich, pulled a piece of crust off. "I don't know what else, but this feels big to me."

Taka stopped chewing. He swigged half his beer to wash the bite down and then shifted towards her and took her hand. Taken aback, Andrea straightened up, wary. "On my best cases, the ones where I feel like I've accomplished something, I get this feeling at the start, like a hollowness and a fullness in my chest all at the same time and my stomach gets all squirrely. When I picked up Billie Mae's dirty, tiny, white shoe in my hand? That's the feeling I got. We can do this, Andrea. There's a reason—" His gaze darted away while he searched for the word he wanted. "Billie Mae's acting out," he finally said. His expression darkened. "That boss of yours, Waltham? You're always saying research is his thing. What better way to use his library than to research this case right outta the closed case files and then see her Ma set free like you told that lawyer? Billie Mae's brother would like that, too, right?"

Andrea's boss was energetic and always enthused. She knew he didn't think the library's full potential had been reached yet, knowledge which resonated with her own epiphany while speaking with Jessica Hiller. She didn't know his feeling on the paranormal, though since he had allowed a whole department for it, he must have some thought on it. She barely knew him. "My boss is Waltham's nephew, Taka. And I've only met him twice. When I was hired and that day he came in asking about Civil War era bullet shapes and powder loads. He's either socked away in his office and private stacks or out in the field."

"So go see him, ask for his help. For Etta Robbins. For Billie Mae. For you. Someone's close. Someone who knows what happened that morning. Someone we need to find."

Andrea's stomach curled up on itself. She'd never asked a personal favor of the Walthams. "Okay, Taka." She squeezed his fingers. "All right."

They finished eating in silence. Taka lifted the TV remote and turned up the volume on the football game, Titans versus Jaguars, before plucking a file up and starting to read. Andrea followed suit.

"I DROWNDED."

Rolling over, Andrea studied Billie Mae in her little white nightgown, relieved to see her dry, her hair glossy and clean.

"I drownded all by myself."

"You didn't drown, Billie Mae. I know that for certain now."

A fierce frown transformed her beautiful face and she stomped her foot, her fists clenched tight. "I did," she shouted, but then she startled, looking up and to the side and she was gone. Andrea flailed upright, heart leaping against her closed throat.

Still half asleep, Taka murmured "What's wrong?"

CHAPTER THIRTEEN

AT ELEVEN AM, a general wave of discontent swept the bull pen, causing Taka to lift his head from the new Excel sheet he was building from what they knew of Adam Ward to better compare his timeline to Billie Mae's. Taka frowned when he saw faces turned his way. Dan Cozner came through the door from the hallway and straight to him at a fast walk. Taka stood up, cold heat surging into his veins, blood rushing in his ears. His cell phone rang on his desk.

"Taka," Cozner said. "It's Zach Taylor. He's dead."

Glancing down, Taka picked up his phone. Carson. He thumbed it open, waited for the line to open. "I know."

"You want to get out of there?" Carson asked.

Cozner looked like he was waiting for Taka to do something, be upset, turn his desk over? But Taka was a soldier before he was a cop and he'd been a cop for eleven years now. Even as a kid, he'd been trained never to point a gun at anyone or anything you weren't prepared to kill. He felt bad, but the kid had made his own choices. What he needed to do now was come clean to Carson. "Yeah. Garage."

They drove through the heavy mid-day traffic to Adelphia's and scored the back booth. The chatter of the swelling lunch crowd, talking over the canned music while they eyed the games playing on the TVs hung everywhere, created nice cover for a quiet conversation. Carson ordered them both burgers although Taka didn't want one. He spun an extra coaster around and around on the table while he gathered his thoughts. First scrolling through his phone and then beating out texts or an email or whatever with his thumbs, Carson let him stew.

They played poker once a month and Carson's partner Bobby never failed to suggest strip poker with a sidelong glance at Taka. He could be a little sharper than Carson at times. The waitress came back and slid their meals onto the table. Carson set his phone aside. Taka stalled for a few minutes longer by slathering mayo on his burger and shaking out ketchup on his fries.

"Just tell me what you're thinking, Taka," Carson finally said. "It's okay if you don't feel as bad as you think you should. Zach Taylor committed murder before he fired a gun at you. He constituted an imminent danger to your life."

Taka shook his head and pushed his plate away. "It's not that. It's Dewey Sanderson."

"One good thing about the County investigating is that it puts Dewey in a tighter corner. He'll have more trouble messing with you without his relationship with Taylor going public."

"That's just it."

Carson took another big bite of his burger. Taka watched him chew. Carson said nothing after he swallowed, just took another bite. Taka sighed, noticing that his hands had found the coaster again. Silence was a great tactic in interrogation and Carson did it well.

"Bobby's not wrong, y'know," Taka tried. Maybe Carson already knew, or had guessed.

"'bout what," Carson asked around a mouthful of fries.

"Me."

Exasperation crossed his face and then Carson was wiping his hands and tidying his space although half his burger remained. "You know

Sanderson from the gun club. You were young. You got some kinda long term grudge against each other. We know he's definitely pissed at you now. What's that got to do with Bobby?"

"Look, Carson, you aren't stupid. You've heard the rumors about me. They're true."

Carson did a good job controlling his expression, but he was clearly surprised.

"I have a hard enough time being a multi-ethnic POC. I don't want to be CPD's... hell, West Virginia's first openly bi cop."

Carson held his gaze, but Taka could see the lawyer in his eyes, calculating and discarding responses until he hit the one that mattered most.

"Are you ashamed?"

"No, I'm a cop. In West Virginia."

Carson nodded. "And Andrea?"

"She's always known. Dewey's the only substantial relationship I've had with a guy."

"Oh." Surprised again, Carson didn't catch himself before those familiar damning words that Taka hated escaped. "You're one of Dewey's boys."

"*That's* what I'm ashamed of."

NODDING AT CARSON when he stopped at the elevators in City Hall, Taka took the stairs to the third floor for a quiet moment by himself and a deep breath before traipsing into PSD's hallowed suite at one sharp. O'Malley, from the prosecutor's office, was waiting with Carson, who was repping CPD in this meeting, the first of several informal meetings and formal hearings to come once Taka's Shooting Board was fully assembled. In this setting, Taka was contractually required to answer questions or lose his job. They all shook hands.

Greg Stack, head of Pro Standards Division and an automatic member of Taka's Board, strolled in and ushered them towards the conference room. "Let me grab my file, be right back," he said.

A box of glass walls partitioned the small conference room off from the main room. Taka knocked the glass twice seating himself on the far side of its wooden rectangular table. It sat eight. He couldn't imagine being wedged in with seven other people. Just the three of them had his triggers bristling. He rolled his shoulders and his head, listening to his neck creak.

Carson poured two glasses of ice water from the pitcher on the table and slid one Taka's way.

O'Malley studied his face and then said, "Admin leave not agreeing with you, Taka?"

Taka shrugged, reminding himself that O'Malley was good at his job. That didn't mean he had to like him, though.

"Look," O'Malley offered in a conciliatory tone that didn't ease Taka's mood one bit. "I read the reports, but I still gotta follow up. Zach Taylor was Councilman Miller's nephew. His sister's screaming in his ear every day. Swears up and down her son wasn't doping."

Stack walked in, smiling. He slapped his files down and dropped a handful of pens onto the table. Taka wondered if there was some deal in the offing or if Stack just liked to be prepared. He must've frowned at the pens because Stack laughed and said, "The last bid on office supplies must've been cheap; most of the pens don't work and we went from twenty-bond paper to ten. Bureaucrats."

Carson snorted. O'Malley fumed. Taka laughed in surprise.

"What's up, O'Malley?" Stack continued. "Our guys say the shoot was good."

"The councilman's all over me. Wants us to wait while the family arranges a private autopsy." He slid a file to Stack. "Just got this. Bloodwork's clean. No drugs in his system according to the hospital. ME's going to waive it."

"Shit," Carson whispered under his breath.

Taka's chest closed. That boy was high as a kite. He took a breath so he could speak. "He was shooting at us, O'Malley."

"He was a diabetic," O'Malley said, measuring each word out for maximum effect as he leveled his gaze on Taka. "Didn't eat, had just come from playing flag football. He was hypoglycemic."

Carson shook his head.

Taka leaned forward. "He was shoo—"

Carson grabbed his arm, cueing him to shut up.

Stack made a thoughtful sound deep in his throat. "The gun was his."

"Legally permitted," O'Malley agreed, turning his focus back to Stack.

"Do you know if he was wearing a med-alert bracelet?" Stack asked.

Taka tensed. What difference would it have made? The boy was firing on multiple officers, Taka fired back.

Carson shook his head. "You can't expect officers in danger to check for a med-alert."

"He was shirtless," O'Malley said. "His bracelet was clearly visible. It was removed from his wrist by the ME and entered into evidence."

Taka racked his brain. Had he seen it?

"O'Malley, the courts are clear on this." Still standing, Stack rested his weight on both fists and leaned across the table, glowering at the asshole, who appeared unruffled by the pose. "Officers can counter lethal force with lethal force. They can't be held accountable for this shooting, even if the kid was having a medical emergency. They had no reasonable way to know that was the case."

"They have to take every measure available to them, Stack, before they use lethal force. As lead officer, Detective Taka should have taken more time to assess the situation." O'Malley was really going to take the investigation down this rabbit hole. The kid was irresponsible, period. It killed him. Period. Taka wanted to feel sorry for him, for the circumstances that led to his death, but he didn't.

Glancing at Carson, Taka said, "Did he have a concealed carry permit?"

"Wouldn't have mattered," O'Malley immediately objected. "He couldn't be denied for a non-mental illness. The gun was visible when officers arrived on the scene."

"I'll take that as a no," Taka said, as Carson squeezed his arm and Stack, dropping into his chair, said, "No, he didn't."

"We just wanted to give you a heads-up that the County's interested and we're giving the family some leeway to run with their own exam." O'Malley lowered his head to catch Taka's glare, aimed at the tabletop. Taka met his eyes. "It isn't personal, detective, I know I come across as a hard ass, but I'm just doing my job—"

"Yes, sir," Taka interrupted, knowing that was the only answer he was allowed.

Greg Stack tapped the table with one of his pens. "I don't like this. So far we're seeing a good shoot. We'll look at the time line, but I think you're keeping a good officer off the streets just to placate a politician, O'Malley, and we need him out there."

O'Malley spread his hands in a "what do you want me to do about it" gesture.

"I'm taking it up with your boss," Stack continued. "See if we can move things along."

"Your privilege," O'Malley said. "This was a courtesy call."

"MRS. HOOPER?"

"Yes?"

After a morning spent with a researcher from West Virginia State who needed specifics on crop rotations in a certain county between the years of 1760 and 1780, Andrea introduced herself to Etta Robbins' sister-in-law and Steven's guardian. She told her about meeting with Etta and about the research she was doing to document Etta's case. "Could I speak to Steven?"

"I don't know, Miss Kelley."

"Andrea, please. I'd really like to get his thoughts. Maybe not even about Billie Mae, if he's uncomfortable with that. I'd really like to know how he feels about it all now, about his mom, and what he remembers about the days before Billie Mae died, when she left the house. Her mother wasn't clear about why she was running away or why she'd gone out in the yard the next day."

"That sounds like a lot of questions about Billie Mae to me."

Andrea quailed. "Yes, it does, doesn't it? I thought I'd be happy with background, what he remembered doing, but I guess I really do have a lot of questions specifically about her after all."

"Steven's spent years in therapy. I just don't know that he'd want to speak to you."

"Has he ever spoken to you about those days surrounding her death? Would you talk to me?"

"No, he hasn't. But I know he remembers them quite clearly for his age at the time."

"I'm especially interested in why Billie Mae went into the yard that day, and where exactly Mrs. Robbins found her"—Andrea caught herself before she said "body"—"laying."

"Did she tell you that? That Billie Mae was laying out in the yard?"

"Yes," Andrea agreed, cringing a little, but hoping Mrs. Hooper would confirm what Mrs. Robbins had not.

"She told me that as well, after the trial, but it was too late by then. Steven's never told me anything. I used to ask, but I haven't in years now."

"Was he ever interviewed by the police? There's not a witness statement from him."

"He wasn't. They tried, of course, but he wouldn't say a word. He didn't talk at all for nearly eighteen months afterwards."

"At all?"

"Wouldn't even ask for water, or new shoes, or... anything. We stopped talking to him about Billie Mae a long time ago."

"Oh." Andrea was nonplussed. She wasn't sure what to do with that info. Steven was technically an adult, but she could still offer to have a therapist sit in on the interview?

"I can..." Mrs. Hooper stopped. After a long moment she sniffed and cleared her throat. "I can ask him, if he'd like to talk to you. He hasn't seen his mother in five years. He might want to talk to you about her at least. I can ask if he'll talk to you about Billie Mae. The therapist he was seeing said he might talk about her more as he got older."

"I'd appreciate that, I really would. It would be really helpful to me to have his insight. I'm not convinced that Mrs. Robbins was rightfully convicted."

A long breath came down the line, ending in a little hiccup. "I've never believed she did a thing to that child. I never have."

"Even if Steven won't talk to me, will you? I'd like to know more about Mrs. Robbins."

"Etta was a dear sweet girl all her life. It's so hard to believe that we're here talking about this. I never would've thought this is the way it would turn out, Etta locked up in that place and Steven here, with me. Etta didn't kill that girl. She didn't."

Andrea didn't know what to say. "I'd like to prove that, Mrs. Hooper. With your help and Steven's, if he'll talk to me."

"I'll ask him, I surely will. What was your number again?"

Andrea repeated it and hung up. She took a deep breath and realized she was shaking. It was true. She didn't believe Billie Mae's mom had killed her.

CHAPTER FOURTEEN

ANDREA MADE THE next call on her list, to Taka's police captain and requested permission to interview the officers involved in Billie Mae's case investigation. Rebecca Cahill was gracious and interested in Andrea's independent project. She asked her to make the request in writing. Andrea agreed to drop it by the following day.

The rest of Andrea's afternoon flew by, as she delved into the soil analysis reports she'd received from the ag station in Berkley County regarding the abandoned garden site at Antebellum plantation Berrylane and then tracked down topography maps of the watershed surrounding it. Her fabric samples for the same project had been sorted by an intern: photographed, sampled for labs to determine content, weave, and dye sources, the individual design elements graphed and drawn individually. All the information would become part of Waltham-Young's permanent collection. She stopped in at the research room to collect them.

The room was busy, with three interns and two fellow archivists scanning documents, pulling files, and poring over old documents spread across the big oak tables. Just walking into the room was a guaranteed pick-me-up. The thrum of discovery lay thick in the air.

"Hey, all," Andrea called out.

An assortment of hellos followed her entrance. She collected the samples and intern's report from her bin and then threaded her way through the tables to Ben. He finished writing the note he was making and then smiled at her. "What can I help you with today, Miss Andrea?"

"You know the girl in Paranormal, right?"

"Karie? Yeah. We've been out."

"Is she the sort that's passionate or is she a skeptic?"

He laughed. "Both. She's passionately skeptical, but there have been a couple of cases that rocked her world a little. Why? You got ghosts?"

Andrea forced a chuckle.

Ben cocked his head. "She'll keep your secrets. Waltham's good at getting peeps to toe that line."

As an organization they were discreet, but Andrea knew that inside the building everything was fair game for gossip. "I just don't want everyone knowing, or y'all are gonna be getting on my every nerve every time I turn around."

"Naw. She's not like us," he said, grinning. "Her stuff's too sensitive. Starts arguments at the drop of a hat. You gotta tell me later, though. I love a good mystery like a coon loves corn."

She laughed, for real this time, and waved her hand at the huge room. "We all do, Ben."

Back in her office she set her paperwork and samples at her work bench and picked up her directory, flipping through it to find Karie Wilson's extension, but then decided better.

She'd wait until after her scheduled call with Bobby Waltham, who was far afield somewhere, to recruit help. Just run it by him so she didn't cause waves. She checked her voicemail, making note of phone numbers and jotting down the time for her speaking engagement at an upcoming historical society meeting. The deep male baritone of a stranger tickled the hairs in her ear as he said her name. Static filled the line, but she could still hear his next words. "I know where you live."

Andrea hit the right key to save the message, every sense alert, her heart racing on an adrenaline spike. A thousand thoughts swirled through her head. The easiest to grab? Call Taka and buy a large dog. She needed something besides grizzly repellant in her room at night. Taka, her innermost voice whispered. Yeah, she wished she could count on that.

Her strong common sense prevailed. Calls came through the switchboard, and the number would be recorded at the main phone. There'd been no specific threat. Did she really want to interrupt Taka's day over a voicemail? Was there anything else in her life besides Billie Mae that would really piss somebody off? She ran through her recent projects at Waltham.

There'd been that native weapons cache that required archeologists on site, holding up the demolition of slave quarters and a plantation house. They remained standing only because of the termite nests shoring them up. The Rec League hadn't been happy; they needed the extra fields.

Often, she had no idea what consequences she was stirring up for other people. She just did the work she was being paid to do and let the chips fall where they may. Generally she was on the side of historical preservation, whether that meant actual preservation or simply preserving the elements for the inevitable time when the setting was no longer available, which was usually, but not always, due to land development.

Billie Mae's killer had no idea she was looking for him. It had to be related to something she was working on at Waltham.

She buzzed the front desk.

"When did it come in?" Marji asked once she had the call sheet displayed on her monitor.

"At two forty-eight."

"Unknown number, doll."

"I thought those were blocked?"

"Only if they go straight through. I took that call and the caller asked specifically for you. Said his name was Bruten Wilder."

"Okay. Thanks, Marji."

Andrea sat back and spun her chair from side to side, thinking. She didn't know the name and suspected it was false, though she had no reason to think that. She tapped it into Google. A 2015 obituary for a local state trooper came up. Further surfing revealed lots of Wilders, but only two Brutens, and they lived in Arkansas and California. Andrea decided to wait and see if the man called back. If he did, she'd tell Taka and employ her other resources then.

Berrylane wasn't due for a month. The Rec League's property was on hold for the foreseeable future, but not shut down altogether. If that was the issue, it should be a while before real trouble reared its head. None of her other projects were close to final report, so shouldn't be raising tempers yet. She'd never imagined being an archivist would be as intriguing and sometimes dangerous as her career had turned out to be. Spinning her chair towards her bench, Andrea jumped up and put her brain to work on the fabrics waiting for her.

ANDREA OPENED THE mudroom door into the garage for the fourth time, thinking she'd heard Taka's Yukon pull into the drive. It was eight o'clock, pitch black, and wet out. Taka wasn't answering his cell. She went back into the kitchen and tapped her fingers on the counter. Finally she snatched up her cell and dialed the precinct.

"Detective Taka, please," she said when the call was answered.

"Hang on," the sergeant replied, his voice made of gravel. Andrea wondered if it hurt him to swallow.

"Hang on, transferring."

Andrea was surprised he was still there, but the tight knot in her chest loosened. She hadn't even known how tense she was until then.

"Taka."

"Taka!" she said. "I was kind of expecting you at my house tonight."

"No, you were suspecting I was down at Sam's getting hammered."

"Well, maybe just a little." She felt sheepish, but she *had* thought it.

"If I'd been you, I'd have thought that, too, Andrea. Sorry I didn't call."

"No, I mean, it's not like you normally call me every night, I just thought—"

"I thought so, too, but actually, I need to go home tonight," Taka said, each word firm.

Andrea stepped over his bag in the living room, shirts spilling out of the top, and folded herself onto her couch in the dark.

"Are you okay?"

During the long pause while she waited for him to answer, she knew he was chewing his bottom lip, trying to decide whether or not to share. The volume of the officers talking and laughing around him was lower than during the day. A single phone rang and then stopped.

Taka drew in a long breath and let it out slow. "O'Malley's gonna pound me on the shoot. Says the kid was having a medical emergency and we should have done more to ascertain his condition before we shot back at him."

"But he was shooting at you!"

"That's what I said. Several times."

"Taka."

"Yeah, I know, Ands. Listen, don't worry about me tonight, okay? You and Billie Mae sleep good."

Andrea thought about the shoes flying around her closet.

"Andrea?"

"Yeah?"

"Are you scared?" he asked, his tone teasing.

"No," she said. She hoped it came out as staunchly as she intended.

"Right," he said, drawing the word out before he sobered again. "Hey, if she gets stirred up, call me. I'm just a heartbeat away, okay?"

They hung up. That was what scared Andrea. Taka really was just a heartbeat away. How attached could a person get to someone without it spilling over into love or sex somehow?

She had a feeling she might find out, even if it broke him.

TAKA MANAGED TO avoid the little cluster of reporters that ran down the block towards him when one of them caught sight of him leaving. After picking up a six-pack of Rolling Rock, he drove straight home. But once there among the detritus of his broken relationship, the bottle of Jack he kept on his bookcase kept drawing his attention until he poured a shot.

He knew he had a tendency to wallow in the grey zone between "moderate" and "abusive" use of alcohol. For one brief period he'd let the alcohol dictate his days and that had been such a disaster that he'd been able to waver on the side of moderate ever since. Taka ignored the knocking at his door while he poured his fourth shot. He might cross the line tonight. He downed it, plucked a second beer from the six-pack on the coffee table, twisted the cap off, flicked it in the general direction of the kitchen trash, and kicked back on the couch again. But just tonight. He'd change the channel from ESPN's umpteenth repeat of the day's news in sports, but he wanted to see the catch of the day again.

His phone vibrated somewhere under his thigh. Taka lifted his leg and fished it out from between the couch cushions. Scott. *I know you're here. Let me in.* The problem wasn't letting Scott in, the problem was getting him to leave if Taka let him in. The phone buzzed in his hand. Scott started banging on the door again. *Answer the door.*

Taka sighed and hauled himself to his feet. He flipped the deadbolt and cracked the door open. Scott shoved it open as Taka retreated to the couch. "Are you okay?"

"No." Taka grabbed a beer, flopped down, and held it up in invitation.

Four more shots and another two beers in silence later, Taka turned his head to look at Scott.

Picking at the label on his second bottle, Scott glanced over, and then back at the TV. "Tell me."

"I killed a kid."

"I know. I saw it on the news."

"He was Dewey's."

"I know. I met him." Scott worked as a bartender at the nightclub Dewey Sanderson pretended not to own. Taka went by there a couple-three times a week for bar food or a drink. It was loud and crowded and everyone moved to the beat. The other dance club in town didn't compare. Andrea didn't get the allure and only rarely met friends there. They might go dancing together a couple of times every summer, when the local bands played and the party spilled into the street, but the Coliseum was his place, his hang-out, not a place he ever took his girlfriends.

When Dewey was present, Taka ignored him and Dewey returned the favor. Dewey liked thumbing his nose at the cops that came in, while keeping them coming in as an extra deterrent against late-night lunacy.

Scott had become a friend these last couple of months, a confidante, after they started talking one slow night about a book they'd both read and Scott confessed to having thrown across the room after finishing. He wrote crime fiction, and gave Taka one of his unpublished novels for feedback on the law enforcement aspect of it. They'd talked procedure for all of ten minutes and then segued into the true heart of the story, the motivation and emotions of people willing to put themselves in danger for the rest of society. Scott had a keen insight into the spirit of enforcement.

"Tell me."

Taka dropped his head back onto the couch and closed his eyes. "You just want it for fodder."

"I'll never use it. I want it because it's hurting you. Give it to me."

Taka rolled his head, opening his eyes to look up at Scott, slouched comfortably on the couch, one leg propped across the corner of the coffee table, still contemplating his bottle. The TV cast shadows over his earnest, all-American-boy features. He looked like a cop, gave off that indefinable taint of having seen too much of the human underbelly. "Why aren't you a cop?"

"I told you," he said, glancing over. "I wasted my youth on school and writing." He looked back down. Turned the bottle in his hands to pick at the other side. "My dad was a cop. MP. Marines. I grew up on base and I hated it. But then I couldn't stop writing about it."

He wouldn't tell Andrea about Scott. Couldn't. When he was with her, he was her Taka. She knew all of him, no words needed, accepted his moods as they came, and let him be when he needed it. Taka didn't know what to do with Scott, who always pushed for words.

"Tell me," Scott said again.

Taka didn't know why he always gave his words to Scott in the end, but he did, every time. He sat up and poured another shot. He left it on the table though, and he began to talk.

CHAPTER FIFTEEN

SHE SAT STRAIGHT up at zero dark thirty, heart pounding. Screaming. Outside. No. Not screaming. Yelling. Someone yelling. Andrea slung her feet out of bed and into her slippers and crossed fast to the window. Not yelling. There was a loud murmuring, like voices, but not.

She pushed on her plantation shutter, inching it to a wider opening, and peered out into the yard. Lit by a three-quarter moon, the yard was empty of anything unusual. The muttering voices grew and then faded a little before surging again. Water. Running water, but not from a faucet. From a creek. Or a running hose.

She walked through the dark house, flipping on lights. Downstairs, she opened the back door to the cold night and cautiously peered out. Nobody. A car passing on Timber Way. A little breeze in the trees. And running water. Ducking back in, she slid on the rubber clogs she wore in the yard and a fleece jacket before going outside to check the hose. It sat coiled neatly against the house, the water off, but the sound was louder here. She walked past and it faded. Walked towards the hose and it built. She reached down and turned the hose on. When water gushed from the hose, she spun the spigot closed again. Silence. "Okay," she said to the thin, cool air. "Okay, Billie Mae, I'll think on hoses." And wet girls lying out in their yards.

Andrea retreated, chilled by more than the cold dark and Billie Mae's new trick. She sat at the kitchen table until the sky began to lighten, then got up and made coffee. Sipping from the warm mug, she trailed back through the house. The neatly boxed files in the living room caught her eye. Plucking up the file of canvass interviews, she found Jason Cobb's on top.

His account was sparse. He helped Mrs. Robbins out a couple of times, didn't know the kids well, didn't see anything out of the ordinary. She slapped it close and decided he'd be her very next interview on Billie Mae's behalf. She rifled through the rest, looking again for any mention of Dr. Huntley and came up empty. She had hoped to talk to him with Taka last night, in person. He would be her second call. Then it occurred to her that she had to be in her office early to take Bobby Waltham's scheduled call from the field. Her watch said she had forty minutes. She bolted to her room, dressed, splashed water on her face, ran a brush through her hair, poured milk and coffee into a travel mug and broke every speed limit on the way to work.

TAKA WOKE HUNG-OVER, the scent of smoke and burnt flesh slow to fade. He groaned and rubbed his head before rolling onto his back and staring at the white ceiling. He'd tried, last night, to dream himself into seeing the shoot over again, really see it, see if he could remember more than he'd told Scott. Remember if he'd noticed anything wrong with the kid, anything at all that should have made him take pause.

Zach Taylor had turned his head, seen them. Lean muscle, ripped jeans, a band of black something around his throat, shaved head. A pistol hung from his right hand, by his thigh. They called out, both he and Tracy, yelling "CPD! Stop!" and "CPD! CPD! Stand where you are!" even though they'd been chasing him for miles and he knew who they were. Patrol, then, a jumble of voices, "Drop your weapon, drop it now, right now!" The kid's hand still came up, the muzzle spit flame before he had it raised level at a uniform caught in a bad position. Taka took his first shot, Tracy right with him, and kept firing.

The kid spun from the force of a hit, facing them now, pulling the trigger again and again, his hand and the gun jerking up with the release of each round. Despite the muzzle blasts and deafening cracks of the bullets, Taka heard the whine of a ricochet before the thwock and the hard shove as it planted itself in the padding of his vest, between his shoulder blades. It knocked him to one knee, tipped him forward to the ground. He'd gone with it; re-braced his grip hand, the gravel from the pavement digging into his forearms; followed center mass on the kid staggering towards them, the pulsing light from the squad cars revealing his progress in sharp red relief one second and hiding him in blue the next. The final lift of his gun jerked upward in frames of red. Taka squeezed his finger back, pressing his grip hand forward and emptied the rest of his magazine, his own muzzle flash blinding him to Zach Taylor's fall to the pavement.

He couldn't remember registering any hint of metal at the kid's wrists in the wash of lights. No watch, no bracelets, though his wrists had been bare, his arms bare, his man-boy chest bare, until his blood painted it all. The only thing that Taka saw on him besides the kid's jeans and his soccer cleats was the wide leather choker. Probably a gift from Dewey Sanderson.

He never saw the medic alert bracelet. Even if you had, Scott asked him last night, would you have held your fire? No, he'd said. And then he drank the shot of whiskey waiting for him.

"No," Taka whispered again now.

They had fallen silent. Taka woke on the couch to the clunk of the deadbolt sliding home from the outside. Head reeling, he'd staggered up to find the coffee table clean, the remaining Jack back where it belonged, and Melinda's key missing from the kitchen hook. His bed had welcomed him, falling up to meet him.

Taka groaned at the dizzy sensory recall and rolled over, dropping his feet to the floor. His muscles were heavy on his bones today, his ankles ached. He argued himself into submission, though, stripped yesterday's clothes, emptied his screaming bladder, and then tried to push some blood around with twenty push-ups. Held a plank for a two-minute count and then since he was on his belly anyway, and he hadn't puked yet, he fished his pull-up bar from under the bed and restored it to the frame above the bathroom door.

Melinda didn't like the way it looked there, so it had been under the bed for months. He did pull-ups and then flipped the shower on, letting the hot water work through the pipes while he fought with the aspirin bottle and swallowed three with handfuls of tepid water from the sink faucet.

Dropping his briefs on the floor, he turned to see what he could of the large bruise between his shoulders. It was fading. He yanked the shower curtain back, stepped under the spray, and yelped at the ice-cold water. He spun the temperature control further left, but the water didn't warm. Goosebumps pimpled his skin and his balls pulled up tight. Gritting his teeth, he shampooed and soaped and rinsed and then slapped at the tap, shutting the water off.

Cold, damp towel looped around his hips, Taka lumbered to the spare room closet and yanked the door open, expecting a flooded carpet, or at least a cold water heater, but it was warm to the touch under its insulation blanket. He frowned and went back to shave. The water was scalding at the sink.

"Well, shit," Taka muttered and got on with his day.

"ANDREA," BOBBY WALTHAM said, voice booming through the satellite phone from his remote camp in Belize. "What can I do for you?"

"Hi, Bobby, thank you for speaking with me."

"Since I ran out of coffee three days ago, I'm truly sorry I'm not there in person," Bobby cracked and then laughed.

"I've come across an interesting murder case I'd like to document. I'd like to use some of Waltham-Young's resources to pursue it."

"Current? Well-known?"

"No, it's a local case, closed, with the mother serving time at Lakin, but a recent discovery of possible items connected to the child involved piqued my interest in it and my friend, Detective William Taka, suggested I might investigate it since the original case took place in my house. There's the possibility my work could be used legally to free the mom and get her the mental health help she needs."

Wind buffeted the speaker and Andrea could hear a bird calling.

"Bobby?"

"I'm here. Just thinking the ramifications through. This would be on your own time?"

"Yes, sir."

"How about you avoid using our name to get you in places, but if you manage to get a lawyer interested, you include us as your research base and list the resources we provided you along the way?"

Too late on the first point, considering her new relationship with Etta Robbin's defense lawyer. And her call to Captain Cahill. But score on the second. Andrea swallowed against the rise of her nerves. "Yes, sir, that would be fine, thank you very much."

"Could you keep me in the loop? Provide my office with a detailed schedule of the research, personnel, and departments you've accessed every month on the tenth?"

"Of course, thank you."

"Thank you, Andrea, you've been a valuable asset to Waltham-Young. I'm happy to help. Is there anything else?"

"No, sir. Should I send carrier pigeons with coffee beans?"

Bobby laughed again. "Bye, Andrea," he said and disconnected.

Her stomach twisting, Andrea set her handset down onto the cradle of the desk phone with exaggerated care. She almost wished he'd said no. Now she had to move forward and find out what really happened to Billie Mae. Whatever that might be, Andrea knew it would be horrific.

A BLACK IMPALA cruised along behind Taka at about forty yards back. They weren't trying to conceal themselves. He couldn't think of any reason feds would be on him, and didn't have much doubt they were Sanderson's men. Private security, maybe ex-military, now on Sanderson's payroll.

He kind of wanted to pull a TV move, flip around and stop them, but in real life, that didn't stop anyone but the occasional amateur out for revenge who could be scared into quitting. Instead, Taka rolled his shoulders and opened his mouth, forcing his jaw open, consciously trying to relax the muscles in his shoulders, neck, and face. He sighed.

At HQ he parked in his assigned spot and stood at the back of his car while the boys parked in the visitor spaces close to the street. When they climbed out, he gave them a two-finger salute and they settled back with their butts on the passenger side quarter panel to await his next move. Taka turned and went inside, leaving them to cool their heels.

In the bullpen, he snagged Oscar, a rookie, and pointed out the men from the window. "Give those two something to do besides wait on me, why don't you? Get creative."

"Who are they?"

Taka shook his head. "You know that shoot last week?"

"Yeah."

"They got something to do with that. Maybe Sanderson's men."

"Sanderson, as in Senator Sanderson?"

"As in Dewey Sanderson," Taka corrected, and then shut his mouth on the explanation he wanted to offer. The fewer words out of his mouth, the better.

"Okay," Oscar nodded. Even the rookies knew Dewey played dirty, though he'd never been charged with a crime. "I can think of something, sure."

"Awesome," Taka said, with no enthusiasm. He wondered how depressed you were if you sounded flat even to yourself.

He left Oscar to his hopefully creative machinations and buried himself behind the understood shield of his computer monitor, cluttered desk, and the shadow of the window shade blocking the morning light. Ignoring the standard morning chaos of the bull pen, he dove back into searching for info on Andrea's neighbors.

CLIMBING THE STAIRS at Waltham-Young, Andrea hoped that Paranormal Investigator Karie would be in her office at this time of the morning, but not yet immersed in her day. The third floor was different than the first. The offices were smaller and opened off a long sunlight-filled hallway sided in narrow, horizontal windows that overlooked the parking lot and the front gardens.

Karie's door stood open, the natural redhead herself seated at her L-shaped desk, back to the door. Andrea knocked and said hi at the same time. Karie jumped and jerked one AirPod out, spinning her chair around.

"Oh, I'm so sorry, I didn't mean to scare you!" Andrea gasped, hand at her throat.

Karie gave her a dazzling smile. "It's okay, I'm just usually the only one up here this early. It's Andrea, right?"

"Yes, it is," Andrea said, stepping inside with her hand out. "Andrea Kelley."

"Karie Wilson. I heard you caught the Berrylane project. There's stories about that place, do you need my help?"

Andrea was surprised. She hadn't come across that aspect of the house's history. She tended to concentrate on the concrete. "Really? Like what kind of stories?"

Karie grinned. "Ghost stories," she intoned, a gleam in her eye. She waved at a chair, inviting Andrea to sit. "Lots of them."

Hooking the chair with her foot, Andrea dragged it closer to Karie and sat. "Okay, spill."

"You know about the soldiers buried there."

"I know it was used as a field hospital, I assumed burials."

"No doubt, but the Union also executed six deserters there, and there's several more stories about civilian deaths. Their burials are undocumented."

"So how do they know they're there?"

"Oh, they're there," Karie said.

"And now you're going to claim to know that because of a few ghost stories?"

Karie clutched her hands to her heart. "A skeptic! I think I love you already."

Andrea blushed. "Um. Not exactly."

"What does 'not exactly' mean?"

"I actually came to ask you about a ghost at my house."

Karie laughed. "Oh. Sorry. I tend to leap in with both feet."

"No, no, I want to hear about Berrylane, but I need help on something different, too. It's not an official case, but Bobby's given me permission to use Waltham resources."

"Intriguing," Karie said. "Go on."

"I'm documenting a law enforcement case." Although it wasn't a part of her job she had explored before, she felt more empowered every time she said it. "A murder that occurred in the house I rent."

Karie's eyebrows rose. "A murder that spawned apparent paranormal activity?"

"Um, yes." Now that the time had come for Andrea to share Billie Mae with someone else, reluctance filled her. A vague sense of protection cooled her sense of urgency. "Apparently."

Seeming to sense her sudden reticence, Karie spun her chair back to the desk, opened a drawer, and fished out a case form. Every Waltham case started with a simple form. She slid it onto a clipboard and handed it to Andrea with a pen. "Maybe this will help you get started. It'll help me when we start digging a bit more. She watched while Andrea filled the top portion out, giving her time to gather herself, before she said, "Can you give me the basics?"

Andrea finished her sentence and then rolled the pen between her fingers. "A little girl, Billie Mae Robbins, was found strangled in a bathtub, fully clothed. She was wet, but the tub was dry when police arrived. One of her shoes was missing and never found. The ligatures on her neck were eventually identified as possibly resulting from the use of a croquet wicket, based on the statement of the victim's mother."

"A croquet wicket?"

Andrea spread her hands, her lips twitching up. "Apparently?"

Karie grinned. "Apparently's a good word for an awful lot of paranormal work. I use it like, thirty-six times an hour. Go on."

"Billie Mae's mother confessed, but never shared the details. There weren't any other viable suspects. Billie Mae's younger brother wouldn't talk about the circumstances leading up to Billie Mae's death. He was only four. Mrs. Robbins is currently incarcerated at Lakin Correctional."

"And how did you get interested?"

"I live in the house. There's been... activity."

"Paranormal activity."

Andrea nodded.

"Want to describe it?"

Andrea took a deep breath. "Um. I've seen her. Billie Mae."

Karie straightened, her shoulders coming back. "Describe her."

"She looks real. I can't touch her, but she can touch things. She appears in different clothes. Sometimes a nightgown, sometimes what she died in."

"Does she talk?"

"Yes."

"Random phrases, or does she make sense?"

"She talks to me. With me."

"You mean, like actual interaction? She responds to you?"

"Yes."

Karie sat very still, her lips clamped down in a straight line.

"I have a friend who saw her yesterday," Andrea continued. "And then he heard her laugh, but he hasn't heard her speaking to me."

"You're completely serious."

"I am."

Putting her pen down, Karie sat back and steepled her fingers.

Andrea bit the inside of her lip, wishing now that she hadn't thought to ask for help.

"There are people," Karie finally said. She took a deep breath and started again. "There are people who do, apparently, communicate with the dead. I'm sure you've seen them on TV. Psychics, for all intents and purposes, who claim to receive mental images of objects or numbers or feelings that grip them, usually fear or love. They interpret this as interaction with spirits, souls who have crossed over. No one can actually prove or disprove this. A lot of them are simply well-trained observers making educated guesses or possessing information on a particular mark that they've gleaned from social media before meeting said mark for a pre-scheduled appointment. Some of them? They're the ones that keep people like me passionate and interested because—y'know—we just don't know.

"Then there's the reports of ghostly apparitions, usually partial, even photos that may or may not have captured those images. There's poltergeist activity, which, in all likelihood, is physical energy manifested by a living person, except there's also those odd borderline cases that can be neither proven nor disproven. There's even some compelling eyewitness accounts of haunted places where you really might be taking your life in your hands to stay for any length of time. But it may be more a fact that science hasn't caught up yet than actual proof of an afterlife."

Andrea nodded after a moment of silence, not sure what response Karie was looking for from her.

"It's very rare to hear someone describe a full apparition, one that actually speaks using words, and interacts directly in response."

"But it does occur," Andrea asked around the dry scratchy spot in her throat.

"It's very rare," Karie repeated.

"Okay," Andrea allowed, letting the word hang.

"What kind of information are you looking for from me?" Karie said, her tone changing as she distanced herself, sounding more detached and professional than just a minute before. "Do you want me to launch a full official investigation?"

Struggling to pick up Karie's non-verbal clues, Andrea shook her head slowly.

Karie's eyes narrowed and she nodded.

"No?"

Karie suppressed her smirk.

"No," Andrea said, her tone firm now. "I just need some background, some advice as to what a full paranormal investigation would look like. I'm not sure what tack I'm taking with the story yet."

"Okay," Karie agreed, relaxing. "Let's scrap this," she said, stripping the paper from the clipboard and waving it in the air. She fed it into the shredder atop the trash can next to her desk. "How about we meet over dinner later and I'll give you the lowdown on skeptical paranormal investigation."

"Do you know Louie's?" Andrea asked and at Karie's nod, said, "At, say, seven? Do you mind if I bring my friend along?"

"Let's do it," Karie said, standing. She walked Andrea out of her office. "I think you'll find it all interesting. Might give you some ideas about sussing out those unmarked graves at Berrylane, too."

Andrea laughed. "Who told you about that, anyway?"

"Tall, dark, and geeky. He can't resist a good mystery."

Andrea rolled her eyes. The description fit Ben perfectly, but she'd bet Randy had tipped him to the Berrylane project. "Ben said you could keep a secret."

"He's right." Karie said. They stopped at the head of the stairs. "I'll see you tonight."

Andrea immersed herself in the minutia of her day, sorting through the various documents she'd collected that described the interior of Berrylane and similar properties in the area in first person accounts. Deciphering the scratch of cursive in many different hands was a challenge. She took notes as she went along, in case she couldn't decide later what translation she had made originally.

When her cell phone rang around noon she picked it up absently. "Andrea Kelley."

The caller hung up.

Shaking her head, she set the phone aside only to have it ring again immediately. A local number. She picked up again. "Andrea Kelley."

The line went dead.

She frowned at her home screen, a distant shot Taka had taken of her climbing at Seneca Rocks. It rang again. This time she paid attention to all the numbers. Her land line. At home. She hit "accept." The line opened with that echoing hush when no one's speaking. Andrea could almost hear something. Her landline buzzed with its own tinny ring. Ignoring it, she closed her eyes and her brain registered the sound's increasing volume. Her landline fell silent. Running water. The sound was running water. Her heart stuttered in her chest. She hung up. Stared at her ascent of Fear of Flying. It rang again.

CHAPTER SIXTEEN

"TAKA," SHE SAID, breathless.

All thoughts of a late lunch fled Taka's head. "Are you okay?"

"I think so." She was obviously on the move.

Standing, Taka started closing the windows he had open on his desktop. "You *think* so?" he said. He hit the off button on his monitor, already digging for his keys. "Where are you?"

"At work."

Taka took a deep breath and slowed his feet a little. "So what's wrong?"

"I think I need to go home. I think..."

Andrea's voice trailed off in a way Taka didn't like much. He nodded at Cozner, mouthed "lunch" and then pushed out into the hallway. "I'm on my way."

"What? No, Taka, it's okay. It's just..."

"I'm on my way. I'll take you home. I have stuff to share with you anyway."

"Okay. I'll, um, I'll wait out front."

Pounding down the stairs, Taka said, "I'll be there." He hit end, trotted through the front lobby and shoved out into the sunshine. He remembered his goons as he unlocked his car and looked up, but there was a blue Honda parked where the Impala had been earlier. He grinned. He'd have to remember to thank Oscar later.

He got three blocks west on Kanawha Boulevard before the Impala appeared in his rearview mirror. He sighed. The relief that wicked through him at the sight of Andrea standing on the front curb at Waltham-Young surprised him. She ducked as he rolled up and yanked the door open, almost falling into the passenger seat.

"Let's go."

Taka threw the car into park and turned to look at her. Her cheeks were flushed in her pale face. "What's going on?"

"Drive, Taka. I think Billie Mae called me."

The words didn't make sense.

"Taka," Andrea demanded. "Drive."

Closing his mouth, Taka slammed the gear shift back into drive and hit the gas pedal. Turning right out of Waltham left the Impala facing the wrong way. Satisfaction warmed him as the back-up lights flashed and the sedan reversed into Waltham's drive, only to get left behind as Taka jumped a yellow light to turn north towards Kanawha Boulevard. He turned his focus back to Andrea, who was sitting tense beside him, one hand on the dash.

"Come again," he said. "With an actual explanation this time."

"My cell rang. When I picked it up no one was there, but then the person called right back. The third time, I just listened. After a few seconds, I could hear the sound of running water."

"That's all?"

"Last night I heard it at home. I couldn't find it in the house, so I went outside and it was the hose, only the hose wasn't on. When I opened the faucet and closed it again, the sound stopped."

"Andrea—"

"It was my landline, Taka."

Andrea's landline existed only for the security system and 911. Taka didn't even know the number. "Are you sure?"

"God, yes. That call came from my house."

He grabbed his radio mike, lifting it to his lips, his thumb already depressing the push-to-talk button before he stopped himself. "Billie Mae's... She can't have an emergency, right? She's..." He couldn't even say it. What kind of a fuck up was he, anyway? A homicide detective who couldn't spit out that a certain little girl was dead already, therefore, by extension, she couldn't possibly suffer personal harm. "Billie Mae's..." The word stuck on his tongue. Low in his throat, Taka growled at himself. "Was the alarm on?"

Andrea sighed and tucked the hair hanging in her face back behind her ear. "Just drive, Taka."

FROM THE MUDROOM, Andrea could see the house was ransacked. All her hoodies were dumped in a heap, her boots and muckers pulled out onto the floor. All the cabinets in the kitchen stood open and empty boxes lay strewn about everywhere. Flour, sugar, Bisquik, and Cheerios littered the floor and counters. Taka disappeared into the entry hall, gun drawn.

Tiptoeing through the mess, Andrea followed him, glancing left into the living room and right up the staircase. Since Taka was disappearing into the upstairs hallway, she entered the living room. The flipped over couch sat tipped against the coffee table, which was covered in stuffing from the slashed cushion of the chair by the window. Andrea's gut threatened to dump itself the same way. The TV lay in front of the small entertainment console it usually sat upon, the screen smashed in. The stereo lay upside down. The fabric on the speakers were ripped and thumpers torn. The box holding Billie Mae's case was gone from its spot beside the couch.

"All clear," Taka said, trotting back downstairs. "The guns are all here. The upstairs is untouched. Can you tell if anything's missing?"

She shook her head. "I don't know, except for Billie Mae's files. They're not here. My office is fine. The TV's trashed, but here, the stereo's here. The files are gone. What does that mean?"

"An interruption." Taka fished his phone from his pocket and called Charleston PD.

Still talking to CPD, giving the dispatcher on duty Andrea's address, Taka strode over and visually checked the lock on the door and the alarm keypad. Taking a pair of gloves from his pocket, he opened the door and peered out. "Yeah," he said to the dispatcher. "Yeah, of course."

Stepping out on the porch, he waved at a car down the street.

"What are you doing?" Andrea asked, following him out.

"I need to know if these guys have any surveillance going here. Maybe they can tell us something."

"Wait. What guys? What surveillance?" she said, trotting to catch up with him.

"I don't know that they do," he said, stopping halfway across the brown grass of the front yard. "No, I'm not talking to you. Do you have someone coming? Bryson? Good." He punched the phone with his index finger and shoved it into his pocket, glaring at the guys who were propped on the hood their car, watching him.

"Stay here," he said, glancing over at her.

"What? No."

"Please? I just need a word with them."

"I'm not going back inside."

"Fine. I'd rather you didn't, anyway."

Andrea crossed her arms over her chest and watched him stride down the street to confront the two men. His body language spelled out his anger, one hand slashing the air when he got close. Their raised voices carried, but she couldn't make out their words. All three men abruptly swung around to look across the yard at the nearest house. Taka waved at the homeowner, who had now stepped out on her porch to make go-go motions at the men. Random strangers didn't park along your bit of road frontage, not in West Virginia.

The men climbed back into their car. The slam of their closing doors echoed up the street. Taka started walking back up the center of the street, stepping aside to let them by. They pulled into her driveway and parked behind Taka's Yukon, but sat inside talking at each other with scowls and short hand-waving exchanges until Taka caught up. Andrea deduced some sort of threat from Taka was involved in coercing their cooperation.

They got out with reluctance and flashed their state police badges at her.

"BCI. Second Lieutenant Hoyle," the shorter of the two said, and pointed a thumb at his younger partner. "Sergeant Detweiler."

Andrea didn't know much about the structure of the West Virginia State Police, but she knew BCI stood for Bureau of Criminal Investigations. Hoyle was maybe thirty-five, blondish, with dark brown eyes, and rugged in a way that screamed West Virginia native.

"They've been on me all morning," Taka said, without further explanation and speaking as if they weren't there. "I thought they were private security, either Dewey's or the senator's. A game Dewey was going to play. But as BCI, they're either major crimes or intelligence. I'm not sure what they're after."

Andrea nodded.

"They might have surveillance on the house."

"This house?" Andrea asked. "My house?"

"We don't." Detweiler said. He was taller than Taka, with a square, earnest face and A-frame shoulders.

"And maybe you can access said surveillance and find out who broke into my house?"

"We don't have surveillance on the house. I'm sorry you had a break-in. We're just keeping an eye on Detective Taka as we were assigned to do. You're within the Charleston city limits, so I suggest you or Detective Taka call CPD. Or we can," Hoyle said.

Andrea looked at Taka, but Taka was unfocused, staring into the middle distance.

"Okay," Andrea said.

Hoyle nodded at Detweiler. Detweiler pulled out his phone, turning on his heel to stand halfway across the lawn while he waited for a supervisor.

He mumbled for a few minutes, and then heaved a big, shoulder-high sigh and pocketed his phone as he walked back, shaking his head. He didn't bother to hide his irritation as he rejoined them. "You already reported the crime."

Taka grunted.

"Audio or visual?" Andrea asked.

Hoyle and Detweiler exchanged a loaded glance.

Andrea wanted to stomp her foot. She dredged up her librarian voice, the one she used with the more recalcitrant ladies of the DAR and little kids when they got too loud. "Audio or visual?"

"That's..." Detweiler stopped, looking a little scared as Andrea squared her shoulders.

"Irrelevant. We don't have surveillance on or in the house," Hoyle finished for him.

Andrea shook her head, her chest compressing until her breath whooshed out. "Warrant?"

He nodded his chin at Taka. "His problem. Not yours."

"We don't need a warrant to investigate Detective Taka's public activities," Detweiler added.

Hoyle glared at him before turning his attention to Andrea.

"Can you tell me who was in my house?"

"No."

She nodded. Pulling her jacket closer around her, she turned to go back inside.

The men fidgeted behind her, the scrape of their shoes loud in the clear, cold air.

"Don't touch anything," Taka told her.

She left the door open and stood in the hallway, staring into the mess of the living room. How would anyone know about Billie Mae's case files? And why would they care enough to break into her house?

After a while she heard the officers' car start up and pull out of her drive, but Taka didn't come in.

HE WAS SITTING on the front step, staring out across the yard at the dusk drawing down. "I'm sorry," he said right away.

She sat down beside him, folding her knees up tight and wrapping her arms around them. "It's not your fault."

"I didn't believe you. And that shoot was my fault. I shouldn't have come here afterward."

"Taka," she said, but then the rest of the words got stuck in her throat.

"The shoot was bad. They might charge me with negligence or worse. He was a damn diabetic. They're saying hypoglycemic rage, but I don't know. He probably would've passed out on his own if we had waited a couple more minutes. He was wearing a med-alert bracelet, but I swear I never saw it. None of us did. These state guys, Detweiler and Hoyle, they're either investigating me for criminal homicide or as part of Criminal Intelligence, organized crime, maybe corruption?"

Andrea's gut twisted, her stomach lighting up with acid burn. "Oh, Taka. Because of Dewey?"

He bit the inside of his lip and his eyes never shifted from the horizon. After a long moment, he nodded, the movement sharp, abbreviated. "They've been trying to pin Dewey down for years. We help out now and then when they need info. They either have something new going and I'm just of interest because Dewey wants my head, or someone, maybe Councilman Miller, maybe Dewey, got O'Malley's boss to request a criminal homicide investigation through the state's Attorney General." He drifted off again and then grimaced. "Or Senator Sanderson asked the Governor for a special favor. BCI jumps at his command."

That seemed like a lot of possibilities to Andrea. Or grasping at straws. The senator would probably be happy Dewey's latest was no more. Taka might be right, though, if the senator was worried about

Dewey's exposure as a gay man with many very young lovers or his past relationship with Taka coming to light. The State could get gag orders issued all around and throw Taka down a dark well with no way out.

He stood up fast, making Andrea's pulse rate shoot up again. He checked the road, but the Impala was gone. Andrea trailed behind him as he went and stood behind his Yukon, contemplating. He felt along the wheel wells and then the front bumper, peered into the front grill, and into the gap between the windshield and the hood.

"What are you looking for?"

"GPS tracker."

"Really? Is that legal?"

"If they have a warrant. Or if it's not theirs." He knelt and ran a hand along the inside of his back bumper. Leaning over, he stretched and then grimaced and jerked his elbow back. He withdrew a black box about the size of a playing card. He stared at it, his face a blank mask. Shoving it into his pocket, he turned on his heel to re-trace his path to the front step. "I shouldn't have come here," he repeated.

"Should we destroy that?"

He shook his head. "Then whoever will know I found it. As long as I know about it, I don't care. My advantage."

Andrea settled again beside him, taking comfort from the heat of his shoulder against hers. "If the break-in were related to the shooting there'd be no reason for Billie Mae's files to be taken."

"Except to fuck with me. Why else take obvious law enforcement documents and nothing else? It's exactly the kind of thing Dewey would do."

"Point. Maybe."Or someone knows we have them and thinks there aren't copies?"

"Maybe the same person who had Billie Mae's shoe and broke in before," Taka muttered, staring straight ahead, his tone dark.

"There was no person. That was Billie Mae."

Two uniforms showed up to take her report and Taka's statement before they could get into it anymore. Andrea tried to be civil. In the name of multi-tasking and the efficiency spouted by the Chief of Police as central to Charleston's shortage of funds, as well as the fact that nothing of cash value had been stolen, the detective who followed in their wake dusted the door and around the desk himself, lifting several distinct prints while Taka snapped his photos for him. After having her sign off and reminding her to go have her own prints filed to rule them out, he shook Taka's hand and went to talk to the uniforms, who were knocking on her neighbors' doors. Again.

"What now?" she asked.

Taka shrugged. "We clean up. We regroup. We hope your neighbors have redirected their cameras towards your house. We figure out what the fuck is going on."

CHAPTER SEVENTEEN

THEY MADE LOUIE'S on Hale Street in downtown with ten minutes to spare, but Karie was already sitting at the bar, a martini in front of her.

"Hey, Karie, this is Taka," Andrea said. Karie's eyes widened as she took Taka in. She couldn't help but notice how small Karie's hand looked in Taka's as he took it in greeting. She always forgot how big he was until she introduced him to someone and saw him anew.

"Hi," Karie breathed. "Karie Wilson, Waltham-Young."

Although still subdued, Taka rumbled out an appropriate form of his name and a how do you do. Karie looked like she might faint.

"Stop that," she hissed.

He shot her a smoldering sideways glance that made her lower belly clench. "I can't ask how she is?"

Karie frowned, her gaze bouncing between them.

Thank you, Jesus, that Louie came through the swing doors to the kitchen and into the bar, calling out their names when he spotted them. The son, grandson, and great-grandson of working chefs and the great-great-grandson of South Carolina plantation slaves, Louie was a gourmet magazine darling for his unique blend of Southern cuisine incorporating wildcrafted vegetables and organically raised game meats.

"Could we get a table tonight, Louie, maybe in the back?"

"I think Daisy can arrange that," he purred.

"Daisy?"

He nodded, his chin drawn up to keep his lips closed, although his eyes crinkled with amusement. "Yes, indeed. Daisy came looking for a job just this week. Ya'll be kind to her," he said, before he raised his voice to call Daisy over.

The blondest Southern belle Andrea had met in the last five years minced around the corner from the larger dining room. Andrea waited for Taka's normal peacock response, but it didn't come.

"Daisy," Louie spoke up from behind them. "I think I'll seat my good friends myself. Please send Julia for their order."

"Yes, sir, Mr. Louie," Daisy said, gathering their menus. She extended a graceful arm to direct them into the next dining area, handing off the menus to Louie in a practiced move. Andrea had to give her credit for being capable of pivoting with the mood.

They passed into Louie's smaller dining room, a dozen four-tops and a couple of tables for two, but currently occupied by only two other patrons. Louie gave them the dim corner table farthest from the rest of the room.

They perused the simple menu, which changed daily. Karie exclaimed over the game selections and chose the elk on familiar server Julia's recommendation. Taka and Andrea settled on venison steaks. Wine delivered and dinners ordered, Karie leaned forward with her hands crossed on the table. "Now." She glanced at Taka. "Andrea says you can corroborate her ghost."

Taka nodded.

Gaze sharpening, Karie shifted into work mode. "Visual apparition, poltergeist activity."

He glanced over at Andrea, but then said, "Yes."

"Have you ever heard her?"

Andrea wondered if he'd go through with it.

"She laughed," Taka said. "I heard that."

"No words, though, no conversation between you and her?"

"No."

Karie breathed through her nose and sat up.

Andrea dried her palms on her thighs.

Julia came back with bread on wax paper and set it down, her lips pursing at the tension permeating their little corner. "Everything okay here?"

"Yes," Karie said, smiling up at her.

Taka cleared his throat and set his glass of Malbec closer to Andrea. "Could you bring me a Woodford? On the rocks."

"Yes, sir," Julia said and left them. Andrea tore a hunk of the always exquisitely fresh French loaf off and moved it to her bread plate.

Karie seem to consider them, sizing them up, maybe sizing up the link between them, visibly gathering her thoughts. "A full-scale investigation requires time, experts and equipment. It attracts media attention if the investigation begins to gather proof, even if it's technically a closed investigation. That is, everyone participating signs nondisclosure agreements, what amounts to a gag order. When proof begins to stack up, those kinds of agreements spring leaks like the *Titanic*. And every single one that's gained attention has ultimately been explained by existing scientific theory or proved a hoax.

"That's our truth and we're sticking to it. But Andrea, Taka..." Karie glanced between them, thoughts percolating. She rubbed her hands together in a nervous gesture, then linked her fingers together, placed her hands on the table, and steamed on. "There have been a couple of experiences like yours that continue to persist unexplained. The people involved don't talk about it. True proof of a continuing afterlife, it's like UFOs. Do you really want to know? Go on NBC and CNN and prove it without a shadow of a doubt? Or try to, anyway? Between the religious pundits and the fear it would engender in the general public..." She shrugged. "A lot of great minds have batted it about over the years and the highest levels of government hold more secrets than the public would care to know."

"Billie Mae's real," Andrea blurted.

They fell silent as Julia returned with Taka's drink. Karie tilted her head, her eyes soft as she continued. "She might be. Both of you would have to submit to batteries of psychological exams. Every square foot of your home and second of your life would be recorded for an undetermined length of time. Equipment that measures energy fields, magnetic fields, light across all spectrums would run twenty-four seven. Audio meters that catch everything from subsonic to supersonic sound waves would record continuously.

"I think that sometimes the equipment alone changes the parameters of the events in such a way that if there really is a paranormal event happening before everything is put into play, that event subsides in response. Or the way in which that event has been able to be captured by the involved individuals—the way spirits or entities or whatever come through—is altered in such a way that they can no longer be perceived. Or they escalate briefly, kill the batteries on everything, and burn out.

"In that case, your neighbors get a laugh, your employer, if he'll still have you, shakes his head and watches you a little closer, you second-guess every noise and flash of light or floater in your vision for the rest of your life. But it passes. It's a good way, actually, to get rid of your experience.

"But if the paranormal disruption persists or even strengthens, if it withstands the assault of scientific inquiry, that can be worse. The only two investigations whispered about by my colleagues? The two that supposedly provided valid scientific proof? The people involved lost themselves. One committed suicide. And even in the few cases in which nothing can be proven, but nothing can be disproven? The evidence gets confiscated sometimes. Other times it just gets roundly discredited by government types whose credentials are as bogus as their degrees and jobs.

"In one of my cases, a fire took everything. The clients kept the property. It's chain-linked and razor-wired. The husband took off, ended up in Colorado where he's still institutionalized with severe amnesia after fifteen years. The wife drifted to Florida, lives in one of those little trailer parks on the beach as a functional alcoholic.

"I know there are cases that spontaneously resolve and everyone keeps their mouths shut because they weren't investigated, or nothing can be corroborated, or it's proven to be natural phenomenon. Those people get to tell a great ghost story on Halloween now and then. So, yes, there are things out there we can't explain, but they are very rare. And they don't usually talk back."

"What about EVP?" Taka said, his voice low.

Andrea whipped her head around, surprised he would know the term.

"Electronic Voice Phenomenon," Karie said, making sure they were all on the same page. "Most of those recordings are hoaxes. Or random static and suggestible minds. Proven fact. The rest can't be disproven, but to the skeptical mind, that is far from proof that the voices come from the spirit world. Why? Is that how you guys are hearing this thing?"

"Billie Mae," Andrea croaked through her tight throat. "Her name is Billie Mae."

"Okay," Karie soothed. "I'm sorry."

"I just hear her," Andrea said. "With my ears. Clear as day."

"Can you tell me?"

Andrea leaned into Taka, checking the room. A couple more of the four-tops had been seated, but the tables near them remained empty. "She comes in the mornings, and if I make bacon, and sometimes she just shows up," Andrea started, and then her throat closed up again. She choked up unexpectedly, dismayed to realize she was close to tears.

Taka lifted his arm and she shifted over until he had her tucked in close. He leaned in and kissed her head. "What does she wear in the mornings," he murmured.

"A white nightgown. Her hair is long and blond. Her eyes are this brilliant shade of cornflower blue. Sometimes she's wearing cutoff jean shorts and a yellow top and white Keds. That's the outfit she, um...that's the outfit she died in."

"Did you see her before or after you knew she was dead and what she wore?" Karie asked.

"I started seeing her eight months ago, in March, right after I moved in. She scared me the first time. I didn't realize, you know, thought she was a kid who had wandered in. It was the nightgown that first time. But I saw the other outfit several times before I managed to locate the information on her. My landlord wasn't exactly forthright about the circumstances at first. He was tired of losing renters."

"The house has a history of events before you?"

Andrea nodded.

"Anyone actually see Billie Mae before you?"

"Kenny said it was doors shutting, moved items, water in the tub for no reason. He owned the house when Billie Mae died, but he didn't really associate the occurrences with her. The house was built in seventy-four and Kenny... I don't know. He just didn't really think of it being her until I came up with the name. I actually found the newspaper articles at Waltham first and then Taka found the case report for me."

Karie glanced at Taka and then back at Andrea. "You've known Taka for how long?"

"Since middle school."

"Cool!" Karie crowed, with a genuine smile. "When did you first see Billie Mae, Taka?"

"I *think* I saw her last week, maybe."

Andrea straightened, Taka shifting to let her without letting go. "Taka—"

Karie plowed on. "But you've known Andrea was seeing something since you pulled the case file, right? How long ago was that?"

"Six, seven months ago?"

"Were there photos in the file?"

"Yes. Andrea recognized Billie Mae right off. But she'd seen her photo already."

"You never saw her until now."

"No. And I don't know if—"

"Did you believe Andrea?"

Taka bit his lip.

"It's okay," Andrea told him.

"Not really."

"It didn't concern you? That she was hallucinating? You hear her talking, right? One-sided conversations with Billie Mae?"

"Yeah, but—" He looked down at Andrea, tightening his hold on her. Andrea frowned up at him. "What?"

"You, uh, you had that accident in Virginia, a couple of weeks before you moved into the house."

Karie's gaze shifted to Andrea in question.

"You mean when I fell from that old loft?"

"Yeah."

"That was nothing, Taka."

"You had a concussion. Seven stitches."

Andrea pulled away to glare at him. "And you thought what, 'oh well, Andrea's seeing a little kid now who's not really here, but that's just fine?'"

"I kind of called your doctor?"

She had to run the words back through her head before they clicked. "You did what?" She wanted to hit Taka so hard right now, or maybe curl up against him and cry. He was her medical proxy and present during her treatment. Calling to ask a question wasn't unreasonable, but still, really? She inched away from him, rigid. His fingers closed in her sleeve and he jerked her back against him.

Before Andrea could counter-act further, Karie said, "TBI is—wow, I can't believe this." She didn't look disbelieving though, she looked ecstatically stoned.

"TBI?" Taka muttered.

"Traumatic Brain Injury."

"I know what it stands for," Taka said. "I served. It's never good."

"It was a mild concussion," Andrea clarified. "Seriously, headache for a couple of days mild. Very mild. Didn't even keep me for observation mild."

Karie wriggled forward, hunching closer to them over the table in her excitement. "TBI is an instigating factor in many disproven cases of reported spectral sightings. Basically, brain injury can cause visual and auditory hallucinations and physical sensations of movement, being touched, unusual heat or cold, almost anything. You know, spine-tingling, hair raising, whatever. All the ways in which people describe their paranormal experience, in an infinite combination.

"But a head bump? In people who have no previous ability to detect unusual occurrences in the natural world, a seemingly inconsequential knock can awaken parts of the brain that see what we normally don't. There are people who can actually see heat signature after a concussion. You know the people that read auras? Auras are energy fields. They can be detected and measured. There are people born with abilities science has been slow to understand, and then there are people who acquire those abilities."

"Are you sure you're a skeptic?" Taka asked.

Karie laughed. "I'm a scientist. And I'm only human."

Despite herself, Andrea found herself relaxing against Taka again. He loosened his grip on her in response, his fingers smoothing her sleeve, straying onto the skin of her arm in soothing sweeps of calloused warmth.

"I'm just saying that if it can be proven that Andrea had no previous knowledge of Billie Mae, no knowledge at all of her death before she first experienced Billie Mae's presence, her mild concussion is one more rung, from an anecdotal viewpoint, in circumstantially proving Billie Mae's existence. We add that to any scientific proof we can gather and bingo, proof of the existence of black helicopters will be yours."

Andrea shuddered. Julia's approach across the room caught her eye and she nodded towards her. "Food's up."

The room was starting to fill, only three of the ten tables remained empty. After they'd been served, Karie glanced over her shoulder before deeming it safe to speak again. "I think, maybe, that you have a very provable case of ghost on your hands, Andrea. I want in. I want to know if she's your brain or an echo or really, truly, proof of life beyond death. You do not want any of this recorded. You do not want an official investigation. You do not want any breath of her involvement in research as you document her case. Trust me."

Andrea stole a peek at Taka and he gave her a sight nod. "Unofficial then. Can we still use the lab for analysis if we need it?"

"Yes," Karie said. "I can put stuff through as long as I report directly to Bobby Waltham, regardless of a full investigation. I'm assuming he's requiring full written disclosure of all Waltham provided research from you anyway?"

Andrea nodded. "He gets to say what gets credited or not to Waltham-Young if my research becomes public."

"Okay," Karie said, picking up her silverware and preparing her attack on her meal as she talked. "Unofficially, I need as much info as you can provide me. I'll leave a bunch of paperwork for you."

Daisy brought a party of six to the table next to them.

"Take your time," Karie continued after savoring her first bite. "I want details and dates, as close as possible. Just call me if you've got stuff for the lab or *think* you have stuff for the lab."

"Good point," Andrea agreed.

Taka shifted, settling in the way he always did when food was placed in front of him and steered the conversation to figuring out if they had mutual friends, where to find Charleston's best burger, lamenting the lack of Thai takeout, mutual recognition of Louie's choice in background music as the latest album of a West Virginia band, and the local music scene.

An hour later, Taka followed Karie and Andrea as they threaded back through the dining rooms into the bar to head home. He nodded at Daisy as she passed them and glancing away, found Dewey Sanderson's brilliant blue eyes locked on him from across the bar.

CHAPTER EIGHTEEN

TAKA FLUSHED HOT under Dewey's burning gaze and stopped.

Andrea and Karie continued towards the door, unaware.

Peripherally aware of both Dewey's bodyguards rising from their seats, Taka absorbed Dewey's palpable rage as he stalked through the crowd, his thick shock of white-blond hair glowing under Louie's dim lighting. One of his goons moved to intercept the women. Taka exploded forward to block him, the loud cacophony of the bar fading to a rush of nothing in his ears.

They collided just behind Andrea, Taka ramming his right forearm across the man's chest to keep him from touching her. The hard elbow jab to Taka's ribs wasn't surprising. Spinning into it, Taka clenched his fingers in the guy's jacket to hold him in place and struck back. The upward lift of the idiot's torso forced him to step back and Taka followed, landing another punch before a hard thump into the bullet bruise between his shoulder blades loosened his grip on the guy's jacket.

With goon number two crowding his back, Taka kept hold of the man in front of him, fist raised. Dewey pushed between them and laid his hand flat on Taka's chest. Through the fabric of his thin cotton shirt, Dewey's palm reflected the depth of his emotion with a radiating heat that forced Taka's attention onto him.

Shorter than average, but powerfully built, Dewey was still ripped after fifteen years. Taka couldn't remember every place they'd tackled rock together, there'd been so many. Dewey had bought him chalk and shoes and hooked him on free climbing before introducing him to other highs. Trail running, BASE jumping, mountain biking. With anticipation of death defying acts conditioned into him, Dewey's touch alone doubled Taka's heart rate. He drew in a sharp breath. Sweat beaded at Dewey's hairline. Taka could map the exact location of each of Dewey's fingers on his chest without looking.

"How could you?" Dewey snarled.

Working to keep his expression neutral, Taka stared into his eyes. "Take your hand off me."

"Or what. Trevor," Dewey said to the man behind Taka. "Escort the women out while we sit down to chat."

"Don't, Trevor," Taka snapped.

Dewey rolled his eyes. "Or what, William," he spat. "You gonna make a move, tear up Louie's nice establishment here, maybe take out a couple of his customers the way you took out Zach?"

"He killed that girl."

"She was a bitch."

The spike of rage in Taka's gut thrust itself hard against his diaphragm. "She was somebody's daughter, Dewey," he rasped.

Dewey's tilted his head and leaned in, his voice dropping. "They've been compensated."

"Are you admitting complicity, Dewey?" Taka said, just as quietly.

"Zach was mine to punish. The least you could have done was—"

A loud crack rent the dead silence of the bar.

Crouching, Taka spun to his left, drawing his gun up and over Dewey's broad back as Dewey ducked for cover. Taka aimed high as

Trevor trained his own pistol low. The backbeat drum of the faint music and louder hum of conversation drifting from the dining rooms washed over them.

Louie, unassuming in his plain white apron, stood next to the bar. Customers remained seated at it, craning to see, though everyone standing had moved to his right, giving him a clear path forward and behind. He rolled his wrist and snapped his hand down. The lash of his grandfather's hunting whip spoke again. Taka flinched at the report. He'd never seen Louie take it off display before, let alone use it. Louie raised his forearm, poised again for immediate action. "Young misses, you come over here," he ordered.

Holding Karie's hand, Andrea brushed past the brave diners standing closest to the fight, prepared to defend their dates. Dewey's fingertips trailed over Taka's lower back as he turned and crossed behind him to stand near Trevor, who had straightened and was tucking his gun back under his suit coat. Dewey smoothed his hair back with both hands. By sheer force of will, Taka shook off his momentary physical freeze in reaction to the second crack of the whip and holstered his gun before anyone could notice. He hoped.

"If you take it outside, gentlemen, right now, I won't call the police," Louie said. "Unless you want me to, Mr. Taka?"

Dewey patted Trevor's back. "Let's go. I'm very sorry, Louie, for the disturbance."

"I'm sorry for your loss, Mr. Sanderson. From now on, you call me first before coming in. Same goes for you, Mr. Taka."

"Yes, sir," Taka said, but held his ground.

Dewey and his men eased by him to get to the door. Trevor kept his eyes locked on Taka, the four of them turning together in a move coordinated to keep each one facing the others. Trevor reached back to grab the door. It opened, a cold gust blowing in, and a couple came in, the man laughing, the woman talking to him over her shoulder.

As if cued, everyone in the bar area began to talk at once. The very picture of cool calm, beauty queen Daisy swept by from seating a party to greet the couple. Dewey and his men stepped aside to let her usher the couple further inside. Trevor caught the door before it swung closed and held it open.

Once all three men were out on the sidewalk, Taka glanced back at Louie, who was coiling the whip and saying something to Andrea and Karie. They both nodded. Taka crossed the short distance to the front of the bar, people quickly shifting to let him pass. The diners seated at the two tables situated against the large, plate glass window facing Hale Street watched him with nervous flicks of their eyes that made Taka's skin itch.

A black Mercedes E550 slid to the curb. Trevor tossed Taka a withering glare before he got in last. Nodding at Louie's uncomfortable customers, Taka stationed himself at the heavy wooden door. When Andrea arrived, she reached past him and tugged it open without speaking to him, Karie on her heels.

Taka followed them down the sidewalk, swinging his head left and right, checking windows and roofs. The block was busy, with several crowded bars, a bluegrass joint, and an art gallery filled with yuppies sipping wine and talking with their hands, gesturing at crazy, bold colored canvases and weird metal sculptures that resembled exactly nothing but twisted metal slag. Two guys stood outside the tattoo shop on the corner across the street, smoking and arguing. The harsh bite of their words cut through the rising fog.

"Stop," Andrea said, apparently watching him with the eyes in the back of her head.

Taka shook his head in response, even though she couldn't see him. Staying observant wasn't a fault, it was a survival tool. "Sorry you got caught up in that, Karie," he offered out loud.

"I saw the story in the papers. It just didn't occur to me that you were the cop involved. Is Mr. Sanderson related to Zach Taylor?"

"No. He was a family friend." The semantics came easy. Taka could still feel Dewey's hand on his chest like a brand. He didn't want to explain Dewey to anyone right now, certainly not to someone Andrea worked with every day.

Karie nodded, willing to let it lie, for which Taka was grateful.

THE FIRST FLOOR of the Huntington Bank garage was nearly full, but devoid of people. They waited while Karie organized herself and started her car. Giving her a little wave as she watched Karie drive out of the lot, Andrea said, "Take me home."

He studied her a minute, biting his bottom lip before he caught himself and stopped. "No. You're coming home with me."

"I'm fine. I want to go home."

"The door lock needs fixing and we didn't clean up."

"The lock still works, Taka, I tried it. I'll get another deadbolt tomorrow. And I have a security system."

"It only works if you turn it on, Andrea."

"So I'll turn it on. Promise."

He shook his head. "No."

"Dewey doesn't scare me."

"He should. Andrea, you know who he is. People disappear around Dewey when he's pissed. And you're—" He bit his lip and looked back down the block.

"I'm what?"

Mine, and he knows that. Taka shoved his hands deep into his pockets and blew out the breath he hadn't realized he was holding. It condensed on the cooling air. No fucking way he was taking Andrea home. And he was tired, the letdown catching up to him. At Andrea's he'd be on alert all night, expecting Dewey and probably getting Billie Mae instead.

Andrea opened her mouth and huffed. The white streamer rose, drawing his reluctant attention. She tilted her head back to consider the stained concrete above. "Fine. Just tonight."

They walked back out under the dark, clear sky to his Yukon in silence. Andrea kept her head turned down and her hands buried in her coat pockets, her shoulders hunched up against the cold breeze blowing into their faces. Taka resisted the urge to tell her to keep her hands free and head up. He became conscious of a car driving slower than the rest of the traffic, pacing them.

He stopped and turned. Lieutenant Hoyle grimaced at him through the windshield of the Impala and sped up, before slowing down again to pull into the curb past the Yukon.

Taka sighed.

"My FX," Andrea said, as he opened her door for her.

"Yeah, okay."

On the short drive out to the river and over to Waltham-Young, Taka brooded over his shit day while Andrea stared out her window. Andrea's car looked lonely in the corner of the Waltham's main lot, far from the five or six others parked near the better-lit area by the library's entrance. He glanced in the rearview mirror at the Impala trailing them a hundred yards back before he made the turn off the street.

"I'm gonna check your car."

"For a tracker? Really?" Andrea asked, her voice warmer than he expected given her silence.

He felt along the back bumper first, but didn't find anything. He ran through the same search as he'd performed on the Yukon until he was standing back where he started. Nothing.

"You never drive my car, Taka. There'd be no reason to track me."

"You're my best friend, Andrea. Everyone knows that." He scruffed both hands through his hair, frustrated that he couldn't stow away the static of his adrenaline fatigue enough to concentrate.

Andrea swung her arms wide, taking in the large lot. "They'd have more time to place one here than they'd have at CPD or at your condo. Fewer people wandering by."

"All right, that's true," he agreed, grateful she was giving in to his paranoia. Returning to the Yukon, he opened the passenger door and plucked his small flashlight from its velcro strip under the dash. He searched the interior of the FX, the glove compartment, under the front seats, and riffled through the gas receipts, ballpoint pens, and tampons in the console bins before moving to the rear. The spare tire well would be a terrible location for reception, but he checked anyway. Shaking his head, he slammed the rear hatch closed.

"There's no reason for them to track me," Andrea repeated.

"It's Dewey." And you're mine. His heart thumped painfully out of rhythm on the sudden spurt of possessiveness that colored that old, familiar thought. He'd never wanted to say it out loud before. The words were too stark. He'd felt it, took action on it, teaching Andrea to protect herself, running background checks on dates and boyfriends, shelling out or pitching in on a security system everywhere she'd lived since he'd come home and joined the CPD. He turned his head, checking on Hoyle and Detweiler. The Impala's lights were doused as they sat waiting, but the low rumble of the engine carried through the thin fog. Although he was standing with his back to her, Taka could feel Andrea roll her eyes at him. But he knew, just knew, the car was bugged. It was what he would do.

Sticking the flashlight between his lips, he lowered himself to the ground, rolled onto his back, and scooted underneath the back bumper of the car. The tracker was lodged up high, snugged against the wall of the left rear wheel well. It was smaller than the other, now sitting in the Yukon's console.

Andrea turned the tiny magnetized device over in her hand when he handed it to her and levered himself upright again. "How long?"

He shrugged. "No longer than a day, I'd think. Since Taylor died. I'm sorry."

"Taka! Stop saying that!" And good, here was the anger he expected, stiffening her limbs, coloring her cheeks, filling her voice. "Those guys"— she flung her hand out towards the Impala—"have no right second guessing you, and none to follow me just because I know you. They could have no possible probable cause."

"Probable cause is just a matter of perception, Andrea, but the State doesn't have the money for tech that high end," he bit back, stabbing his index finger at the tracker. "And if they did, why are those guys still following us so close? One way or another this is all on Dewey and whatever strings he's pulling now. I'd stake my life on it."

"Yeah, well, if it is, we're grown-ups now, Taka, and we know a few people of our own these days."

"They'll find out, Andrea. I can't—" He couldn't look at her. He studied the rise of the Impala's exhaust instead. Those two pricks probably already knew. It was only a matter of time before all of CPD knew. "I told Carson. If I end up being the first outed, c'est la vie, but I don't *want* everyone to know I was just another one of Dewey's boys, even if I was legal."

"It was years ago, Taka. You didn't know. It's time Dewey got some kind of payback for hurting you. For hurting all of you."

CHAPTER NINETEEN

ANDREA WOKE ON Taka's couch to the sound of running water. She froze, staring hard in the direction of the maddening gurgle. Taka appeared in the doorway of his bedroom, frowning, head turning to locate the sound. Dread pooled in Andrea's belly. She gagged when the room spun as she struggled to sit up.

"You okay?" Taka asked in a low voice.

"It's Billie Mae."

Taka shook his head, easing over to her. "You're here. With me, Andrea. At my place."

"Do you hear that?"

He sat down on the edge of the couch, Andrea scooting back to make room for him. "The running water? Yeah."

"That's what I heard the other night and again on the phone."

"It's just a pipe that broke or something." He frowned at her and laid his hand on her forehead. "You look really pale."

She felt pale. Washed out and nauseous.

"It's Billie Mae."

Taka's lips flattened and twisted. "I'm going to take a look around."

ANDREA CLOSED HER eyes. She looked as white as a damn ghost herself. He didn't know if her non-response meant agreement or resignation, but he knew damn well the noise wasn't being caused by Billie Mae.

Barefoot in the hallway outside his apartment, Taka paused to listen. You'd think they were at sea, the water was so loud. But it was definitely coming from further to his left. He padded several steps that way. The hallway smelled vaguely of smoke. A door opened as he passed it and he startled, spinning around and dropping into a defensive crouch.

Mr. Talbot held his hands up. "Easy there, Taka," he exclaimed.

Taka straightened, forcing a smile onto his face.

"You looking for the burst pipe?"

"Yes, sir," Taka said, trying to keep the surprise off his face. Despite his determination to find the source, he found himself relieved that someone else could hear it, that it really wasn't Billie Mae, somehow loosed from Andrea's house to his place. He felt again the pressure on his bicep, her forearm under his fingertips, the rigid heat of her against his side as they talked about her concussion with Karie and his doubt in Billie Mae's existence.

The fall had scared him, the call from the hospital, the vivid, blood-crusted line hidden in her hair, laced with tiny purple stitches. And then when she'd started talking about hearing things in the new rental, had tentatively asked him to look up the name, "Billie Mae Robbins," his heart broke for her. Her doctor reassured him, told him to make her an appointment for further evaluation. But after he found the case files, after he'd talked to her landlord about who had lived in the house before Andrea, trying to find out how she heard the name, and when she didn't show any further symptoms... he let it go. So what if her brain had tangled the facts up a bit? He still loved her. No one else, aside from her landlord, had to know.

"Sounds like it's next door, doesn't it?" Mr. Talbot said. "But there's nothing wet in my place, at least not yet." He stepped out and they walked down to the next door.

It was one thing for Taka to wonder if he had seen Billie Mae at Andrea's. He heard about her enough, knew most of the lines of the one-sided conversations he heard through the bathroom door or in the kitchen by heart. Andrea had him jumpy and spooked and convinced it was real. But this was another thing altogether, Andrea claiming this unknown problem as Billie Mae's doing even though they were here, at his place.

Taka would've preferred to slam his fist through 311's door. He knocked.

God damn it, he should have known. Made that follow-up doctor's appointment for her.

No one answered.

Mr. Talbot gave the door three good fist poundings and they waited. Nothing.

"Is this unit even occupied?"

"I think so," he said, pounding one more time. "There was a lady going in and out the other day with boxes. Suzanne? I think she said she was Suzanne. I was in a hurry."

"Huh," Taka said, listening to the sudden silence.

"Do you think that's good or bad?" Mr. Talbot asked, cocking his head and putting his ear to the door.

Taka shrugged. "I guess that depends on if we have water in our apartments still."

"Let's see," Mr. Talbot said. Taka followed him back into his apartment, loitering just inside the door. The older man reached over the kitchen counter from the entry hall to flip on the faucet. Water spewed out.

"Guess we're good then," Taka said with forced cheer. "Have a good night, Mr. Talbot."

"You too, Taka. Stay outta the papers!"

"I'll try, sir." Taka closed the door behind him and took a deep breath. Did that mean Mr. Talbot had seen the article on the shooting in the paper or that he hadn't? Stupid Zach Taylor, stupid Dewey Sanderson, stupid him for going into law enforcement in the first place.

Closing his own condo door behind him, he leaned back against it, not meeting Andrea's eyes, although she watched him with a solemn expression from where she sat cross-legged in her blankets on his couch.

"Five doors down. No one answered the door and then it stopped."

"I heard voices in the hall."

"Mr. Talbot. He has the apartment next to that one. Said there wasn't any water seeping through. No wet carpet or wall or anything."

"It was Billie Mae."

Taka's heart dropped. He looked up at her. "It wasn't, Andrea. It's just a pipe or something. I'll report it tomorrow morning if no one answers the door on our way out."

"It's Billie Mae. It means something important, Taka."

"It doesn't!" he yelled, before he understood the catch in his chest, the pulse of furious energy carrying him forward. He stopped himself two strides from her, lowered his raised hands before he could grab her. He wanted to shake her, make her stop all this. "Look," he said. He closed his eyes, concentrated on stilling the quiver of his anger. When he opened them again she was standing, dark eyes wide and jaw set, fists clenched at her side. "Talking to Karie tonight made me remember a few things I'd forgotten about along the way."

She raised her chin.

"This." He threw both his hands up, palms up, trying to indicate everything that had happened over the last few days. "All this. It's—I shouldn't have let it escalate. I shouldn't have bought into this."

"My crazy?"

She might as well have sunk a knife into him. The stabbing pain was the same.

"Explain. Explain it then," she challenged. "Explain the fact that you saw her, that you heard her. Explain the shoes and Mr. Huntley seeing the girl with the snake on our steps."

He couldn't. But there must be some explanation other than ghost. And he suspected Huntley could enlighten him on at least the snake and the shoes.

"My steps, my front steps," she corrected herself when he didn't say anything.

Did she really think he cared about that slip? At all? All he cared about was her and whether she was okay or not.

"I love you, Andrea," he said. And god damn. Each word tore itself off his heart. "I love you."

He stepped forward and wrapped his arms around her as she started to cry, unyielding and braced against him.

ANDREA WOKE LATER in the morning all cried out. Her nose was stuffy and her eyes burned. The shower was running. She peeled herself up and rinsed her face with cold water from the kitchen sink and brushed her teeth and re-packed the go-bag she'd taken from her car. Fortunately, since she'd been up half the night, she didn't need the bathroom at all, so she just let herself out.

Five doors from Taka's end unit, she noted the condo number and knocked. There was no answer. Outside the day was already bright, the sky a brittle blue with high, flat clouds and the incoming cold front delineated to the south. In the parking lot she said hello to Taka's elderly neighbor, Miss Betty, and cooed at Miss Betty's equally old schnauzer.

She opened her car door and then had a thought. She called out, "Miss Betty! You don't know who's moved into 311, do you?"

"I think he said his name was Vernef Itch, sweetie. I made him repeat it. Maybe it's Russian, or something? He seemed real nice."

Andrea bit the inside of her cheek to keep from laughing. "Thank you, Miss Betty!"

On the river road Andrea's phone sang out Taka's tone. She didn't pick it up, just let it ring through, tears pricking her eyes. A minute later the voicemail pinged.

She'd shaken herself into a semblance of research mode by the time she turned into the Waltham's parking lot. She had to focus on her clients this morning before turning her day over to Billie Mae.

AT NOON, ANDREA checked her phone and found six messages from Taka and one from Etta Robbins's sister, Mrs. Hooper. Her heart beat harder as she listened to Mrs. Hooper state that Billie Mae's brother wanted to talk to her. She could call back after seven in the evening, when he got home from baseball practice.

She pulled out the yellow legal pad on which she'd made notes from her interviews with Mrs. Robbins and Mrs. Hooper. Reading over them made her wonder again about the missing wicket. Phone still in hand, she speed-dialed her landlord.

"Meyers," Kenny answered. He was older, a full-time landlord who did all his own maintenance and renovation.

"Hey, it's Andrea. Listen, thank you for being patient with me the last few months. Did you see that two kids were pulled from Lake Vickers last week?"

"Yeah," he said, his voice softening. "Saw it in the paper."

"I found a kid's shoe in the yard, a blue Keds. The police confirmed it belonged to the second kid, Adam Ward."

Kenny made a distressed sound, low in his throat. "Geesh, Andrea, really? That wasn't in the paper. No one's called me."

That was something Andrea hadn't considered, either calling him before now or not saying anything about the shoe. "Yes. I'm sorry. You should probably be prepared to talk to CPD if they call you," she said, while typing on her keyboard for the latest news updates, seeing reports on Adam's death right away. She skimmed the first article, relieved to see physical details. She sat back to concentrate on the conversation. "The thing is, Billie Mae's been really, really active. You know me, Kenny, I'm an archivist. I'm addicted to research. I've decided to document her case from the ground up. Maybe I can prove her mom didn't kill her."

"Andrea," Kenny said, the word full of warning.

"It's a matter of public record, Kenny. Billie Mae's still here for a reason. She's haunting your house. Etta Robbins' sister-in-law and her lawyer never believed her confession. I just need to know, Kenny. Please? You were there. I need answers."

"I wasn't there, not when it counted."

Andrea frowned. "Of course not, it's not like you lived there. Wait, were you there?" If he had been, Detective Ford didn't know, or didn't talk to him, anyway. Or the interview wasn't in the file.

"No, not until afterward. Bob Huntley called me. I got there just after Billie Mae had been taken out."

"Was Mrs. Robbins still there?"

"She was. She was in shock. Acted like she didn't even know who I was, kept asking for her husband."

Something in his tone made her inner ear prick forward.

"Did you know her well?"

Silence crackled down the line. Faint music played in the background, a car radio maybe. Creedence Clearwater's "Bad Moon Rising." "I knew her like i know you," Kenny sighed. "I spent a bit of time there with her and the kids when she needed help. She made me an occasional home-cooked meal."

"Oh, God, I'm so sorry, Kenny. I didn't know."

"No way you could." He cleared his throat.

"We, uh, we found Billie Mae's missing shoe. Planting blueberries near the carport. We also found a dog burial."

"Shit," Kenny breathed.

"Is that the Robbins' dog?"

"Yeah. I buried it. Poured the carport concrete a couple of years later."

"Do you know what happened to it? Mrs. Robbins doesn't."

"Dog was dead, Andrea. Just laying there in the kitchen. The cops noticed, when they took Etta's boy, Steve, out of the house. I wrapped it in a blanket off the dryer and put it outside, but it took me a couple of days to bury him. That was...yeah... not so good by then."

"That blanket was Billie Mae's. There was a stuffed rabbit, too. Mrs. Robbins said Billie Mae had one."

"Fortune, the sleepy rabbit. That's what we all called it. Etta was in custody, already confessed to... you know. Her sister-in-law made all the funeral arrangements. She didn't come back to the house, didn't ask for anything of Billie Mae's, so I put the rabbit in with the dog, figured Billie Mae'd have liked that. She loved that dog. He went with those kids everywhere."

"I'm sorry, Kenny, to ask, but was there blood on the dog?"

"No, nothing like that. Older dog. Just bad timing, that's all."

To tell or not? For all Andrea knew, the dog's skull fracture happened after he died. She glanced at the questions she had scrawled in the margins of her notes. The word "wicket" jumped out at her. She'd underlined it three times.

"Do you know if the Robbins owned a croquet set? "

"Etta said something about a wicket the one time I gone over to Lakin. I cleaned the house out. I don't know what she was talking about. I don't think she did it. None of us did. Not me, not her sister-in-law, but Etta, she said she did it and the cops didn't look any further."

"One cop did, Kenny. I have his notes and I have Billie Mae."

"Okay." He took a quick, shallow breath. "Okay."

"Did you know Mrs. Robbins carried Billie Mae in from outside?"

"No." His dismay was evident in his voice. "How do you figure that?"

"She told me."

"Billie Mae?"

"No, Mrs. Robbins, when I spoke with her."

"Can you really believe anything she says now?"

"I don't know."

"She wasn't—Etta wasn't wet. There wasn't blood on her clothes, just on her hands, on her face. The kitchen floor had streaks of mud, but that was from Billie Mae tracking through. And the dog. That's why Etta was upset with her. Why would she tell you that?"

"I don't know. Maybe because it's been years since anyone last asked her?"

"I don't believe her, Andrea."

Maybe she could talk to the ME's office. Maybe someone could explain the autopsy report to her, tell her if it was even a possibility Mrs. Robbins could have physically strangled Billie Mae without her shirt getting wet or bloody. "Do you remember seeing Billie Mae's missing shoe when you buried the dog? Maybe it got caught up in the blanket somehow?"

"I can't."

He sounded broken. She didn't even know why she had asked him that. Her stomach turned over on itself. She tapped her pen on her notes, flipped the page. A name caught her eye.

"I have to go, Andrea."

"Wait! Do you remember ever hearing the name Jason Cobb from Mrs. Robbins or in the neighborhood?"

"No, don't remember a Cobb. I don't know everyone on the street, though."

"Thank you. I'm so sorry for bringing all this back up."

He muttered, "See you later."

She hit end and covered her face with her hands. The hollow emptiness in her chest felt terrible. Maybe she wasn't built for this. She had probably not only ruined Kenny's day, but his week. Maybe his month. She knew Taka could have talked to Kenny and stayed objective, but right now Andrea had no idea how. No idea how he did his job at all.

Her hands were shaking when she lowered them to scroll through her phone again. She found Taka's voicemails and listened to them. The first three were "call me." The fourth was a threat of sorts. The fifth was a real threat to call the front desk and make sure she was there at work and safe. The sixth said that yes, since she was there at work and safe, he'd wait for her to call him.

.

CHAPTER TWENTY

TAKA WAS ON the phone when Detective Chief Ronnie Horton entered the bull pen and stopped to get his bearings. He turned his head left and caught Taka's gaze from across the room. He watched with a sinking in his gut as Horton threaded his way through the desks and around the clumps of cops talking to one another.

"Hey, Lieutenant," Taka said, when Horton finally fetched up in front of him.

"We finally ID'd the first kid we found, a girl. Kayla Anderson, ten. She went missing twenty-eight months ago. Mother's long gone. Father waited two days to file. Said she was supposed to be at a friend's house. That friend lives a few houses down from Adam Ward."

Who was pulled out of Lake Vickers a couple of days after Kayla, his missing Keds found in Andrea's yard. And shit, yeah, Taka remembered the search for Kayla. He was working a double homicide, but they had all been roped into the search for several days. She had lived out near the airport and the search had covered miles of land and trails north and east of it. There had been absolutely nothing to go on at all.

A web of cold nerviness spidered out from his spine, tightening his skin onto his bones. Maybe the break-in wasn't Dewey harassing him. Billie Mae's purloined files were gone. By silent agreement, neither of them mentioned that missing item to the responding officer, since they were still waiting for their official copies to be granted. "And the Wards live a street over from Andrea. Did this friend see Kayla the day she disappeared?"

"Yes. She said Kayla came home with her after school. A lot of miscommunication ensued and Dad didn't even know she was missing for over twenty-four hours. Dad drove over to look around for her, but Kayla had a history of disappearing with friends, so he waited. Didn't want to cause a commotion. We looked at him, but never found a reason to pursue him."

"How old was she again?"

"Ten. Adam was seven. Kayla's dad ran into an older man out walking, who tried to reassure him that kids don't go far and that she'd turn up."

"Robert Huntley."

Horton shrugged. "Mr. Anderson didn't get his name, and couldn't positively ID him from the photo we showed him, but we're going to bring Huntley in, see what he has to say."

"Are you including the Robbins case in your investigation?"

"For now, on the QT, as a long shot. These are crimes of opportunity and we have the Robbins girl walking back into her house that morning, but that case has always been hinky."

"You want to withhold giving copies of the full case files to Andrea," Taka guessed.

"It's public record, so we can't say no if she pushes, but yeah, we want to stall other eyes on this. Captain's going to deny her request for officer interviews for now."

"You know, she's just trying to make sure Etta Robbins isn't doing time for confessing to killing her kid if she's actually innocent. She's on our side."

Horton spread his hands. "Talking to the choir, Taka, but do you want anything screwed up on a technicality if she trips over something before we do? Or hell, do you want her hurt if she's right and somehow figures this out before we do? She lives right there and we've got other missing kids going back two decades."

"I know, Chief. I get it. You having the lake dragged?"

"Trying to get approval right now." He shifted, his gaze darting away over Taka's right shoulder. "Look..."

Taka sat back in his chair, aware Horton hadn't given him Kayla's Anderson's file to look at himself. His breath thickened in his lungs, the familiar sweaty, musty, staleness of the old building sticking in his nose. "Captain wants me off this." "Yeah. Sorry, Tak. That video making the rounds today has her turning colors."

Someone had shot video in Louie's and originally posted it to Facebook, but Karl had shown it to Taka on Twitter. It started with the second whip crack and Trevor blocked any view of Taka except for his gun pointed over Dewey's back. Dewey was just visible in the lower left. Louie filled most of the frame. CPD was taking a vocal social media beating for what some citizens believed to be just another instance of their failure to properly police Charleston. Taka shuffled paperwork around on his desk and handed Adam Ward's file over.

"She wants to see you."

"I'll bet."

"I heard about the Councilman's nephew being diabetic. O'Malley's a prick," Horton said, backing away already.

"Thanks, man," Taka muttered, mind turning to what he needed off his desktop. No doubt the Captain intended to suspend him without pay while Pro Standards sorted his shit out. As evidenced by the presence of Hoyle and Detweiler and the damning trackers, Councilman Miller and Dewey Sanderson were no doubt using different forms of clout to lean on all sorts of higher-ups at the State Police, and possibly the Governor's office, who in turn would be pressuring the County and CPD.

Taka already knew from glancing at the morning paper that the Councilman was going high, the public route. Dewey would be navigating the underground, using secrets to insure compliance. The senator wouldn't be happy, but Dewey's relationships with his boys was an open secret. At least they weren't minors anymore, though that past could rise up and bite Dewey on the ass one day. That'd be the only line of threat Daddy would be covering beyond a well-placed whisper in the ear here and there to ensure Taka kept his mouth shut. On that point, none of them had anything to worry about.

He emailed the map of Andrea's neighborhood and his Excel timelines of interviews and the cops involved in both Billie Mae and Adam Ward's cases to Ronnie Horton and then erased the drive on his desktop. If push came to shove, Carson could argue Taka was rattled when he used his personal instead of intra-department email. Whoops. it wasn't illegal for him to have the files of a closed case in his possession and he'd been asked to look at Adam Ward's. He had additional info on five of the nine neighbors on Andrea's cul-de-sac.

After piling the rest of the hard copy forms Pro Standards wanted him to complete on the shooting in a folder, Taka powered down his desktop and headed to the captain's office. Debbie, who kept track of everything in the Bureau Chief's office, waved him in and down the hall to Rebecca Cahill's door. He knocked on the frame and waited until she finished typing on her keyboard and glanced up to smile at him.

"Detective, please come in." She didn't stand. Taka couldn't tell if that was a good sign or a bad one. She waited until he settled in one of the two scarred wooden chairs in front of her desk to continue. "Greg Stack sent some paperwork over I need you to sign. You're being temporarily suspended with pay while the inquiry into the death of Zach Taylor continues. Should actual charges be brought against you, your pay will also be suspended. Taka, the Kanawha County Prosecutor's Office is already talking about convening a Grand Jury."

Taka swallowed the bitter fumes of bile rolling up from his belly and burning his throat.

"It's an impossible situation. I have no doubt you did the right thing. The courts will see that if this gets pushed hard enough to land in front of a judge."

"Dewey Sanderson has a lot of friends."

"I know the senator isn't happy with his son, so that might throw up some road blocks. Personally, I'm more worried about the councilman. I'm sorry this happened to you."

"Has Tracy been cleared?"

Rebecca was a good cop and a better administrator. She followed his lead and relaxed her commanding professionalism an ounce. "Yes. I just put him back on active duty. I'm going to have him break in Fields while you're on suspension. We need both of you to keep a low media profile on this one, Taka, and don't think I don't know that's you in that damn video. Be grateful that you're unidentifiable. The Gazette's already called twice asking for confirmation. You need to go home and stay there."

He wouldn't insult her by denying it, but he wasn't going to acknowledge it, either. And he wasn't going to go home and watch TV. "Are you aware my friend Andrea Kelley is working on documenting the death of Billie Mae Robbins for the archives at Waltham-Young?"

"I am. I'm denying her request of officer interviews."

"For what reason?"

"I'm not required to give one."

She didn't say anything else. Taka didn't try to fill the silence. He waited for her to insult him by reminding him not to speak with Andrea about the current investigation.

Her landline beeped and she reached over to press the intercom.

Debbie's voice filled the empty air between them. "You have a call on hold, ma'am. Mayor's office."

"I need your badge and service weapon, Taka."

He stood up, unclipped his badge, and set it down on the desk beside her name-plate before he unbuckled his belt and slid his holster and gun from it.

Reaching out to take it from him, she said, "Good luck, Taka."

Taka swallowed. He didn't think he could squeeze out a reply. He simply walked out, listening to her pick up the phone and greet her caller in a forced, chirpy tone.

"No, everything's fine," she reassured her caller, and then he was standing in the hall at the top of the stairs and nothing, nothing about this, seemed fine to him.

HOYLE AND DETWEILER were waiting for him, looking completely bored. Taka waved at them and then took them on a long meandering drive, crossing the river on Dickinson Street and then driving down Creel to Ferry to MacCorkle to the 36th Street Bridge. He cruised back up Kanawha past Waltham-Young to the Patrick Street Bridge, crossed into South Charleston, and drove right by their home, the West Virginia State Police Headquarters. The stark, white, low slung buildings didn't look like much for such a big title.

He turned here and there randomly until he came upon a Panera's and remembered he'd skipped breakfast. His stomach woke up, grumbling at the injustice of his day. He checked his mirrors, noted the lack of curbside parking, and cranked the Yukon around into an illegal u-turn. The screech of the Impala's tires to avoid rear ending him hurt Taka's ears. A Mustang rocked on its frame as its driver came to a complete stop behind Hoyle and Detweiler. Hoyle maneuvered into a proper three-point turn. Idiots. After parking at the back of the lot, Taka walked to where Hoyle was backing into a spot on the far side.

He ducked down and waited for Hoyle to open his window. "You do realize I'm letting you follow me, right? Wasn't like you were going to lose me if you safely went by me and turned around."

Detweiler shot him the bird from the passenger seat.

"Fuck you, Taka," Hoyle spat. "Get me a coffee."

At the counter he ordered a turkey sandwich with an apple and two coffees, fully leaded, because he was a damn pushover. He knew Detweiler and Hoyle were just doing the job they'd been ordered to do, whatever that job was—follow a violent cop? Harass a cop possibly

ELLE ANDREWS PATT// 183

involved in wily local mogul Dewey Sanderson's suspected criminal doings? A new thought occurred to him. Were they his protection from local mogul and suspected crime lord Dewey Sanderson?

"Anything else, sir?"

There was cream soda sitting right there on ice. Taka wanted one, but they were just that much too sweet and Andrea wasn't there to split it with him. But with his whole day freed up, hell, his whole week, maybe his whole fucking life, there was no reason that he couldn't deliver her half. Glancing at his watch he saw it was only one. He'd left his last message for her at nine-thirty.

"Cobb salad, blue cheese, cream soda, two waters." So what if she was still mad at him? He could still feed her. She never ate when pissed anyway, so taking lunch was a good bet. He paid, the cashier handed him a pager, and he sidled over into the small crowd loitering in front of the pick-up counter. He was still working on his defense for bringing her lunch when the pager joy-buzzed his palm.

ANDREA LOGGED ALL her sources for the Berrylane job and started her report. Going through her notes she saw that the historian in Camden had never returned her call regarding the Berrylane drapery fabrics. She called again and left another message. It would be really nice to gain whatever historical context she could get before having the fabric re-created. When she'd worked through all the details she could fill in so far, she started a list of questions to help pinpoint the remainder of the research she needed to complete.

She added the need to collect the related ghost stories Karie had mentioned to a separate list of project tasks. Ghost walks or hunts might add a marketing angle her client could exploit to raise funds towards the grounds maintenance. She shot off an email to Karie requesting her sources.

Her desk phone rang and she picked it up while scrolling her email. "Andrea."

"Hey, doll," Marji said from the front desk. "Your best boy is here with lunch in hand."

"Taka?"

"Looks edible?"

Andrea sighed at the inside joke. "Yeah, that's the one."

"I wasn't aware you had more than one best boy."

Taka's thunderous protest at Marji's quip rumbled through the line. Andrea sighed again.

Marji's voice sobered. "Do you want me to let him up?"

If she refused him, he'd just wait outside for her. "Yeah, Marji, but tell him I'm mad at him."

"All right, doll." She set the receiver down slow, allowing Andrea to hear her telling Taka to watch his step before the line slammed closed.

Andrea replaced her own handset and then cleared a spot at her bench for their lunch by filing what papers she could and tacking the rest to the project boards hanging above the bench.

"Hey," Taka said from the doorway.

"Hey, yourself," Andrea answered without stopping. She snatched up the drawings of her three fabric samples to tack them up.

"What is that?" Taka asked.

She glanced over her shoulder at him. "What?"

He swung the bag in his hand at a paper tacked sideways to a cleared area of the cork next to her right elbow. "That. Is it your neighborhood?"

"Yeah. What about it?" And yes, she knew she sounded defensive, but Taka could go screw himself.

"I have one, too. And a timeline. It's not quite finished," he said, still staring at the Google Earth printouts she'd taped together. "What's that reflection?"

She looked back at the map. "Maybe a koi pond?" She stabbed one last tack into the final drawing and turned around. He looked ridiculously sexy in a pair of faded jeans and a black polo with the CPD logo on the left breast. Sizing him up, she did the math. The timing for an apology made sense given the Billie Mae mess and the fact that she was angry with his about-face on where he stood regarding his belief in the whole situation, but his attire didn't. "Let me guess. You've been reinstated and assigned undercover."

He frowned. "What?"

She waved her hand at him. "Middle of the work day. No badge. No gun." On his hip. Well, outside his hip. She knew damn well his own Glock was in a Super-tuck holster inside his jeans. And he might or might not have something at his ankle as well, depending on his level of paranoia.

For a second the expression on his face was tight and unreadable, but then he smoothed it out into pleasant. He held the bag out until she took it and then set the two bottles of water in his left hand on the bench and grabbed the cream soda bottle from under his arm. He cracked the cap and took a long swig before handing it to her. Andrea frowned, but accepted it. She took a big swallow. It was cold and sweet and despite herself, she smiled at him.

"Salad in the bag. For you," he said.

"Okay."

She pointed at her work stool and pulled her cushioned office chair out from behind her desk for herself before unpacking the bag. They ate in silence, passing the cream soda between them. Halfway through her salad, Andrea cracked. "So. Tell me."

"Suspended with pay until the shooting investigation is complete or charges are brought against me."

She wasn't hungry anymore, but she took another bite and chewed hard to keep from blurting out anything she would regret later. Taka put the remainder of his sandwich down and didn't pick it up again, staring past her instead at her cork board. No, at the taped-together aerial map of her neighborhood on the corkboard.

"Rebecca Cahill is going to decline to allow your interviews and the case file copies you requested. She's also revoking your official access to the original case files."

"So we can't get replacement copies for the ones that were stolen."

"No."

"I thought they were public records."

"They are. You could push, but..." Taka shrugged.

"You don't think I should."

"No."

"You don't think Billie Mae's case is related to these new ones."

His expression unchanging, Taka slid his eyes over to meet hers. "I didn't say that."

Andrea dropped her fork and wiped her mouth. "Why are you even here?" She didn't wait for him to answer, just closed her salad up and stuffed it back into the bag. Taka crumpled the paper around his sandwich and she snatched it up, dropped it on top of the salad, and threw the bag into her trash can.

"Do you have an extra flash drive?" Taka mumbled.

She rolled her eyes, but dug one of her extras out of her desk and handed it to him.

"I'll be back," he said and even though he wasn't playing, wasn't doing a Terminator impression, it irritated her.

"Whatever."

He hesitated in her doorway, but then stomped away down the hall towards the stairs. She untacked the piecemeal map and slapped it down onto the bench. The stack of unfinished project files on the left-hand side of her bench yielded the red file into which she'd been compiling everything related to her neighborhood search. She reclaimed her stool and pulling out two transparent sheets meant for opaque projectors, scotch taped them together, slapped them down on the map, and started filling out the names she knew or had collected in red marker. Scott, Foreman, McMullin, Pepper, Larsen, Johnson, Huntley, and Scofield. She marked her rental with a big X.

Footsteps came down the stairs, a click-clack of heels and then voices, a woman and a man. She spun on her stool.

"Hey, Andrea," Leslie called, walking past with Ben in tow.

"You get with Karie?" Ben asked, pausing at her door.

"Yes, thank you. She was really helpful."

"I want the scoop!" he said. Looking down the hall, he raised his voice. "Hi, Taka, good to see you!" He sketched her a two-finger salute and then trotted after Leslie.

Andrea spun back around to her map. The hairs on the back of her neck stood up as Taka came in behind her, close enough she could feel the heat of him on her back, and placed the flash drive down next to her hand. She expected the firm touch of his hand on her neck, the spill of his rough fingertips across her collarbone, but he only leaned forward until his breath brushed her ear. She couldn't help closing her eyes. "I'm sorry," he said, keeping his voice low and even. "That has the info I managed to get on your neighbors and the timeline I put together from the case notes. It's not complete, but it's better than nothing."

She nodded.

"Is it all right if I go to your house? I'll start cleaning up."

She'd rather camp at Waltham overnight than go home and face hours of sorting and putting away, knowing someone had been in her house with their hands all over everything she owned. "Thank you."

Taka shifted and kissed her temple. "I'm sorry," he said again and retreated. Andrea wanted to ask him what he was sorry for, exactly. Not believing in Billie Mae, despite the fact he had seen her, or not believing in her. Instead, Andrea let him go.

CHAPTER TWENTY-ONE

ANDREA ABANDONED HER Waltham projects to concentrate on the timeline Taka had put together. The afternoon slipped by. Naturally, the bulk of the work on Billie Mae's case took place in the four or five days following her death, but Detective Ford had followed up on various leads for almost two years. Those leads included an alien abduction, sightings of Etta Robbins around town both before and after the killing, and two reports of a man crossing backyards on the next street over.

Her neck was getting stiff when her phone beeped. The text from her friend Lauren, a fellow archivist who lived in Texas, read: *OMG! I just found out where Hoffa's buried!* Andrea smiled and stretched before texting back. They hit several different topics for ten minutes before Lauren asked about Taka and when he was moving to Texas. Andrea texted back that Texas was welcome to him and then spent another five minutes expounding on Taka's live-at-Andrea's-until-they-leave girlfriend policy, rather than explaining the real reason she was pissed at him, before Lauren had to jump into a meeting.

Turning her focus to her map, Andrea looked at the way the backyards lined up with the backyards of the street behind in a wavering line. Some houses had fences, most didn't. She'd have to compare residents at the time of Billie Mae's death to current home owners or renters. Her arrival and Jason Cobb's departure couldn't be the only changes on the block. She wanted to talk to Dr. Huntley about his conversation with Etta on the street and ask him if he'd spoken to Billie Mae that night. The white pages in her telephone book yielded zip, but a computer search turned up a landline for him. He didn't answer Andrea's call. She didn't leave a message, deciding to walk across the street and knock on his door later.

The Scofields lived next door to her, on the north side, closer to Timber Way. Paulette, a brunette with thick strips of highlighting in her hair and a love of long skirts with boots worked as a realtor. She'd left flyers on Andrea's door a few times. John, a physical therapist, was tall and athletic, his dark hair cropped close to his head. Andrea saw him out on her runs sometimes, though they usually ran different routes.

Susan Pepper lived on the other side of Andrea, to the south. Her property straddled the dead end of the cul-de-sac. Andrea wrote her particulars in red marker across the top of her house, noting that there had been an interview with her in the case box. The moldy papers. They had sneezed and sneezed when Andrea pulled the pages apart. According to the tax records, Ms. Pepper had been living there nineteen years, almost as long as Dr. Huntley.

This time, the white pages on her desk coughed up a number and Andrea dialed, not expecting an answer.

"Susan Pepper, may I help you?"

"Andrea Kelley. I live next door? I love your landscaping, especially the day lilies."

Ms. Pepper's tone changed, warming. "Thank you so much. What can I do for you, Andrea?"

"Actually, since I'm living there, in that particular house, I've become interested in the death of Billie Mae Robbins." Silence met her statement. Andrea plowed on. "I'm researching the case in hopes of unearthing new information. I've interviewed her mother."

"You have?" Ms. Pepper breathed.

"Yes. I know the police interviewed you. I've reviewed the full case documents."

"Can you do that?"

"Yes. The case has been solved, so...yes."

"Oh. Well, I don't know that I have much to say. It was very sad."

"I know you travel a lot for your job, but I'm not sure what you do."

"I'm a pharmaceuticals rep."

Andrea waited, but Ms. Pepper didn't elaborate. "Were you home during the days surrounding Billie Mae's death?"

"I came home early that afternoon, the day she died." Ms. Pepper paused for long enough that Andrea checked to make sure the call remained connected. "It was chaos."

"Could you describe it?" Andrea cringed. Fisting her free hand, she thumped it lightly on the file. To her own ear, she sounded clinical, the question peeling out of her like this was just another Waltham project, even though she'd already ruined Kenny's day and thought she'd felt bad about it.

But Ms. Pepper answered, her voice thoughtful and clear. "I'd been returning from three days away on business. Cell phones weren't as prevalent then, so although my brother was here and I carried one, he hadn't thought to call me. When I pulled in about noon there were still police cars, a van, and three or four other cars parked on the street. Oliver was sitting out on the porch. He had seen that poor girl just that morning. It was such a gorgeous day. It just didn't seem right."

Distracted by the name, by Taka's voice saying something clichéd, colloquial, from one of the police reports, Andrea scribbled down "Oliver," then said, "What didn't seem right?"

"It was brilliant out, sunny, and the sky that amazing blue it gets sometimes. I'll never forget that. One of those days that makes you happy to be alive and here that poor child was dead. In the bathtub of all things. I've never been a parent, but really, you'd think people that have them would treasure them more."

"Did you have any contact with the family?"

"Not really," she said. Andrea imagined from her voice that Ms. Pepper was looking out the window at the flowers surrounding her beech trees out front, twirling the phone cord around and around her finger. "Those kids played in the yard with that big dog they owned for hours on end, yelling and running around. They were forever trampling my hostas and foam flowers."

Baltimore, Oliver from Baltimore, Susan Pepper's brother. Who spoke to Billie Mae the night before. "You said Oliver saw Billie Mae that morning? The police interviewed him as well, correct?"

"Yes, before I arrived home. Apparently the little thing was out in the street alone, looking for her dog."

"That morning?"

Ms. Pepper said nothing. Andrea could hear Oprah speaking in the background.

"Ms. Pepper?"

"Susan, please. I'm certain Oliver said he saw her that very morning. Looking for her dog."

Mrs. Hooper had said the dog stayed with the kids, always. "You said the kids played with the dog a lot? Was the yard fenced back then?"

"No, none of the yards were. Times change. The dog didn't dig or go far, but he did roam the neighborhood a bit. And he loved water. Jumped in the kiddie pools in the summer. Bob didn't care for that much."

"Bob?"

"Bob Huntley. He lives just across from you?"

"Of course, I'm sorry," Andrea said, shaking herself. "I've got a lot of information percolating."

Ms. Pepper laughed. "I imagine you do. I tried writing an article for my garden club once and I'll never do it again."

Putting her Taka voice and whatever it was she knew she was missing regarding Oliver aside, Andrea tried to re-focus. "How many of the families living on the street were there when Billie Mae died?"

"Oh, I'm sure I don't know for certain. Bob, of course, and the Johnsons. I remember the Scofields had just moved in, because, you know, how terrible for them, all excited about their new home. That house, second from the corner on your side. They were there."

Glancing at her map, Andrea said, "The Foremans?"

"Is her name Marcy?"

"I don't know. I'll find out. Anyone else?"

"The people with all the kids. They were here back then. I can't think of anyone else."

"Thank you so much for your time, Ms. Pepper. Could I call you again if I have more questions?"

"It's Susan, Andrea, I insist. And yes, or just come knock if I'm home. I always have iced tea on hand."

"Do you think your brother would talk to me?"

"I could ask him."

"Is he still in Baltimore?"

"He's just moved back to Charleston. Can I get your number?"

Andrea gave it to her and exchanged goodbyes, promising to come for tea soon.

She made notes on her legal pad, recording her conversation, adding question marks around Dr. Huntley not caring for the dog and that Oliver told his sister the dog was lost the morning Billie Mae died, before continuing to rack her brain, the tax records, and the internet search engines for info on her neighbors.

The Larsens had three kids and three vehicles. She saw the blue minivan pulling in lots of nights as she came home. The boys played basketball in the driveway. Andrea bought two truly terrible cups of lemonade from their daughter one weekend. She couldn't find out where they worked and didn't recall seeing a notation on them in the case files.

Janet Johnson had come out to quiet Taka and the state cops last night. A lawyer with Ferguson and Sung, her husband's name was Tony. Google coughed up the fact that Tony's daughter from a former marriage was a competitive gymnast.

Andrea's desk phone rang and she scooped the handset onto her shoulder, tapping Cindy McMullin into her next search. "Andrea."

"I'm here." The voice was male, very deep, and hoarse.

"Excuse me?"

The call disconnected with a clunk that echoed into dead silence. Goosebumps raced up Andrea's arms.

Heart thudding, she jumped up, spinning to look out her door. No one. Of course. She tip-toed to the door and peered down the hallway in both directions. Nothing. No one visible. Bluesy music, with the scratchy static of a very old record, drifted up from the office of the resident music historian on the second floor.

Andrea walked down the hall to the next occupied office, relieved to find Leslie chatting on her own phone in her cheery surrounds, her feet propped on her desk, her back to Andrea.

Sturdier, Andrea marched back to her own office. Where was "here"? It could still mean here, at Waltham, or maybe it meant "here," meaning at wherever the call was originating. She could call Marji. Again. Her knees weakened. She sunk onto her stool. Was it the same caller from before again? Wilder? Bruten Wilder. Now that she had thought it, she was almost certain the voice was the same. What was his issue?

She called Marji, who rattled off a familiar number this time. Her house. Holding her breath, Andrea dialed back and let it ring six times, willing Taka to answer, before she hung up. She plopped the handset on the hook and lunged for her cell phone on the workbench.

His cell went to voicemail. She hit end and tried again. And then tried a third time. It rang four times and went again to voicemail. No time to panic. Not allowed. Andrea slid the map and thumb drive and her project files into her portfolio case, grabbed her purse, and forced herself to walk, not run, down the empty hallway.

In the lobby, she lengthened her stride, nearly trotting to the double doors. Behind her, Marji's voice drifted from the very far side of the lobby, a goodbye or take care, maybe. Andrea didn't have a hand to wave with, but she half-turned as she hit the crisp outside air, shooting a smile that felt more like a grimace in Marji's general direction.

The lowered grey sky filled with darker storm clouds as she tried to stay within ten miles of the speed limit. She didn't want a ticket, it would take too long. She'd have a heart attack if she had to stop. She tried Taka again, and again her call went straight to voicemail. She held the cell in her hand, wondering if she could reach Hoyle through the state police number. But she didn't know for sure anything was wrong. She was probably being stupid. The recording of her phone number played over and over in her head. She pressed harder on the accelerator, although she had no idea what she would do when she got home.

Her street was quiet. The Larsens' blue van was absent from their drive. Dr. Huntley's porch lights shone through the gloom of the late afternoon. The state police car sat parked along his curb. Hoyle and Detweiler both looked at her as she drifted past. Taka's Yukon stood in her drive. She pulled up behind the Yukon instead of into the carport. Brad and Cindy McMullin's beagle barked as she opened her car door. She stared at her house. It seemed fine. But deserted. That odd feeling when you know no one's home even before you check to see if it's true.

She walked to the Impala. Hoyle's sandy brows rose and then he was opening the door and clambering out.

"I received a phone call from my landline about twenty minutes ago. It wasn't Taka. An unfamiliar man's voice said 'I'm here' and then the call ended."

"No one's entered the house since Detective Taka arrived and he hasn't left."

"When did he get here?"

"About two-thirty. We came directly here from Waltham-Young."

"Why are you following him?"

He tilted his head, his lips twisting as he considered his answer. "I was ordered to do so."

Andrea shifted, the bramble vine of her instinct climbing into her throat, but her head telling her she should believe Hoyle. He was a cop doing his duty. No one but Taka was inside her home. She nearly choked on her own spit when she swallowed. She nodded.

"We'll go in with you," Hoyle said.

Andrea hesitated.

"Are you sure it was your landline?"

"Yes."

Detweiler's voice rose from the other side of the car as he opened his door. "Then we're going in with you."

She opened the front door and they entered ahead of her, guns drawn. The house was silent. Detweiler swept the hall and living room, while Hoyle eased up the stairs. The hallway was clean, the living room straightened, her smashed TV gone altogether. Other debris lay in small piles, a stack of books here, the broken lamp there. A handful of papers lay spread out on the coffee table. Andrea squinted at them. Stray sheets from Billie Mae's copied case files. The files that had been missing entirely after the break-in. Wrinkled. Streaked with brown smears.

The floor squeaked above, Hoyle's footsteps steady as he entered her bedroom.

"Clear," Detweiler called from the vicinity of the mudroom.

Hoyle's "Clear," rang out from overhead. He came galloping down. "Let's check out back," he said, but Detweiler was already opening the kitchen door.

Something black caught her eye under the edge of the couch and she crouched to look. Taka's personal Glock, where he often parked it at her house.

The kitchen was clean and swept, but not mopped. There was a pile of flour and spices pushed into a small mound on the table. The empty glass salt shaker stood by it. The pepper was completely full. She thought again about sneezing and sneezing when they read Susan Pepper's statement at the table.

Taka's key ring sat on the usual mudroom shelf.

Footsteps traversed the hallway upstairs. Andrea froze. She tiptoed into the kitchen. Neither cop was visible through the window.

"Taka?"

The house absorbed his name and gave nothing back. There was nowhere to hide in her house. The layout was small and simple. The only closet big enough to house a man was in her bedroom. Did Hoyle check the closet?

She pulled her dry tongue off the roof of her mouth. "Taka?"

Leaning out the kitchen door, she swept the yard, but Hoyle and Detweiler were elsewhere.

Swallowing her heart, Andrea ducked into the hall and listened. Nothing. Dead silence. Deserted silence. Office clear. Feeling self-conscious, she darted into the living room and scooped up Taka's Glock. She dropped the magazine to check the contents. The click as she slid it home again echoed in her ear. Fair warning for anyone who might still be lurking upstairs, although already, she was almost certain no one was there. She worked her numb legs up the stairs, easing up one step, listening, then easing up the next. The hall was clear. The bath. The spare room, empty except for an old desk and a double bed. Her bedroom door stood open. Renewing her grip, she entered gun first, but it was deserted, too.

A scattering of papers covered the bed, all fonts, different shades of grey ink. More of the copied case notes that had been missing. Here again. Like the earrings Chuck had given her, like Billie Mae's shoe. She picked one up. Page two of the interview with Susan Pepper. The next was a page from Etta Robbins' testimony at court, about Billie Mae being scared of a man she had seen the night before she died. The next was a page from Detective Ford's notes. He had underlined the name Fitch three times.

Fitch. Who was Fitch? The thought she couldn't catch hold of while talking to Susan Pepper came thundering back, Taka saying Billie Mae had a firecracker lit to her tail. Oliver's words. Susan Pepper's brother, who's last name was Fitch. Glancing across the remaining sheets, she saw his interview sitting right in the middle. "Billie Mae?" she whispered.

The temperature plummeted. Andrea jerked upright, certain someone was standing right behind her. She whirled around. No one. Her panting breath frosted on the frigid air. "Billie Mae?"

The papers rustled and Andrea whipped back to stare at them. They rose in a swirl from the bed, but there was no breeze. They dropped all at once and the temperature shot back up, dragging a gasped yell from Andrea's throat. Taka's phone sat in the center of the bed within a ring formed of papers, lit up, the announcement of a new voicemail from 'Jay-Super' squared up in the center of the screen.

Trembling, Andrea knelt on the bed, grabbed the phone, and then flew back down the stairs and out the front door, letting it bang wide open behind her. Hoyle, in the front yard on his phone, whirled around to face her.

It took three tries to get Taka's code keyed in properly, the gun in her hand scraping across the edge as she worked. She tapped at the phone icon and then the voicemail, ready to scream. Stabbing her finger at the play button, she accidentally paused it. Cursing as Hoyle stopped in front of her, she tapped the screen again and lifted the cell to her ear. "Hey, Taka! Got your message. There's no broken pipe and no water in that unit. Mr. Fitch said to thank you for checking on it. Guy's nice, his name's Oliver if you see him around. I checked all the units around and above you, but there's nothing, man. Don't know what you heard."

"What's happened?" Hoyle demanded, reaching out at the same time to take the gun from her.

Andrea turned it to him grip first and let him have it. His phone rang before she could slow her thoughts enough to tell him anything. The running water had been in Fitch's condo. That statement, Fitch's statement, reappearing. What did it mean? Could those calls she thought were from Wilder actually be from Fitch? Was he in her house? Why?

Hoyle dropped the Glock's magazine, cleared the chambered round, pocketed it, shifted the gun to his other hand, and dug his phone out of his pocket before she could spit out, "That's Taka's."

"Hoyle," he barked into his phone, glaring at her. His brows rose, his lips parting with the motion. "Yes, sir. Yes." He thumbed his phone off and then frowned at it. "We've been pulled for a new scene."

"That's Taka's gun. There's—" She stopped herself from saying more. Something scary upstairs? Someone? "There's no note or anything."

Pulling out his phone again, Hoyle hit a single digit and waited. "Detweiler's on the street behind your house," he said to Andrea, and then "See anything?" into the phone. He shook his head at her. "Maddox called. We've been pulled unless this is something we need to stick with." He disconnected and gave Andrea a long, searching look. "What spooked you?"

"I—nothing. There were just some papers upstairs. And Taka's phone."

"That's Taka's?"

"Yes. And his gun was on the floor in the living room. There's a voice—"

Hoyle's phone trilled again. He glanced at it and shoved it back in his pocket. "Does he ever go out without it?"

"No. Never."

"Not even if he goes for a run? He had a really bad day."

She chewed her lip. What could she tell him that didn't sound crazy? There wasn't a single reason Fitch would have to feel threatened. There wasn't a single reason he'd even know she was interested in talking to him the first time he called. She'd only just spoken to his sister before she came rushing home. Hoyle tilted his head with a considering look before he gave her a small, crooked smile.

Taka didn't run when he was tied up in knots. He worked out. He drank. He rarely went anywhere unarmed. His phone was purposefully placed. With Fitch's interview. "I think this might have something to do with a guy named Fitch."

"Fitch? You mean Verny Fitch?"

"Verny?"

"Yeah. He's private security for the Sandersons?"

Her throat closed up so hard, she coughed. "Is Verny short for Oliver?"

"Yeah. But we were watching. No one came. Taka had to have left out the back."

"That's his gun." She held up his phone. "This is his phone. So where is he?" she asked, spinning, searching the yard. Her gaze fell on Susan Pepper's house next door. What if Taka had gotten the same info she had from—not Billie Mae—whatever that was upstairs? Would he have gone over to ask about the man? If he had, he wouldn't have left his phone and gun. "Oliver Fitch's sister lives next door."

"Shit."

"And Oliver Fitch lives in Taka's building."

Hoyle's eyes narrowed as he thought. Probably the same thoughts she was having. The condo was convenient. It wasn't the greatest place ever, but it was the only mid-size residential complex between downtown and her north side neighborhood. It wasn't a stretch they'd both be living there. But if Fitch worked for the Sandersons and had his sister for cover, Andrea's house would be a lot more private for a face to face confrontation over Zach Taylor's death than Taka's condo. Except no one else had been there.

"Hey," Detweiler said, coming out the open front door. "We've been ditched, looks like. Trooper's got remains on the highway for us."

"Great. Andrea here has just informed me that Verny Fitch's sister lives there," he said, pointing at Susan Pepper's house. "And Fitch himself lives in Taka's building."

"Fitch? Really?" Detweiler held his phone up. "What do you want to do?"

Hoyle considered the sky for a minute. "Send someone by Taka's place. See if he's there. Find out Fitch's new address at the same time. Wait for me in the car."

"Got it, boss."

Andrea could see the dismissal on Hoyle's face before he opened his mouth. "Look, Andrea, we were watching the house. No one came or went on the street at all. I know you had the break-in last night, but did anything look different today to you?"

Besides magically appearing papers? She shook her head.

"I'm sorry," Hoyle said. He held her gaze. "There's no reason to assume he didn't leave on his own. In fact, considering our presence, we have to assume he's avoiding us."

She could tell he was carefully phrasing his words. They had never said exactly why they were watching Taka in the first place. Andrea couldn't think. "He's a good cop," she said.

"I called it in. There's already someone contacting his Chief. CPD will evaluate and decide on an appropriate level of response, okay?" he said, holding out Taka's gun.

She took it. The situation was desperately wrong, but Andrea didn't know what else to do. He gave her the magazine and crossed the street to the Impala, before he turned to her again. "Catch," he said and soft-tossed her the extra bullet he'd removed from the Glock's chamber.

CHAPTER TWENTY-TWO

AFTER THEY LEFT, Andrea looked again at Susan Pepper's house. Maybe Taka had the same thought she had when she saw the full pepper shaker on the table. Maybe despite his stubborn reversal on the reality of Billie Mae, he had thought about the clues she was throwing at them. She knew right through her core that he would not have left voluntarily when he said he'd be waiting for her.

The swirl of papers on the bed rose in her mind's eye. They had not been in the house after the break-in. She forced her feet to move. That brutal force in the bedroom was not Billie Mae. Cold air rushed over her sun-warmed skin as she crossed the threshold and closed her front door. Through the arched doorway to the kitchen, she could see that the previously spotless floor was littered in dirt smeared papers. She dropped to her knees when she reached them. They all came from the case box. The torn one under her left hand sported her own notes in the margin. Her skin pulled tight and hot. She might burst.

Sweating, she let Taka's gun slide from her hand and swept the papers up in messy piles, depositing them on the kitchen table atop the mound of flour and seasonings Taka had made. If she could just figure this out, if she could just find the dates, get them sorted again. Her hands scrabbled over them, flipping pages, straightening, turning them upright while she watched, aware, but unable to stop her tears. She gulped in air on a harsh breath.

The temperature plummeted again. A gale force wind ripped the papers from her hands, sent them off the table, skittering and flying, pummeled her. She covered her hot wet face from the assault. It howled and bit and tore at her hair and clothes. It stopped. Outside, the beagle howled, long and mournful. Andrea peeked out from between her hands. Every single sheet of paper hung in the air. The howl dissolved into rabid barking. All the papers dropped at once. Everything on the table and counters had been swept to the floor. Except the pepper shaker. It sat upright in the exact middle of the table.

"Okay, okay," she said out loud, hearing how her voice shook. "Okay."

Andrea left the kitchen without touching anything. She floated in a daze up the stairs and into the bathroom. Her heart contracted painfully. Billie Mae sat in the tub in her yellow shirt and shorts, shivering, wet, her legs drawn up and arms wrapped around her knees. Her beautiful blond hair hung in limp tangles around her face. As she looked up at Andrea, the deep red line across her throat gaped open. A faint purple blush crept over her skin from the edges of the raw wound, deepening in color every second.

Hand pressed to her aching chest, Andrea bent over, braced herself on her knees and tried to breathe. "Okay, okay, okay," she breathed.

Her battered muscles didn't want to cooperate. She stumbled the two steps she needed to lean against the counter and somehow her fingers turned the cold water on. The first trickle of water she patted onto her face helped steady her. She managed to get both hands into the stream and cup them to really splash herself. She rinsed her face several times and then turned the water off, dripping over the sink until she could make herself reach for the hand towel folded on the counter and dry her face.

Billie Mae was gone, but for the puddle in the tub and the earthy damp odor that followed her.

In Andrea's bedroom, everything was as she'd left it. She held her breath as she slid the closet door open, but nothing waited for her. After entering her code into the gun safe, she withdrew her compact Heckler and Koch, already loaded, and sheathed it in its belt holster. She changed quickly into jeans and a blue tee shirt. Sliding her belt on, she paused to thread it through the loops of the holster and the buckled it tight. The holster sat snug inside the waistband of her jeans, against the rise of her hip. From a pile of well-worn Henleys, she pulled her favorite, a grayish green, and pulled it on. She could face anything to come in a Henley, right?

She transferred the one twenty-dollar bill she had and the small pocketknife she always carried from her work pants to her jeans. What else might she need? If Taka didn't appear in the next five minutes and wasn't over drinking tea with Susan Pepper, what would she do? Go to his condo. If he wasn't there, go knock on Oliver Fitch's door down the hall? Maybe she could get Ms. Pepper—Susan, she had insisted—to call her brother, see if he would let her interview him for the project. She needed a couple of extra mags, her wallet, stripped down to license, insurance card, Waltham ID, maybe her ATM card. Too warm for a jacket with the Henley until the sun went down. Andrea eyed her small leather backpack purse. She loaded it up and grabbed her black leather jacket. Back in the bathroom, she brushed her hair into a ponytail, secured it, and checked her mascara. Armored up, she bolted downstairs.

"Taka?" she yelled, hoping maybe he'd come back in, but there was no answer. She collected Taka's gun and phone from the kitchen floor, treading careful and fast, not wanting to touch the papers and precipitate another fit. She secured the gun, left Taka a note on the table in the hall, and locked the house up.

Opening her car door, she threw the jacket in the passenger seat, pocketed the keys she'd left on the driver's seat earlier, and shoved her mini-Maglite into her pack, which she dropped on the floorboard.

Rolling her shoulders back, she surveyed the street. It looked like every other day at this time, the sunlight filtering low between the houses and through the half-shed hardwoods. Two of the Larsen kids were playing some kind of hopping and running game on their driveway.

Susan Pepper's house looked much like Andrea's, wood frame and brick, a modest ranch. Painted a common slate blue with a dark asphalt roof, only the landscaping distinguished it from every other home on the block. Heavily textured, Susan Pepper put a lot of thought into the placement of the graceful beds interspersed among the dogwoods, maples, and beeches. A massive, old oak dominated the back yard on the left side, close to Andrea's yard, and loomed over the house. A winding walk connected the concrete drive to the wide, roofed porch, which held two chairs with a small round table between them to the left side of the front door and a double swinging chair on the other.

Andrea hesitated, not sure whether to knock or ring the bell. Deciding she wanted to be sure Susan heard her, Andrea pressed the bell. It was a standard tone and the sheer normalcy made Andrea feel that much more insubstantial and unsure of herself.

A voice made her stay her hand when she moved to hit the bell again. Susan opened the door, a questioning look already pasted on her round face.

"Hi, I'm Andrea," Andrea said, sticking her hand out. "From next door."

Susan took it. "Of course, dear. Hi, I didn't expect you quite so soon."

"Actually, I was just wondering if my friend was here. He isn't at my house, although his car is there." Andrea waved at the Yukon over her shoulder.

Susan leaned out, craning her neck to see. "I'm sorry, I haven't seen anyone this afternoon. I've been busy inside since you called. I can't imagine why he'd come here. Maybe he went for a walk or something?"

Andrea shrugged. "I don't know, I just thought...I don't know. I have some time this evening, would it be possible to get your brother's contact information from you?"

Checking the street beyond Andrea again, and then looking her up and down, Susan considered her answer. "I guess it wouldn't hurt to give you his number."

"Thank you so much."

Susan's mouth turned down at the corners. "Could you wait here?"

"Yes, no problem."

She shut the door. Firmly. The deadbolt clicked.

Andrea wondered what she looked like, to worry Susan so much. She smoothed her hair with her hands and checked that her HK wasn't showing through the Henley. Taka had spent a lot of time helping her choose outfits and holsters that she could carry with and have no one the wiser. Sometimes she wondered if he was too paranoid, if she had caught it from him. He'd told her it was the one time in her lifetime she needed it that she would regret not having it and she'd taken that advice to heart.

A truck started on the next street over, chugging with a throaty diesel blub. Andrea tried for a reassuring smile when Susan opened the door again, but she didn't look impressed. She gave Andrea a sticky note with the name Oliver and a number written on it. "Thank you, Ms.—Susan."

"You're welcome. I left him a message, just a heads up that you'll be calling and why."

Andrea tried not to let her face fall, but didn't think she was very successful if Susan's frown was anything to go by. She held up the note. "Thanks. Have a good evening."

She felt Susan Pepper's eyes on her back all the way down the front walk. Movement caught her eye. Billie Mae stood among the daylilies massing along Susan Pepper's four-board fence. Andrea slipped into the shade of her carport and out into her own backyard. Billie Mae was gone. Andrea let her gaze travel over the daylilies to the wooded cover along the back of Susan's house, but if Taka had witnessed the paper display and gone poking around, there was no evidence of it. "Taka?" she called out across the yard. A burble of running water answered her. She swiped her phone from her jeans pocket and dialed Fitch's number. No answer. The running water was now a babbling rush in Andrea's ears.

She nearly ran to her car, got in, and slammed the door, shutting off the awful sound. Was it possible Oliver Fitch had come for Taka? If Dewey was involved, Taka might kill someone before it was all over.

"I'M GOING TO kill you," Taka growled, his mouth filling with blood from cuts on his gum and the inside of his lip. He spat, but most of it landed on his own jeans. He sat on his ass on cold bare earth, handcuffed to a PVC pipe that ran just above his head. His captor made to kick him in the face again, but then just laughed and stepped back, shaking his head. His cell dinged and he went back to texting whoever he'd been in communication with since Taka regained consciousness. Taka's scraped fingers hurt. Blood trickled down his forearms from where the cuffs cut into his wrists every time he braced himself against attack. His hands were already numb. He clenched them into fists a couple of times to get some circulation going and then tried to rub his fingers together. At least his head didn't hurt, though he was horribly dizzy.

He was in an unfinished basement, one bare bulb doing a shit job of lighting the large space. The ground was uneven within the concrete foundations, the ceiling varied in height, and parts of it were obscured by beams and a haphazard pile of boxes. The boxes were marked but Taka couldn't make anything out. A kind of gardening station ranged down the long wall closest to the full-size door—a bench with hand tools and pots on it, with tools hung overhead and two rows of deep drawers below. A tangle of coiled and uncoiled hoses lay heaped to the side of it next to a clump of thin white wire and tomato stakes. Rakes, a shovel, a tarp. Nothing useful. Another ding from the phone drew his attention back to his captor.

The guy in front of him was average. Five-ten. Not overweight, but not thin either. Thinning brown comb-over, dark eyes. An average everyman who didn't stand out in black slacks and windbreaker.

The distant peal of a doorbell floated down from above. Footsteps that faded.

Taka had no idea why this everyman was beating on him. "What the fuck do you want with me?"

The everyman chuckled and eyed Taka over his phone. Taka tensed, already drawing his knees in when the everyman stepped forward and kicked him again. His boot skidded along Taka's ribs instead of landing in his belly. Everyman grunted and raised his foot yet again. Taka twisted, lashing his legs out in a scissors-cut to take the everyman down, but he only trapped one leg. Everyman smashed his boot down onto Taka's thigh and then stood on it while he wrenched his captured leg out of Taka's weak grasp, laughing again. "Dewey's gonna eat you alive," Everyman muttered.

Taka tried to slow his breath. Shoving both feet against the frozen dirt, he scooted back up against the wall, taking his weight off his screaming wrists. Why would Dewey come after him? Harass Andrea, yeah, as a provocation, bring Taka to him. But taking Taka? After he killed Dewey's boy? The bastard was shady. He had control issues. But Dewey's dirt never came home. "After Louie's?" he heard himself mumble, and got lost for a long moment, Dewey's fingers burning on his chest. He trembled, cold in his sweat-dampened tee. There'd been a couple of dozen witnesses. "Dewey's not stupid."

"We'll see," Everyman said, looking pleased as he watched Taka struggle to stay upright. Taka had been hot with the desire to drive his fists into this guy's face, but now he had to clench his teeth against the shiver that shook him. He stared back at Everyman and shut it down by forcing himself to relax. As he let go, Taka's eyelids grew heavy. He blinked. The everyman watched, gaze never shifting, until his phone dinged and he went back to his conversation.

PART II

CHAPTER TWENTY-THREE

THE GOLD DOME of the State Capitol building threw blinding flashes of reflected sunlight at her as Andrea took the curves through the Charleston foothills too fast. She joined the heavy evening traffic backed up on west 64. The red sunset stretched itself across the ridges, creating deep shadows in the hollows and setting the Kanawha river alight. The constant slow and go corkscrewed the swarm of black gnats swirling in her belly, sending them into her throat so that she had to keep swallowing.

She picked up her phone three times to call Taka's more-often-than-not partner, Tracy Manners, but put it down each time. It seemed unreasonable that Taka's truck sat at her house, that his gun lay in her safe, that his phone was tucked into her purse, that he had ditched the state cops by skulking through her backyard and what? Met someone who drove him somewhere. For something. He would have left her a note. A voicemail. Something.

Pressing the accelerator harder, she swerved around the BMW dragging ass in front of her, only to get blocked by a Yellow Freight truck in the next lane. It seemed just as unlikely that Fitch or anyone else could...what? Subdue Taka and kidnap him from under Hoyle and Detweiler's noses? Dewey was too smart to try.

Three long miles later, she got off at Taka's exit and crept over the surface streets for another half mile before traffic loosened up and she could move faster, twisting up through the heavily wooded residential streets, irritated by the half-gone sun flickering through the mature hardwoods.

Finally she pulled into Taka's lot, threw the car into park, and scrambled out while slinging her pack over both shoulders. She ran to his building, up all three flights on the outside stairs, and down the inside hall, slowing as she passed Oliver Fitch's unit. Billie Mae had been practically screaming at them last night by manifesting that burst pipe and Taka had chosen that moment to shut himself off to her. Anger spiked in her chest, which at least quieted the cloud of swarming gnats in her belly.

With her keys in hand, she pounded on Taka's door to give him a heads-up if he was there. The key slid and stuck before it clunked home. She threw the door open, yelling, "Taka!"

The condo was dark. She flicked the overhead light on. He'd cleaned up before he left. The blankets she'd left folded on the couch were put away. No laptop on his uniquely Taka-organized desk, the opened and unpaid bills stacked to the left and the paid, not-yet-destroyed bills to the right. He made fun of her for keeping her paperwork longer than a month. No glasses in the kitchen sink. In his room, which appeared spartan without Melinda's pillows and throw and her scarves draped all over, the bed was neatly made. The bathroom spotless. She walked into the living room. The TV cabinet remained neatly organized, nothing out of place. Taka's worn heavy bag hung, as always, from a reinforced corner frame tucked behind the front door. A few mismatched hand weights lined the baseboard beneath it. No Taka.

Andrea tugged her phone from her back pocket and dialed Oliver Fitch's cell while she locked Taka's place up. She walked back down to 311 and listened to the silence inside. Fitch had left the standard greeting on his voicemail. The vaguely haughty phone woman demanded Andrea leave a message. She introduced herself, but then the lady cut her off. She hit the number to start over and then talked fast, requesting an interview.

In the parking lot, the streetlights buzzed overhead, warming up. Two girls in bright, mid-thigh dresses and heels giggled and talked their way to a lime green Ford Sentra. Andrea knew the club they were headed to, but it sounded like a different place through their eyes. She wondered how good-looking Jayden must be to have them counting his eyelashes and the freckles on his nose. They were both so enamored, it might be his lucky night. The back edge of her leather holster rubbed against her skin with every step she took and sweat rolled down her spine. She tried to think of a time when she was ever like those girls and couldn't.

Billie Mae and whatever else was in her house wanted her attention on Susan Pepper and her brother. Susan was home. Oliver Fitch wasn't. Fitch worked for the Sandersons. Her next logical step was to locate Dewey. A CPD squad car turned into the condo complex as she was pulling out.

Driving through the lights of Charleston to Waltham-Young, she called both Tracy and Carson, to make sure Taka wasn't with them. Tracy's phone went to voicemail, but Carson picked up right away. As promised, the state police had already informed CPD of Taka's vanishing act and Captain Cahill had notified Carson. "The official state police take is that he dodged them. The captain's inclined to let it lie a full day," he told her.

"I just want to scream, Carson, this is ridiculous. The man left his gun in my house. His phone is in my purse."

"Listen, the cap'n can't do much. State police said no one entered your house. Taka's after-incident was clean, he was suspended with pay, and he didn't take his gun, which is a positive in their view."

"It's Dewey, Carson. I know Taka told you about him. About them."

"I know there's a lot of talk about the Sandersons and what they're capable of, Andrea, but no one's ever provided proof," Carson reasoned. "Taka's too public right now for Dewey to make a move. And they're adults now."

"Doesn't mean Dewey won't hurt him."

"Yeah, okay, even I was talking about how Dewey wants Taka's head, but I meant it figuratively. Dewey wants him charged for Zach Taylor's murder. He wants CPD dragged through the mud without any splashing on him. But that video showing him at Louie's has the senator bulgy-eyed already. Dewey's not going to push it. Everyone's more worried about what it is Taka's doing. Cahill posted a BOLO after the state informed her that should Taka approach Dewey, he'll be taken into custody."

"But what if Dewey's already approached Taka?" The Waltham parking lot was half-full, reminding her that the historical society was holding a genealogical seminar that night.

"I think you're jumping to dangerous conclusions."

"I'm filing a missing person's report," she said, pulling into her regular parking space.

"I'm sure he's fine, Andrea, but I think that's a sound plan. CPD is legally required to report to the filer when the missing person is located. They can't tell you where he is unless he gives consent, though, just that he's safe." Carson cleared his throat and Andrea could hear it coming as she turned the FX off. "He's probably just holed up somewhere with a bottle of Jack."

"Yeah," she breathed. "I'm sure he is."

She lowered her phone and hit end as Carson was saying, "He'll show up in the morning, you'll—"

She slung her pack over one shoulder and grabbed her portfolio case. Entering the Waltham lobby, she waved at Dave, who was nighttime security. Andrea hurried down the darkened hall, wondering who else was in the building. She put her bags down in her office and checked the time on her desk phone. It was just after seven. Picking it up, she tried Randy's extension, but he wasn't in. Karie was the only other co-worker who had an inkling what was going on, but Andrea didn't know her well enough to know her connections in town.

There was something Karie could help with, though—dealing with whatever or whoever the other presence in her house might be. She dialed Karie's extension. Tears filled Andrea's eyes when Karie answered. Unexpectedly relieved, she sank down into her chair as Karie chirped her greeting.

"It's Andrea." She stopped to pull herself together. Why was she crying? Once her throat loosened she said, "I need your help."

"Okay. Right now?"

"Yes, in my office."

"Are you okay?"

"No, I'm really not."

"On my way."

Andrea set the phone down and let herself cry, let all her half-formed what if thoughts tumble unchecked, hating herself for it, even as she knew she needed it to clear her head. This was the problem with her. No one she cared for lasted. Her mother, her brother, the only man she'd ever loved almost as much as Taka, even her few girlfriends had all moved away. She didn't have close friendships anymore. Except Taka. And only that because she'd had him through all the rest. She couldn't afford to lose him. They both knew that's why they'd never move beyond friendship. Though really, friendship? They were in an open marriage without the good part, the last step that would either sign his death warrant or drive him away. It was a wonder he was still around as it was. She'd missed him so much the years he was gone in the military. She couldn't lose him again. She wouldn't.

When Karie rushed in a few minutes later, breathless and wide-eyed, Andrea wiped at her cheeks and hiccupped.

"What's happened?"

"Taka." Andrea's breath caught on another hiccupped sob. She was not the center of the universe and she was not cursed. Shit happened. Sometimes it happened more to some people than others, but it happened to everyone.

Karie bent over and wrapped her in a hug. "Is this about the video?"

Carson had mentioned the same, but then run right into saying everyone thought Dewey was the one in danger and she hadn't asked. "What video?"

Karie raised her brows. "You haven't seen it? The video from Louie's."

Andrea shook her head.

"CPD's getting crap over it, but Louie's getting pats on the back. It might go viral."

"Is that why Taka was suspended?"

Karie shrugged. "You can't see him in it, but people saw him there. What's going on?"

"He was at my house, but now he's gone."

"Like he left you gone?"

Andrea shook her head and straightened up in her chair. Karie let her go but didn't step away. Spotting a napkin left over from lunch she whipped it up, handed it to Andrea, cocked a hip onto the edge of Andrea's desk, and waited. Andrea blew her nose and sucked up her fear, tucking it back away. "We're not together. I meant he's missing."

"Explain."

Since Karie was the one standing in front of her, Andrea did.

"Why are there state cops watching Taka?"

"That shooting. That man last night was Dewey Sanderson, whose dad—"

"Is Senator Sanderson," Karie interrupted. "I didn't realize last night exactly who he was, but it's been all over social media today. Rumor has it that Dewey had a thing for the guy Taka killed. And this guy Fitch works for him? Do you think Billie Mae is pointing you at Fitch because he broke into the house?"

"I don't think it was Billie Mae."

Karie frowned at her.

"I know it sounds even crazier than—" Andrea waved her hands in the air. "Taka decided after we talked to you that maybe it's all just my head and I'm influencing his perceptions because he wants to believe me so much."

"How did he get that out of what I said?"

Andrea shrugged. "Because we were at his place, not mine. I think it scared him that I was claiming that burst pipe was Billie Mae when we weren't at my house."

"Did you feel tired? Maybe sick?"

"How did you know?"

"Billie Mae's not ever appeared away from the house before, right?" Karie said. She tapped her teeth with her bright blue fingernail while she thought. "That takes energy. In theory, she wouldn't have any practice drawing it from unfamiliar things. What makes you think the poltergeist activity at the house today wasn't Billie Mae?"

Thinking, Andrea worried the inside of her lower lip. "It felt different."

"How?"

"Darker? Stronger. I saw Billie Mae. She was in the tub, soaking wet and scared."

"Have you ever seen her like that before?"

"No."

"You think Fitch has something to do with Taka. And maybe Billie Mae, too."

Checking in with her gut, Andrea let herself think that thought, fully formed. "Yeah, I do. And I think we need to find his boss, Dewey, to find Taka. They have history."

"HEY, VERNY," A man called out.

Adrenaline shot through Taka. His heart thudded and nausea made him flush hot. He cracked his eyes open, alarmed that he'd almost dozed off. This second man was definitely one of Dewey's. He was taller than the everyman, and thick, with a bull neck and massive hands. A Sanderson cousin named Cody Smith. Taka had seen him standing behind Dewey in media pictures of the Sanderson clan attending charity functions and basketball games.

"Cody."

"What we doing?"

"Taking him to the cabin." Everyman, Verny, glanced up. "Sue still home?"

"Yeah. Watching TV."

"I told her we were moving these old boxes of mine to a storage unit. We got room for both?"

"Brought the Escalade." Cody said, coming closer to inspect Taka.

Taka held himself still.

"Hey, scumbag," he said and kicked Taka's foot. "What the fuck are you, some kinda mixed-breed nigger?"

Suppressing his instant reaction to the familiar insult, Taka rolled his head up to let it rest against the wall and studied Cody. Dressed in dark grey slacks and a black crew neck sweater, he looked ready for dinner at Laury's Steakhouse or the theater, not hauling boxes and bloody, half-breed cops.

"Tough guy, aren't you?" Cody continued. "Shooting diabetic kids."

Taka ground his teeth together and kept his mouth shut.

"You know Dewey liked that boy. He was a good kid."

Yeah. And Taka had been a good kid once, too. He knew all about Dewey and what he considered good. Dewey could care less about the color of his skin. The nausea rose up again and he closed his eyes. Saliva filled his mouth.

"Open your eyes, nigger." He kicked at Taka's foot again, but hit his ankle. Taka glared at him. "There you go. We're gonna give you to Dewey. Let him do the honors." He slid a Glock from his waistband and pointed it at Taka's chest with both hands, his finger heavy on the trigger. "Unless you fuck it up, in which case we got no problems just giving him a piece of you." He glanced sideways at Verny, who stood with a casual manner, his hands buried deep in the pockets of his slacks, as if he were hanging out on a sidewalk chatting up an old friend. "Go ahead, Verny, I got him."

Pulling a pre-loaded syringe from his jacket pocket, Verny walked forward and crouched beside Taka. It took every ounce of courage Taka possessed not to strike out with his legs, not to get himself killed right there. Verny pressed Taka's shoulder back against the wall as he drove his knee down into Taka's hip, pinning him in place. He was stronger than he looked. Taka did kick out, twisting without effect when Verny drove the needle through his shirt and into his shoulder below his collarbone. Verny just moved with him as he pushed the contents of the syringe and then stood up. "What is it?" Taka asked, his voice hoarse.

"Not the same trip," Cody answered, grinning. "This is gonna knock you flat."

Within moments a warm tide rose up inside him and Taka remembered it. Remembered sinking onto his knees in Andrea's living room as he went up—layers and layers of life laid out before him. The never-ending walk. Flickering trees. Painful grate across his nerves at the creak of a gate. The sharp scent of raw earth. Cody said something else. Taka opened his eyes to look at him but then he was gone, Verny's laughter riding into his head on a wave of black.

CHAPTER TWENTY-FOUR

FORTY MINUTES AFTER a frustrating call with one of Taka's fellow CPD detectives to file her own missing Taka report, Andrea had a dozen articles open online with pictures of Dewey Sanderson at various events around town, but not much personal information and no address. He'd been just out of college when she'd last spoken to him, still living at a house his dad owned. The numbers they located for him rang to an impersonal answering service and a business line that went unanswered. As far as she or Karie could tell Dewey worked as a "consultant," but had no business address and no references online. He bought and sold vintage cars, but all contacts were funneled through a garage manager. Andrea didn't leave a message. The images of Dewey included business associates, family, and pals. None of them included Oliver Fitch, whose photo she had pulled from Susan Pepper's Facebook page.

"Bingo!" Karie crowed. "Dewey owns that nightclub, the Coliseum, on Quarrier."

"How did we not know that?"

"It's buried behind two limited liability companies. His father was an early investor."

Andrea's cell rang, but she didn't recognize the number displayed. "Andrea."

"It's Jimmy Hoyle. Did you locate Detective Taka yet?"

"No."

"Look, I did talk to my chief. We weren't on protection detail, just surveillance. There's nothing I can offer you officially until you file a missing person's report, and then only if our help is requested by CPD. You might try getting that done sooner by declaring he's a suicide risk due to his circumstances, but—"

"He didn't take his gun, he was suspended with his pay intact, and his after-incident follow-up didn't indicate he was a danger to himself or others."

"I'm impressed."

Andrea rolled her eyes. Karie managed to look both impatient and curious while she waited for Andrea's full attention. "I called the friends he might've called. I filed the report. I need to find either Oliver Fitch or Dewey Sanderson."

"I don't think they'd be stupid enough to grab him. The family's gotten everything they've asked for so far."

"But Dewey's not family and he won't ask for anything, Officer Hoyle, he'll just take it."

"Lieutenant," Hoyle corrected. "But call me Jimmy. It sounds like maybe you have personal experience with Mr. Sanderson."

"So does Taka."

The silence that met her statement was damning. "Well, shit," Hoyle finally breathed. "Where are you?"

"At Waltham-Young, trying to figure out where Dewey might be tonight."

"At his office in The Coliseum until one am."

"Where were you an hour ago?"

"Um..."

"That was rhetorical. We just found The Coliseum."

"Again, I'm impressed. Not many people know he owns it. Who's we?"

"A researcher friend."

Hoyle cleared his throat. "You can't just go traipsing in there, you know."

"Watch me," Andrea spit.

"Okay then, I'll meet you two blocks west of the club, in front of the Federal Center, in twenty minutes."

Andrea stood straight up, startling Karie.

"What," Karie said, as Andrea said, "What?"

Hoyle hung up. Andrea hit his number. It rang once and jumped to voice mail. "Fuck."

"What," Karie demanded.

"One of the state cops is going to meet us at The Coliseum."

"Why?"

"Dewey will be there until one according to him."

"How does he know?"

Andrea shook her head. "I guess we'll ask him that."

"We?"

"Slip of the tongue," Andrea said, leaning over her desk to click out of all her open web pages. "Crap, I was supposed to talk to Billie Mae's brother tonight."

"Billie Mae's brother? Was he there?"

"He was. He's never talked about it."

"Then I'm definitely going. I'll drive, you call the kid."

THE CARPET UNDER Taka's aching head was damp. It stunk of wet dog and gasoline. It dropped out from under his cheek and then slammed back into his face. Pothole. Everything else filtered in as he kicked and squirmed onto his side, the quiet throb of the engine, the radio. Joe Mile hawking the latest Chevys on the lot. Push, pull, or drag your clunker in for a great deal. The car dropped again, crunching his shoulders and slapping his head again. "Ow!" he yelled and kicked out as hard as he could manage with his hands cuffed behind his back and his feet tied together.

Male laughter and a resounding thunk from the back seat above him. "Shut up."

He inched around, trying to see if he could get up. He was too big for the cramped space. A wool blanket lay over him, suffocating him. He wriggled, trying to figure out what he was stuck between. A solid wall, in front, which would be the rear door of the Escalade, and golf bag at his back. His fingers found a zipper, but were too clumsy to let him open the pocket for a tee. Too bad he couldn't maneuver enough to get a club into his hand.

The car bounced hard. Taka's stomach lurched with the spike of pain in his head. He gagged and dry-heaved, his eyes tearing up as he fought not to vomit. When it passed, he panted, every breath coating his tongue with the flavor of rancid carpet.

"MRS. HOOPER, IT'S Andrea. Is this a good time to talk to Steven?"

"I'll just get him for you," Mrs. Hooper said, her voice very soft and unsure.

Karie drove with her hands at ten and two, worry written into every tense muscle.

"It's okay," Andrea said, while she waited for Steven to come to the phone. "You can just drop me at the club. I just want to see if Dewey's there."

They stopped at the light at Kanawha and Court Street. Andrea could see the back-lit police department window nearest Taka's desk.

"And then what, ask him if he kidnapped Taka?"

"No." If only he were up there right now. "I don't know."

Karie asked, "Do you even have a plan?" just as Steven said, "Hello?" into her ear.

Squashing down her fear, Andrea tore her gaze away as Karie accelerated down Kanawha. She held a finger up to Karie and said, "Hi, Steven. I'm Andrea. Thank you for agreeing to speak with me."

"Yeah, okay," he said. She wondered what he looked like, now, almost three times as old as Billie Mae.

"I'd really just like to hear what you remember from that day."

"Oh. Um, not much, really."

"Do you remember Billie Mae?"

"I do. I remember playing trains with her. She used to let me wrap her hair around my hand when we watched TV on the couch."

"Do you recall what happened the night before she died?"

"I know she ran away. But we found her."

"And that morning?"

Karie turned left onto Summers Street.

"Billie Mae wasn't in her bed when I woke up, or in the bathroom, so I went downstairs. There was a cereal box and bowls on the table, so I sat down and ate dry cereal," Steven said, his voice falling into a steady tone that told Andrea this was the story he told, the one he'd practiced, either in therapy or in his head, over and over again. "I was happy I got to use the blue bowl, because Billie Mae usually got it first. I didn't notice anything wrong until my Mom ran by me and out the door. Billie Mae was limp when she carried her in and I asked if she was sick. My mom said, stay, Stevie, you stay right there, don't move, so I didn't, until the cops came. They were banging on the door and I was scared, so I crawled up under the table with Tuck."

Etta Robbins had said the dog was with Steven when all the men were there. "Was Tuck inside when you sat down to eat?"

"No. He was crying at the door and I got up and let him in. I didn't— okay, yeah, I guess I did move after she told me not to, but..." Steven drew in a shaky breath as Andrea held hers, a little shocked she'd obviously thrown him a curve ball. "I don't know what happened to him after. I don't remember seeing them take Billie Mae away, either. I remember the cops and Dr. Huntley being there and Miss Susan and the guy from across the street."

The man's name stuck on the tip of Andrea's tongue. "The guy from across the street?"

Karie turned her head sharply and then just as quickly re-focused on her driving, turning left again to drive past the busy club.

"Yeah. He used to help my mom out and he played with me, sometimes, gave me airplane rides, you know, when you swing a kid around?"

There were two bouncers on the door and a crowd of dressed-up co-eds loitering on the sidewalk out front.

"Did you see the guy from across the street earlier that morning? Before the police came?"

"No."

Hoyle's Impala was parked just where he said he'd be. Andrea pointed at it and Karie snagged a spot just behind it.

"Do you remember Dr. Huntley?"

"Yeah, he used to play Tee-ball with me. He comes to my games sometimes, takes me to see the Power play."

Now that was interesting. She really, really needed to talk to Dr. Huntley. "Thank you, Steven, for speaking with me. Would you mind if I called you again sometime? I still have a lot of research to do and I might want to ask you some more questions about Billie Mae, about what you remember about your life in general at that age."

"Sure," Steven said, though it was hesitant. "I guess that'd be okay."

Andrea asked him to take her number in case he had questions to ask her and they disconnected. "What was that about the dog?" Karie asked

"Steven let it into the house that morning. My landlord said it was dead by the time he got there. Its skull has a big crack in it. Maybe the dog was outside with Billie Mae and tried to protect her?"

A tap on her window made Andrea jump. Hoyle stood next to the car. She had been distracted, but not so much that she wouldn't have seen him get out of his car, which meant he'd been lurking on the sidewalk, waiting for them. She glared at him and rolled her window down.

"You're not going in. Who's that," he demanded, popping his chin out towards Karie.

"My friend and coworker, Karie Edwards. And I am going in."

"He'll be out by one fifteen. We can just observe."

"You can observe us going into the club," Karie bit back, opening her door.

Andrea did the same, but Hoyle didn't move. She drew the door back and shoved it outwards harder, hitting him. He threw his hands up and stepped back.

"How do you know for sure he's there?" Andrea asked.

"We have eyes on him. He's a slimeball but not much of a criminal. His schedule rarely varies."

Karie came around the front of the car to stand next to Andrea. She scanned Hoyle from his short, unruly blond hair to the toes of his black Doc Martens and back up again. "How do we know you aren't trying to keep us away from him?"

"I am trying to keep you away from him," Hoyle retorted.

"I mean, how do we know you aren't working for him?"

Andrea tilted her head in consideration and then smirked at Karie. It hadn't even occurred to her to question Hoyle's motivation. Looking back at Hoyle, she let her smile drop. "Why do you care if we go talk to Dewey? I've known him for years. We're just going in to say hi and chat him up."

"It'd be enough that Detective Taka killed his latest boy, but you said they have history. We've never been able to tie anything to Dewey, that's why we can't go rushing in just because Taka may or may not have slipped us. People have a tendency, once they've crossed Dewey, to show up far, far away. Most of them still alive, but none of them willing to talk. Taka's a cop and he knows Dewey on a personal level. He'd talk. We're kind of hoping one of them makes a move."

"One of them makes a move? Taka's gone! Dewey's already made his move."

"You don't know that. It's just as likely Taka's going after Dewey because of his suspension."

Carson had said the same thing. Andrea's ears filled up with the rush of her blood. Her vision narrowed, until all she could see was Hoyle's flat stare, the slight flare of his nostrils, his flattening lips as she tried to understand him. "That break-in? Taka said it had Dewey written all over it. Oliver Fitch was in my house! And then today he called. From. My. House. Dewey wants Taka back on his knees so he can fuck him up all over again!"

Hoyle's dark eyes widened, his lips parting as he stared at her. Andrea covered her mouth with both hands, her eyes burning, her lungs too tight to breathe. She turned back to the car, fumbling with the door. Hoyle pressed against her back to hook his arm around her chest and drew her back enough to get the door open and then help her sit. She folded over on herself, unable to stop the deep hitch of her chest and the hacking sobs that hurt her ears.

After a few minutes she became aware of Karie crouched beside her in the crook of the door, sitting below her on the frame and stroking her thigh over and over again.

Pissed at herself, Andrea sat up, rubbing the tears away from her eyes and off her face with both hands. She pushed her hair back roughly. "Shit," she said and reached up to yank down the passenger visor, hoping it had a vanity mirror. It did. Her eyes were red, her face swollen and tear-streaked. "You have mascara?"

Karie reached in and opened her glove box. A little tapestry bag nestled beside the revolver inside. Andrea laughed, a harsh bark. "Good, that's good," she said.

Karie smiled, yanked the bag out, and shoved the compartment door closed. "Girl's got to carry protection, right?"

Andrea laughed again.

"You do have—" Hoyle started.

"Yes, I do have a license," Karie said. "And mascara," she added, pulling it from the bag with a flourish.

"Do you have eye drops?"

"No, sorry."

Hoyle sighed. "I do, but you aren't going in, so you don't need them."

"I am," Andrea told him, holding his fierce gaze. "I'm going in with my girlfriend and we're having a drink. You may come with us if you like."

Hoyle dropped his head, his chin resting on his chest before he heaved another huge sigh and lifted it to meet her eyes. "I will." He reached deep into his trousers pocket and held the eye drops up.

Andrea swiped them from him. "Thank you."

"Are you really a blond?" Karie blurted.

"Like I haven't heard that before," Hoyle said, letting his irritation leak into his tone.

Andrea tipped her head back and positioned the dropper.

"It's just—"

"Yes. Ma had brown eyes. No. Blond hair and brown eyes is not a myth."

"It's hot," Karie assured him.

Blinking hard, Andrea grimaced and restrained herself from hitting Karie. "Oh my God, the mascara, please."

CHAPTER TWENTY-FIVE

THE COLISEUM WAS booming, literally, the techno-beat loud and disorienting in the dim light. The crowd shifted and swayed. Andrea hung onto Karie's arm as they entered and walked fifteen feet in to survey the room, Hoyle trailing them. Every ten feet along the walls a massive surround-sound speaker hung near the ceiling. A long bar ran down either side of the club for thirty feet, with tables and high tops staggered around the space between them before the club opened up at the back into a much larger space. Round booths hugged the sides of a huge dance floor dominated by a platform in the middle. Andrea had seen plenty of bands perform there, but tonight a DJ was running the program, and club girls shared the platform, dancing like their lives depended on it.

She pointed to the left-hand bar, where there were scattered stools available. Weaving around tables and working their way closer, Andrea scoped the faces around her, knowing eventually she'd spot someone both she and Taka knew.

At the bar Karie and Andrea claimed free side-by-side stools. Hoyle leaned over between them and caught the closest bartender's eye. The tall blond worked his way down before nodding at Hoyle, placing the last draft beer he'd pulled on the bar for him. Andrea caught Karie's frown and directed the same at Hoyle. He picked up the beer and shrugged. Andrea pointed at Hoyle's beer and Karie, shouting, ordered a vodka and cranberry before Andrea spun back to Hoyle, who was squinting back toward the DJ and his girls.

She pulled on his sleeve and lifted a brow when he shot her a questioning glance. Shuffling closer, he bent over to talk into her ear. "I come here a lot on weekends. The bartender's a friend of mine from back home."

"He works for Dewey."

"Yeah, he does, but I don't, I swear. And he's only ever talked to Dewey once, anyway."

Andrea pulled back and he took the hint, eased away without giving up his spot at their backs. She smiled at Karie's concerned look and flapped her hand in a whatever gesture. When the drinks came, Andrea slipped a twenty on the bar. She sipped enough of her beer to make it easier to carry. "Ready?" she shouted at Karie, who nodded and stood up. Standing in their way, Jimmy Hoyle closed his eyes for a second like he was gathering his patience before he opened them, his misgivings right on top, and then moved.

The back room was cooler, big vents on the ceiling throwing cold draughts down on the sweating crowd. Andrea dropped her shoulder to slip into the writhing mass, swaying to the beat as she crossed left to right and skirted the platform.

Someone caught her right bicep. She stopped, juggling her beer, and the guy let go, laughing as she recognized him. "Sorry!"

"Hey, Matt!" Andrea yelled back. He was someone from school, a hard drinker, looking a little worse for wear than when she'd last seen him. "You seen Taka here?"

"No, not yet. He coming?"

She shrugged and lifted her beer towards a booth being cleared. "Catch you in a bit," she said, Hoyle moving past her to snag the booth.

Karie sat down across from Hoyle, but since Hoyle was facing the rear of the club, Andrea slid in next to him, forcing him to scoot closer to the wall, his eyes narrowed and lips tight.

She flipped her hair and took a tiny sip of her beer and watched the dancers near them before she let her gaze roam, looking for Dewey. Hoyle leaned close. "All the way back. VIP."

The sheer curtains on both VIP lounges were tied open tonight. Curved couches filled the back and side walls. The big man sat with three of his posse in leather club chairs at a low eight-person table. A pretty brunette in short shorts and a halter leaned over the table, a tray expertly balanced on one hand. She laughed, her long hair cascading over her shoulder as she set their order down. Dewey brushed it back with one hand and kissed her cheek. She gave him a big grin and left the table, sashaying back towards the bar on her super high heels with a confident stride.

"She attends to Dewey's every need while he's here," Hoyle offered. "Fetches food and drink and pretty girls, though we think the girls are mostly for show?"

All for show. Andrea kept her gaze on Dewey. If Hoyle wanted info, he needed to give info. "What other properties does Dewey own?"

"Do you really think you can find Taka this way? The most you can do is drive by. How would you be able to tell? Go home. Report him missing again tomorrow if he still is, tell them you suspect Fitch was in your house. Find out if they can process those prints from the break-in faster."

She wasn't good at lying, but he didn't know her. "We found his home address," she tried, turning to face him. "What else does he own?"

Hoyle sighed. "A warehouse buried in Boone county. Storage units on seventh and in South Charleston. A second house on the Gauley outside Summersville. His Dad owns multiple properties all over the state."

"Can you get me a list?"

"No."

She sipped her beer and went back to sizing Dewey up. He didn't look much different than he had back when they were high school seniors and he'd come around every few days to pick Taka up. Tow-headed blond and blue eyes. Handsome. Andrea hadn't liked him then and didn't like him now. He wasn't tall, maybe five-nine, but built, with broad shoulders and a big personality. He liked adrenaline sports, which is what had drawn Taka into his web.

Kayaking on the New River, in the gorge, they'd swept around a wide rocky bend and been treated to Dewey on a climbing line, scaling a sheer face with deceptive ease. He missed a hold, dropping several yards before his friends yanked the slack. When they'd caught their collective breaths, Dewey leaned back in the harness and let out a long whoop and then laughed and laughed.

"Dewey!" someone called from up top. "Are you okay?"

"Fuck, yeah!" Dewey yelled back and laughed some more.

"That's Dewey Sanderson," Taka told her, his eyes bright. "I met him at the range." And then he was shouting to him, "Hey! Hey, Dewey, shit, man!"

Dewey spun on the rope, looking down at them. "Hey, Taka! You climb? I'll call you!"

And Taka, at eighteen, had fallen as surely as the middle school boys had, though his lures were alcohol and motorbikes, shotguns and BASE jumping. Ten months in he caught Dewey with a boy who was only sixteen and finally realized that not only were they far from exclusive, but at twenty-three, Dewey was committing statutory rape. And didn't care. A little digging gave him Dewey's sordid past and enlightened Andrea to her passion for research. Taka promptly got as far away as he could by joining the Army.

Since then Andrea knew he looked sometimes, occasionally touched, but he'd not had a serious boyfriend since Dewey. And only one serious girlfriend, though he had a proclivity for letting any of his girlfriends move in with him for months at a time. Alison lasted two years before deciding she needed more purpose in her life and moved home to South Carolina. Taka took six months to get back into the game that time.

Taka didn't go to great lengths to hide his bisexuality, but West Virginia's general anti-gay sentiment followed by his exposure to "Don't Ask, Don't Tell" had shaped his silence at a young age. And he'd be humiliated if his fellow cops found out he'd been one of Dewey's boys. Her heart clenched at the fact that she'd spilled his secret to Hoyle.

Dewey laughed and took a sip of his drink, his gaze meeting hers for a millisecond before a dancer blocked it. A moment later, he was on his phone. Taka didn't have much occasion to run into Dewey, but when they had, so far, they did an admirable job of acting like they had no familiarity with one another. Until Louie's. Andrea hoped she was the only one who'd seen the way Dewey turned Taka inside out.

She dreaded what Dewey could do to Taka in revenge for his latest boy.

Karie took her hand, startling her. "Stop staring, you'll draw his attention."

"I want to talk to him."

Someone filled her peripheral vision. "He wants to talk to you, too," Dewey's brunette said, the empty tray tucked against her side. "We could've all caught fire over there, you were so laser focused."

"Oh, sorry," Andrea said, not sorry at all.

A genuine smile rose on the girl's face.

Andrea tilted her head in appraisal. "When did Dewey start going for the smart ones?"

"Oh, he doesn't, believe me," the brunette said. "He likes his boys kinda clueless. I think he must've been burned before in that regard." Although they had leaned close together, to hear each other, Andrea didn't miss the understanding that lit up Hoyle's face. "Anyway, he requests your company, Andrea."

"Ah, I was wondering if he remembered me."

"I'll go with you," Hoyle said.

"This is a single invite, cop, sorry about that."

"I'm not—"

She winked at him. "Sure, and I'm just a barmaid." She spun on her heel, headed again for the bar. "Don't keep him waiting, Andrea," she threw back over her shoulder.

"Do you want me to go?" Karie asked.

Andrea smiled as she watched the brunette sashay away. Dewey might regret that hire. "No," she said, glancing at Karie. "Sorry to drag you into this. I'll be fine."

Leaving her beer behind, Andrea wove a path through the gyrating crowd to Dewey's lounge, watching him watch her progress. He gestured at the chair across from him and waved off two of his bodyguards. Pointing at the third, sitting beside him, he said, "You remember Trevor. He knows everything."

"Wow. What's the square root of the hypotenuse on an angle of one hundred forty-six degrees?"

Trevor sneered at her. She tried to sneer back, but wasn't sure she succeeded when Dewey just grinned at her. "Are you bringing me apologies from that son of a bitch?"

She shook her head, trying to think through his question. Was he playing a game?

"Well. What are you here for then?"

"I want Taka."

"Best to take that up with him then."

"I know you have him."

Dewey narrowed his eyes. "I don't understand your statement. I haven't had William in any way in a very, very long time."

Could the man not think in anything other than a sexual manner? Really? "Your man Fitch has taken him."

"My man, Fitch." He sat back in his chair, stretching his legs out so that his calves bumped hers. "Hear that, Trevor? My man Fitch. I can assure you he has not, in fact, taken," he said, using air quotes for emphasis on "taken," "William anywhere."

"Taka was in my home when Fitch called me from my home, on my landline, and now Taka's gone, leaving his phone and gun behind. Tell me what you want for him and I'll get it for you."

Dewey's eyebrows inched up his forehead as he leaned forward again. "I don't have him. If I did, what I would want is Zach back." His expression shifted, his brows drawing down and chin drawing up as he clenched his jaw down tight. "They never should have shot him, but I—" His breath caught and Andrea thought he'd stop, but he only swallowed hard and continued. "I have more reason than his family. I've seen that boy on a low. I know how he could be. He probably did kill Deborah. He got out of his head when he crashed. As for Verny?" Dewey grated the name out in a furious growl. "Verny was supposed to make sure that didn't happen. Verny probably overdosed him on the damn insulin because he wasn't paying attention." Dewey took a deep, calming breath before smoothing his hair back over his scalp. "Verny no longer works for me."

Trevor cleared his throat. "Why did Verny call you from your house?"

Looking back and forth between them, Andrea decided she'd shared enough. "I don't know."

"How do you know it was Verny?"

Andrea chewed the inside of her lip. She couldn't exactly tell him a ghost told her. "Security."

"Dewey, would Verny ever go in somewhere without taking down the system?"

Relaxing once again into his comfortable slouch, though his face was still flushed, Dewey crossed his arms. "No, Trevor, I don't believe he would."

"Mr. Sanderson hasn't disappeared your boyfriend, and I seriously doubt Verny has either." Trevor pushed his chair back as he stood, proving himself the same size and disposition as the closed door behind him. "May I see you and your friends to the door?"

CURLED ON HIS left side, Taka woke to darkness on a rough wood floor, his nose filled with must. A thin rim of flickering light outlined a closed door, with voices and music beyond. His stiff neck bristled with pain as he lifted his head, the movement awkward because his hands were again cuffed above his head. Small room. A bed to his left. He frowned at the dark hulk to his right. A water heater. Another door standing partially open to the dark beyond.

Letting his head hit the floor again, Taka tried rolling onto his back, finding it easy to do. He tilted his head back to look at his numb, but tingling hands. About six inches above the floor, a three-inch diameter metal pipe ran along the length of the bedroom's wood-paneled wall to the right. The fingers of his left hand rested on an elbow joint. The connecting pipe ran through the wood panel to the outside. The pipe was cold on his skin. Cold water pipe to the water heater. Check.

Fumbling his hands against the wall, he pushed himself away from it so that he could straighten his arms, every movement seeming far distance from the control of his brain. He tilted from side to side, letting his shoulders stretch one at a time against his restraints. Rocking his hips, he tried to work some feeling into his left butt cheek. As slow as a dream, Taka scissored his legs open over the uneven planks of the floor. Snow angel. A bubble of sound escaped him. Half. Half an angel. He bent and straightened each knee to ease the aches. He didn't seem to be actually hurt, though his wrists were still complaining about the handcuffs and his hands about the lack of circulation. At least this time he wasn't hanging. His arms appreciated that.

The chain-linked cuffs, probably his, wouldn't allow him to turn over, but by twisting his body and working one knee under himself, he managed to slouch upward, which helped the insistent thumping of his head. "Hey," he croaked. He worked some spit into his mouth and yelled again, getting some range this time. "Hey! I need to piss."

He closed his hands into weak fists and tried to slam them into the wall. The limited movement made a soft unsatisfying thud, but the cuff rattled on the pipe. That was an easier motion. He jangled the cuffs.

Rang the bell. "Hey!" Thank God his hinged cuffs were in his truck. He'd have no mobility in those. "I gotta go."

Light and the swell of voices filled the room as the door swung open. Taka winced and shut his eyes, disappointed to find it was just the TV. More people meant more mistakes. He squinted through one eye at the painful light. "Hey," he croaked again. "I gotta piss. Come on, man."

"Cody," Verny said from the doorway. "Come un-cuff him."

CHAPTER TWENTY-SIX

TAKA TURNED HIS head away from the harsh light, letting both eyes slide open. With better visibility, he could see that his lateral movement was limited by the structure of the wall to about two feet along the pipe. No escape there. Cody clomped in. A safe distance away, Verny held a shiny 1911 in a two-handed grip and kept it aimed at Taka's chest. Taka had to give him props for being smarter than your average asshole.

Cody crouched down in front of him and fiddled with the key. While waiting, Taka thought of four different ways he could maybe make this an escape opportunity, but between his bladder, his head, his throbbing wrists, and Verny's unexpected caution, he wasn't up to trying. Something else would present itself. Cody finally got the cuff on his right hand open. Taka's arms fell. His right hand hit his thigh, the other bounced off the floor, the bracelet gouging into raw flesh. Taka winced and tried to bring it to his chest.

"Don't move, Taka," Verny warned him.

Taka glared at him while Cody re-cuffed him, letting him keep his hands in front.

Standing up, Cody crossed the room, shoved the half-closed bathroom door open, and flicked on the light as he disappeared inside.

"Okay, get up. Keep it slow."

Taka didn't really have a choice. His body protested every inch he gained from the ground. He gimped his way to the bathroom. Jack and Jill. Grungy. Old. Cody stood positioned in front of the closed second door, presumably into another bedroom. "Make it quick," he said.

"Keep it slow, make it quick, y'all need to make up your minds."

"Shut up, Taka, or you can just piss your pants," Verny said, following him as far as the doorway.

He shuffled to the toilet, glad for once that the Army had beaten all need for privacy out of him because he didn't think he could stand. He took care of business, groaning with relief.

"I never used that shit before," Cody said. "Your head hurt?"

"Just from banging it around, I think. You suck at driving."

"It's the road, jerk-off."

"You know what's bad? The aftertaste." He smacked his lips. His tongue tasted like a wet wool sock left in a hot trunk to ripen and mold over an entire summer. "When's Dewey coming?"

"When he comes," Verny snapped. "Jesus Christ, that is a record piss."

Taka's belly rumbled and cramped. He groaned and folded over, closing his eyes and let his gut work.

"Fuck that reeks. Here."

Verny had vacated. Cody had his hand over his mouth and nose, but was offering Taka a roll of paper. Taka thought he contained his surprise, but Cody said, "Man shouldn't die with shit up his crack."

Thankfully it was a clean sweep. His hands were fucking pins and needles now.

"That drug is wicked," Cody said.

Standing, Taka hitched his pants and briefs up and zipped.

"Flush already, man."

Since it seemed to be a civilized kidnapping now, Taka said, "Mind if I rinse some of this blood off my hands?"

At least the water was hot, but holding his hands and bloody wrists under it got them bleeding again. The water stung. Dizzy and fading now that his most immediate needs had been met, Taka propped himself up on his elbows. "Grab him," Verny said, impatient.

Cody reached past him and shut the water off.

Back in the bedroom, the window he hadn't seen before wasn't covered. No outside lights were visible, save for the moon's. Against the far wall, a stained, striped mattress lay on a metal frame with no headboard. A damp cold pervaded the space and the only sound remained the TV, which had become an annoying buzz of discordant voices. He knew it must be a hunting cabin, but not one of Dewey's, or at least not the ones Taka knew. Dewey did neither primitive or old. Though if rumor were true, maybe Dewey needed a place like this for people like him these days.

"Taka," Verny said sharply. And how had he ended up sitting on the floor again? Verny kicked his leg. "Drink this."

Opening his eyes which were, for some reason, closed, Taka saw the bottle of water Verny held just inches from his face. He fumbled his drowsy hands up and took it. Verny took it back and opened it. He poured a third of it over Taka's upturned face, shocking him awake. "Fuck," Taka spluttered.

"Drink it," he ordered, shoving it back into Taka's grasp.

"That shit's *really* wicked," Cody said, his tone easy, like he was watching the Discovery Channel instead of standing guard over a kidnapped cop. Swallowing the water down in big gulps, Taka threw evil thoughts at him. Cody's gentle smile in return confused him. Maybe he'd wake up next to Andrea any second now. Maybe now. Maybe now.

Verny jerked the crushed bottle from his fist and jerked his head at Cody, who crouched down and cuffed him to the pipe. Taka startled hard when the bedroom door slammed shut, leaving him alone in the dark. His wrists throbbed with his pulse. His stomach gurgled and jumped. Squirming around until he was lying down again, Taka let the chemical exhaustion take him.

WAITING IN THE dark of the Impala beside Hoyle as they staked out the Coliseum, Andrea's legs itched to move. Every hour, it seemed, Taka felt further away.

"Don't you have to be at work tomorrow?" she asked.

He grunted. "Nothing on the burner Andy can't handle."

"Andy?"

"Detweiler. You know this isn't necessary, right?"

"What makes you so sure Taka walked away?"

"He wasn't particularly cooperative," Hoyle said, and then added, "though he did bring us coffee."

A laugh bubbled up into Andrea's throat, but she bit down on it, afraid if she started, she'd not be able to stop. While she wasn't prone to hysterics, she was definitely riding a hard, tired edge of anxiety. She nodded instead, blinking back tears.

"You and Karie work together?"

"We're both on staff at Waltham," she said, wiping the tears from her lids with both hands. "We've only just met, though, on a mutual project."

"Big staff?"

"Sixty full time, fifteen part-time and about double that number in various interns, residents, grant recipients, students, and guest researchers at any given time."

"I didn't realize."

Most Charleston residents didn't know they had the largest repository of information on historical southern culture and one of the largest repositories of all human culture in the world sitting right in their backyard. If their collections didn't meet their client's needs, Waltham staff knew where in the world to find it. They had ties to every major library and museum in the world. The Waltham staff were trained master networkers and seldom burned bridges. "Most people don't."

"Is she single?"

"Who?"

Hoyle grinned. "Karie."

"Oh. Yes? I think?"

"And you and Taka? How long?"

"How long?"

"Have you been together?"

"We're not together."

"Really?"

She rolled her eyes. "Twenty questions over?"

He nodded and settled back, attention fixed on the club entrance.

"What if Dewey goes out the back?"

He pointed to the left. "Alley dumps out there and it's one way. This late, they use a black Escalade and a yellow Corvette."

"Okay."

They waited in silence. Andrea's phone lit up, the text tone singing out. It was Karie. *Home. Call if you need me.*

Andrea texted *ok- Jimmy wants coffee with you sometime*

Not my type, Karie sent back. *C U tomorrow at nine.*

With the windows only cracked open to the cool October breeze, the car grew warm and Andrea started to drift. Taka called her name and she startled awake to Hoyle starting the car. He pointed up the street at the hulk of the Escalade rolling towards Court Street.

"Dewey's in the back," Hoyle said. "Can I ask you what you meant before?"

"When?"

"Dewey wants Taka back on his knees?"

"No."

"Was Taka underage?"

"No, he wasn't. That's all I'm saying about that except that you're not to repeat it. To anyone."

They threaded along the one-way streets of downtown, making multiple turns before Hoyle said, "He's going home." They turned left off the Southside Bridge and onto Louden Heights Road. Past the dark smear of the Kanawha below, Charleston's lights filled the river valley and then scattered themselves up the far hills, twinkling from beneath the unseen trees.

"Maybe Taka's there."

Hoyle shook his head. "We have a unit there. No unusual activity at all. No way we can get in to check the place."

"There must be someth—"

"No. There's not."

They followed the Escalade onto Dewey's looping, narrow street and then cruised past the driveway as it turned in. A low stone wall framed a paved driveway and half an acre of middling steep grade sloping up to a large house with four stone columns and a wide front porch. The Escalade headed for the portico on the right-hand side. Ground level lighting and floodlights on the front corners showed the house's wide white plank siding and black shutters. Red tip hedges, crepe myrtles, dogwoods, and strategically placed Bradford pears achieved a casual southern look. To the left of the house an enormous old beech anchored the design of the front yard.

An innocuous blue Kia sat alongside the curb down the street. The man slumped inside raised a finger at Hoyle. At the end of the block Hoyle flipped them around and drove back past. Dewey stood out in the drive and waved at them. Andrea twisted in the seat to watch as he turned and headed into the house through a side door.

"Your car's at Waltham?" Hoyle asked.

"It is," Andrea said, dropping back to face forward. Depending on when Dewey's home was built, the county might have floorplans. All the way back to the library she made notes on her phone, strategizing her approach and prioritizing her research.

As she got out of the car, Hoyle closed his hand around her left wrist. "Stay away from the Sandersons."

She shook her head at him. "This has to do with Dewey, Hoyle."

"It's Jimmy. You have a one-track mind."

"You don't know me, Jimmy," she said, letting her frustration rise, over-enunciating his name. "Or you'd know how many different tracks I'm operating on right this second and you'd agree that they all lead to Dewey."

The drive home was a blur and the house too empty when she walked in. Devoid of life. She walked through the hall to the kitchen. It seemed like a stranger's home. Turning on her heel, she reversed course and dragged herself up the stairs. She stacked the papers strewn across the bed and laid them on the floor. Sitting on Taka's side of the mattress, Andrea tugged one boot off and then the other, dropped them to the floor, and then collapsed fully-clothed.

CHAPTER TWENTY-SEVEN

TAKA GROANED AND shifted again, trying to sit up a little and relieve his sore back and neck. He was cold. His fingernails were sore and three of them bleeding from picking at the layers of tape covering the pipe's elbow joint. The birds outside had gone from sleepy questioning of the low dawn light to raucous name-calling as the sun began to thrust itself through the dirty glass panes of the window and finger the crack along the top edge of the open beam roof, but no one came to check on him.

A sound like water slapping at pilings beat a rhythm he couldn't quite hear without holding his breath. He listened until he made himself faint, straining to hear what he could.

Still no one came.

He wasn't going to last much longer without pissing his pants. What happened to civilized? "Hey," he tried to shout, but he was congested from the dust. He cleared his throat. "Hey, Cody! C'mon, man."

The silence of a deserted house absorbed his hoarse voice, drawing it through all the room's cracks and crevices, scattering it to the gusty morning breeze rattling what must be loose portions of a tin roof.

Scooting down onto his back and reaching his tired arms up once more, Taka tugged at the pipe for a thousandth time. It made the same inch-and-a-half shift he'd been working on for hours, but refused to give further. Once more, he tried to get a good grip on the joint and twist, but the handcuff chain wasn't long enough to allow him any leverage. He rested and tried again, his palms and fingers red and blistered.

Blowing his breath out on a grunt, he gave up and walked his feet out to let his body lie flat. Arms hanging from the cuffs, he caught his breath. Positioned as he was, he couldn't get any working room to damage the wall and he couldn't gain enough leverage or pressure to snap the chain off one of the cuffs without a broken wrist for a reward. Or a broken wrist for no reward if the chain didn't snap.

He repeated his efforts. A trickle of warmth ran across his chilled thigh and then he couldn't stop it, as his bladder finally let go in a painful spasm. He closed his eyes in hard relief as the urine soaked his jeans. The strong odor burned his nose and reminded him again of his thirst. Swallowing with a dry click, Taka breathed through his mouth. Maybe that was the last of the drug out of his system. Shutting out the birds' annoying trills and caws and shrieks, he imagined Andrea's heat draped over him, the quiet dawn hush of her room. After a minute he raised his hands and tried again to get a grip on the joint.

THE MORNING DAWNED grey and cloudy. Billie Mae stood at the side of the bed, the very definition of mournful.

"Hey, there," Andrea whispered without lifting her head. "Who took Taka, Billie Mae?"

"I drownded," Billie Mae whispered back.

Planting her palms in the tumble of sheets and duvet, Andrea sat up. "Where, Billie Mae? Where did you drown?"

She pointed, like always, towards Lake Vickers.

Andrea's breath caught, her heart speeding up. A little closer to home, she was also pointing in the direction of the back yard. "Your back yard?"

Billie Mae shook her head.

Andrea got up and walked to the window. She looked out across her own yard. Angling her line of sight with the direction of Billie Mae's index finger, she found herself staring out across Susan Pepper's yard. Susan's voice filled her head—*those kids were always trampling my hostas chasing after that dog.* Could it be? "Ms. Pepper's back yard?"

She turned around.

Billie Mae was gone.

After calling in sick, she checked in with Captain Cahill, who warned her away from any contact with Zach Taylor's family or friends. "Friends," Andrea grumbled to herself as she hung up. Too late for that. She fired up the coffee pot and started cleaning. Two hours later, having worked her way upstairs, Andrea remembered the coffee and went back down to pour herself a mug. Opening the fridge to grab the milk, she spotted Taka's stash of doublestuff Oreos and pulled them out.

She sat down at the kitchen table with her coffee and ate two cookies Taka's way, unscrewing them to eat the cream first and then eating the two cookie halves one at a time. She wondered if Taka's phone would reveal anything more— texts, maybe voicemails. Had Dewey called him? Had Fitch?

Retrieving her small backpack from the mudroom coat hooks, she rummaged inside and found his phone. The display said she had missed nine calls and eleven texts. Her heart seized. What if, knowing his phone was in her house, Taka had called and she had missed him? Glaring at the screen, she punched at the side buttons on the phone until she got it off "mute" and turned all the way up. Slightly panicked, she ripped her own phone from her hip and checked to make sure it was working and turned all the way up. It was. No one had called. There were no texts.

She took a deep breath and scanned through Taka's recent texts. Three inane ones from Melinda, and five from someone named Scott, who wanted first to borrow a certain book and then to grab a beer and finally for Taka to call him. Three from Carson. Carson's were all along the lines of "where the fuck are you?" Of the recent calls, four were from Carson, two from Tracy Manners, and one from CPD. There were only three voicemails he hadn't picked up. Two from Carson demanding he call—before Andrea had told him she had Taka's phone—and one from CPD.

"Hi, it's, uh, Patrolman Chris Mendel, sir. I'm just going off shift and wanted you to know I followed up on that car fire, sir. There were two other incidents on that same stretch of road, sir. A, uh, Oliver Fitch, who had the same, um, *experience* you had, and, um, going further back, a personal car fire that killed a state trooper, Bruten Wilder? Maybe you remember. He'd been shot, but the, uh, fire killed him. No suspects. I'll leave a file on your desk, sir."

Andrea listened to the shush of the line until it cut off. Hands shaking, she had trouble hitting the touch screen to replay it. She listened to it again, her heart a Luna moth in her chest, her brain stuck on the names. Bruten Wilder? Fitch? Bruten Wilder?

Bruten Wilder was a state trooper. She'd seen his obituary and dismissed it. He had left her a threatening message at work. Her first thought when she'd received the call from her house was that it had been Wilder's voice. She had wondered if Wilder and Fitch were one and the same. "Bruten Wilder is dead," she said out loud. Had been dead for some time. "Why is Fitch pretending to be Bruten Wilder?"

Her mug tipped over, sending coffee across the table. She jumped up, knocking her chair to the floor. Her arms rippled in gooseflesh, each hair standing on end as the temperature dropped.

"Bruten Wilder. You're here," she whispered. The table flipped over, sending the phones and Oreos flying. She watched the mug tumble end over end. It hit the wooden cabinet door below the sink and then the tile floor and shattered. The temperature shot back up. Silence pressed against her ears.

A heavy knocking echoed through the house. Heart leaping, Andrea whirled around towards the sound. Front door. She strode down the hall and flung the door open.

Karie stared back at her with wide eyes, her hand still raised in mid-air. "Um, hi?" she stuttered.

Andrea nodded, but couldn't say anything. After a minute, she stepped back. Karie hefted the huge, black leather duffle at her feet up and shouldered her way in. "What's going on?"

Andrea shook her head, still tongue tied. She returned to the kitchen, Karie trailing her.

"What happened?" Karie exclaimed, taking in the mess, the table and chair on their sides, the spilled milk, the pieces of ceramic strewn across the kitchen floor. "Was it Billie Mae?"

"Bruten."

"Bruten?"

"I think," Andrea said, "it's Bruten Wilder."

"Who's that?"

"A dead state trooper."

Karie's mouth opened. "Oh."

Andrea nodded. Again.

"Well, then." Karie lowered the bag to the floor. "Good thing I brought some equipment." She righted the chair and helped Andrea lift the table. "Where's your broom?"

"I'll get it," Andrea managed.

"Paper towels?"

"By the sink."

They cleaned the kitchen in silence. The salt shaker was toast, shattered, but the pepper shaker survived intact. Imagine that. By the time Karie dumped the last of the mug smithereens into the trash, Andrea could think again. She pulled the second chair back over and fished around in the Oreo packaging for the few Oreos that had survived. She pulled out two and handed one to Karie, holding hers up in a toast. Quick-minded Karie held hers up as well. "To tough cookies," Andrea said.

Cracking a smile, Karie tipped her cookie at Andrea's. "To you, tough cookie."

"I don't feel so tough right now. I'm still shaking." She held her hand up and watched it tremble before looking back at Karie.

"That must've been hella scary. I'd be shaking too. But he won't be back for a while after an expenditure of energy that large."

"Okay," Andrea said, and bit into her Oreo. Karie twisted hers apart and Andrea's stomach flipped. She backed away and took a seat at the table.

Karie leaned back against the counter. "So, Bruten Wilder."

"He called me. At work. A couple of days ago. I thought..."

"What?"

"I thought he was threatening me. And then I thought he was Oliver Fitch. He said, I know where you live. And then he called—no, *I think* he called—when Taka was here. Yesterday. He said, I'm here. And it was from here, from my landline. That's why I came home."

"Did you know him?"

"No. He died on the highway. We had a..." Andrea waved her hand in the air, having trouble focusing. "Weird thing with Taka's truck there. In that same spot. So did—oh, God." She swallowed hard, sure for a second that her Oreo might make a reappearance. Karie came and sat down at the table. She reached her hand out, offering it, and Andrea took it. "So did Oliver Fitch."

"How can we find out more about Bruten Wilder?"

"Hoyle. We can call Jimmy Hoyle."

"You do that. I'm going to set up the recorder with a couple of microphones. See if we can get any communication going with Trooper Wilder."

"He's going to want to know why I want the info."

"I'll call him then," Karie said. "Tell him what I do for a living. Make it sound like casual curiosity. Tell me what happened on the highway."

Andrea explained the weird phantom flames and the message Mendel left on Taka's phone. When she was finished she punched into her recent calls, found Jimmy's number, and slid the phone over so that Karie could dial it into her phone. Karie got up and wandered towards the living room. Andrea called Chris Mendel, but he didn't pick up. She left a message reminding him who she was and asked him to call her as soon as he could.

Karie, propped up in the kitchen doorway with her back to Andrea, laughed. "No, actually I'm calling about something else altogether. You know I work for Waltham. What we didn't tell you is that I investigate claims of the paranormal." She laughed again. "No, I investigate. I haven't found a case I could prove was supernatural yet. Yes, I'm officially a skeptic. Listen, I have this case. A sticky spot in the highway. No, not an actually sticky spot, a spot where there's been multiple accounts of vehicular breakdown—I can't use the word vehicular? I'm technically a librarian. I can use all the words. Anyway. Mechanical breakdowns. Engines stop running and there's a lot of smoky billowyness involved. Billowyness is too a word. I know all the rules so I can break them. Librarian, remember? All these breakdowns happened along one particular stretch of I-79 and that also happens to be the spot where a state trooper by the name of Bruten Wilder was killed a while back. Oh, I'm so sorry. Well, that makes my request more difficult. I was hoping you could give me official copies of the investigation into his death? Okay, thank you. No, I don't think it has anything to do with the coincidence of accidents in the area, but it's my job. I can rule the paranormal out and during the course of my investigation, I might find the actual physical cause. Yes. Okay. I'm sorry I was so cavalier about your friend. I should have realized you would know him. Yes, I'll be talking to her later today. Of course I will."

She ended the call and tapped her phone on her chin as she thought about what he'd told her.

"Did he say he'd help you?" Andrea asked.

Karie turned to face her. "Yeah. He asked if you'd heard from Taka yet. And he asked me to call him if you go sleuthing about again today."

Andrea's phone rang. Hoyle's number. She sighed.

Screwing her face up, Karie said, "Is it him?"

She nodded and picked her phone up.

CHAPTER TWENTY-EIGHT

"ANDREA KELLEY."

"Hey, it's Jimmy Hoyle. Hear anything?"

"No." Her voice was not unfriendly, but held a tone Jimmy couldn't decipher on one word.

"You going back out to Dewey's today?" As he spoke his waitress sailed by, spun, and dropped fresh coffee into his cup with a wink.

"No."

"Do you want me to meet you at CPD and we can talk to them in person?"

"No," she said, sounding distracted. "Taka's captain doesn't see the need for a search. They're worried about his media exposure and they did put out a BOLO, but they want to keep it quiet. Can you get me a list of Dewey's other properties?"

"No."

"Hoyle."

He should have expected her to ask again, but he hadn't.

"Lieutenant Hoyle?" Now that her focus was directed on their conversation, her voice became fuller and louder. He'd been attracted to her from the start, but the tingle that her voice shot through him and into his groin surprised him.

"My name is Jimmy. I have the day off. I can't get the list, but I can take you for a drive."

"Past a few properties I might be interested in?"

"Exactly."

"Can you meet me at Waltham in..." A clicking noise filtered through from the background and then a woman's low voice as Andrea consulted with someone. "An hour?"

"Make it two? Your friend Karie called about some info she needed for some highway project she's working on. Can you leave it for her if I bring it with me?"

"Sure."

"All right then, I'll see you in a couple of hours." Jimmy set his phone down and contemplated the half-eaten omelet in front of him. The diner was his favorite place for late breakfast. He could understand a woman like Karie, a researcher, an investigator, acting quickly on a new connection, but he still didn't believe her story. Last night she was hot on Dewey for Andrea, someone she didn't know well, and brave enough to accompany her into a situation she knew nothing about. Paranormal research didn't seem like the area of expertise Andrea needed to tap in order to find Dewey. So why Karie? He shook his head at his own suspicious nature and dug back into his eggs.

She was doing Andrea a favor, just like him, though only God knew why he had further involved himself. Karie had work of her own to do and apparently Brute's death was part of it. He hadn't been allowed to work the case, but he knew it had gone cold within weeks. If investigating that stretch of road turned up a viable lead for Bruten's case, then more power to her. But even with the Waltham name behind her, trying to get the reports through normal channels for a ghost hunt wouldn't be well received. Jimmy shoved his plate back, swigged the last of his coffee, and snagged his check to pay at the register.

The chilly day shone, the air itself brilliant. Just the kind of weather that would have had Bruten rounding up enough guys for a pick-up football game at UC. Jimmy met him during his first week at the academy, when instructor Trooper Wilder had taken him down on the hand-to-hand mats with a quick stomp to his ankle. Afterwards, Brute had bought first round and offered insight into the years ahead. He sincerely liked helping stranded motorists and his heart broke at every accident scene. But what he really loved was driving the highways, hour after hour. What had he seen out there that got him killed?

After navigating the Impala through Charleston's one-way streets and sparse pre-lunch traffic, Jimmy found a parking space downtown. He walked two blocks to the Coliseum, pulled the door, and made a point to stroll into the dim, empty place like he had all day and owned the place. A frizzy-blond girl cleaning tables near the DJ's booth started towards him. He waved. "Hey, Scott around?"

"Who's asking?"

Jimmy held his hands up. "Just a friend. Know him from back home. You're Angie, right?"

She stopped and tipped her head to squint at him. "Yeah, maybe I seen you around. Scott's re-stocking."

Jimmy flipped his badge open as he approached her. "Jimmy Hoyle. State Police." She eyed the badge and then him while he pulled out his phone and swiped through his photos before turning the screen to her. "You know this guy?"

"Yeah. He's the cop that shot Zach."

"Seen him recently?"

"He's a regular, but he ain't been in. Wouldn't be very welcome if'n he did."

"JJ!" Scott called from the far end of the room. "Hey, man!" The girl rolled her eyes and went back to her tables as Scott joined him, pushing two kegs ahead of him on a handcart. "Want a beer, man?" He parked the kegs behind the bar and flipped a glass from the drying pan upwards, end over end, to fill it at the tap.

"Fancy move."

"I'm Dewey's best bartender," Scott said, placing the beer in front of Jimmy. "What you doing?"

Jimmy took a sip before he spoke. Scott was on loan from North Carolina's State Bureau of Investigation. He understood the differences in small-town undercover from large city work, but his practical experience was all dicey drug cases in Charlotte, complete with covert communications. "Relax. We good?"

"Dusted and cleaned an hour ago. There's no audio on the camera."

"You getting close?"

Scott shrugged. "Man's cagey as hell." He bent to lift the top keg off and roll it into position. "Who were you with last night?"

"Researchers from Waltham-Young. One of them is William Taka's girlfriend. He's gone AWOL and she thinks Dewey has something to do with it."

Scotty finished tapping the new keg before he spoke again. "He hasn't been in since he killed Dewey's boy. Show me the pic."

Jimmy fingered his phone and slid it across the bar, wondering if Taka knew Dewey owned the place and then gave himself a mental head slap. There was no chance at all that Detective Taka didn't know that or that Dewey sat in back more nights than not, even if the general public was unaware of that fact. "He came in before that?" he asked as Scotty made a show of looking at the phone for the overhead security camera.

"Yeah, couple times a week. Lots of CPD in and out of here."

"Any contact with Dewey?"

Scott shrugged as he tapped the second keg. "Dewey stays in back. Cops stay up front. I'm stuck behind the bar."

"You haven't heard anything about him? Detective Taka?"

"No. But I'm in with Trevor now, so I'll ask. Been hitting him up for a move into security. You track that shipment last week?"

"Legit. Has Verny Fitch been around?"

"Heard Dewey canned him. OD'd the Taylor kid on insulin."

"Hey, Scotty, truck's here," the girl yelled from somewhere in the back.

Scott offered Jimmy a fist bump. "Tell Maddox I don't want Oscar in here next week checking up on me. He's too stiff."

Making his way over the river to nearby Dunbar and the Bureau of Criminal Investigation's HQ, known simply as BCI, Jimmy stewed. Nuking Oscar didn't mean much in the end. He'd only been a floater for Scotty's comfort and if Scott didn't need him, that was one less connection that Dewey might discover. Jimmy had eyes Scotty didn't know about in the bar anyway. As far as they knew, Senator Sanderson wrote Verny's paycheck for private security, so he'd been surprised at Scotty's confirmation that it had been Dewey who fired him. Would Verny blame Taka for being on the outs with the Sandersons?

Cadets marched across the State Police Academy's central courtyard as he drove past before pulling onto the concrete apron in front of BCI, a red brick two story front mated incompatibly to an 'L' shaped aluminum warehouse. His little Intelligence unit was housed here, but much of Troop 0 was scattered across South Charleston in individual barracks or wherever there was space, including at Troop 4's detachment and the State Police Head Quarters nearby. He logged in and weaved his way through the barrack to his unit.

Maddox, the only one present, sat with his feet kicked up on Oscar's desk, eating a thick sandwich that had already dripped mustard onto his light blue button down.

"I just talked to Scotty."

"At the bar?"

"Yeah, went in at nine thirty-four," Jimmy said, dropping down into the chair at Oscar's desk. "Stayed less than ten minutes. It was casual. He doesn't want Oscar in there next week, he stands out too much."

Maddox nodded, chewing, and swallowed twice before he answered. "We can do that."

"He's buddying up with Dewey's head of security. Asked for a lateral move."

"That still Trevor?"

"Yeah."

"Dewey take the cop?"

"Not that Scotty's heard. He's gonna sniff around. Taka was a regular until the shooting. Hasn't been in since."

Maddox laughed. "Fucking suicidal if he did."

"Listen, Verny Fitch's sister lives next door to Andrea Kelley. Kelley thinks Fitch was involved in the break-in on Tuesday and that he called her from inside her house yesterday while Taka was there. She's convinced Dewey lied to her last night and sent Fitch to take him. But Scotty confirmed that Dewey claims Fitch OD'd that kid on insulin before Taka shot him and that Dewey fired him for it."

"Where you going with this? If Fitch wanted some kinda backwards revenge on Taka for being let go, he'd just kill him where he stood. Word is Taka does this, Jimmy. He disappears. Did you talk to the sister? Can you put Verny anywhere in the vicinity in the right time period?"

"*Can* I talk to the sister?"

Maddox sighed. "Only if you keep it under the radar. We got no dog in this hunt and getting something hard on Dewey is more important than some damn local who's probably holed up drinking off his suspension."

Jimmy knew he was right. The break-in and Taka's disappearance was Charleston PD's to handle alone unless hard evidence came up that Dewey was involved. They had an FBI liaison and contacts at the Kanawha County Sherriff's office and CPD. They'd be notified if that kind of evidence came to light. Dewey Sanderson was a big, slippery catch and the State's Attorney General wanted him. Senator Dante Sanderson might become entangled in that net as well—which gave Intel all the more reason to stay focused on their own goals. If Jimmy had to guess, he'd say the AG had humored the Senator's request on behalf of Councilman Miller to keep "that monster" under surveillance until his suspension came through to keep the Senator close. It's what he'd have done. But neither Maddox nor the AG knew the Senator was also getting some payback in on one of Dewey's former boys. "All right," he said as he stood.

"You gotta keep that girl of his, Kelley, outta Dewey's hair," Maddox said, waving his sandwich. "We can't afford to lose this op right now."

"I'm meeting her in an hour."

"File your contact report before you leave," he grumbled, mouth full. His phone bleated.

"Aye, aye, Captain," Jimmy said, calculating the time he'd need to do that in his head.

Maddox waved him off and snatched up his phone.

Jimmy wrote up his contact reports on Andrea and Scott with spare detail and shot them to Maddox by email before he rushed to pull the reports he thought would be most useful to Karie and sent them to the printer. Just before he hit the print key, he decided to print Bruten Wilder's entire case file. Maybe she would see something none of the investigators had found. He ducked into the shift supervisor's office with the right form to allow Karie access.

After a couple of perfunctory questions—what, Brute's haunting you, J?—and a warning that she better not see any of the reports showing up in the media, she signed the form. She also gave him a confidentiality form for Karie to sign and said she'd take his firstborn if he didn't bring it back on his next duty shift.

The truth was Waltham-Young was a deep resource for the state police and sharing info was not uncommon. The only question mark was that this particular request came from a paranormal division neither he nor the supervisor were aware existed and weren't about to note. "Make sure you verify her employment before you go handing stuff over to her."

"Yes, ma'am."

A tall balding trooper poked his head in through the supervisor's door with a perfunctory knock on the frame. "Jimmy. We got a vehicle fire out at Copeland Bay. Bodies plural. You in?"

"Got an assignment, Mark. I'll call you when I'm done, see if you still want me."

"Sounds good. I'll text you the address."

CHAPTER TWENTY-NINE

ANDREA LEFT KARIE setting up cameras and other equipment. She pulled Taka's Yukon in under the carport. As she shifted the transmission into park, she noticed the two GPS trackers sitting in the console and picked one up. Plain black. A manufacturer's stamp, but no ID codes or serial number. She examined the second one, which was a little larger, and found the same. No way to tell if it was still working. Would anyone be monitoring them now? One of Dewey's people? A state police officer? Taking both, she got out of the truck and locked it. As she walked back to the FX, she glanced up.

Across the street Robert Huntley stood in his front doorway, staring out at his yard, or maybe her house. He wasn't looking at her, though, she was sure of that. She slid the trackers in her jacket pocket and walked down her drive. Angling across the street to walk up his drive, she raised her hand and waved at him. "Good morning, Dr. Huntley."

He turned his head and lifted his arm on automatic, before he stopped himself and scowled at her. She scooped his newspaper up off the grass near his sidewalk and smiled as she brought it to him. He reached out to take it when she offered it to him. "Thank you."

"Do you have a few minutes to speak with me?"

"Susan said you were asking around about the little girl who died there, in your house. That you're doing some sort of research," he said, his tone hostile.

Unsure how to reply to his anger, Andrea decided to let him lead. "Yes. On Billie Mae Robbins."

"A detective came here yesterday to interview me, but he insisted that I go down to the police station to talk. He asked me about Billie Mae, too. I don't know why. Her mama's been at Lakin for years now. What did you say to them?"

She held her hands up, palms out. "I haven't spoken to them, Dr. Huntley. They did let me review her case file, but denied my request to speak to the officers involved."

"You know two kids were found in Lake Vickers last week. I walk five miles every night." He gestured into the air. "All around here. Saw Billie Mae and Adam all the time. Helped in the search for the little girl, Kayla. Talked to her dad. Talked to Etta Robbins, too. Kids go home when they get tired. When I talked to Adam's mama, I told her to call to the station. But these other kids, Adam and Kayla, the ones all over here that never come home. They have nothing to do with Billie Mae."

"Did you talk to Billie Mae the night before she died?"

"No. Talked to her mama, not to her."

"She told her mother a man spoke to her, that he scared her."

Dr. Huntley shook his head.

"No, it wasn't me. And Billie Mae knew me, anyway. She called me Dr. H. All the kids do. She and Steven played over here sometimes. Liked to hide in my shed."

That made sense. Apparently Billie Mae still did, judging from the paint bucket she borrowed. "Did you see a man that night?"

His brows twitched and he looked away, thinking. "No. Not that I recall."

"Do you know Susan Pepper's brother?"

"Just to shake his hand. He was here at the time. He comes and goes. Why?"

"His statement says he saw Billie Mae just before dark on Cooper Road, running back in this direction."

"Cooper goes to the boat ramp."

"Yes, it does."

"Your name's Andrea, right?"

"Yes. Andrea Kelley."

"That girl was six years old, Andrea, and could be a handful, but she wasn't an overly brave child. I seriously doubt she was down on Cooper after dark. I seriously doubt she went any further that night than the little patch of woods at the stop sign there," he said, wagging his index finger at it.

Etta said she waited until dusk and then found Billie Mae almost home, upset because a man had scared her, which jibed with Fitch's official statement except the location. Susan said her brother had seen Billie Mae on the morning she died, looking for the dog, Tuck. Why didn't he tell that to Detective Ford? Dr. Huntley was an expert on child behavior and he seemed adamant that Billie Mae wouldn't have strayed so far down Timber Way. Who was lying?

Billie Mae and Bruten Wilder had set Andrea on Fitch. If Fitch had something to hide from that morning, maybe he wanted the police suspecting Billie Mae capable of reaching the lake. On the other hand, Dr. Huntley was the only common denominator. And the kids were comfortable with him, a position in their lives useful to a child predator.

"You know something I don't, Andrea?"

"Just trying to remember what I've read," she said, and smiled at him.

"If you talk to the cops, tell them I had nothing to do with any of these deaths. What has the world come to when a man can't even take a walk and talk with the neighbors without being considered suspicious?"

"I'm sorry, Dr. Huntley, I really am. If I have other questions about the Robbins, will you talk to me again? I need a lot of background. I'm hoping to help Etta Robbins. Maybe prove she's innocent."

"I don't know. I'll have to think about that."

"Yes, sir. I understand. One more thing before I go. Steven Robbins mentioned a neighbor who spent time with them, came to dinner, helped with repairs. Do you remember him?"

"Steve spoke to you?"

"Yes, sir."

"About Billie Mae?"

"Yes, sir."

"I thought that boy would never let go," Dr. Huntley mused, relaxing for the first time since they started talking. "Good for him. He's got a great therapist."

"You're proud of him."

"I am. That makes me feel better about this mission of yours."

"The neighbor?"

"Oh. Well." He scratched the back of his neck.

Andrea waited him out.

"I guess Steven's getting old enough, but I don't know if you should really..."

A light went on in Andrea's brain. "Etta had a relationship with him," she stated. "Jason Cobb."

"You already know, then."

She nodded, holding her breath.

"They kept it quiet, but yes, when Jason's wife was out of town, he came and went at odd hours. I saw them kissing at Etta's door once, early in the morning. None of my business, that. Jason put the house up for sale a couple of weeks after Billie Mae died and moved within the month. I don't know where they went."

"Why did you stay in touch with Steven?"

"It was a tragedy what happened. He saw too much that day. I wanted him to know someone remembered, that someone cared. I stayed with him until the social worker came for him. And later..." He looked back over at her house. "I wanted him to have a connection to someone who was there. Who knew him then, knew what had happened to him because they saw it happen to him. I think that's important as we grow."

His words forcibly reminded Andrea that Dr. H. was a psychologist. A man who had made a career of advocating for the welfare of children's emotions and minds. "Walking the walk?"

He smiled at her. "Yes. No one can think themselves above the call of responsibility. I'll always be available for Steve to turn to if he needs me. Until I join my wife, God rest her soul."

"Thank you for speaking with me. I'm sorry I upset you. You didn't happen to see my friend yesterday afternoon, did you?"

"The big guy?" he said, but continued before she could nod. "No. That little girl, that one who sits on your steps to play with that snake. She looks a lot like Billie Mae."

"Yes," Andrea said, edging back down his front porch steps to the sidewalk. He hadn't said "your little girl" this time, she noted. What would he say if she told him "that" little girl *was* Billie Mae? "Yes, she does."

"Good luck to you."

"Thank you, sir."

SHAKING ON THE cold floor, Taka curled into the cramp eating his stomach. When it released, his belly rumbled and growled. He bit the inside of his dry lip to keep from wasting his energy by shouting in frustration, aware of how his tongue stuck to the roof of his mouth and his throat hurt. In contrast, his jeans weren't drying at all. The skin of his thighs and balls and butt was starting to itch. It was maddening. Shifting his weight to the opposite thigh and hip, he tried once more to catch the weld of the handcuff chain on the edge of the pipe's elbow joint at the right angle to pop it. When he jerked his upper hand over, the chain slid, racking his bloody knuckles on the wood paneling yet again. "Fuck!"

He leaned his forehead into the wall. He wanted to demand to be released, that Verny get his fucking ass in here right now and let him go. But there was no one here. No guard. No one to stop him from leaving if he could just break the fucking chain or loosen the joint or pull the pipe out far enough from the block of wood to get past it and break the PVC connectors on the water heater. He wanted out of his jeans, a hot shower, a gallon of water, and food, the bloodier, the better.

The sun crept closer and closer until it pooled all around him. He stretched out on his back and soaked in its wan heat, trying to still his trembling. After hours of sitting up and working his hands and arms enough to keep his circulation moving as he tried to free himself, lying down felt good. His stomach gurgled, but the hunger pangs had calmed. He counted backwards, tightening his quads and butt on each odd number to distract himself from the itchiness and the cold.

CHEWING OVER HER talk with Dr. Huntley, Andrea's thoughts circled back like a relentless terrier to Verny Fitch. At a red light, she pulled up her last calls list and thumbed Patrolman Mendel's number. The muted sounds of the CPD bull pen stole through the receiver beneath his voice. He gave her his condolences and reassurances on Taka's disappearance in one breath before telling her about Fitch's incident report from the highway fire. Taka and Fitch were the only phantom fire victims at the site of Bruten Wilder's murder. She hung up with him. Taka and Fitch. And her. Her house, her ghost at both her and Taka's homes. Fitch a neighbor at both. Had Billie Mae found Bruten lurking there, at Fitch's condo?

She took a deep breath and tried Fitch's cell number again.

The call only rang once before a mild voice said, "Fitch."

"Hi, Mr. Fitch, I'm Andrea Kelly, your sister gave me your number? I'm researching the murder of Billie Mae Robbins?" The light turned and she followed the car in front of her as it accelerated.

He cleared his throat. "She told me."

"Can I ask you a few questions about Billie Mae?"

"There's not much to say, Ms. Kelley. That girl's mother killed her."

"But you saw her? Looking for her dog that morning? That's not in the statement you gave the police, but your sister mentioned it?"

Long silence. He was sitting somewhere with voices all around him. Maybe a shopping center? Maybe a coffee shop. Andrea crossed over Lee and stopped at the next light.

"Sue's mistaken. She's not as sharp as she used to be and that was years ago. I saw the little girl the night before, down at Cooper Road. She was a tiny thing and there was no one else around. I tried to talk to her, make sure she was okay, but she got scared and I drove on. That's all I know. I wouldn't have even known it was her except my sister and I were out on the porch when she came back down the street and met her mother."

"Your sister wasn't out of town?"

"Out of town? No."

A horn honked behind her. Andrea jumped and hit the gas to cross the intersection, cars streaming by her on the left. "My mistake. I haven't typed out my notes yet." She forced a laugh. "Can't read my own writing. She said she's out of town a lot as a drug rep."

"Yes, she is."

"But she was home that night."

Fitch once again let the background noise around him fill the line before he spoke. "Yes."

"You were living in Baltimore?"

"Yes."

"So you didn't know Billie Mae or her family," she confirmed, turning onto Kanawha. The sight of the river did nothing to ease her tension as it usually did.

"No."

There was nothing else she could ask him about Billie Mae. All the other questions she wanted to ask him burned in her throat and chest like verbal indigestion. *Did you break into my house? Do you know where Taka is? Did you kill Billie Mae? Did you kill Bruten Wilder? When will you be home so I can...* do what? There was nothing she could do right now. She cleared her throat. "Thank you, Mr. Fitch, for talking with me."

"I'd prefer you don't use my name in whatever it is you plan to do with this research." Despite his previous single word answers, his tone remained mild, though the way he said "research" implied air quotes.

"It's a matter of public record, Mr. Fitch."

"If I see my name, I'll do what I have to do."

Andrea's hackles rose at the menacing shift in his voice. "I'm certain I'll be combining eyewitness reports in a neighborly composite, Mr. Fitch. I won't need to use your name."

"Good," he said. "That's good."

He disconnected without warning.

Andrea pulled her phone away from her ear and watched her new home screen replace the call. Screenshot Taka smirked at her, all happy eyed and crooked grin. "Where the fuck are you, Taka?" she asked out loud. "And why did Susan Pepper lie to me?"

CHAPTER THIRTY

AT WALTHAM, ANDREA stopped to dump her belongings in her office and check her employee directory for Daniel Wilkins' office hours in hopes she wouldn't have to go hunting for him through the labyrinth of libraries and research rooms. He was in. She dialed his extension and when he answered gave him a heads up that she was on her way over.

He met her at his door with a roguish smile brightening his otherwise long, somewhat homely face. "Haven't see you in this hallway since that goldfish debacle on the Cameron project."

She laughed. "That was one screwy project. Though, now that you've reminded me of it, I might need to assess a historical client's security protocol for their exhibit when it gets a little closer to completion. If so, I'll certainly recommend that we do that for them."

"Appreciate it, Andrea. What can I help you with today?"

She drew the two GPS trackers from her pocket.

Daniel lifted his gaze to meet hers. "Those are interesting."

"You don't have to help me. They aren't related to a Waltham project."

He looked at her for a long moment before he reached out and grasped her wrist, drew her into his office, and shut his door. He plucked the trackers from her hand and let her go. "Sit down. Let me look at these." He sat at his desk to examine the trackers with a handheld magnifier. "I take it they aren't yours."

"No. But can I reuse them? If I get a base unit of the same brand?"

Daniel was already shaking his head. "These are newer tech. No base unit needed. As a matter of fact, these are probably being tracked right now on a smart phone. They'll be registered with a company that provides that service to whoever contracted it. Whoever owns these undoubtedly knows they're here at Waltham-Young. They might even know that they're here in this particular office."

Andrea's stomach dropped, her blood running cold, despite knowing Taka had left them in his Yukon on purpose. He had called it an advantage, not to destroy them. Then again, he was convinced they were Dewey's work and he didn't want Dewey following her. He probably hoped to provoke a situation in which he could control the outcome in a way that ended with Dewey at CPD. Was it a stupid boy thing or a stupid cop thing? Jimmy Hoyle said he was hoping for the same, except he wanted Dewey at State Police headquarters

Daniel cleared his throat. "Should I destroy them?"

"Then they'll know they were destroyed."

"True," Daniel conceded. "Who is 'they'?"

"I don't know for sure." If it was Hoyle, then he already knew they'd found them. If it was Dewey and he already had Taka, because he'd left them in his truck at her house, on purpose, like a dumbass, then they'd know she had them. If it was someone else altogether, CPD? A reporter? A Zach Taylor family member? Then they'd have to find Taka another way.

"I can't let you leave here without knowing you'll be safe, Andrea. I can call Tim in to set up security for you."

"No," she said, holding her hands up as if she needed to physically stop him. Tim was head of Waltham-Young Security. Daniel worked closely with him, but Daniel was an archivist like her, specializing in the current and historical use of security technology—everything from sharpened sticks as a palisade to the advanced devices in use by the world's most covert operations. "You've met William Taka."

"Ah," Daniel said. "Related to the shooting he was involved in last week?"

Somehow. She nodded.

"Are you in danger?"

"No," she said, but it felt like a lie. She noticed her hands twining nervously in her lap and planted them on her knees. "No," she said again in a firmer voice. "I'm also spending part of today with a state police detective involved in Taka's case. I'm fine. I'm working on a personal project approved by Bobby Waltham and I was wondering if I could use these, but I guess not."

"What do you need to track?"

Her gut held her tongue.

"Okay." He spun around on his chair, stood up, and opened a wall cabinet. He pulled out a soft-sided case, laid it on his worktable, and unzipped it. "I have a friend who's in R and D with a company bringing better personalized GPS tracking to the general public." He unzipped another small case and spilled several black rectangles into his palm. "These aren't going to be available for a while. They're in beta and we're using them here at Waltham for some of the more expensive equipment Security signs out to researchers for field work. They can be permanently mounted on items like laptops or dog collars or attached by magnets if the item's metal."

Andrea bit her lip.

"I'll give you two plain and two magnetized. I'll make you a sub-account under Waltham's. Just..." He tilted his head, considering her. "Be careful, okay?"

"How do I track them?"

"You have an iPhone?"

"Yes."

"They have an app for that," he said, grinning.

"Really?"

BACK IN HER office, Andrea wrote up her conversations with Steven and Dr. Huntley, and then went searching for Jason Cobb. She found him living in Dunbar. After jotting down his address, she noted his landline and cell numbers on her updated task list. Her phone burped with a text from Jimmy Hoyle that he was headed over to pick her up.

After twenty minutes of skimming every news article, blog post, or Facebook account on Bruten Wilder that she could dig up, she gathered her purse and the bag she had loaded with water bottles, protein bars, her Sig, and spare magazines. He was coming up the steps when she ducked out through the double doors. She smiled at him, tucking her hair behind her ear when it swung forward.

"Good timing," he said, grinning up at her. He smiled with his whole body. Struck by the thought, Andrea could only nod in return as he turned and fell in step with her.

The Impala was clean on the inside and smelled of aftershave and coffee.

"Where are we going first?"

"Out Corridor G almost to Midway Road. I gotta check in with a trooper about a scene. Make sure he gets what he needs. What can you tell me about Verny Fitch's sister?"

Andrea glanced at him. "Nice diversionary tactic."

He waited her out.

"Look, I'm documenting a legal case. A little girl named Billie Mae died in my house under unusual circumstances. Her mother confessed and is serving a life sentence for her murder. I talked to Susan Pepper about Billie Mae playing in her yard and about her brother's conversation with Billie Mae the evening before she went missing."

"They had contact?"

"They did. Billie Mae was upset and ran away. Fitch saw and talked to her, but she got scared and he left her alone. A few minutes later, her mom found her outside, near the house."

Jimmy grunted.

Turning her head to watch downtown Charleston slide by as they headed for the on ramp to cross west over the river, Andrea debated telling him the rest.

"When was this?" Jimmy said. "What year?"

"2003."

"You suspect Verny, don't you? Despite the mother's confession? That's why you mentioned his name in the first place. But Verny Fitch has been in Baltimore until recently. He's technically employed by Senator Sanderson as a security consultant which, in this case, translates to bodyguard and gopher. The senator moved him back and placed him with Dewey."

She examined his expression, wondering how sincere he was in wanting to help her. "Whether or not I suspect Fitch in a child murder has nothing to do with Taka's kidnapping."

"You mentioned his name first when Taka went missing," Jimmy pushed. "You didn't know he worked for Dewey."

Because Bruten Wilder had thrown a shit fit with Billie Mae's missing files and practically laid Fitch's witness statement down in her lap. Only the files weren't missing now. A funny faint feeling lightened her head. At the time of the break-in, she heard the sound of running water when Billie Mae called her, that call a second new trick Billie Mae had never done before. But Billie Mae had startled the morning before, looking at something Andrea couldn't see and Bruten had called her at work later that same day. Unknown number. Her house. Her ghost. Fitch's sister a neighbor. Fitch a neighbor of Taka's. Just moved in.

The running water. The bone-chilling cold she'd never experienced around Billie Mae. The call during the break-in. The energy-sucking nausea at Taka's afterward, the running water that woke them, drawing their attention to Fitch's apartment all the way down the hall. The phantom fire where he died. It was all Bruten.

Billie Mae didn't find Bruten lurking at the condo. Bruten found Billie Mae—while what? Haunting Fitch? She couldn't talk to Jimmy about that. Aside from the fact that he'd known Bruten Wilder, he'd think she was crazy. Andrea couldn't stop the tears from welling up in her eyes.

"Look," Jimmy said, softening his tone. "Like I said before, I hope Taka's going after Dewey. That'd be a win-win for us. We're going to stay on this."

She shook her head. The grey river roiled beneath them, throwing itself against its banks. Andrea could relate. She knuckled the corners of her eyes to dry them. "We had copies of Billie Mae's case files at the house. If Dewey sent Fitch to scare Taka by tossing my house, maybe Fitch saw the files and got worried. If he hurt Billie Mae, that'd give him his own motive for going after Taka."

"Okay," Jimmy said and subsided into a thoughtful silence.

Andrea watched the miles go by. They were out on 119, also known as Corridor G, in the suburbs southwest of the city, near the massive shopping complex Southridge. Housing developments and strip centers had crept through the hills like a fancy fungus, leaving pools of scraggly mountain land and sheared rock walls among the sculpted terraces and leveled plateaus of pavement and lawns. Tracy Manners lived out this way. She realized she'd been expecting him to call about Taka, and then wondered how he was handling the fallout from the shooting.

"You know, the idea of Fitch for the break-in works for me," Jimmy suddenly said. "It makes sense in relation to his employment by the Sandersons and easy access from his sister's house. He's known in the neighborhood. The break-in could play as a scare tactic. Taking Taka for Dewey after Taka had been suspended without pay, though, that's a little dicey. Councilman Miller and the Sandersons have other ways to ruin Taka's career, now that they've got the ball rolling. That puts it back to Taka absconding to retaliate for his suspension. Your suspicion of Fitch regarding the little girl is... faulty. You're being influenced by your affection for your best friend and anger at Fitch. There's what? A witness statement he willingly gave in those files? The mom confessed. Case closed. He knows that, even if he isn't the sharpest tool. Did CPD process the prints?"

"It's only been two days," she whispered. "Low priority, I doubt it." Andrea couldn't fault his logic and she couldn't share her most compelling evidence. She found herself impressed by his careful reasoning.

"I'm sorry," he said.

Andrea looked over at him. He glanced at her, his lips curving up in a slow smile as she continued to watch him. She rolled her eyes and it blossomed. He really did have a great smile. She sighed and answered his original question. "I don't know much about Susan Pepper. She's a drug rep. She gardens. She's lived in her house for seventeen years."

"My boss said if I could manage it without stepping on CPD's toes, I could confirm Verny as in the vicinity. I asked about his sister because I wanted to know if Susan's approachable, if she'd talk honestly about her brother."

"Oh," she said. He really did intend to follow up. "Sorry. I don't know. They told me two different things about Billie Mae."

"They? You talked to Fitch?"

"I called him. He picked right up."

"You talked to Verny."

"I went to his apartment but he wasn't there, so I called him."

"Did you ask about Taka?"

"No. I didn't know how to." All the questions she had wanted to ask Verny bubbled up again. She should have at least asked if he'd been at his sister's yesterday. If he'd seen Taka. "I asked about Billie Mae."

"You are..." Jimmy shook his head. "Either stupid or brave."

"I'm loyal, not stupid. I didn't want to spook him. Taka's gone. Fitch took him. Fitch works for Dewey. Dewey's still my strongest bet for finding him."

"Taka's gone. He thinks he's fucked. Dewey's the easiest person in this equation for him to go after and—" Jimmy glanced over, but if he thought he could spur a reaction out of her, he was wrong. "According to you, he's already pissed at Dewey on multiple levels. Dewey's still *my* strongest bet for finding him."

"I thought you had the day off."

He shrugged. "I happen to find Taka lurking, my career gets a boost."

There was nothing more to say. At least she knew why he had changed his mind about helping her.

Traffic started slowing on a four-lane section of the corridor past Little Coal River and the flashing lights of an accident scene became visible around the next curve. They crept up on the scene. Two private cars and a police vehicle sat in the median crossover for Owen Drive to their left. Police, state, and sheriff's cars, along with an ambulance, blocked the right lane in their direction on both sides of Owen Drive.

The cars ahead of them merged left. Jimmy hit his lights and pulled to the right. He bounced them onto the grass of the shoulder to the cluster of law enforcement vehicles. Twenty feet off the corridor, through a barbed wire fence that had been cut and folded back, two fire engines, a pick-up truck and another sheriff's car sat at hard angles to a shallow gully and copse of trees. Among the beeches and redbuds, a line of three deputies stood facing a herd of curious cows not far from the smoking hulk of a blackened SUV.

A few yards further and the SUV would have flattened itself against one of the rock walls that gave the 119 corridor carved through the hills its nickname. A tall state trooper detached himself from the officers documenting the scene and walked their way. Jimmy parked and rolled his window down, letting in a horrible scorched rubber stench redolent with melted electronics and plastic and underscored by a sweet, putrid, burnt roast scent that rolled Andrea's stomach. The trooper leaned down and rested an elbow on the frame. "Definitely two bodies. But it's still too hot to see if we can get a VIN."

"They go through the fence?"

"Yes. Witness who called it in said she noticed smoke and then it flamed up as she drove by."

"Anybody else see it?"

"Two motorists going the other way," he said, throwing his thumb over his shoulder at the vehicles in the median behind them.

"And this was at—"

"Ten-twenty-eight. Fire was intense by the time Rescue arrived. Plates were already melted."

"Anybody talk to the property owner?"

"Closest building is a quarter of a mile. Says he didn't hear anything. We think it's a Hummer, an H3."

"Keep me in the loop, Mark."

"Will do. Thanks, Jimmy."

As they pulled back onto the corridor, Andrea said, "You're what, a supervisor?"

"A lead. I'm in Criminal Intelligence. Mark's an investigator. We work in teams. With sick days and mental health days and family leave and vacation and injuries and our budget, we all have to keep a hand in where we can. Make sure no balls get dropped. The highway's ours, the field is the Sherriff's. Looks like this is ours, so we want our asses covered."

Andrea nodded, not sure if that made her more confident in law enforcement or less. "Some days Waltham's a ghost town."

"Our next stop's just two miles from here. There's an industrial complex on the other side of Old Beegum Road. Dewey has storage there."

CHAPTER THIRTY-ONE

THE NONDESCRIPT WAREHOUSE was low slung and sprawling. Three cars sat in the otherwise empty lot. Jimmy swung around and parked the Impala down the street, in front of an abandoned concrete storefront.

"We can't tell anything from out here," Andrea said, leaning forward to study the building.

"We can't just go strolling in."

"I can."

"And say what?"

"I'm lost." She picked up her phone and pulled up her GPS. Tapping in the tiny community's name, she enlarged the map and found the name of a little road nearby. "Can I use the phone to call for directions because my cell is dead. And the rest room. "

Jimmy looked at her through his lashes. "We could employ a little patience, watch for a while," he suggested in a tone that said he knew he was just wasting breath.

Andrea opened her door. Jimmy didn't try to stop her. She slung her bag over her arm and gave him one last chance, raising her eyebrows at him.

"Give me your phone," he sighed.

"Why?"

He made a grabby motion with his fingers. She handed the phone to him. "Your phone's dead, you don't have a car charger, why carry it in with you? Leave your purse here, too. Take my keys."

"You're more than just good looks, huh?"

He grinned at her. "More than ten minutes and I'm coming in with my lights on."

"I have your keys," she said, as she got out and shut the door. After crossing the street, she looked back, but Jimmy wasn't behind the wheel. She frowned, but continued on her way.

The warehouse was just that. Andrea let Jimmy's keys dangle from her hand. A receptionist gave her the building's address and let her use the phone. Suddenly nervous, she called her own number and tried not to sound too fake as she talked to herself. The bathrooms were in the rear of the warehouse and the woman escorted her through the vast space holding huge palletized cardboard boxes, some wrapped in plastic. Two men rode forklifts, shifting the pallets from place to place. A third emptied one of the big boxes, counting out the smaller cardboard boxes it contained into piles of ten. There was writing on the smaller boxes, but Andrea couldn't read the labeling from her location. Two offices built above the lobby space, accessed by a staircase in the warehouse itself, appeared dark and unoccupied. A chain looped around the bottom of the staircase marked them as off-limits.

Back outside Jimmy remained absent as Andrea strolled across the parking lot. She wasn't sure what to do, so she crossed the street and climbed into the driver's side of the Impala. Jimmy yanked on the passenger door as she started the engine.

"Get directions, honey?" he said, as he got in.

"I did," Andrea said brightly. "You?"

"No one home."

Andrea pulled out, making a careful three-point turn, and proceeded to leave the community behind. "Okay, where next?"

"Back to town. We can check out one of the senator's businesses on the west side."

She pulled over in a wide spot and they got out to swap seats. As they passed each other in front of the car, Jimmy caught Andrea's hand, arresting her forward motion. His brown eyes searched hers. Andrea couldn't decipher his intent. Finally he said, "You hungry?"

Wondering what he really wanted to say, Andrea shook her head.

The drive over took thirty-five minutes through the lunchtime traffic.

The large building hosted an active business, with employees out on the two loading docks and twenty cars or more in the lot. "What do they do here?"

"They wholesale irrigation hose, greenhouse supplies."

"How very politically correct," Andrea muttered. "There's too many people here, no way they could conceal a snatched cop."

"There's a mini-farm," Jimmy offered. "Backs up to Woodrum Lake east of Romance."

NEITHER THE LAKE, a long, narrow, multi-branched body of water at the center of a state park, or the farm was visible from the road.

"Ready for a hike?" Jimmy asked as he cruised past the correct address.

"Go in through the woods?"

"Yeah." He pointed out the "For Sale" sign further up the road verge. If we're confronted, we'll just say we're looking at property for sale."

"Checking out the boundaries?"

"Good. That works."

They parked near the sign and pulled their jackets on against the chilly air as they got out. Bordered by a barbed wire fence, the property appeared to be vacant land, with no buildings on site. Hickories and oaks were taking over the scrubby pines, with plenty of azaleas and rhododendrons filling in the understory. Several different kinds of birds darted through the air, startled by their presence. Blackberry bushes crowded thick along the road, full of mature berries. Andrea picked one and popped it into her mouth. It burst in her mouth with an Indian summer sweetness that made her nostalgic for the warmth of August. Wondering if Taka had eaten, if he'd be okay when they found him, Andrea picked another handful, but only held them.

They found a narrow tire-rutted trail, wide enough for an ATV, leading onto the property. Jimmy picked up his pace. Fifty yards in, he struck off to his right through the woods, in the general direction of Dewey's farm. Andrea let the warmed blackberries fall from her hand and followed. When they had zigzagged all the way to the barbed wire on the house's property line, they turned towards the lake, but kept the fence in their sight as they wound their way through the trees. A couple of minutes walking and the house itself appeared.

A large colonial with a wraparound porch, it appeared well-maintained. Two cars sat in the drive and a truck was pulled into the open garage. Two kids in jeans and sweatshirts played catch on the back lawn leading to a small barn with a center aisle and attached shed holding two kayaks and a canoe on open racks.

Jimmy stopped and stepped back a little further into the cover of the woods, drawing Andrea with him. "Let's just watch a little."

Andrea's anticipation drained away. She felt certain this wasn't anywhere Taka could be if there were kids playing in the yard. "Who are they?"

Jimmy shrugged, his lips pulling down at the corners.

A door slammed and a lean man with shaggy blond hair came out of the garage, a black and white dog on his heels. "That's Dewey's brother-in-law," Jimmy said. The dog halted on the gravel drive, ears perked, looking directly at them. "Okay, start walking," Jimmy instructed in a low voice. "Down the fence line."

They started working through the brush again. Growling, the dog came rushing forward. The man turned, his gaze scanning the woods. Jimmy stepped into a clearer space near the fence and waved. "Hi!" he called. "Sorry to bother you!" The dog dug its heels in and skidded to a stop three feet from the fence and Jimmy, barking wildly. Jimmy shouted over it. "We're just walking the property line. Sorry."

Dewey's brother-in-law waved and called the dog off. The dog huffed and stopped, but stared at them with a ferocious focus. "Duncan," the man called again, "Here!" The dog cocked an ear at him, but held its ground. "Here!"

Duncan sneezed and spun, bolting back to his master.

The man waved again. "No bother."

He turned away, talking to the dog who was looking up at him, anxiety written all over its taut frame. The kids went back to playing catch. For show, Andrea and Jimmy kept going, walking deeper and deeper into the woods along the narrow track until the fence ran out about a hundred yards from what must be a branch of the lake.

"It's pretty," Jimmy said.

And it was. The water rippled with a light breeze. Andrea's jacket was too thin to stand there long without freezing. Two birds carved white lines into the water's dark surface. The sky stretched high and blue and cloudless in all directions. The woods came down to the shore in several places and being, undoubtedly, on state land now, there were no houses to be seen from their vantage point. "It's gorgeous." She'd love to be out on it in a canoe with Taka, just drifting.

"I have a boat," Jimmy said, reading her mind.

"You do?"

"A little pontoon boat. It's peaceful."

"We're not going to find him this way."

"No, we're not. We're not going to find him at all, but his buddies at CPD might. If there are cameras on the traffic light at Timber Way. If someone saw something. If he shows up at his place or yours or Dewey's Charleston house or the Coliseum."

"You're just babysitting?"

"They've got two guys out in your neighborhood right now, Andrea. They're looking. No one wants you hurt. "

Andrea walked closer to the water and sat down on the bank.

Jimmy followed her, but left her some space as he sat, too.

"Why do you care?" she asked. "You were assigned surveillance. You did that. Your job's done."

"Look, I don't like being used. And being assigned from up top to follow Taka around until his suspension came through didn't sit well with me. He was just doing his job. Just because the asshole he shot was a councilman's son who happened to be associated with Dewey Sanderson doesn't mean he was wrong to do so. But I have a state investigation to protect. We have people on the ground who have a better shot than you at finding out if Dewey has anything to do with Taka disappearing, whichever one's being the idiot. I don't need you crashing around accusing Dewey and jeopardizing whatever deals he has going down."

"Is that really Dewey's brother-in-law?"

"I'm not that big an asshole."

"Is that a yes?"

Hurt flickered over his expressive face before he glanced away. "Yes."

"I need to get home. Karie's coming back over."

"I have some information she requested," he said, his voice stronger. "Are you working with her on the highway thing?"

"Yes."

Jimmy picked at the grass in front of him. "I knew Bruten Wilder."

"Karie told me. I'm sorry."

"He mentored me out of the academy. His case has been cold for months. Tell me the deal with this roadside trouble you're looking into."

Andrea turned her head. He looked back at her, intent on her answer, his lips pressed together. A faint scar bisected the lower one. His nose had been badly set at least once. He wasn't classically handsome, but his irregular features lent him a ruggedness that she found attractive. He seemed solid. Kind. His phone vibrated and he lifted it from his hip to read the message.

After he silently replaced it, she said "Your friend was shot and the car lit on fire to cover his murder."

Jimmy dropped his gaze to the grass and nodded before he looked away, past the lake, to the mist-shrouded foothills in the distance.

"Nineteen months later, Oliver Fitch pulled his car over in the same spot after his engine cut out. Two witnesses stopped to help. Smoke poured out from under his car's hood and actually caused a minor traffic back-up when it drifted over the nearest lanes of traffic, obscuring the view. A fire truck arrived, followed by a trooper. Flames were visible, but in the time that most cars would be destroyed, the car wasn't engulfed, the interior wasn't on fire, and the metal wasn't melting. While everyone watched, the firefighters opened the hood, but nothing was burning. Once the hood was up, the smoke stopped. There was no evidence of fire. No soot, no scorching, no damage. One of the fire crew got in and started the car. It ran fine. Nothing wrong. A half-mile of road and shoulder were searched for anything unusual that may have gotten caught in the grille or undercarriage and burnt."

Jimmy frowned at her. "Let me guess. They found nothing suspicious."

"No, they didn't. And then last Sunday, Taka's Chevy did the same. A CPD officer who stopped said he remembered another incident like that, so we had him look it up. It was Wilder, Fitch, and us."

"Only Bruten died and you guys didn't. There is no Waltham or WVDOT project is there?"

Since they were being honest, now... "No."

"What's going on, Andrea? I know there's something I'm missing here, but I can't figure it out. You and Fitch have a personal issue? Revenge? What?"

"No. It's a lot more complicated than that. And it's a really long story."

He stood up and held his hand out. "It's a long ride back to Charleston. Will you please fill me in?"

CHAPTER THIRTY-TWO

A LATE MODEL Jetta sat behind Taka's Yukon when they arrived at Andrea's house. Jimmy pulled his car alongside. When they entered the house through the kitchen, Jimmy whistled. "That is some serious gadgetry, ladies."

"Only the best at Waltham-Young, sir." Karie grinned. "I have equipment ghost hunters would die for."

Jimmy walked around the boom mike attached to a sliver chrome box about the size of a shoebox and sporting several gauges. "What is it?"

"EVP recorder emitting a forced frequency field. There's two down here and one upstairs."

"And this," he asked, nodding at a little black cube on the counter.

"A motion sensor connected to that." She turned and pointed at the camera and laser grid in the doorway between the kitchen and the living room.

Andrea stood marooned in the mudroom.

"Hey, come on," Karie said to her, pulling a chair from the kitchen table. "Sit down."

"I will," Andrea said." I just need a minute." She turned and walked back out into the carport. The door closed with a soft click.

Jimmy turned to Karie. "Do you really believe in this stuff?"

"I'll tell you what I told Taka and Andrea. The two or three cases I know of that were legitimate were devastating for the people involved. If this is for real, we can't let anyone else know."

"Like, real. Really real." He lifted his hands, wiggling his fingers. "Life beyond the grave, ghosts, evil."

Karie sighed and gave him a disgusted look. "You asked. I told you. Evil has nothing to do with it. Well, human evil, maybe, on this side of the veil."

Jimmy shook his head. "How do we tell? Check this stuff?"

"Yes, but it may or may not have captured anything during the time it's been set. I've asked questions out loud periodically."

"You guys set it up this morning?"

She slid her cell out of the back pocket of her jeans and checked the time. "Seven and a half hours ago. We can dump the data and let it keep running while we check it."

"What do you need?"

"I have my laptop and we could probably use Andrea's as well."

Jimmy had been wandering around the kitchen. Neat and clean. The worn white appliances and butcher block wood reminded him of his ma's kitchen back home. He picked up the Ziploc with the dog skull inside and squinted at it. "This the Robbins' dog?"

"Maybe," Andrea said, coming back in. "Circumstances say yes. I emailed a zooarchaeologist who consults with Waltham and he said he'd look at it for us, though we don't know how that might help yet. What do you need, Karie?"

"Laptop, if you have one?"

ANDREA RETRIEVED HER laptop from her bedroom, skirting the equipment and noting that today nothing was out of place in the room. In the kitchen, she set the computer down on the table, where Karie was busy marking the SD cards she'd pulled. "Great. We can both watch different feeds. We can slow, fast forward, and rewind if we see anything while we listen to the audio."

"Jimmy," Andrea said. "Will you stay and help?"

"I was planning on it."

"Good. If you'll work with Karie, I'm going to call for pizza, look at that file you brought on Trooper Wilder, and check on a couple of calls I made earlier on a different project."

After Jimmy nodded in distraction as he watched Karie, Andrea took Bruten's file from the table and retreated to her office. Before she was settled, Karie flitted by the door. "I'm just going to retrieve the data from your room," she called. Andrea nodded even though Karie was already by her.

She rolled her head on her neck, rubbing it. A small headache had set up in her forehead, but she knew it was only stress. She called Giorgio's first and ordered her usual, plus a large cheese and pepperoni, and a large Greek salad. Then she called Carson.

"Anything?" she said as soon as he answered.

"No. I'm sorry, Andrea. He'll turn up. He always does."

"This isn't—"

"I know. They're looking for him. I talked to Captain Cahill this afternoon. They've been to all his usual haunts, they've checked in on the Sandersons and the Taylors, and they've put out a statewide bulletin."

"Can I ask you a favor?"

"Sure."

"Can you find out whatever you can about an Oliver Fitch? Apparently he's called Verny. He's living at the same complex as Taka, just a few doors down from him. He's recently moved here from Baltimore and his sister lives next door to me. Technically, he works security for Senator Sanderson, but he was watching Zach Taylor for Dewey."

"You mean, like, background check, criminal records, that sort of thing?"

"Yes. The state police are running an investigation on Dewey and they're aware of Oliver Fitch, but I don't think I can ask them for information on him."

"Why do you need it?"

"That's why I can't ask?"

Carson tsked and then shifted, his movement rustling across the line.

"All I have are suspicions."

"Okay. I'll do you one better, *I'll* ask the state police for info on him."

"How?"

"He was present at the shooting."

Cold hatred swept through Andrea. "Bastard."

"I take it you think he had something to do with Taka going AWOL?"

"Yes."

"Take it to the cap'n."

"I already told her, but she said Verny's proximity to my home and Taka's isn't enough for them to go knocking on his door. And besides, I already did and he's not there."

Carson's silence said more than any words could.

"He wasn't there. I am perfectly fine."

"Where are you now?"

"At home with a work colleague." She so did not want to explain Jimmy right now, so she omitted him. She had no idea why he had been nominated to babysit her. And now he knew about Billie Mae and Bruten Wilder and the whole unreal situation.

"Stay there. Please?"

"I'm fine, Carson, and I will, okay? Will you please get me the info on Fitch? If you do I won't have to go looking for it. I'll sit right here at home and dink around on my research project."

"Okay, I will. I'll call you as soon as I have anything."

Andrea flipped her desktop tower switch and thumbed her monitor on, hoping Billie Mae had spent her energy playing for the cameras and didn't have anything to say. While the computer booted up, she thought about how to go about tracking any other murders with similar circumstances. She decided to start with a few simple keyword searches before hitting news sites and newspaper archives for Charleston and Baltimore. She could widen her search by county and then by state, if necessary, before she started networking her contacts, checking in with the forums she used to track people down. With time, she could locate enough info to write a decent biography on Oliver Fitch without ever speaking to him again.

But first she surfed to Snowfoot Tracking, logged in, and activated two of the GPS units Daniel had given her. The one she'd placed under the wheel well of Hoyle's Impala popped up at her house on the digital map. She wondered how many laws she was breaking putting a tracker on a state-owned vehicle. To its right, the other one burned bright at Susan Pepper's. Maybe Taka had already checked into her background. Taking her jacket from the back of her chair, Andrea pulled the flash drive from its pocket and slid it into her tower's USB port.

THE DOORBELL RANG. Jimmy glanced at Karie, but she was frowning at the laptop in front of her and when it rang again a minute later, Jimmy paused his own video of the empty living room to get up and answer it. Rifling through both front pockets he came up ten dollars short. "Hey," he called. "I need another ten dollars. And a tip."

Andrea ducked out of her office with the cash and handed it to the grateful delivery girl. She took the bag on top of the two pizza boxes Jimmy held as she closed the door. "Thank you."

"You're welcome," he said. "Karie's glued to the Casper show in there, but all I've seen so far is nothing and more nothing. What are you so intent on over here?"

"I have all Fitch's previous addresses and I'm checking for homicides in those locations that have similar details to the recent deaths here or homicide-arsons like Bruten's."

The FBI suspected Dewey had ordered seven different homicides involving arson of cars or buildings, but they'd never had the hard evidence to prove that, despite issuing multiple search warrants. Jimmy's team was hoping to take Dewey down on arms sales, but since he ran a legitimate gun supply wholesale, it was proving difficult. "And what are you finding?"

"Nothing on the kids, but four similar murder-arsons."

"Four. I'm impressed," he said.

Andrea set her bag down on the counter by the sink and looked at him sidegogglin. He figured she was trying to decide if he was humoring her or making fun of her. "If you're part of the team looking at Dewey," she said, "I'm sure you already know the information I'm finding on Fitch, but you haven't offered it."

Perceptive. She was very perceptive. "I do," he agreed. "And I haven't."

"I take that to mean you can't."

He gave her a little bow. "Where are the plates?"

She pointed at a cabinet. He retrieved them while she removed an iced tea pitcher from the refrigerator.

"Can I have a beer?" Karie piped up.

Andrea laughed. "Yes, you may. I think I will, too."

She raised her brows at Jimmy, who shrugged. "Sure."

Andrea replaced the tea and grabbed a Morgantown growler.

"What kind?" he said.

"Alpha Blonde Ale."

She really needed to stop being just the kind of girl he wanted.

"Find anything, Karie?" she said, retrieving glasses.

"I've marked two places to review and I'm pretty sure I have EVP at those spots as well."

"You don't stop to analyze as you go along?" Jimmy asked.

"Nope," Karie said. "I'm a scientist first. This is a step-by-step approach. Find the useful data and then objectively analyze the data. Wash and repeat."

"Do you eat while you work?"

"No," she laughed. "It takes too long to eat while I'm concentrating." She closed her laptop and held it up for Jimmy to take, which he did, placing it out of the way on the counter.

"What about you, Andrea?" he asked, taking two of the beers to the table.

"No, I'll take a break." She grabbed the last beer and brought it over with a roll of paper towels.

The first few minutes, they ate in silence.

"If my boss blamed me for killing his boyfriend after said boyfriend was shot to death by a cop, I'd feel pretty justified in saying it wasn't my fault," Andrea ventured.

After a long moment of chewing, Karie said, "I'd feel hurt."

"I'd be pissed," Jimmy said.

"If," Andrea said.

"If? You said Dewey fired him for it," Karie pointed out.

Andrea glanced at Jimmy. "And Jimmy said Fitch actually works for Senator Sanderson."

Jimmy choked on the bite he was swallowing. He cleared his throat and took a swig of beer. "I did not mean to imply the senator has anything to do with this. Or Fitch either, for the record."

"He's not Dewey's to fire," Andrea said, her voice soft. "What's to say dear old Dad isn't engaging in a little over-protectiveness on his son's behalf?"

"Seriously?"

"And doing someone a favor at the same time. Councilman Miller's an old friend of the senator's," Karie added. "They both graduated from my high school. They played football together."

Jimmy snorted. "That doesn't mean—"

"The years they both attend our largest fundraiser, they always sit together, laughing like twelve-year-olds."

He looked back and forth between them.

"Just saying," Andrea said and tore a huge bite off her pizza.

Could Verny have taken Taka? Sure. On his own? Jimmy doubted it. Verny followed orders. He excelled at following orders, but he couldn't manage an operation on his own. He'd fuck it up and get caught in rapid order. Still, the senator had never been implicated in any wrongdoing, despite his son's unsavory dealings. "If Verny had anything to do with this, which I doubt, he's acting on his own and he's going to make a mess of it sooner rather than later."

Andrea took another bite of her pizza, watching him while she chewed. Jimmy wondered if she was thinking of Taka or Verny. He couldn't tactfully talk to her about Taka and wouldn't tell her about Verny.

"Has he screwed up before?" Karie asked.

"They all have," Jimmy blurted, and having said that, immediately broke on not telling them about Verny. "The last time Verny was unemployed, he tried to run a protection racket on a few small-town merchants where he was hiding out in Maine. He did eighteen months for assault."

"So *if*," Andrea said. "*If* Fitch took Taka of his own volition, either Taka won't last long or Fitch will make a mistake," Andrea said.

"Sooner rather than later," he agreed.

TAKA'S ARMS WERE numb and his hands hurt. Dark shrouded the room, drawing his thoughts to the memory of peeking beneath the cover his mother drew over the parakeet cage every night. He always wondered how the birds felt about dark dropping over them so fast. The scrape of a key broke him from a vivid waking dream in which he was sorting dead birds into bins.

Verny came and stood silently in the bedroom doorway, his face screwed up at the rank odor in the room. He'd morphed from Everyman to average-redneck in a black tee shirt and well-worn cowboy boots. "Not such a smart cop now, are ya?"

Someone slammed in through the cabin's front door. The crinkle of bags accompanied footsteps to what Taka assumed was the kitchen. "Beer?" Cody yelled.

Taka's stomach rumbled. Verny laughed at him and closed the bedroom door. The TV came on. Wheel of Fortune. Biting his lip, Taka wiggled upward, hands and arms stinging with vicious prickles of pain. He clenched his eyes shut and tilted his head back, screaming in his head. When the sensation eased, he opened and closed his fingers and shifted his legs. His butt was numb and his skin was itch-burning now from urine scald and the rough rub of his wet jeans, but there wasn't much to do about that.

"Painting the town red," Cody shouted.

That was good. He could do that. He focused on listening to the players as they asked for letters, to the number of them turned over, trying to unscramble the jumble revealed. It was impossible in phrases rather than seeing single words as the letters turned, but he kept right on trying.

ANDREA'S PHONE VIBRATED on the table with a call from Carson.

Just then Jimmy jerked his phone from the clip on his belt and stared at the screen. "I gotta go," he said and stood up, his chair skidding back and his napkin dropping to the floor. Her breath caught. "I'll call later," he added and strode out through the mudroom, punching buttons on his phone.

Andrea's phone vibrated again. She snatched it up. The mudroom door slammed.

"What is it?" Karie asked, her eyes wide.

"Taka's lawyer." Andrea breathed. Too fast for info on Fitch. She hit accept.

Jimmy's car started up with a roar.

It had to be Taka.

"Carson," Andrea said, getting up to go to her office for privacy. "What's wrong?"

Karie rose with her and started clearing their half-eaten dinner. "Tracy Manners is dead."

CHAPTER THIRTY-THREE

ANDREA STOPPED HALFWAY down the front hall, her cell phone pressed hard to her ear. Maybe she had heard him wrong. "Tracy's dead?"

"He and his dad were both shot in his Hummer, and then it was set on fire," Carson said. "The IDs have to be confirmed, but they just matched the VIN and his mom said they left together not long before the fire was reported this morning."

"What took so long?"

"The fire was hot. They had to wait for it to cool."

"Carson—"

"They were lucky to find a VIN."

"Taka wasn't—"

"Taka's disappearance has just jumped in priority. CPD is locating all parties involved in the Taylor shooting again, asking questions. The state police are backtracking Tracy and his dad's activity the last few days, seeing if there's any leads that don't come back to the shooting, if he or his dad was involved in anything that could have bit them on the ass. Please, can you just lock the doors and stay home until it's sorted?"

Andrea swallowed. "Sure," she said. "I can do that."

"I'll call you when I know more."

She had been there. It had been Tracy Manners in that smoking hulk. Quiet, confident, quick-witted, full-of-easy-grace Tracy. And his dad. Andrea found herself sitting at her desk. She pulled up the Snowfoot site to watch Jimmy's Impala speed along Greenbrier on the way to 64.

"What's happened?" Karie asked from the doorway. Andrea turned to look at her. "Tracy." Speaking hurt her throat. Pinching the bridge of her nose, she tried to stop the tears already spilling over onto her cheeks. She sniffed and swiped at her cheeks. "Tracy Manners, Taka's partner on the Zach Taylor case, was killed this morning. In the same way as Bruten Wilder."

Kari stiffened. "But they wouldn't be related."

"We don't know that they aren't. Two Charleston LEOs shot and left to burn."

"Leos?"

"Law enforcement officers."

"I knew that," Karie said. "Sorry. I just..." She crossed the room to drop into the extra chair. Pointing at Andrea's monitor, she said, "And what's that."

"That's Jimmy."

Karie raised her brow.

"And the other?"

"Susan Pepper."

"What are you thinking?"

"That I'm going to keep digging into Fitch and then you're going to see if Billie Mae or Bruten Wilder have anything to say about him."

"I meant..." She circled her index finger at the monitor and Jimmy's moving dot.

Andrea's throat closed back up. She didn't really know why she'd done it, but she knew that if she got into trouble over it she didn't want to drag Karie into the deep end with her. She shrugged.

"All righty then," Karie said. She got up and checked the camera in the corner, which was aimed to capture most of the room. Her gaze fell on Bruten Wilder's case file. Andrea handed it to her. "I'm going to see what I see in this file. And then I'll keep reviewing video. Yell if you need me." She was one foot out the door when she stopped and turned back. "I'm so sorry, Andrea, about Tracy. Whatever I can do to help you, I'll do. I just don't know what that is."

This time Andrea couldn't stop the tears and didn't try. She nodded. "You're doing it."

Watching Jimmy's progress through Charleston, Andrea could tell that he was headed to the State Police barracks. She suspected he'd gotten the same info that Carson had given her. Her stomach gnawed on itself. Dewey might be an asshole, but his relationship with Taka had been consensual and for a time at least, exclusive. Only four years older, Dewey had meshed right into their lives and she had been there during the good times, invited for camping trips and long hikes and barbecues.

Despite a streak of cruelty and an acid tongue, he had always been generous with his time, his money, and his genuine affection for Taka. He might be pissed enough at Taka to rough him up, but he wasn't a killer. Or at least he hadn't been. She thought about the confrontation at Louie's, how Taka had flushed when Dewey stopped him with a hand on his chest, the low rumble of words she couldn't hear, and how utterly believable Dewey sounded when he'd asked her if she were there as Taka's go-between last night.

If Taka's disappearance and Tracy Manners' death were related, either Dewey was a very changed man or he had nothing to do with either. In that case, "I hope Fitch is acting on his own," she whispered out loud. A cool puff of air lifted her hair from her face. She leapt up, her heart racing. "Is it Fitch?" she said aloud. Nothing. But then she remembered Billie Mae's case files, the papers spread everywhere, with Verny Fitch's statement lying center stage on her bed. "It is Fitch."

Nothing.

She sat back down. She snatched up her cell phone and hit Verny's number. His voicemail picked up after five rings. She re-dialed. It rang once.

"Fitch," he growled into the phone.

"It's Andrea Kelley, Mr. Fitch, is this a bad time?"

He made a strange noise. It took her a second to realize he was laughing. The Wheel of Fortune theme song played in the background. He sucked in a strangled breath and cleared his throat. "What do you need, Ms. Kelley?"

"I should have asked earlier, but I've just realized you may have been at your sister's yesterday and I wanted to know if you saw any activity at my house yesterday afternoon?"

"What kind of activity."

"Cars? People?"

"No, I didn't."

"My friend went missing. It just occurred to me that maybe you saw him."

"No, I didn't. You've got balls, though, I'll give you that," he said, and hung up.

Andrea lowered her phone. "You got something to say, Bruten, say it now."

CODY CAME IN and uncuffed one wrist. Taka's arms fell, his hands smacking onto the hardwood and shooting pain all the way up into his shoulders. Cody toed him in the ribs until Taka rolled over onto his tingling hands and tried to stand. But then Cody dropped a knee into his back, laying him down flat on his belly, grabbed the cuffs to pull his right hand back, and then pulled his left up and closed the dangling bracelet around it, securing his hands together behind his back. He wrapped a hand around Taka's bicep and pulled up.

Taka clenched his jaw shut and scrambled to get his feet under him. Cody half carried, half shoved him into the bathroom and dropped him into the tub on his face. Taka kicked and got over onto his back in time to catch the first blast of cold water from the shower head high on his chest. He shook his head, turning his face away, but swallowed the water in his mouth, grateful for it. The pressure had to be ten times his condo's, and the old shower head allowed a deluge of water. Gasping, he tried to breathe and catch a mouthful of water from the ricochet at the same time, but only got two swallows before Cody adjusted the spray. He let the water run to hot across Taka's torso before cranking it to full cold again, making Taka shout. With his right leg crammed into the tub, knee fully bent and taking up the full width, and the left sticking out, Taka felt like a turtle on its back. He couldn't even sit up.

Verny came in and stopped short, the expression on his face changing as he watched Cody move the shower head again to fully soak Taka's thighs and right leg. "Get out."

Cody looked up, his brows dipping down between his dark eyes.

"Get out," Verny shouted.

"Yeah, boss, you got it," Cody said. He let go of the shower head and tried to walk by, but Verny was frozen in place. Wriggling, Taka tried to brace his left boot up on the edge of the shower surround, so he could shove himself up off the bottom of the tub, but it kept slipping, the ancient white tile crumbling away under the force of his efforts. Cody sidled past Verny and disappeared. Verny reached back and closed the bathroom door.

"What," Taka said, acid roiling up to burn his throat.

Verny stepped forward and reaching up, adjusted the shower head so that the full stream hit Taka's crotch and then flipped it up to catch Taka full in the face. Taka sputtered and turned his head away, his mouth open to gulp whatever air he could, swallowing water compulsively every time he tried to clear his mouth by spitting it out. Verny pressed down on his left leg and wormed his other hand down past Taka's right calf. Taka lunged, getting his shoulders up before he fell back again. Verny smirked and held his wet hands up. "Not a faggot, cop." The tub began filling.

Twisting, Taka kept trying to brace his feet to shove himself up the back slope of the tub, out of the spray. Using his foot, Verny knocked him off balance again and again, not caring that he was getting soaked in the process. The pointed toe of his cowboy boot scraped up under Taka's jaw as Taka slid down yet again. Some rational part of him made Taka quit before his strength gave out. In reward, Verny lifted his boot from Taka's chest. Head turned from the full frontal blast of the spray, Taka gulped in air as well as he could and let the tub fill around him.

The water temperature changed. For the first few seconds, Taka welcomed the warmth, but then the heat jumped up. He yelled, heard his own whine as he rolled from side to side to spread the pain, hunching his shoulders up in vain until he forced his eyes open to glare up at Verny. With his foot perched on the rim of the tub and a distasteful look on his face, Verny looked like a demented Captain Morgan. He reached out and cranked the heat down and the cold up.

Panting, swallowing water he no longer wanted, Taka shook his head to fling the wet hair out of his eyes and went back to trying to breathe, tilting his face away from the constant stream to keep his mouth from filling too fast. Verny turned the heat back up, taking it slower this time. Taka let it build until he couldn't take it and glared back up at Verny. Verny spun the water cooler. Okay. Lesson learned. Verny smiled. Bastard asshole.

Taka's abs were burning and his fingers cramping from trying to spread them on the bottom to help hold his head above the deepening water when Verny shut the shower off. Breathing hard, Taka shook his head again.

"That woman called me. Twice."

Taka kept his eyes on Verny as he sank. His left hand slid away and his whole body tipped sideways, his chin dropping into the water. He scrambled and got his fingers re-positioned, spit water out of his mouth.

"Your girlfriend. Andrea? Is that right?"

Taka's heart about stopped, pounding with a sudden lurch, but he had nothing to say about that. How did Verny know Andrea?

"She was asking me about that girl that died over there. The one whose own mother drowned her in the bathtub. I didn't have nothing to do with that. Nothing."

He seemed to expect something, some reply. Taka stared at him. Who the fuck was Verny?

Lunging forward, Verny pushed down hard on the top of Taka's head with both hands, sending him under.

Taka bobbed back up, his wrists screaming. "You bastard," he sputtered, but his voice carried no volume. Verny laughed and tried to dunk him again. Taka braced his right leg and shoulders, tightened every ab, and resisted. Verny let go and brought his boot back down on Taka's chest, then leaned forward, using his weight to drive Taka down.

Taka choked coming back up. The first real tendrils of cold fear wormed into his heart.

"Those kids were always mudding up the goldfish pond. They let the dog dig up her flowers. She understood why the mom did it. Those kids were hellions. Shit, the dog was a beast. He bit her that morning. Does your girlfriend know that? My sister," he said, and fuck. Oliver Fitch. He was Oliver Fitch, the visiting brother who talked to Billie Mae. "Made me shut my mouth about it because she didn't want to cause more trouble. She could've sued."

And gotten what? Taka wanted to ask. Nothing from nothing equaled nothing. He kept his mouth shut, which was good because Verny shoved him down again with only a sip of breath. But then let him bob right back up. Taka heaved the cold heavy air in, sucking up water, which made him start coughing all over again. He must've looked bad, because Verny grabbed his hair and held him above the surface for a minute until he recovered.

When he let go, Taka almost went under on his own. He caught himself and re-braced his fingers and arms and knee and boot, pressing his elbows against the sides of the tub, the very inside edge of his left boot against the wall. It was reverse bouldering. That's what it was. Fingers and toes. His core taut with tension. All he had to do to survive was not fall into the water. Verny dialed up the cold water tap and let the faucet run. Taka hadn't thought he could be more miserable. He couldn't stop the muscle tremors making it hard to keep himself braced.

Verny pulled his phone from his back pocket, grimaced at it, and then pulled a Glock from the super-tuck concealed at his hip and pointed it at Taka one-handed. Like Taka was going anywhere. Glaring at him, Verny said, "Yeah?" into the phone.

The volume of the woman caller's anger made Verny hold the phone away from his ear and Taka could hear every word. *"How could you shit where we eat? You just got here. What is wrong with you?"*

"He's not feeding me anymore," Verny snapped back. His lower lip slid out.

Taka frowned at his petulance, trying to work out who could make a grown man of Verny's ilk pout. Wife, lover, mother.

"Because you're a dumb shit. I can't believe you. What are you going to live on if he fires me, too?"

"I've got savings," Verny muttered.

"Bullshit, because you're a stupid fuck. And if you think you're touching our principal and getting caught in the process, I should just shoot your ass and be done with you. You've always been worthless."

The gun didn't waver, but Verny's eyes were distant, unfocused. Taka got his right leg sorted enough to partially straighten it.

"That's not what you said in Detroit when I saved your ass," Verny said.

Taka moved slow, sliding up a few inches before throwing his shoulders forward to sit up. Verny absently planted his boot on Taka's chest before he could make it vertical and shoved him back down.

"... you, Ollie."

Taka sputtered and gagged, trying not to swallow more water as he fought to re-brace himself just a little higher. Cold water continued to gush into the tub.

"Don't you fucking call me that."

"I'll call you whatever the fuck I want to call you, asswipe. I should've finished strangling you when we were little. Stupid shouldn't ever grow up."

Sister, Taka realized. Susan Pepper.

Verny lifted the phone as if to throw it, but didn't. Instead, he rubbed it across his head, his fingertips spiking his hair up on one side.

"Whatever you're driving better be clean," his sister ranted. Verny put the phone back to his ear. *"I'll be at your place at four in the morning. We have tickets out at six. If you're not there, I'm leaving your ass, Ollie. Don't say I didn't warn you."*

"Dad'll kill you."

"Daddy was mad I didn't let you rot in jail the first time."

Verny growled. "Leave me the fuck alone."

"You aren't there and I will."

He stood still for a long moment before he pocketed the phone. "She's pretty, that girlfriend of yours. I'm gonna enjoy fucking her after your funeral."

He stepped down hard on Taka's chest, forcing his air out as he went under.

Taka flushed hot in the icy water, lungs aching, heart slamming at his ears, legs pedaling, boots skidding on the wall tile. Air. Before he could react, the water closed over him again. Verny's boot crushed down. Muscles clenching, Taka's mouth gaped open. The rush of water burned his nose, blew up his sinuses. The back of his head hit the bottom of the tub.

His hair drifted at the edges of his vision. The white tile surround wavered, far above. The rush of his blood faded. He was going to die. Right here. Right now. He hurt. His arms spasmed. The cuffs chewed through his skin, into his bone. Unrelenting pressure encased him. Bright flare of pain in the soft spot below his creaking sternum. Verny blocking out the light. White flash of his teeth as he grinned up there in the air Taka needed, needed right now, right now, right now.

He came to shaking, head just above the water, with Verny sitting on the lid of the toilet watching him, wetter than not. Verny smiled. He stood up and Taka flinched, which made Verny chuckle. He sat himself back down with deliberation.. "How many people have you killed?"

Taka just looked back at him, unable to pull words from the nothing in his brain. Verny surged off the toilet, grabbed his head, and pushed him back under. Taka thrashed, kicking, twisting, jerked free, but then he couldn't find up. Verny laughing. Solidness against his face. Tub. Pressing against the solid with his forehead, Taka bowed his back, struggled to brace his knees. Utter black invaded his vison before he flung his body straight up, gasping in a great breath. Water ran down into his eyes and mouth as he panted.

Verny stood facing him. He shoved Taka's chest with both hands, but Taka only rocked back onto his heels.

"You liked killing that boy. Gave you a rush."

Taka shook his head.

"Gave me a rush, watching."

Taka looked at him, at the grin on his face.

"Yeah, I was there, of course I was there, he was my charge."

Taka's brain wouldn't let him grasp that properly or understand what Verny wanted from him.

"I saw you smile," Verny said.

Tracy had said, damn fine shot, Taka, and Taka had smiled, pleased himself that he'd used a minimum of ammo, controlled the scene, not endangered the public more than necessary, that every bullet hit its mark and not some bystander. "I'll smile when I kill you," Taka choked out.

Verny just laughed again, a sound full of light, dismaying in its total lack of fear. "Yeah. Sure, boy. Stay." He stepped back, but was too smart to turn his back. "Hey, Cody, come get this piece of shit."

Sitting there, teeth chattering, sure he'd never catch his breath, Taka gnawed on his intense fear, his panic, the terror that coursed through him when Verny sent him under that last time. Thirty minutes ago, he was fine with the concept of dying. When faced with the absolute certainty of it... A swirling wash of sick tumbled through his belly. He leaned forward and puked into the water.

CHAPTER THIRTY-FOUR

STARTING WITH THE internet fishing lines she already had out, Andrea reeled in the info to her many inquiries tiny piece by tiny piece. Bits on Fitch, on Dewey, on the senator. Zach Taylor lived on through social media, a sort of half-life extension that would long sustain his memory. Ninety minutes in, she scanned her gathered facts sheet. Susan Pepper stood out for her lack of internet presence. She had a Facebook that revealed her as either the most boring or most circumspect of users. Ditto her few entries on a Twitter account. Taka had noted his fruitless search as well.

Andrea keyed in search terms using various spellings of Susan's first name with her last. She found her public records, her two bronze medals for prize lilies, a few scattered entries in various forums for Apple, GE, a plumbing site, a poetry site. Frowning, Andrea blew through pharmaceutical and sales terms and started in locating and keying in drug manufacturers, drug wholesalers, and regional reps to see if Susan Pepper's name came up anywhere. She posted inquires to her network and then returned to Taka's info to sort through Dr.

Huntley's particulars and decide what questions she needed to be asking about him. Letting her back-brain simmer on the spare info Taka had gathered, she circled back to her forums and private messages on seven different sites. Andrea drew in a sharp breath. There it was. Two child murders with the same characteristics in Charlottesville, VA.

"Andrea!" Karie yelled from the kitchen. "Come here!"

Andrea tabbed an open window and looked at Susan Pepper's former addresses. Charlottesville. That funny-swirly feeling of discovery, of knowing she was on the verge of breaking open the next level of the hunt lit her up inside.

"Andrea!"

It was the same pulse that colored the tone of Karie's voice.

"Come see if you hear what I'm hearing on this EVP!"

Energized, Andrea strode briskly into the kitchen. A visual wave of sound throbbed across Karie's laptop screen. "Here," she said, resting a hand on the back of Karie's chair to look over her shoulder.

Karie stripped off the headphones she was wearing and handed them back. "These are clearer. It's on repeat. Just listen a couple of times and when you're sure, say it out loud."

"Which unit is this from?"

"Your office, while you were talking to Fitch."

"While?"

"Yes. It carries one full word into the silence after you told Bruten to speak up, but the clearest recitation is towards the end of your conversation with Fitch. That's the one I isolated and cleaned up. Listen."

The palpable thrum of her excitement scared Andrea a little. There was no taking this back. Bruten had bulled his way into her life and she'd let Karie in herself. It wasn't just she and Taka and Billie Mae anymore. Never again. A chill skittered down her spine. Please, please let Taka be okay. Let him come home safe.

Andrea straightened up and slid the headphones on.

"I'll," a male voice said. Static filled the next two seconds. *"Fire."* The word changed in pitch from beginning to end, as if coming through on

a bad station. Crackles, hisses, and shhhs entwined every syllable, yet the words were unmistakable as she listened through the audio twice before she spoke out loud. "Fivemile. Fire. Fivemile. Fivemile. Fivemile. Fitch. Fitch. Fitch."

TAKA'S BREATHING SLOWED and he made himself stop gulping air. When Cody failed to return, he took a deep breath and stood, his weight heavy on his bones, the water sloshing over onto the floor. He parked himself on the rim of the tub and slung one leg over and then the other. Nearly fell standing up. He shuffled to the bathroom door and peered into the bedroom.

The door was closed. Light flickered under it. He squelched through the room, turned around, and tried the knob. Locked. On the other side Cody and Verny argued in low voices. Taka crossed to the window to peer through the gloom at the casing around the window. He could break the glass with his shoulder or possibly his back, but he didn't really want to risk bleeding to death if it broke wrong. There weren't paramedics standing by like on a raid.

The doorknob rattled. Taka spun, dropped onto the bed, and slumped over onto his side. Cody came and stood over him. He shoved at Taka's shoulder. Playing opossum, Taka closed his eyes all the way and let himself fall back onto the musty mattress. Cody huffed. He cracked a water open and dropped it on Taka's belly. It rolled off. After the door snicked shut behind him, Taka continued to lay still, mustering his energy to get up again. Now that he was lying flat, even though his weight rested on his aching arms, exhaustion overwhelmed him.

A BRIEF MOMENT of deja vu made Jimmy stand up, pushing his chair back until it hit something hard. Seated to one side behind him, Nina grumbled in irritation. "Sorry," Jimmy said. "You want coffee?"

"Cream, no sugar," Nina mumbled, without looking away from the monitor on the desk.

"I'll take black," Bill added.

On call, seething with adrenaline, the three of them had rushed to their unit room at BCI only to sit for the next two hours, scanning every bit of video footage Charleston PD patrol officers and Kanawha County deputies were dropping off to the State Police investigators down the hall coordinating the effort. Flash drives, security tapes, and emails from the field or DOT poured in as eighteen units canvassed the area immediately surrounding the murder scene at Copeland Bay. It would have been a big manpower case anyway, but the fact that cops were involved and one might still be in danger added an extra urgency.

Pouring coffee into three mugs, Jimmy hoped on the one hand that Taka was holed up in a no-tell motel drinking himself blind and on the other hoped he wasn't, because if he was, Taka was going to be third degree scalded by major hot water when he surfaced.

Rejoining his team, Jimmy's gaze was drawn to the movement of vehicles on the left-hand-side of the monitor. In the lower right hand corner, a door opened. A man came out of a store carrying two cups, walked towards the camera, and then dropped into a patio chair still in frame. "Hold that," Jimmy barked.

Bill swung his head around as Nina paused the film.

"Run it back. Watch the guy on the right. He look like Verny Fitch?"

"Who's Verny Fitch?" Bill asked as Nina stared at the man walking out and sitting down again.

"Yeah, bub, I think so," Nina said. He rewound again.

As the man handed the cup to someone out of frame and sat, Jimmy felt almost sure it was Verny.

"Who's Verny?

"He's so good at that," Nina muttered. "Damn chameleon."

Jimmy held out Bill's coffee and Bill took it, frowning up at him. He wasn't in on the Sanderson investigation, but Jimmy might be able to leverage more man hours out of BCI if they connected Fitch to Tracy Manner's death. "Verny Fitch works for the Sandersons," Jimmy told him.

"So?"

"He was next door when Detective Taka walked away," Nina said, leaning forward to snatch a pile of papers off the desk in front of the monitor.

"Seriously?"

Nina shuffled through the papers, which detailed the sources and locations of the footage. "Pretty sure."

Jimmy set the coffees on the desk. "Where was that footage taken from?"

"Edward's," Bill said. "Independent coffee shop on 119. Nearest coffee to the Manners house."

"Got it," Nina grumbled.

"What," Jimmy asked.

"The view from the jewelry shop next door shows the parking for Edward's." Nina typed the file number in, then hit play and fast forward when the window came up. A black Escalade pulled in and a big guy got out of the driver's side. Verny came around from the passenger side.

"You got the CPD canvass report from Timber Way?" Jimmy asked. He was certain an Escalade had been caught on camera in the vicinity of Andrea's house the evening of Taka's disappearance.

Nina typed.

The report was several pages long, but Jimmy had already read it. Leaning over the desk, he knocked Nina's hand off the mouse, ignoring her swipe back at him, and scrolled down to the list he needed. "There," he said, pointing. "Black Escalade. Plate obscured. Can you get facial recognition from this? Confirm it's Verny?"

"Yeah, no prob," Nina said.

"And find out who the big guy is. Bill, go pull the ballistics from the federal task force file on Dewey Sanderson. The unsolved homicide-arsons. Take copies to the lab yourself. Tell them when the bullets come from the ME on Manners, I want those comparisons first. High priority. Then get your ass straight back here."

"Got it, Boss."

"I DID AN investigation in Fivemile," Karie said.

Andrea pulled the headphones off. "You think he means Fivemile Road?" she asked, still staring at the audio waves bouncing across the laptop screen.

"Or the community."

"There's a community?" Fivemile was a hilly area northeast of Charleston proper. While not far overland, driving there by car on the winding two lane backroads took more time that you'd think. All she could remember were the steep hills all around and cracked concrete front steps of the few homes set on shaggy lots cut into the thick forest crowding the roads.

"Well, a township."

"Township doesn't equal community," she said, thinking out loud.

"One stoplight," Karie clarified. "And just one building for town business and voting, but yeah, it's not just a survey marker on the county map."

"But it's not a community."

"That's not the point."

"I'm processing," Andrea snapped.

"Okay, but we need to process faster," Karie said, standing up and taking the headphones from Andrea's hand. "The point is that something's burning out there."

Andrea paced to the sink and then back to the table. "Is he talking past or present?"

"Bruten's accident happened on I-64 here in Charleston, so he's not talking about that."

"Do you think Fitch is in Fivemile? Now?"

"I don't know, Andrea. This has never happened to me before."

"Maybe Jimmy can send somebody that way." She called his cell number, but it went straight to voicemail. Leave a message or not? "It's Andrea. I think Fitch is out in Fivemile or maybe set a fire in Fivemile. Please call me." Ending the call, she turned back to Karie. "What happens if we call it in?"

Karie shrugged. "They're going to ask for an address."

"I see smoke. I smell smoke. I don't know where exactly, but I'm in Fivemile. Will that work?" Would it be now? Had it already happened? Andrea wondered if she were just being overly-dramatic. Maybe she'd read too much fan fiction. Maybe she should stick to fiction and her job and leave the true-crime sleuthing to someone else. But if she did that, maybe Billie Mae would wake her every morning for the next ten years and Taka would just be gone.

She frowned, staring down at her keyboard as she packed her sudden fear and grief back down somewhere in her middle. She didn't know exactly where it went, only that the tight coil of it slithered and slinked into her core until it all but disappeared. It was there, but not. The first time she'd experienced the depth of her middle, she'd been seventeen and her mother was three months from dying. She thought about it little since then, but it was always there, as deep, as endless, as unknown as outer space. Infinity. The place she buried everything that got in the way of now. Right now.

And right now, she needed to know where Taka might be. If he might be burning, burnt, or about to be on fire in Fivemile, the stuff of his most vivid nightmares.

"I just don't know," Karie said. "We don't know the timeframe. Intelligent contact is rare."

Andrea looked at her tight face, the fear in her eyes.

"For you to have two—"

"I'm calling," Andrea decided. "Just in case."

"Okay."

Andrea held her phone up, her thumb poised over the keys. She had no idea how the Kanawha County cell towers were positioned, but she knew that at least seventy percent of 911 calls made from inside a building from a cell phone couldn't be located reliably. She closed her eyes on a wave of indecision. The image of Tracy Manners' burned-out car assaulted her. "Fuck it," she said, opening her eyes, and dialed 911.

"What's your emergency?"

"Fire."

"Your location?"

"Fivemile."

"Fivemile Road?"

"I don't know exactly," Andrea said. "I see smoke."

"From a building, ma'am?"

"No," she said, holding Karie's gaze. "I was driving and saw smoke."

"Could it be fog, ma'am?"

"It smelled like smoke."

"Can you see flames?"

"No, there's, um." She turned away, catching the blur of light reflected in the window like… "There's smoke obscuring the road."

"Can you give me a cross street, ma'am?

Andrea spun back around to Karie, her heart sinking.

"Ma'am?"

She mouthed "road name" at Karie. "Uh, I'm looking."

"Ma'am, my data is showing me a location for you in north Charleston, is that correct?"

Andrea closed her eyes. Was Fivemile part of larger Charleston?

"Ma'am? Can you tell me where you are?"

"Charleston."

"I'm triangulating your location, ma'am, and police are on their way to you. Can you give me a cross street? A building name? Anything that may help us find you?"

"I'm calling about a fire in Fivemile."

"Yes, ma'am. Can you still smell smoke?"

"No. There's a fire burning in Fivemile."

"It's okay, Andrea. I'm here with you. Can you stay on the line with me? Are you at 653 Double Branch Lane?"

Andrea threw her free hand up. "They're coming here," she said to Karie.

"Here?"

"Andrea? Is there someone there with you?"

"Yes."

"I've notified the officers. Are you safe?"

"Yes. It's just a friend."

She could hear the sirens now.

"Just stay with me, Andrea, help is on the way."

"I don't need help," she said. "I have knowledge of a fire out in Fivemile."

"All right, Andrea. We'll take care of that. What are you wearing?"

She frowned. What did that matter? "A blue sweater over jeans."

"Can you open the door and step outside?"

She hurried through the hall to open the door. A Charleston police officer with his hands on his gun stepped in, pulled her out, and whisked her to one side. "Are you alone?" he said, and then she recognized him as Corporal Mendel, the officer who knew about the phantom highway fires.

"No, my friend's inside."

"Is there anyone else inside?"

"No."

"What's her name?"

"Karie."

He nodded, frowning past her. A second officer she hadn't noticed sidled through the door from the other side, gun drawn. He disappeared inside.

Another car pulled onto the street, lights on, but sirens off.

"I'm so sorry," Andrea said. "I didn't mean for all this—" She waved her hands around.

"Are you okay?" Mendel asked, a sincere concern reflected in his eyes.

"I am. I had word that there might be a fire in Fivemile. It might involve Taka."

"I'll call off the troops and we'll talk inside."

"Fivemile's small, could you please get someone looking for smoke at least?"

He searched her face for a long moment before reaching for his radio mic. "Stay here," he said to her and then, "Dispatch," into his mic as he turned away to meet the incoming officers in the yard.

He kept his word, managing to calm the response and send his fellow officers back into the night a little curious, but perfectly willing to let Mendel and his partner handle the paperwork. His brows rose at the set up in the living room and his head swiveled as he peeked into her office even as he was calling out to his partner, in the kitchen with Karie.

Forty minutes after arrival, Mendel was sitting at the kitchen table with coffee in his hands while his partner sat in their cruiser transcribing his notes into an incident report. "You're going to have to make a court appearance. With three officers responding, I can't just make it disappear."

"I understand." She sat down next to Karie, warming her hands on her own cup. "I didn't know what to do. I was hoping 911 couldn't locate my cell phone."

"Some can get location within 300 yards. Kanawha can't, but they get the info on the nearest tower and obviously you aren't anywhere close to Fivemile, but you're close to the address associated with your cell number."

"I forgot that they could look up my number."

"We're going to pretend you haven't incriminated yourself repeatedly just now," Mendel said. "What's your lead? Is it reliable?"

"Well." Andrea's gaze strayed to the equipment set up next to them.

"When I lived in Atlanta, I had a lot of free time. I was a member of a paranormal investigation team. Are you fixin' to tell me a ghost tipped you off? 'Cause this looks suspiciously like an investigation. Does this have anything to do with the weird car fires?"

"How crazy do you think I am right now?"

"I've seen some weird shit, excuse my language. But only a handful wasn't explainable."

"How about fucking weird shit?" Karie said.

He grinned at her. "Hit me."

Karie handed him the headphones and played the EVP for him.

He listened with his eyes closed, head cocked to one side. "My uncle is a volunteer firefighter out in Fivemile. Let me give him a call."

TAKA WOKE CURLED on his side to utter darkness. Shifting in discomfort, the sharp bite of the cuffs reminded him why his hands were trapped behind him. Someone was snoring in the living room, a loud buzz-saw grind with a wheeze at the end. He wormed around, his lower arm dead from lying on it, and located the water bottle on a wet patch of mattress. It felt light, only half full, and water trickled over his hands as he turned it. Letting go of it, he rolled the other way and slid his legs off the bed to land on his knees on the floor.

He leaned forward on the mattress and grabbed the bottle's loosened cap between his teeth. When he tilted his head up, the water leaked into his mouth. Of course he choked on it two swallows in. He dropped the bottle, coughing, and then held his breath, waiting to see if he'd woken Cody, because he was reasonably sure Verny wouldn't be playing guard. The snoring continued unabated.

Cautiously, he stood up. Except for his hunger, a crunchy kind of headache, and the rub of his jeans on his irritated skin, he felt reasonably able. Experimentally, he swung his arms back. Sharp pains shot up them and into his shoulders. Gritting his teeth, Taka worked them a little and shrugged his shoulders several times. Once he could feel his fingers, he eased over to the door and quietly jiggled the handle again. Still locked.

JIMMY DISCONNECTED WITH Captain Maddox, his immediate superior, after waking him up at home to hammer out his current plan of action. On review, both men had agreed that Fitch's proximity to Detectives Manners and Taka and unconfirmed proximity to Zach Taylor, the kid who precipitated this tangled mess by beating Deborah Watkins to death in her dorm room, wasn't enough evidence of a common denominator to get a warrant for a real-time location search on Fitch's cell number, let alone a warrant to search his apartment or Susan Pepper's home.

The past-locations search Nina had pushed through on emergency gave them only expected numbers and locations, nothing in Fivemile to link to the "anonymous" tip he'd received and a quick, covert check showed no activity out that way.

So far no hard evidence tied his team's Sanderson investigation to Tracy Manners' murder or Taka's disappearance. None of them wanted to haul Dewey in and alert him to it by asking questions about his relationship with Fitch. "Bill, you got a plate on that Escalade, yet?"

"No, Boss, been back through the footage once and I'm going through again."

"Dewey's crew owns two," Nina added. "But that big guy with Fitch at the coffee shop is Cody Smith and he has one."

"The wannabe?"

"Yeah. Sanderson cousin. Works the door at the Coliseum during events. It's probably his at both the coffee shop and out on Double Branch Road."

"Which wouldn't link Dewey. I'll write up the report. I want locations on all three Escalades. And call over to Charleston PD. Ask Detective Chief Ronnie Horton if CPD interviewed Fitch for either Deborah Watkin's homicide or their shooting investigation. If we can nail a warrant down for the Manners investigation, we can tag along on the searches, see if there's anything that'll help us with Dewey."

"Should I call Scotty on his burner?" Nina asked. "Give him a heads-up on Fitch in case he shows up at the Coliseum?"

"No. If we need contact, Andy Detweiler's taking over surveillance at two am. But we're not risking our case over this if we can't connect Dewey to it. The feds are already nervous about Senator Sanderson's exposure. If it intersects, it intersects, but Scotty's cover isn't getting blown over it unless I'm arresting Dewey on murder charges."

Turning to his monitor, Jimmy tuned their voices out as they went back to work. After attaching the pertinent clips from the video footage, he summarized his conversation with Maddox and started proofing the completed reports on the reasons Fitch should be considered as, at the very least, a person of interest in the murder of Tracy Manners.

"Hey, Boss," Bill said. "CPD says no, they didn't interview Fitch. No one involved with either Deborah Watkins or Zach Taylor mentioned him in connection to Taylor. They'll make the rounds tomorrow and see if they can corroborate his presence."

"Damn. Plate?"

"Not gonna happen. Too obscured."

Jimmy finished up in minutes and emailed the report with all the necessary CCs attached to the State investigator in charge of the Manners case before immediately calling to lead him through it. The tall trooper who had met him at the scene on Corridor G what felt like days ago answered his call on the first ring.

His deep voice made Jimmy's belly loop over at the remembered stench of roasting Hummer and then again when he realized Andrea must have known Tracy Manners and probably knew she'd seen him burning by now. The image of smoke rising from what little remained of Bruten when he'd arrived at the scene on I-64 last year was seared into his brain.

"Hoyle? You there?"

Jimmy cleared his throat. "We might have a suspect off the security video," he said. "He's a security consult for Senator Sanderson. He may have been working for Dewey Sanderson and he may have been associated with Zach Taylor."

"That's a lot of maybes."

"His sister lives next door to the house from which Detective William Taka disappeared and he was having coffee on Corridor G shortly before the 911 call on Manners came in. Dewey told a Waltham-Young employee that he fired Fitch after Taylor's arrest. But it'll be she said-he said, so not useful." Winnowing it down to the facts, not willing to out Scotty as an inside confirmation, and omitting Andrea and Karie's crazy made that entire statement so thin that he almost hung up on himself.

"Was Fitch at his sister's when Taka disappeared?"

"We have him a couple of miles away on a cross street traffic cam later that evening."

Mark sighed. "Better than no lead at all, which is what we have right now. I'm meeting with representatives of all the agencies assisting us at Charleston PD in an hour, why don't you pick me up at Troop 4's barrack and brief me on the way."

CHAPTER THIRTY-FIVE

"ALL'S QUIET ON the Eastern front," Corporal Mendel said when he eventually returned to the kitchen. "But my uncle said he'd call if anything comes up in Fivemile."

"Thank you," Andrea said, standing up to meet him.

Mendel waved a hand at the computers and recorders spread across the kitchen table. "You get any more tips from the other side as to the timing of this supposed fire, let me know, okay?"

Andrea blinked away the sudden tears that stung her eyes.

"Hey, now," Mendel murmured, stepping next to her with one arm open, which he closed around her shoulders. "CPD's gonna find him. Just a matter of time."

She nodded. "Thank you. For everything."

He squeezed her and let go. "My partner's transmitting the report right now. It'll be available online tomorrow and you'll be notified of your court date next week. I'll see myself out." He nodded at Karie, who sketched a wave from her seat, and took himself off.

Andrea watched the moonlight-silvered tree branches in the backyard sway until the front door snicked closed. She should probably call Carson, ask what kind of trouble she was going to be in. Bobby Waltham probably wouldn't be happy with either her or the fact she had involved paranormal investigator as well. Where the fuck was Taka? Wrapping her arms around herself, she rubbed her arms.

"Thanks a lot, Bruten," she said out loud, startling a laugh out of Karie.

"It's still a phenomenal EVP," Karie said. "If it doesn't hold up, we may have to concede it's not an intelligent communication, but it'd be hard for anyone to claim it's a coincidence of random sound confluence. Of course, we can't prove it's not exactly that either. Such goes the study of the paranormal."

There were way too many words in that declaration. After a long moment in which Andrea could only think about the useless tour Jimmy took her on after they left Tracy burning, the blackberries bursting on her tongue while Taka was god knows where, she said, "I guess I'll get back to it."

Karie rubbed her eyes. "It's almost midnight, we should quit for tonight. I'm staying over, though."

Andrea sighed. Although her body felt worn, she didn't think she could sleep.

"A shower, two or three hours sleep," Karie coaxed. "Billie Mae shows up in the mornings, right? Maybe everybody'll be recharged with a little shut-eye."

What wouldn't Andrea give to be waking up in a few hours to Billie Mae's plaintive statement of "I drownded" and Taka warm beside her? Hot water sounded good. And everything she'd put out to her network needed time to connect, for people to find the info she'd requested. The rest, sorting through data, the info she'd dredge up on her own, would be there in a few hours. She nodded. "Okay."

IN A SECOND-FLOOR conference room at Charleston PD, Jimmy glanced down at his phone on the table as it vibrated. Jesus. Two-twenty am. Already.

Dewey ditched us

"Fuck," he said out loud.

Charleston PD's Detective Chief, Lieutenant Ronnie Horton, stopped talking. Jimmy looked up from Andy Detweiler's text to find himself the center of attention in the nine-member multi-jurisdictional meeting to coordinate activities and update information in the search for Tracy Manners' killer and William Taka's whereabouts and motivation for leaving.

Glancing at Mark's questioning expression, he picked up the phone as he stood. "I gotta step out. Different investigation."

Mark nodded his okay. Jimmy had remained largely silent, simply upping the quotient of State power in the room as a show of force to reassure the locals. He'd never worked with Lieutenant Horton before, but the man was organized and calm and Jimmy appreciated those traits. Everyone at CPD was gnashing their teeth, wanting to do something, but Horton had them in check so far. The last thing Charleston needed was another officer involved shooting because every LEO in town was hunting for a cop killer.

In the hall, he called Andy, his thoughts a whirl, all of them focused on Verny Fitch, courtesy of Andrea Kelley. "Tell me."

"Not much to tell. I came on at two at the house. Mathers handed Dewey to me at 2:18, but it was Scotty who got out of the back of the Escalade."

"You call him?"

"No," Andy said, his dismay at the question clear in his tone.

"Good," Jimmy said. Scotty would contact them as soon as he could. Undercover work sometimes meant you ended up colluding by accident. Nothing to be done about it if you wanted convictions that lasted. "Ideas?"

"We've been on Dewey six weeks, Jimmy. The only thing that's come up until now is this situation with the cop."

Jimmy blew his breath out through his teeth. All they had on Dewey regarding Taka was threats. Everything—everything— else, from his statutory rapes to questionable business deals to unsolved murders to all the tidbits in the federal task force files, added up to a whole lot of circumstance and not much fact, but you never knew who might be holding the key piece of info to tie it all together. Jimmy hoped it might be Fitch. "We have no idea what car Dewey's in?"

"None of his."

"Did Mathers actually see Dewey get in the Escalade?"

Silence on Andy's end was all the answer he needed.

"So we don't even know what time he left." He squeezed the phone in his hand hard enough to bruise his palm, but managed to avoid throwing it smack against the wall. "Leave someone on the club and someone on the house. I want you back at BCI. Pull up everything the task force has on the homicide-arsons we were trying to link to Dewey. Bill's already run a request over to the ballistics lab for comparison. Get him to help you correlate the info we have on Verny Fitch through both Sanderson investigations." There was one more idea Andrea had planted in his head that he wanted to follow up on. "And see what connections exist between the arson-homicide victims and Senator Sanderson."

"Seriously?"

"Yeah, Andy, you sound like Bill. Seriously. You work for Criminal Intelligence. Analysis is your fucking job," Jimmy half-yelled. "We've been casting around for two years now. There's something we're not seeing in all that paper we've generated." He spun on his heel and paced back down the hall.

"The senator does write Verny's paycheck," Andy allowed.

"Yeah," Jimmy breathed. "Tiptoe through it. I don't want the Feds getting upset. I'll call when I'm leaving CPD."

"SHUT THE FUCK up," Verny shouted.

Cody's snore cut off mid-breath as he yelped. "Damn it, Verny, that hurt."

Sitting across the bed with his back to the side wall of the cabin, Taka had been resting, but awake. He didn't bother opening his eyes.

"Get up and make some coffee."

The light came on under the bathroom door, staining the inside of Taka's eyelids with a red overlay. The TV erupted, disturbing the night silent bubble Taka had been almost enjoying. The babble of channels being rapidly changed resolved into a weather forecast he couldn't follow.

Eventually the scent of coffee seeped into his room. The men settled in the kitchen, their voices occasionally reaching him through the wall. Taka was staring out the window at the lighter-than-the-room night, not aware of doing so until headlights slashed across the trees it framed. The car's rumbling engine crunched closer on the gravel drive and then shut off. Doors opened and slammed. Voices rose in greeting and then fell off again before escalating.

"Are you fucking insane? I already have the state police on my back and Taka's girl came around last night blaming me for this." Dewey's voice. His enraged tone. "What the hell do you think I want with him?"

"He killed Zach."

"*You* killed Zach."

"The senator wanted him gone, he's gone. I did my job."

"What the fuck you talking about, Verny? "

"I'm talking about getting fired for doing my job!"

"I can't even..." All of Taka's concentration focused on the closed door in the dark, the sliver of light at the bottom flickering with shadows. He could practically see the scowl on Dewey's face, the outrage vibrating from him, the swing of his hand through the air. "Done is done. I need Trevor to make that clear to you?"

The gunshot that followed echoed in the small space. Taka shoved his shoulders back against the wall, shifting the bed away from it. Another shot boomed. He rolled-fell off the bed into the space he'd made. Panting open-mouthed through the pain it caused him, he crouched against the wall. A bullet punched through the bedroom door a millisecond before a third boom accompanied the shattering of the window and light punched through a hole in the room's front wall. Illuminated glass fragments showered onto the bed, the floor, and Taka.

Footsteps pounded through the outer room and out the front. A short exchange of shots outside followed, and then silence. Taka stood and listened. A muffled thump, not inside. He kicked the bed onto its side and darted around it to the bedroom door. The wood was too splintered around the fist-sized bullet hole for him to see anything through it. Standing to one side, he tilted his head near the frame where a vertical line of light shone through. Nothing. A chill skinned his damp back as he turned it to the door and tried the knob again.

He still wore his soggy boots. Mule-kicking his way through a door that opened towards him, even a cheap one, was still a long shot. And loud. The broken window might be a better bet.

Shards of sharp glass stuck up and poked down. Angling himself sideways, he fumbled his cold hands up his back and took a stab at knocking the nearest shard out with his bent elbow. It cracked, part of it falling away. The remainder sliced the underside of his forearm with a dull burning sensation. Probably a bad thing that it didn't hurt like hell. His blood was warm, at least. A scrabbling at the back wall. He ducked to the side as the first bullet entered the window, and tucked himself down as tight as possible. The gun barked again and again, holes appearing in the far wall with each muzzle flash. A man shouted, but with his hearing destroyed, Taka couldn't make out the words.

Liquid splashed onto the broken window and down the outside wall. The odor of gasoline bit the air and climbed into the room. Taka scrambled back to the door, praying the gunman had moved on, put his head down, and mule-kicked as hard as he could. The door shuddered. He aimed better and did it again. The frame cracked under each blow. On the fourth kick, it gave way, but Taka's boot stuck. Between the twisting door, shards of broken wood stabbing through his jeans, and his hands behind his back, he couldn't keep his balance.

He fell. His shoulder folded under his weight as his head smacked into the floor.

He lay stunned, unable to gather himself. A whoosh filled his deafened ears and a blast of heat from the explosive flame shriveled the hairs on his arms. He tugged his foot up and then kicked with both until the surrounding wood gave way. The bedroom door still lay in his way, blocking the opening. Rolling over on his side, Taka put the fire climbing the window frame to his back.

"Motherfuckers," Verny yelled from the front room. "Fuck you."

Black smoke rolled past Taka from the burning back wall in clouds, obscuring his view. Verny stood beyond the open front doorway, watching. He lit another book of matches and tossed it over the threshold into the cabin. Flames scorched along the trails of gasoline to light up the inside front wall and then the couch. A low whump thumped Taka's eardrums as the right side of the room went up.

Verny sent a line of bullets in through the door and Taka cringed, curling up tight as he could, sure it wasn't enough.

CHAPTER THIRTY-SIX

ABOVE THE CRACKLING hiss of the fire, an engine cranked over. The stifling heated air hurt Taka's lungs and cooked the heat into his skin and bones. He coughed, fighting the heaviness of his own body as his chest expanded against the dirt under him. Grass roasted under weeks of unrelenting sun pressed against his cheek. He knew this. He lifted his head.

Through watering eyes, Taka watched the flaming suicide flail in the gas station parking lot until the woman caught his attention by tugging on the sliding door of the mini-van. "Hey," the stranger lying in the ditch beside him said. Taka glanced over only to see his brother's familiar features. He lay on his back, his face turned towards Taka, his eyes closed. Wide, wet bandages exposed weeping burns from the fire that swept across the aircraft carrier's deck. Angry raw flesh covered his chest and belly, his groin, his thighs, circled his arms. Someone leaned over Taka, pressing hard into his shoulder. It hurt.

He tore his gaze from his burnt brother. Blood dripped off Dewey's blond bangs onto Taka's face and ran down his neck, leaving a cool trail on his skin. He watched Dewey's lips move. The fire roared inside his head.

He shook it.

Why was Dewey in the ditch?

"Get up," Dewey shouted right into his ear. He yanked on Taka's arm and Taka got a boot braced on the door frame and rolled onto his knees and forehead, then fought his way up to his feet.

He stumbled out over the door of his makeshift cell through the black, cinder-filled smoke. Snaking up under his feet, an electric cord sizzled and popped. Coughing, Dewey lumbered into him and fell.

"Dewey," Taka said, his voice muffled and strange, and then choked. Nose streaming, he coughed and tried to blink the smoke out of his eyes. Found the hard floor under his knees. He leaned over Dewey to yell in his face. "Fire! Get the fuck up!" Dewey lurched upward, smacking Taka in the face with his shoulder as he listed sideways. "Get up," Taka screamed, his jaw stretching tight.

Dewey rolled onto his hands and knees. An explosion in the flames across the room. Sparks hit Taka's back like a thousand needles sinking home. He jerked upright. The cuffs tore into his damaged wrists, the cotton padding his senses ripped away.

Dewey. Cabin. Fire.

Red embers sunk into the back of Dewey's jacket, the exposed skin of his neck.

Kitchen. Gas.

"Dewey," Taka screamed.

Head hanging, Dewey lifted a hand and found Taka's shoulder. Levering himself up, he struggled to his feet. A racking cough closed his fists. His nails dug through Taka's shirt into his skin as Dewey whined deep in his throat with the effort to quit. Sweat and blood ran down his face and dripped onto the floor. Reaching down, he wrapped both his hands around one of Taka's biceps, bracing himself against Taka's weight to help Taka stand again.

The cabin walls were fully engulfed in flames, but most of the flammables and sparse furniture hadn't caught yet. Taka heard the echo of an Army instructor's voice barking, flashover, flashover, flashover. He plowed through the room, dragging Dewey along as he clung to Taka's arm. Four steps from the snapping, ash blown night just visible through the flames, they stumbled over someone's legs.

Taka caught them both before they fell again. Cody lay face down, a big hole torn through his back. A mighty cough climbed Taka's throat. He made himself move. One step, and then another, until they ducked out through the fiery front doorway.

Every bit of fresh air trickling down into his lungs made Taka cough harder. Dewey beat at his shoulders and back as Taka tried to sink onto the flattened grass and rutted dirt where Trevor lay on his side, his eyes open.

Growling, Dewey kept him on his feet for several more yards towards the tree line before he finally let Taka go to his knees. Dewey leaned over, coughing and wheezing, until he gave up and wilted onto the ground. The fire talked, scolding and roaring, reaching into the cold, dark sky as it greedily devoured the dry hardwood of the cabin. The slight breeze drew the swirling smoke above their heads and over the tops of the trees.

Taka wondered if the flames would be visible from whatever road lay out front. To the back, there was only the cloaked landscape of a creek lying hard against mountainside. Snuffling, he shrugged his shoulders up and wiped his streaming eyes and wet face on each in turn.

Dewey patted at his pockets. "No cell," he coughed. "My fucking head is killing me."

"Trevor?"

Dewey careened up and forward to check. He came back empty handed and stood swaying.

"Sit down," Taka ground out between coughs.

Dewey did. They watched the fire burn. It ran off into the dew-soaked grass in one direction, then petered out. As long as the wind didn't shift too much or pick up, maybe the thing would just gut out on its own after the small cabin burned.

ANDREA WATCHED THE shadows on her ceiling for a while. Finally she rolled over to check the time. Four minutes after three. Too early for Billie Mae. She got up. Concentrating on the cold press of the hardwood on her soles, she walked to the window and looked out towards Susan Pepper's yard. Lights were on in the house. They reflected off a rippling surface peeking out from between the crepe myrtles and butterfly bushes and daylilies Billie Mae had stood in just beyond the four-board fence. The possible koi pond shown on the Goggle Earth map pinned to her corkboard at work. *What's that reflection?* Taka said again in her head.

Andrea's nose filled with the must of that first time they opened the ruined box of Billie Mae's case files. They'd been trading explosive sneezes and then she'd picked up Susan Pepper's statement and Taka said, I don't think we're in Kansas anymore. She thought about the pepper shaker standing alone on the table after Taka disappeared. She thought about the fact that Taka's flash drive contained more notes on attempts to collect Susan Pepper's background than anyone except Dr. Huntley.

Two. In the small amount of time she'd put in so far, Andrea had already found two unsolved child murders near addresses where Susan Pepper once lived. Both were strangulations. Both occurred during the time periods when Susan lived nearby. There was no evidence Susan was the pharmaceutical drug rep she claimed to be. How those two facts fit together, Andrea couldn't fathom, but she knew both to be true. How delusional was she to accuse a man of kidnap while suspecting him of murder and then to turn around and accuse his sister of the same?

The koi pond stole her attention again. She thought about the sound of running water. Shallow ponds like that lost water to evaporation. Small pre-formed ponds like that were filled using hoses. She loved to play in the hose as a kid. Stomping through the puddles it formed in the grass. Holding a hand over the end to spray water high into the air to make rainbows. Cold droplets on hot skin. Captive fish. She could see her little girl hands in the cool rippling water, the flash of white and gold darting away from her touch. A joyful hound dog leaping in past her, sending glittering water into the warm sky.

Lost in thought, Andrea pulled her robe on and shuffled down the stairs to check her internet fishing lines.

TAKA AND DEWEY moved further from the intense heat after something inside burst spectacularly and sent the flames shooting higher into the black sky. Taka worried about the scattered trees nearest the cabin catching fire, but they had only charred, the flames dying within minutes every time one caught. The overhead electrical line burned through and fell, throwing off fitful sparks every few moments.

A car rolling down the gravel drive broke Taka from his resigned zone-out. Dewey had tried unsuccessfully to break the cuffs. Taka's wrists were too abraded and Dewey's head hurt too bad to let him get the torque he needed to snap the weld. Blood kept running down into Dewey's eyes, annoying him.

"Hey, hard head," Taka said, kicking at Dewey's ankle. "Someone's coming. "

Verny had taken Dewey and Trevor's guns with him, along with their cell phones. He'd shot the tires and windows out of the BMW Dewey said he'd borrowed. The fire was no longer raging, but it hadn't laid down yet, either. There was nowhere to hide.

Dewey swiveled his head towards the noise and then squinted back at Taka before breaking the tense silence between them. "My family is my business, Taka. You owe me that."

"I don't owe you anything, Dewey," Taka bit back.

"I know I hurt you, asshole, but if you ever felt anything for me, let it go. You at least owe me that for Zach."

A forest service truck nosed into the clearing, blinding them in its high beams as it turned in their direction. The headlights dimmed and then died, leaving only the running lights, flashing red lights, and top spotlights on.

The driver eased out into the flickering light, the shadows crazy between the truck and the flames, a hand on the bulge of a gun. "Y'all okay?" a woman asked. "Can you stand for me?"

"No," Taka called back to her. "I'm Detective William Taka of Charleston PD. This is Dewey Sanderson, of Charleston. Guy near the house is dead."

"Can you raise your hands?"

A male voice from inside the truck threaded inaudibly between her words.

Taka nodded at Dewey and Dewey duly lifted his hands. "I can't, ma'am," Taka said.

"Are you injured?"

"Handcuffed. He's been shot in the head."

The woman conferred with her partner as he continued talking to what Taka could only hope was dispatch. She reached in and popped the headlights back on. Dewey growled, turning his head away and covered his face with his hands.

"Okay," she said. "Ambulance is on its way."

Her partner, white, rangy, and bearded, got out and came around the front of the hood, carrying a small tackle box. She walked forward and covered him as he approached them in the bright light. He glanced at Taka and then crouched near Dewey. "I'm Bryan," he said, opening the box. "My partner there is Mary."

After snapping on gloves, he asked Dewey to lower his hands and evaluated his pupils with a penlight. Liberating a stack of gauze from its paper wrapping, he swiped at the blood on Dewey's face, dropping the used gauze on the ground as he went until he found an entry wound. He applied pressure with one hand, his fingers spread over the top of Dewey's head while he used the other to search for the protrusion of flesh that marked the bullet's exit. "You're a very lucky man, Mr. Sanderson. Can you hold this?" Dewey pressed his fingers against the gauze while Bryan prepared a compression bandage and then carefully wrapped it around Dewey's head to cover both wounds.

In the far distance, air raid sirens wailed. It had been years since Taka had heard one. All across West Virginia, fire houses were staffed by volunteers and the air raid sirens called them in as needed. In many counties they were still more reliable than cell service.

"Detective?" Bryan said, turning to him. "Are you injured?"

"No. Just pissed."

Bryan laughed. "How'd the fire start?"

"My kidnapper splashed some gasoline on the place and threw lit matchbooks until it started burning."

"Good one. Kidnapper?"

"Yes."

"But you aren't injured?"

"My wrists are kinda torn up."

"What about your lungs? Breathe a lot of that smoke?"

Taka resisted the tickle in his throat just thinking about taking a deeper breath caused and said, "Better now."

"Your head?"

"It's better now."

"What was wrong with it before?"

"They drugged me with something, but I don't know what."

"Injectable?"

"Yeah."

All the while, Bryan had been checking Dewey's lungs, his pulse, his blood pressure. Now he scooted over and shifted his ministrations to Taka. After listening to Taka's chest, he pulled him forward a bit and shone his penlight down his back to look at his wrists. "Ow," he said. "You know what they hit you with?"

Taka shrugged.

"Hey, Bryan," Mary said, walking over to join them, her gun holstered. "We've got confirmation that Detective Taka was officially reported missing yesterday morning. His department's being notified he's here."

"Get the bolt cutters," Bryan said.

Mary returned to the truck and opened one of the side compartments, plucking the cutters off their hanger, while Bryan went to confirm Trevor's death. Murder. Whatever.

"Hey," Bryan called. "I'm guessing the perpetrator left here in an SUV of some sort."

"Cody Smith's Escalade," Dewey muttered. "Black. 2008."

"Smith the suspect?" Mary asked.

Taka shook his head. "That would be Verny Fitch. Oliver Fitch. He's supposed to meet his sister at his place at four a.m. but I don't know where he lives. She's Susan Pepper, Double Branch Lane in Charleston."

"I'll call it in, Bryan." She set the cutters down by Taka's thigh.

Oh, well. His arms and butt were numb, anyway.

Bryan came back. Something in the house cracked with a groan and hiss. They all jumped, watching the flames for a minute before Bryan asked, "What's dead guy's name? He with you or the bad guy?"

"Trevor Parsons," Dewey said, his voice a little stronger. "He's my bodyguard. Was. Shit. And Cody Smith is still inside the house."

"Who is he?"

"My dumb fucking cousin."

"Was he also shot?"

"Yes."

"Are you Senator Sanderson's son?"

"I am."

Bryan looked at Taka. "And you're the cop that shot that diabetic kid in Charleston?"

Taka sighed and nodded.

"I thought I recognized your name. Do you know each other or were you both kidnapped?"

Taka glanced sideways at Dewey. He knew what he'd heard, but did Verny really lure Dewey here in order to give Taka to him as a gift? Or had Verny intended to kill them both all along? Why kill Dewey?

"I didn't have anything to do with it," Dewey growled. "The asshole got me here on false pretenses."

"The asshole?" Bryan asked.

"Verny Fitch."

"And how do you know him."

"He was on my security team. I fired him last week."

"He took me hoping to get his job back," Taka croaked, his throat closing, which set him off coughing again, pain shooting through his arms.

Both Dewey and Bryan ignored him, Bryan talking to Dewey instead. "Did you know Detective Taka before today?"

Dewey nodded.

"Do you know the reason why Detective Taka was kidnapped?"

Dewey shook his head.

Taka didn't like this guy overstepping his legal bounds, but he didn't want to get into dicey territory with him right now. Or open his mouth about Zach Taylor without a lot of thought about it first.

"Okay, then," Bryan said. "Detective Taka, can I help you stand?"

Mentally congratulating the guy on knowing when to shut the fuck up, Taka said, "If you'll cut these fucking cuffs off now."

Bryan just reached down and hauled him up.

The painful motion made him dizzy and he started to cough. Bryan steadied him.

When he calmed, Bryan said, "Why are you wet?"

"Verny tried to drown me." Which wasn't strictly true, since if Verny had wanted to drown him, Taka couldn't have stopped him.

"Hey, Mary? Could you call in a second ambulance, please? And bring me the O$_2$ tank."

Holding onto his left arm, Bryan led him to the far end of the service truck and sat him down again in the dimmer light. "Sorry, Detective. I could tell that line of questioning wasn't going anywhere and I don't want to run afoul of CPD, so I'm not going to ask him anything else."

"You're a fire investigator?"

"I am, with the Fire Marshall's Office. And a supervisor with the Division of Forestry. Just putting in some volunteer overtime, brushing up on what our people in the field are facing these days. I've heard things. Did Mr. Sanderson have a role in your kidnapping?"

"Can you cut these off?"

"How long you been restrained this way?"

Taka shrugged. "Since yesterday?"

"Yeah. You're not going to be talking after I do that." Scowling, he shifted his attention to Taka's arm. "Did Sanderson play a role in your kidnapping?"

There were fire sirens winding along the road towards them, throbbing over the cabin's death throes and Dewey's soft words with Mary and the dullness of Taka's fatigue. "I don't know," he said. "I don't think so."

"You know him? Besides from tonight?"

A hot brand of pain flared across Taka's upper left arm under Bryan's fingers and stole his breath.

"Sorry," Bryan said, digging in a little deeper.

Taka breathed in through his nose, intending to blow it out through his mouth, but the deeper breath got him coughing. He coughed until he choked, his eyes tearing. Breathing shallow on small sips of air, he blinked blearily at Bryan, who promptly fitted a mask attached to an O_2 tank over his mouth and nose. He tried not to suck the sweet, moist air in too deep while he concentrated on killing the urge to cough again.

"To add insult to injury, Detective," Bryan said lightly, "I do believe that's a bullet hole in your arm." He held up the long-handled cutters. "Ready?"

CHAPTER THIRTY-SEVEN

JIMMY COLLARED RONNIE Horton as the meeting broke up. "Could I talk to you, privately?"

"My office?"

Papers were stacked on top of the dingy grey metal filing cabinets filling one wall of the cramped office and on the only chair besides the one Horton occupied. Jimmy leaned on the doorframe. "It's no secret that the Attorney General's been after Dewey Sanderson for a long while now. Charleston PD has had their fingers in as many Sanderson pies as the state. I know y'all have kept us apprised over the years of CPD's own interests in him, but I need a favor, and I want it kept between us."

"Us?"

"As in the two of us. You and me."

"Tell me first."

Smart man. Jimmy knew he liked him in the meeting. He waited until two officers passed in the hall before he spoke again. "Off the record, I'm building a timeline. I don't want to draw too much attention accessing local records through the state. I need when and why CPD has looked at Dewey locally and then anything CPD might have on why and when and where that path crosses with his daddy's."

The open expression on Horton's face faded into contemplation, his gaze shifting to the packed cabinets. "How far back are you thinking?"

"Three years should make a start."

Horton nodded. "By myself, it'll take a couple of weeks."

"Yeah," Jimmy said, aware that Mark and three or four others were now in the hall as the stragglers left the meeting room. "You got my number." Jimmy glanced at his watch, wondering if sleep would be an option in the next few hours. Four hours until his Thursday morning meeting at eight.

"Jimmy!"

Jimmy turned to take in Mark's excitement as Horton's phone rang. "They got him! Detective Taka! He's—"

"Fivemile?" Horton said into his receiver

"Out in Fivemile," Mark finished.

A HACKER FRIEND located a receipt for mini-storage in Susan Pepper's name in Arlington. Andrea screen captured it. After typing a quick email reply of thanks, she delved back into her search for any proof that Susan had a legal job of any sort. Headlights flashed across her windows as a car drove by towards the road. Had to be Susan Pepper. Andrea clicked over to her tracker window and watched her turn left out of the cul-de-sac. Swapping views, she saw that Jimmy was also on the move, headed east out of Charleston on I-64.

All her alarms going off at once, she sat straight up. Reducing the size of the window, she arranged the maps on her monitor so she could watch both vehicles at once. Within minutes Susan looped around and parked in the lot of the Foodland at Timber Way and Summit. Jimmy turned north on 73 and seemed to be headed directly for Fivemile. Andrea jumped up, burning with curiosity over both drivers' actions at oh dark thirty, but if Jimmy was headed to Fivemile, so was she.

She ran upstairs and pulled on yesterday's jeans, tucked her holster and sig in place, jerked a fresh henley over her head, and snagged a jacket before hitting the bathroom to throw cold water on her face and tired eyes. Burrito-ed in the blankets of the guest bed, Karie wasn't awake when Andrea cracked the bedroom door open and Andrea decided to leave her to it.

Downstairs, she scribbled a note to Karie, snatched her keys and purse from the hall table, and bolted through the dark kitchen to the garage. Scrambling into the FX, she ignored the biting pre-dawn cold, cranked the little car up, and backed it down the drive.

As she rolled up to the stop sign, a CPD cruiser slowed down on Timber Way and turned onto her street. She watched the rearview for a moment, wondering if they might be coming for her, but the car went past her drive and slowed along the curve of the cul-de-sac. Patrol, then, no doubt stepped up in response to Taka's disappearance and her misguided 911 call.

Minutes later, as Andrea whipped past the first entrance to the Foodland on the way to the highway, she couldn't resist slowing down and craning her head around to see if she could catch sight of Susan's white sedan. It was parked in the rear third of the lot, away from the nearest light, but close to the road. A black Escalade trundled across the lot on a direct collision course with the sedan. The FX shimmied over a lane reflector and Andrea snapped her attention back to the road. Damn. What if the Escalade was her brother's? There'd been one parked at Susan's house when she went knocking on the door two days ago.

She remembered Billie Mae standing in the daylilies, staring at the back of the house as she waited for Susan to return with Verny's number. An undercurrent of both threat and amusement had tinted Verny Fitch's voice when she spoke to him. Could Taka have been at Susan Pepper's house all along? Might he be there still? Andrea slowed down further, and pulled into the dark One Stop gas station half a mile down the road.

Could she lie to Jimmy if she called him at this time of night to ask him what he was doing, while pretending she didn't know he was on his way to Fivemile? Instead, she called Corporal Mendel to ask if his firefighting Uncle from Fivemile had been in touch. It rang several times and went to voicemail. Taking a deep breath, she texted Jimmy. *You awake?*

Tapping her fingers on the steering wheel, Andrea studied the desolate station. The lights on the pumps were on, although the store was closed. A pick-up truck approached on the road, followed by another CPD cruiser, their headlights blinding her for a few seconds as they passed. Her phone beeped.

Working

She bit her lip. *Anything?*

She launched the app for the tracker. He was on Fivemile Road, still driving.

No

Still driving. And texting.

She didn't want to be responsible for his death, so she didn't reply. Susan's sedan remained stationary at the Foodland. If she was there, no one was at her house. If Jimmy was checking Fivemile, Andrea could soothe the knot in her stomach telling her Taka might be right next door and right now, no one was home.

She threw her phone onto the passenger seat and pulled back out onto the road, heading for home. In the Foodland parking lot, Susan and a dark-haired man stood on either side of Susan's car. Andrea didn't want to draw their attention by slowing down too much, but they seemed intensely focused on one another. Leaning forward, Susan raised both her hands in the air, her body taut with anger. Head bowed, rigid under her verbal onslaught, the man had both his hands planted on the sedan's hood. Headlights tipped over the hill in front of her, forcing Andrea to concentrate on her driving.

"HEY, BUDDY. TAKA? You with me?"

The words hung in the air, heavy purple sacs, like raindrops just on the edge of bursting. They beckoned, daring him to touch, but he just didn't care. He was finally warm.

"Hey, buddy, can you open your eyes?"

"My eyes are open," he muttered, conscious of the skin on his forehead drawing down in stinging wrinkles, the distorted muffle of his voice. One of the raindrops trickled across his temple and into his ear. He shook his head.

"Whoa, whoa there. Don't—"

Taka surged up, blinking. Hands shoved at his shoulders, two blurry faces rushing down at him too fast. He shied away, his stomach rolling, and the ground thumped into him. A hand caught the back of his head and eased it down. The ground was soft and... not flat.

"Wait, just chill. It's Bryan, remember me?"

And yeah, ok. Fire guy Bryan. Taka nodded. The slight motion sent him spinning and he closed his eyes again.

"Open your eyes, Detective," a sharp voice barked.

He did. Lights flashed crazy across everything, red and blue, white light too bright, men yelling, the steady roar of water, and still the heat of the flames, now meeting the heat rolling off him. "Are you allergic to morphine, detective?"

Taka shook his head.

"Never had a reaction?"

Mouth too dry, Taka fumbled the words. Bryan reached down, lifted the oxygen mask Taka hadn't noticed, and leaned closer. "Makes me hot. Nauseous. Awake."

"Of course it does," Bryan said, smiling, and fitted the mask back over Taka's nose and mouth. "You can't be average."

Taka squinted up at him, confused by the man's obvious amusement.

The sharp voice said, "I've got it," as he injected something into the IV line inserted just below Taka's elbow, above his bandaged wrists. When did that happen? The light show caught his attention and he watched the colored rays strobe the smoke above him for an indeterminate amount of time.

"Nausea better?" Bryan asked

"Yeah." He was propped on a gurney. He pulled the mask down, letting it rest against his neck, the flow of oxygen brushing his overly sensitive skin. "What happened?"

"Circulation happened," Bryan said, dryly. "You were cuffed a long time. We were loading you when you decided to come around all the way. Nearly took the gurney over. Ready?"

Only then becoming aware of all the motion around him, Taka turned his head towards the only still thing, the man standing by his left shoulder. "Where the hell have you been?" he said to Jimmy.

"Fuck you, Taka," Jimmy said, still looking at his phone. He lifted it to his ear as he said, "We thought you ditched us."

"Let me up," Taka growled, plucking at the strap over his chest.

"Nuh-huh," Bryan said, shaking the bag of fluids he was holding up in one hand. "You're going to the hospital."

"I'm fine."

"You're not. You're half-drowned, you have first-degree burns, and you've been shot. The smoke inhalation and unknown needle stick are bonuses."

Taka stopped scrabbling at the buckle he couldn't quite lever open and considered. He was sore and his chest ached when he breathed in too deep, but no, he was good. "This guy, Fitch, his sister..."

"I know," Jimmy said, pocketing his phone without having spoken to anyone. He moved to help Taka free himself. "They aren't at Fitch's or Susan Pepper's. There's units moving on the airport right now, but no one has eyes on them, yet."

Bryan slapped his free hand down on theirs.

Taka looked up at him. "He threatened Andrea."

"Your girl?"

Taka set his jaw.

"His friend," Jimmy said. "My friend, too."

Although confused by the statement, Taka knew better than to question it. He continued to glare at Bryan. Bryan rolled his eyes and lifted his hand. "Your funeral."

"Like I never heard that before," Taka snapped, tugging at the chest strap while Jimmy moved on to the one across his thighs.

"Hey," the sharp-voiced EMT said, making a reappearance, another liter of fluids in his hands to replace the nearly empty one Bryan still held aloft.

"You're not winning this one," Bryan told him. "Just tape that port in for the inevitable collapse and let him go. I've got your back. Refused medical, didn't stay for you to yank it, yada, yada."

The EMT grimaced, his lip lifting. "Delayed drowning. That's you, Detective. You start getting short of breath or light-headed, clammy, you got minutes, not hours." He nodded over at Jimmy. "Seriously. He starts that shallow breathing shit again and turns grey, call 911."

THE CRUISER WAS gone and the street dark. Andrea opened her mudroom door and paused to see if she'd woken Karie with her activity. The cooling tick of the FX's engine echoed off the tile. It had never seemed so loud before as it did now, bouncing off the deep silence in the darkened house. She lifted the Maglite from its nook and eased the door closed again. Standing just inside the deeper shadow of the carport, she checked the street. Nothing moved. Remembering Taka' advice for illicit entry, she strode out onto her drive, crossed the grass between her house and Susan's and let herself into Susan's backyard through the side gate as if she belonged there.

JIMMY SET HIS phone back into its cradle on the Impala's dashboard. "Morphine really doesn't work on you?" he said, as they hurtled along the cavern-dark two lane through the tunnel of their headlights.

Taka wasn't pain-free, but nothing was screaming. He knew morphine knocked most people on their ass, but it only left him awake and irritated. "Takes the edge off."

"That GSW doesn't hurt?"

Not so much without the edge. It had to have been a ricochet. "Bullet's not that deep. I'm sure Bryan just didn't have the right tool to pop it out."

"You know who Bryan is?"

Taka couldn't decide if that might be a trick question of some sort. Should he know who Bryan was? "Fire investigator?"

"The uncle of a fan of yours."

"Who?"

Jimmy glanced over. "Patrolman Chris Mendel."

It took a minute to place the name, but Taka did. "And?"

"Andrea made a false 911 call, trying to report a fire out here."

Maybe he wasn't as awake as he thought he was. "Where are we?"

Jimmy's eyebrows rose and then he grinned and Taka knew then that Jimmy had been stringing him along, making him work his brain, keeping him from zoning out. "Fivemile."

Shit. He'd lived in Fivemile when he first moved to Charleston. He wasn't as far out in the boonies as he'd thought when he lay shivering on the bedroom floor. "Verny Fitch is meeting his sister at his apartment at four. They're flying out at six."

"It's five-fifteen."

"Fuck. Wait. Where are we going?"

Jimmy thumbed his phone and then waited. His face never changed as he talked in monosyllables and grunts. He disconnected. "Patrol's saying residences are quiet. Smart bet's at the airport. On the other hand, neither the Escalade's tag or Susan Pepper's tag has registered on a plate reader anywhere."

"I gotta call Andrea."

"I have been, ever since I saw you weren't dead. No answer."

CHAPTER THIRTY-EIGHT

ANDREA HELD HER flashlight against her thigh, reluctant to turn it on between the twin worries of a neighbor noticing and the loss of her night vision if she did. Halfway down the fence line to her left, she saw the rounded concrete edges of the koi pond. Stirred by the stiffening breeze, its water reflected dim glimmers of light through the flowers and low shrubs crowding its edges. She hugged the wall of the house, pausing at each of the two windows on that side to listen for any noise within. Her throat ached with the need to call Taka's name, however softly. Instead, she tapped twice, something Taka had done as a teen, tapping on her window so as not to disturb her mother.

At the corner she peered across the wide expanse of the back yard, awash in the impenetrable shifting shadows of the rustling trees. An owl hooted just above her and she startled hard, her heart surging into her tight throat. Straining to hear anything other than the expected, despite the cold wind filling her ears. Steeling herself, she crept around the corner and sidestepped to a short, recessed door set into the back wall of the house that could only lead into a half-basement. She tapped on the door. A resounding thunk answered her. Andrea's stressed heart skipped a beat, her breath catching.

Scrabbling at the door, her fingers refusing for a long minute to work, she finally found the long bolt slid vertically through a simple eye-hook. She lifted it and let it drop on its string as she swung the door open towards her. Something light colored moved away from her, disappearing into the unrelieved dark. Too big to be an opossum, too small to be a person.

She squinted, trying to see anything. "Taka?" she whispered.

Another thump echoed from her left. She patted her back pocket, feeling for her phone and its dimmer-than-the-Maglite screen, but then remembered throwing it onto the seat in her car. "Taka?"

Thump.

Sweating, her pulse pounding, Andrea pressed the flashlight on, as she covered it with her other hand. Spreading her fingers to allow a sliver of light, she swept it along the ground and up to the left, revealing a tool bench with two rows of deep drawers tucked below a butcher-block counter. A scream rose in Andrea's throat as something inhuman rose from the dirt in front of it. It lifted its head. Streaming strands of light solidified into a mud-caked curtain of blond hair even as the shroud it wore became a torn and filthy yellow shirt and ragged denim shorts. Billie Mae turned her dirty face up to glare at Andrea, blue eyes flashing in the light. The red gash across her throat gaped raw and wet. She looked back at the bench and then kicked at the footboard that ran across its entire length.

Thump.

She drew her leg back to kick again, but all of her expanded at once instead, into a Billie Mae fog that sent a cool caress over Andrea's heated skin before it fully dissipated. Andrea shuddered, swallowing her foundered scream before it rose above a whine, though she choked on it, having to blink back tears until she won the fight against her own body. Forcing herself to the bench step by step, now with a deep certainty that Taka was not here, Andrea willed her inner self to silence, focusing only on the task before her. She crouched before the fourth drawer on the bottom and set her Maglite on the damp earth to illuminate it.

Wooden and old, the drawer resisted opening. Andrea tugged hard on the handle a second and third time before the drawer began to move on its swollen rails. Halfway open, it stuck again. She lifted the flashlight to look at its contents. New and broken spray handles, o-rings, pieces of spliced hose, connectors to attach hoses together and more to attach and remove implements. Underneath the sprawl of small parts, a round yellow sprinkler. Rocking the drawer with both hands, Andrea pulled it completely free of the bench and set it aside. Shining the light into the space left behind, she saw the unmistakable dull shine of an opaque plastic box.

Lights flashed across the basement door. Andrea froze. Vehicles. The deep rumble of a truck. Hands shaking, she drew the wide, shallow box out and popped the catch as the car idled and the truck pulled into the drive. The light found a tumble of small treasures. A butterfly barrette. A plastic friendship bracelet. Two pennies. A quartz rock. A pink headband. A small purple sock. She lifted the sock to see what else lay beneath it. A smooth stone. Perfect for skipping, her brain supplied. A rosary. A decoder ring. A woven leather bracelet. A ceramic heart on a silver chain. She closed her eyes to the rest. The truck maneuvered into the carport and shut off. Doors slammed, one behind the other. Andrea closed the box to the unmistakable sounds of the house being entered.

Which had been Billie Mae's? Her shoe had been the only item reported missing, but Andrea knew one of the things in this box belonged to her. It seemed when she drew in her next breath that she drew resolve in with it. Her muscles tightened. For the first time away from her computer since Taka disappeared, she felt completely focused. Ears attuned to the creaks and small noises of movement above her, Andrea replaced the box and then shoved and rocked the drawer closed.

Moving with confidence, she doused her light and slid back into the dark and around the same corner of the house. One step at a time, aware of every leaf crackle under her boots, she eased to the side gate, only to flatten herself against the house when the front door opened and footsteps hit the front porch.

The door closed. A murmur of voices floated to her over the click of the door's lock. She wanted to assume it was Susan Pepper and Verny Fitch, but resisted as her inner voice insisted she wait.

Wait.

And see, that voice said. When had her cautious inner voice started to sound like Taka?

Wait.

Only one set of footsteps clacked away on the concrete sidewalk, but under those, a soft thunk from the back of the house. Trapped between the two, Andrea shifted over into the corner of space formed by the front fence and the house. A man walked fast across the back yard, away from her, past the koi pond, clothes rustling. Listening hard as she watched, she tracked the clacking footsteps down Susan's paved drive, out onto the street, past her location. The man—Fitch, her brain supplied—kept going, deep into the dark of the back corner closest to her house, trailing the odor of wood smoke behind him. Had he been out at a fire in Fivemile? Was Jimmy still there?

Andrea found her gun in her hands. Calming her whirl of thoughts, she dug for the resolve and focus she'd found in the basement and discovered it right there, waiting for her. Wait, she reminded herself. The loud footsteps turned up her own drive.

Silence.

Wait.

Knocking from across the yard, at her front door. Silence. The owl.

The porch lights jumped on.

Andrea held her breath, hoping Karie wouldn't hit the switch for the corner floods and eliminate Andrea's plan to steal across her own yard until she knew what was going on.

She didn't hear the door open, but then Karie's voice broke the pre-dawn hush. Andrea couldn't hear the words exchanged, only the tone. Susan Pepper's soft courteous drawl, speaking to Karie in a rush,

Karie's solicitous reply. The door shutting. Andrea sucked in a couple of deep breaths, gathering herself, and then opened the side gate, wincing now at the slight whine of the hinges. She left it open.

Where had Fitch gone? Crouching by the fence, Andrea scanned her side yard, the recesses of her carport, for any movement, any shadow out of place. She didn't startle when the owl lit off again, but Fitch did, revealing his location outside her mudroom door.

TAKA REACHED FORWARD and punched the dash compartment release with his index finger.

"You think I'm stupid?" Jimmy drawled.

When Taka glanced at him, Jimmy was watching him.

"Road?" Taka said, but Jimmy took another half a second to return his gaze to the highway.

"Under the seat. Got a Bellini scattergun in the trunk."

Pain flared through Taka's arms and torso as he bent to retrieve the pistol. The sleeve of the black hoodie one of the volunteer responders had given him rode up his arm. His fingers found only a rough plastic box. "Seriously?"

Jimmy shrugged. "Technically, I shouldn't need more than the one on my hip."

"What about the one at your ankle?"

Jimmy smirked without looking away from the road as he sailed past a Cumberland semi doing at least fifteen over the limit. "If Verny has a way out of town, why wouldn't he take it? Why go to your girlfriend's house?"

"She's not... He probably thinks he killed us all and no one's going to be on to him this fast. And Andrea called him, questioned him about a little girl who died in her house."

"The ghost. You think he killed her?"

Although it surprised Taka that Andrea had confided in a state cop, the bite of jealousy Jimmy's easy reply caused dismayed him. Tamping it back down, he tried to recall the conversation he'd heard in the bathroom. "Or his sister did."

"And you know this how?"

"The dog bit her. Verny bashed its skull in." He knew they could prove it, given time. There'd be medical records. They had Kenny. Even if they couldn't prove the murder, Carson could spin it circumstantially, there'd be follow-up. There might be more evidence if they could execute warrants.

Jimmy snapped his fingers. "Hey, stay with me here," he said, his tone harsh.

Taka nodded.

"So what if the dog bit her?"

"Verny told me. It was the same day. The same morning Billie Mae died. The dog was outside with her. Kenny buried it after everyone left."

"And Kenny is?"

"The landlord."

"3692," Jimmy said, reaching out to flick on his emergency lights.

Taka keyed in the combination and raised the lid to reveal a compact black 9mm. Lifting it out, he dropped the magazine, which was full, and then slammed it back home and racked a bullet into the chamber. After taking the second full magazine from the box, he replaced it under the seat with a grunt and settled back to breathe for a few minutes. Closing his eyes to the annoying flash of the streetlights and the Impala's throbbing blue light, he soothed his nerves by letting his fingers run the lines of the gun and Jimmy's voice become background noise as he requested back-up.

CHAPTER THIRTY-NINE

"I DROWNDED," BILLIE Mae whispered.

Andrea nearly dropped her gun. She ducked her head, wondering how many adrenaline dumps her heart could take. She blew her shallow breath out, looked up, and whispered back, "I know. Liked the koi pond, did you?"

Lit up by her own unearthly glow, which made her white nightgown and blue, blue eyes luminescent, Billie Mae gave her a brilliant grin and blipped away with a sassy swing of her shiny blond tresses.

The mudroom door swung open, tossing light over Verny Fitch as he jumped away from it. Susan's silhouette filled the doorway. "I know you're out there, Andrea," she hissed. "I'm going to hurt this girl if you don't come in here right now. And if the cops show up, she's dead. Get in here, you loser," she said to her brother, jerking on his arm. They retreated inside, but left the door open.

Wait.

Karie cried out, not loud enough to wake the neighbors, but across the street, the McMullin's beagle barked before Andrea had time to react. Andrea stood, but stayed low. It barked again. A stir of air made her duck further as the owl glided over her, wings outstretched, silent. Huge. It swooped out across her yard and lost itself in the dark beyond. The dog barked a rapid-fire warning of territory. Andrea darted forward. The McMullins' floodlights came on. She tucked herself into the shadow of her carport roof overhang. Torn between wanting Brad McMullin's help and the belief that Karie would pay the price if she revealed herself, Andrea wanted to scream. She clamped down on the impulse.

A low voice. The dog quieted. The lights went off.

If Andrea could sneak around to the back, she could assess the situation. It made sense that Karie would be in the kitchen. If the siblings were separated, maybe she could take one out. Her stomach rolled lopsided at the thought of actually aiming her gun at a real person. Karie yelped and then squealed, a sound cut off just as it started.

Andrea moved, trotting along the overhang to the back yard. Stopping, she peeked out to make sure Fitch hadn't come back out and then ran towards the location of the kitchen. Her boots sank in the soft dirt packed around the new blackberry bushes, her ankle giving, but she caught herself, bolted past the open back door and fetched up against the siding under the window.

Fitch stepped outside, swinging his head to look all around the back yard. Andrea held her harsh breath, her dry throat burning. He peered at the swaying trees, his hair lifting in the sharp breeze, his clothes still bleeding the scent of smoke and sharp tang of spilled gasoline.

Andrea clenched her jaw shut, grinding her teeth together. What had he done to Taka?

Making a disgusted noise deep in his throat, he turned away from Andrea and went back inside.

"She's not out there," he growled.

"This one here says she is. Her car is here. His car is here. This one's car is here. Because of you even that fucking filthy car of Cody's is here. Backed into my carport. Where else would she be?"

Karie screamed, a little louder this time. One of them choked off her following cries amid the sounds of a scuffle. "You lying?" Susan Pepper asked. Her voice sounded so completely different from Andrea's friendly, if nervous neighbor, that Andrea wondered if she'd made a mistake.

She popped her head above the windowsill in time to see Susan's hand swing back, the kitchen camera and tripod tip over and skid across the floor, Karie's bloodied cheek, her hands bound behind her, the glimmer of a knife in Susan's hand. No mistake. Breathing hard as she knelt back to the ground, Andrea ran through her options.

Storm the house, fire at anything—*anyone*—that moved. Get to her car undetected to call 911—*again*—and deal with Karie's death if they sent cars in loud. Call Mendel. Call Jimmy. Too far away, both of them.

Storming the house. Check.

She inched towards the door.

The familiar click of the front door deadbolt unlocking echoed through the momentary lapse of voices from inside the house. Only Taka knew where to find the spare key. Relief made Andrea's arms weaken for just a moment before Jimmy shouted from the mudroom, "State police! Drop your weapon! Drop your weapon!"

Steeling herself, Andrea ducked through the open back door and hunkered down against the end cabinet as Jimmy rushed the kitchen. Shoulders rounded in a half-crouch, Taka crept forward through the front hall, a pistol raised in both hands in front of him. His back to her, Fitch was holding his own gun in his right hand, down along his thigh, and lifted it towards Taka with casual grace.

"Stop!" Susan yelled. Karie screamed, curdling Andrea's gut. Jimmy froze. Glaring at him, Susan pressed the tip of her knife further into Karie's chest and then jerked it sideways. Blood rose, staining Karie's breast. "I'll kill her!"

Taka halted on the kitchen threshold with his gun leveled center mass on Fitch and Fitch's gun leveled at him. Jimmy stood a few feet to Fitch's left, the barrel of his gun aimed at the man's head. Susan laughed. Jimmy was in a no win position, with Karie sitting too close to his line of fire on the far side of Fitch.

"State police," Jimmy barked again. "Drop your weapons."

Sobs hitching ragged in her throat as she panted, Karie lifted her head and met Andrea's gaze. Near the ground, gun at the low ready, hidden from Fitch and Susan, but in full view of Taka and Jimmy, Andrea shook her head ever so slightly. Karie dropped her gaze, her chest heaving, blood spreading across the thin cotton of her tee shirt.

"Step back. Lower your weapon," Jimmy demanded, shifting his aim onto Susan Pepper.

Susan leaned forward, yanked Karie's head back by her hair, and pressed the knife in under Karie's ear. "Shoot him, Ollie."

"If I shoot him, that asshole," Fitch said, tilting his head at Jimmy, "will shoot me."

"All this is your fuck up, loser. He's not going to risk the fucking girl. Now shoot him."

Taka's arms faltered, the nose of his gun dropping.

"Do it," Susan shouted.

Andrea stood and squeezed her trigger, registering another man in harm's way too late. Her gun flashed, kicking back into her hands, report assaulting her ears, once, twice. The bullets tore through the apparition of a stocky state trooper and into Fitch's back. Fitch's gun flashed and boomed. Blood misted into the frigid air, dissipating along with the trooper. Andrea followed Fitch's forward stumble towards Taka with the muzzle of her gun. She fired again into the startled arch of his upper back, Jimmy's simultaneous shot an echo in her ringing ears.

Susan Pepper's scream seemed torn from her. Her knife clattered to the floor, drawing Andrea's attention even as Fitch fell. Susan's fingers scrabbled at her throat. Jimmy slid across the floor into Karie's chair on his knees, gun covering Susan's struggle. He grabbed the back of the chair with his other hand and scrambled up, hauling it and Karie past Andrea into the relative safety of the mudroom.

Susan flailed, hitting through a trooper's materializing shoulders, his head, before she began to sag, her knees folding. She dropped to the ground. The trooper—*Bruten*—followed her down, his fingers sinking into her throat as her lips turned blue.

Andrea tore her gaze away, looking for Taka.

Huddled to one side in the hall, he stared back at her from around the edge of the arched doorway. Wearing the yellow long sleeve and denim shorts she died in, albeit clean this time, Billie Mae appeared in mid-stride behind him, walking from the front door to stop right beside him. She tapped his shoulder. Taka frowned and turned his head to look directly at her. She lifted her tiny hands to pat both his cheeks and then kissed him on the nose. Slowly, he snaked an arm around her, his mouth dropping open to suck in more air as he did.

A little wild-eyed, he stood, lifting Billie Mae into his arms as she smiled at him. He kicked Fitch's gun away and then stepped over his sprawled body. Andrea set her gun down on the blood-spattered floor and met him in the middle of the kitchen. Billie Mae reached out for her and Andrea took her. Wrapping her arms around the warm, compact, little girl, she closed her eyes as Billie Mae hugged her in return. She buried her face in Billie Mae's unblemished neck, breathing in that indefinable baby girl scent and baby shampoo.

"Andrea," Jimmy said in a hushed tone, looking past her. His hands rested on Karie's shoulders where she still sat in the chair, holding a towel against her breast, the same shocked expression as Jimmy's on her face, her eyes wide and mouth open.

Andrea turned, Billie Mae pulling away to look as well. Bruten stood waiting, smiling. His uniform was spotless, B.L. Wilder emblazoned on the silver tag along his right chest pocket and his badges shiny and aligned on his left. He nodded and held out his hand. Andrea set Billie Mae on her feet.

Billie Mae smiled up at her and then went to Bruten, taking his hand. Bruten raised his brows at her and she laughed her bacon laugh and nodded. Digging into the left front pocket of her shorts, she withdrew her fist and held it up before opening her hand.

The decoder ring from the flat box in Susan Pepper's basement sat on it. "Stevie's," she said. She kissed it and then blew on it and the ring sparkled away.

"Thank you," Bruten said in the signature rumble Andrea recognized from his calls to her. His gaze shifted and he nodded at Jimmy.

They faded, leaving behind only the faint tinkle of Billie Mae's laugh. Andrea's reactionary gasp of a sob twisted into an uncontrollable giggle at the sound of it. Taka tugged her into his arms to tuck her against him. She didn't care that he was damp and stunk of sweat and urine and blood and smoke. She cried into his soot-stained shirt, while he whispered nonsense into her hair.

THE NEXT THREE hours were lost to a flurry of motion and questions by law enforcement and EMS personnel. The first officers on scene collected all the weapons involved and separated the four of them, while a fireman-paramedic monitored Susan Pepper until reinforcements arrived. Taka, Karie, and Susan were transported for medical care and both of CPDs CSIs were called in to lead teams through both Andrea's and Susan's houses. Bullets were dug out Andrea's cabinets, the drywall above her stove, the hallway door frame.

Someone came and told Andrea that the opaque box she'd described at Susan's had been located, as had the well-hidden back corner gate in the four-board fence line, and a box containing copies of Billie Mae's case files and her mother's trial documents. Andrea didn't offer up the remainders that Bruten had managed to hide and return to her. Eventually, Verny Fitch's body was tagged and bagged and removed. Carson showed up to drive Andrea to CPD and then the hospital, helping her negotiate the gaggle of reporters waiting everywhere to pounce.

After seeing an exhausted Taka settled in a private room just down the hall from Dewey, uniforms on both their doors, a nurse assistant helped Andrea find Karie in the ER to offer her a ride home through Carson, when he returned to get her. Karie's face lit up when she saw her, despite the bandage on her cheek and large bruise darkening her collarbone. She pulled at the edge of her hospital gown to show Andrea the nine stitches slanted across her left breast.

"I'm so sorry," Andrea offered.

"It'll heal," Karie said, waving her off. "I hope the camera's not broken. I've never..." Tears welled up in her eyes, triggering Andrea's own tears, a lump swelling in her throat. "I've never seen something... Never heard of—well, the stories of the hitchhiking ghosts or the White Lady maybe—"

Andrea laughed and squeezed Karie's hands. "Take a breath."

"She was there. She was actually there. Really there." She gripped Andrea's hand. "We can't tell anyone. No one. I'm certain now that Taka is your conduit."

"Conduit?" Andrea said, and took one hand back to wipe her cheeks.

"He, um, he's like an extra power source for you. The splashiest activity has happened when you're together or at least nearby. You go together, like milk and Oreos," she said, flashing a grin before she sobered again. "I'm just glad you weren't in the house when they came, your neighbor and her brother. Where were you?"

"At her house?" Andrea ventured.

"You broke into her house?"

"Kind of? Into her basement. I saw her at Foodland, with her brother, so I knew she wasn't home."

"What were you doing at—you tracked her on that app! Does Jimmy know?"

"No! Don't tell him if he asks."

Karie nodded with a thoughtful expression, her lips curving up to one side.

"I realized that if Fitch took Taka, maybe he was actually next door, so I went to check."

Karie's whole face opened in surprise. "Andrea!"

Already having been lectured by no less than five different officers despite refusing to say anything at all about her involvement in the scene except to Carson, Andrea pressed on. "Billie Mae was in the basement."

Karie nodded again, back to considering Andrea with regard. "Taka was on his way. He was closer to you and probably focused on you, too. That makes sense."

"I found a trophy case."

"Oh, shit."

"Yeah." Andrea's throat closed again. She held the tears at bay, her fist pressed to her mouth. When she could speak again, she said, "There were a lot of them. Carson said they'll dust it, try to figure out if it's Fitch's or Susan's."

Karie's eyes widened. "Stevie's decoder ring."

Andrea sniffed and nodded in agreement.

"God, I hope that camera didn't break," Karie said again.

"I hope it did since I killed a man."

Karie's hand tightened around hers. "I have a big mouth and a one track mind. I didn't mean... Are you okay with that?"

There were a lot things Andrea packed into her deep spot. Regrets, grief, helplessness. Guilt over Fitch's death wasn't one of them, so far. "I am." She tried to smile, but couldn't quite manage it, and used both hands to brush away the tears seeping onto her cheeks. "I don't want to see a replay, so I hope the camera's shattered, but yes, I killed a man before he could hurt my people. I'm okay with that."

CHAPTER FORTY

THE PIECES STARTED to fall together. The wire Taka reported seeing in the basement proved to be wickets. More were found among the flower beds, being used as hose guides to fill the koi pond. After presenting Susan Pepper and her surprised lawyer the partially completed forensics, her landlord and Dr. Huntley's statements about the dog, Taka's statement regarding the cell conversation he overheard, and proving her bite scar matched the dentition of the dog's skull, she admitted to her actions that led to the death of Billie Mae Robbins.

That's the way Ronnie Horton relayed it as he stood in Taka's hospital room two days later. Susan didn't confess, she admitted to her actions. She found Billie Mae playing with the hose she'd left running and the dog in the pond, chasing the fish. She also admitted to Adam Ward and Kayla Anderson's deaths, but only because that evidence was readily available once CPD knew where to start. The state police lab, backed up for months, would eventually try a new technique to collect DNA off the eleven remaining trophies Andrea had discovered.

The third day found them all cleared and Taka released from the hospital. In cahoots with Etta Robbin's defense lawyer, Jessica Hiller, Andrea met with Jason Cobb two days later. The Kanawha County Prosecutor was already working on Etta Robbins' release, but now questioning whether Billie Mae could have been saved with faster medical intervention. Andrea reported to Jessica, and then called Taka, cooped up in his condo, once she was out of Dunbar and out on Corridor G.

"They slept late and he was still there that morning," she said as she drove back to work. "They saw Billie Mae lying on the grass from the window upstairs and Jason carried her in while Etta called 911. Jason was devastated, in shock. They thought warming her up would help before they realized she was dead. Etta insisted he leave before anyone arrived and when he hesitated, hit him until he left. He said she was inconsolable, already blaming herself for not being downstairs, not taking care of her children. He was sure he'd lose everything, his wife, his job, so he left."

"He just left her to deal with it on her own?"

"She was just a fling," Andrea said, using Cobb's word for the affair. She was sure Taka shared her opinion on Jason Cobb's character, so she bit her tongue on that rant and continued her story. "After Etta confessed, he wanted to go in, tell the police what he knew, but his wife said she'd leave him if he did."

"Will he talk to Hiller now? And the Prosecutor's Office?"

"He's been divorced six years."

Silence met her words and she understood it, thinking again about the sheer amount of emotional pain Cobb could have saved Etta Robbins and her son by stepping forward sooner. After a moment, she moved on. "As an anonymous source, I'm feeding everything I've found on Susan Pepper, her brother, the possible related cases in other states, and everything we put together on Billie Mae to Jimmy. Some of it's going through Waltham-Young and some through that reporter, the one at Lake Vickers, who wanted to speak to you about Zach Taylor.

Jimmy knows her. She'll work with him. I'm still turning over rocks as my contacts get back to me."

"Okay." Still on suspension, Taka was laconic and grumpy. Taking an active interest in preserving their investment in him while they waited the grand jury out, CPD had already scheduled him with an appointed psychologist and informed him he would attend. If the pending charges against him were dismissed, and after the psychologist released him, he'd have to be re-certified by passing both a physical and a range test before he could be reinstated.

"Oh! Jimmy said to tell you the GPS trackers were registered to an email linked to one of Verny Fitch's old burner numbers."

"That's good."

Andrea waited to see if he'd say more, but he didn't. "Do you want me to pick you up after work? Dinner at Louie's?"

"No. I'm tired."

"I'll bring you dinner."

"No. Miss Betty filled my freezer."

Andrea drove around a stalled farm truck filled with bushels of apples. The views from the river road were glorious and bright and Andrea wished she'd taken Taka with her to see Jason Cobb. Even seeing him angry would be better than the silence. "Are you all right?"

Taka sighed. "I'm just tired."

Between the hospital waking him up every few hours and the flames when he did fall asleep, she didn't doubt that. "I love you, you know."

"I know. I love you too."

"I'll pick you up at two tomorrow for Tracy's funeral."

"Okay," he agreed.

"I'll call you later," she said before realizing he'd already disconnected. If she hadn't already taken so much time from Waltham, she'd drive straight over to check on him for real. Hoping he'd still change his mind and come stay at hers for a few days, she resigned herself to calling him again later.

THE KNOCK ON his door startled him. Taka wiped his face but didn't get up, hoping whoever it was would go away. Instead, a key scraped in the lock. His heart jumped with a wild hope that it was Andrea, although he'd made it clear he didn't want her coming over.

"Hey," Scotty said, poking his head around the door. "Taka?"

Taka lifted his hand to wipe his face again and Scotty saw the movement as he came on through the door. Taka waited for him to ask the obvious. Why are you on the floor? Why are you in the dark?

But he didn't. He watched Taka as he gently closed the door and locked the deadbolt. He toed his tennis shoes off and padded over without speaking, turning and lowering himself to sit down on the floor next to Taka, his back against the half wall below the kitchen counter.

Taka's eyes overflowed again. He closed them and laid his head on his folded arms, which rested on his drawn-up knees.

After a while Scotty moved his arm against Taka's side. Taka stiffened, but relaxed again when Scotty simply moved his hand to Taka's upper back. The warm solid weight of it felt good. Taka sighed and snuffled. He wiped his eyes and nose on his sleeve and then turned his head to look at Scotty.

"You're throwing that shirt in the hamper as soon as you get up," Scott muttered.

Taka laughed, a strangled sound.

"Heard you had a rough couple of days." He got up, reached over the counter and held a paper towel down in front of Taka's face. Taka took it. Unfolding, he stretched his legs out and blew his nose as Scott went into the kitchen. The cabinet door dropped closed and liquid filled a glass. Scott came back with a glass two fingers full of amber liquid. He handed it to Taka. "Jamison's."

Taka took a sip and winced, tipping his head back at the burn down his smoke-tender throat.

"You eat, yet?"

Taka shrugged.

Scott sighed and disappeared again.

He rattled around the kitchen. Taka took one slow sip after another as the aroma of onions and beef and cooked eggs filled the room. His stomach rumbled. Pushing himself up, he dragged himself over to lean against the kitchen frame and watch Scott's economic movements as he folded cheese into the scrambled eggs and then slid slices of pan-fried steak onto two plates. He set the pan aside, turned off all the burners, and then split the eggs onto the plates and set that pan beside the other. He slid the silverware drawer open and plucked out forks before holding out a plate to Taka.

Scott followed him into the living room with his own plate in one hand and a bottle of water and the Jamison's in the other. They sat down on Taka's shitty couch and put the plates on the coffee table. They sat shoulder to shoulder and ate in silence, the TV turned to an early afternoon talk show on mute. The sound of cars coming and going along the road drifted in, indistinguishable voices from the parking lot, someone was running a vacuum. Scott opened the water and handed it to him.

Taka looked askance at him, but drank half anyway. When he set it down, Scott handed him the re-filled glass of whisky. Taka smiled. "Trying to get me drunk again?"

"No, trying to get your shoulders to drop another two inches."

Taka rolled his shoulders and consciously dropped them, surprised at how tense he'd been holding them. They finished the steak and eggs. Scott pushed the water at him, while he refilled the whiskey glass and they passed it back and forth until it was empty again.

"Look, Taka . . ." Scott said.

Taka shook his head. "I'm going to shower." When he stood, Scott stood with him. They cleared the table together.

In the kitchen, Scott opened the dishwasher. "Go on, I'll clean up."

Taka chewed on his lip, thinking he should help, but not moving anyway.

"Go," Scot said.

Taka nodded and forced his feet to move him through the bedroom to the bath. He stepped in, closed the door, and stood there, staring at the black-and-white-striped curtain he'd bought one day with Andrea. After a minute he closed the toilet lid and sat down, trying not to think about the water hitting him in the face at the cabin, but failing. The comforting sounds from the kitchen stopped. Taka strained to hear Scott, but then jumped when Scott knocked on the bathroom door.

"Taka, are you getting in or what?" His hand landed on the door again, a gentle bump. Taka could picture him out there, one hand on the door, one on the knob. He should have locked the door. "Taka? I'm coming in."

Taka's tongue refused to move. He swallowed against the tightness of his throat. The draft of air from the opening door raised goosebumps on his arms.

"Taka?" Scott pursed his lips, assessing him with those damn sky-blue eyes that lightened and darkened with his moods. Those eyes made Taka want to hide.

"Shit," Scott said. He entered and brushed past Taka to lean over the tub and turn the water on. He started the shower running and rattled the curtain closed.

Taka cringed at the sounds, closing his eyes.

Scott's hands pulled at his shirt, until Taka lifted his arms and let Scott strip it from him.

"Up, c'mon," Scott said, his voice hoarse, his hand a warm pressure beneath Taka's elbow. Taka stood and let Scott unbutton his jeans and pull the zipper before he opened his eyes again when Scott stepped back.

He stripped, dropping his shirt on top of Taka's. He yanked his jeans open and pushed them down with his boxers, deftly stepping out of them and leaving them puddled on the shirts. "I got your back, Taka, c'mon." He slipped past the curtain and the sound of the water changed as it collided with his taut body.

Taka swallowed his fear and finished undressing.

THE BURR OF Scott's phone woke them late in the afternoon. Taka groped for it on the nightstand and soft tossed it at Scott's chest as he sat up, rubbing his eyes.

"Scotty." Scott inhaled sharply though his nose and threw the covers aside to get up. "Yeah. Yeah." He went into the bathroom, but left the door open as he tugged his jeans on, sans underwear. Of course he'd be that kind of guy, just like his girlfriends. Andrea always said Taka had a type and he was starting to agree with her. Scott nodded absently, holding his shirt in one hand, casting around for his socks. Taka got up and dug a fresh tee shirt out for him. "Be there in twenty. Yeah." He disconnected and stood staring at his phone.

"What's up?"

"Dewey's new head of security is dead. And Dewey's dad."

Everything in Taka stopped for just a second. "Senator Sanderson's dead?"

"Shot. Carjacking."

"Carjacking?"

"One of the Escalades."

My family is my business, Taka, Dewey had growled at him in Fivemile. "If Dewey's security was there, Dewey was, too," Taka said. Dewey had said, if you ever felt anything for me, let it go.

Scott snatched the shirt from Taka's hand. "Thanks," he said, pulling it over his head. "Guy got away. Dewey's fine. They're moving me onto the detail."

Taka shook his head. Scotty had been trying to move up in Dewey's organization since he'd started at the Coliseum. He figured tending bar was his in and now he'd been proven correct. But Taka wanted him out. Now. "You know you could do better than Dewey," he tried. "You could apply to the police academy."

Scott rolled his eyes. "I'm thirty-two, Taka, with an English degree, two unpublished books, and a spotty work history. They need me there early."

Taka couldn't think of anything to say. He couldn't exactly say, hey, I think maybe Dewey killed his Dad. He couldn't say, hey, I haven't fallen so hard for a guy since Dewey. He waved his hand towards the bedroom door. "Yeah. Go."

Stepping close, Scotty snagged the back of Taka's neck. "Look at me." When Taka reluctantly complied, he said, "This isn't a one-off. I'm not leaving you. And I'm not going to be as easy to ignore as Melinda."

Taka didn't know what he was feeling or what words Scott expected, so he just kissed him. Scott deepened it. When they broke, Taka whispered "Stay safe," and let him go.

CHAPTER FORTY-ONE

WHEN HIS CELL phone rang, Jimmy threw his pen down on the Sanderson timeline he'd drawn to plot convergences between the local, state, and federal investigations. "You heard," he answered.

"Yeah," Scott said. "Dewey's third called. I'm in if Maddox isn't pulling me."

"We got a ballistics match on Verny's gun for Taka, Smith, and Manners. We got tape on him near the Manners scene. MO and his sister puts him at the homicide-arsons the federal task force is investigating. She claims they were all hits Senator Sanderson ordered. That her brother confided his sins to her. She was giving up the senator in exchange for dismissal on the child murders and witness protection, but now he's dead. Even with the deal off the table and under threat of the death penalty, she's not willing to cross Dewey. Claims he's clean as far as she knows."

"Nothing on ballistics for either Dewey or the senator from the federal cases?" His breath was harsher in the phone and Jimmy could hear the pounding of his feet, like he was charging down a set of stairs.

"No." But that was just checking against known weapons from casings collected at the range on surveillance. And the ballistics of any particular gun changed over time or could be easily altered. "It's a long shot, but you get a chance, expand our inventory of known weapons and spent casings."

"Every shooter has a favorite gun," Scott said, quoting Jimmy himself. "How'd Verny end up here?"

"According to Susan Pepper, the senator passed him to Dewey for a specific job and then backed Dewey up when he fired Verny for doing it. She also said Verny deserved what he got." Jimmy had watched hours of tape on the woman. She was a real psychopath, but nobody would catch him saying that out loud. He wanted her so deep in the system that she'd be one of those forgotten prisoners lost in solitary, accidentally starved to death, and then buried in an unmarked grave to hide the mistake.

"Shit. He overdosed Zach Taylor on purpose."

"Probably. But it wasn't supposed to get messy or go public, let alone involve law enforcement."

A door slammed shut. Scotty wasn't at the Coliseum yet. And he didn't have stairs at his place.

And an engine started as Scott said, "You still think Dewey's involved somehow in the homicide-arsons."

Life undercover became an open book at trial. Jimmy wondered if Scotty really thought the team wasn't monitoring his whereabouts.

"Jim?"

Jimmy shook himself. He needed the downtime he had just planned with Andrea tonight to keep him from stewing in his own juices. His unit would be heels over asses once the Feds pulled them in on the assassination. Susan Pepper was scary. Dewey Sanderson was just irritating by comparison. And maybe guilty of patricide. "He's guilty of something, I know that. Maddox wants you as deep as you can manage. Does Taka know you're with us?"

Only the hollow rush of background noise came back to him as Scott drove without speaking.

"Does. He. Know." Jimmy repeated.

Scott cleared his throat. "No."

"You don't have to change anything, not right now, Scott. We know Taka didn't come up on the radar until after the shooting and you were already involved. Taka and Dewey have history, that might help us. But..." He wiped his hand over his face, knowing that getting involved with Andrea meant he'd be closer to Taka as well. "Keep lying to him. Got it? He can't know you're with us."

"Yeah. Got it."

TAKA TURNED ON CNN and stood reading the ticker at the bottom of the screen until the anchor worked her way back to the story on Senator Sanderson's assassination. He listened for the first ten minutes, watched the replay of the traffic cam that caught the carjacking, and then turned it off. He'd never known the man except in passing, but he knew Dewey was a devoted son. Had been a devoted son, maybe up until the moment Verny opened his mouth in Fivemile. And if Dewey had drawn the wrong conclusion? If his Dad hadn't ordered Verny to see Zach Taylor dead? What could Taka say to anybody? It was a conversation he overheard under duress and maybe he was wrong, himself.

He kicked around his apartment. He cleaned the bathroom and then picked up the living room. Put the clean dishes away and wiped down the kitchen counter and stovetop. For good measure, he cleaned the refrigerator doors and, after glancing over at the thin layer of grime coating it, the stove hood. He took the trash down to the disposal chute in the hall. Stood in the middle of his silent, empty condo, realizing the couple of reporters still stalking him would be gone, and decided dinner at Louie's sounded good after all. He sat down and texted Andrea. *Dewey's dad is dead.*

I know.

I don't want to be here. Still up for Louies?

Yes. Reservation at 7. Should I get you?

No. CU there. He debated showering again. Just the thought of the water running sent a shuddering chill down his spine. Taka forced his thoughts away from that and stalked into his bedroom. Instead of dwelling, he salved his wrists and re-bandaged his arm before dressing in his most comfortable worn jeans, a red polo, and his old leather jacket. His arms remained sore and his head hurt a little, but other than that he couldn't complain.

His enthusiasm for leaving the dark quiet of his own cave waned as he drove through town. The streetlights were too bright and the oncoming traffic blinding. At just past rush hour, deciding which route made the most efficient path to Louie's door in downtown involved more thought than Taka cared to make. He was already exhausted and losing his appetite when he finally parked.

His phone chimed while he sat debating with himself over whether or not to just go home. *Saving you a seat at the bar. Louie's doing steak au poive just for you. Jimmy's here, too.*

Just great. Taka sighed. He'd wanted Andrea to himself tonight. But with Scott's scent and calloused touch still riding his skin, he needed to suck it up and go in anyway. Andrea had supported all his relationships despite whatever lay unexplored between them and he'd be damned if he didn't do the same.

WONDERING IF TAKA had received her text, Andrea glanced past Jimmy, searching the crowded sidewalk outside Louie's once more. Jimmy laid his hand on hers. "He'll come if he comes. It's a hard thing he's been through."

"I know. Does he know Ms. Pepper confirmed her brother killed Bruten?"

"I told him before he left the hospital."

"I still can't believe they were both murderers. I can't believe she killed kids."

Jimmy looked around and then lowered his voice. "We think she was, at the very least, her brother's brains on the executions he committed. We're searching her financials to match travel dates with child homicides and this afternoon my team found an offshore account in her name. Now we need to find out where the money came from." Off her speculative look, he added, "Don't. We'll do it. Save your hackers for that fabric sample you can't find."

She rolled her eyes. "My little old historian called me back today and hooked me up. The Berrylane project has been saved by a diligent North Carolina preservationist with a scanner. I've already sicced the Waltham textiles team on making me an exact replica of the drapes."

He held up a fist and she bumped it.

"You found it?" Taka said from beside her.

She jumped and sat up, not realizing until then how closely she and Jimmy were huddled together as they talked. Taka's gaze fell onto Jimmy's hand over hers on the bar. Self-conscious, she stood up and hugged him. He hugged her back, his initial stiffness giving way to his usual all-encompassing bear hug as he relaxed.

"Good to see you, Taka," Louie boomed. Taka reached out and shook his hand. Andrea gave him one more squeeze and settled back onto her stool. "Merlot?"

"Steak au poive?"

Louie smiled. "Just for you."

The world shifted a bit back towards normal when Taka grinned at Louie. "It smells divine in here and Merlot would be perfect."

"Detective," Jimmy said.

"Lieutenant," Taka responded.

"Sit down, Taka," Andrea demanded.

"So you found what you needed for the project?"

"I did. I also recommended they use croquet wickets for hose guides in the garden because apparently that's been done way longer than I ever imagined."

Taka frowned at her,

"Seriously?" Jimmy said. "You googled history of hose guides or something after finding out your murdering neighbor used them?"

Andrea shrugged. "Every negative has a positive, according to Grace Speare, by way of a lot of other writers and philosophers."

Taka leaned closer to Andrea to address Jimmy directly. "If you're going to be dating her, you should read Speare's *Everything Talks To Me*. Believe me, that's Andrea in a nutshell."

"Are we dating?" Jimmy asked Andrea.

She shrugged, glancing over at Taka, who just quirked his lips up in a non-committal manner. Her throat closed, deep down at the base, but she liked Jimmy. And she'd told Taka she wouldn't wait on him.

Louie reappeared and set Taka's glass of wine down. Taka nodded his thanks and reached for it as something small fell straight down from above. It hit the bar and bounced. The restaurant's lights glinted off it in bright pinpricks of brilliance as it spun off into Andrea's lap, where she caught it in both hands, her skin burning.

"Ow," she exclaimed, dumping it back onto the bar between Taka and herself.

Steam rose from the twisted silver ring. Andrea looked up, but there was nothing to see on the unmarred, decorative tin ceiling tile. The nearby ceiling fan continued turning as always. The other diners at the bar seemed not to have noticed anything unusual and the usual hub-bub continued unabated just above the music playing in the background.

Jimmy and Taka exchanged a look past her. Jimmy lifted his brows in challenge.

"I'm not picking it up," Andrea said, although she was almost certain that look meant something about her, not the ring.

Taka took a ballpoint from his jacket's inside pocket and hooked the ring, flipping it over to see the other side before he lifted it.

"It's made from horseshoe nails," Andrea breathed.

Louie held his hand out. After a second's hesitation, Taka dumped the ring into his palm. After rotating it, Louie looked closely at the surface. His mouth opened, but he didn't say anything. He examined the ceiling. Andrea tilted her own head back again, but still couldn't see where it might have fallen from.

"There hot water pipes or ducts or anything like that up there? Anything that could heat metal that hot?" Jimmy asked.

Louie shook his head. "No, sir," he said. "No, sir." He turned his back on them and retrieved his great-grandfather's hunting whip from the wall. Andrea glanced at Taka as he watched Louie come back with it, hearing the whip's crack once again in her head. Louie stared at the base of the handle where there was a lighter strip of leather. "It's gone," he said.

Andrea leaned forward, anticipation swirling in her chest. "What's gone?"

"My great-grandfather's ring. It was his father's ring, which his own father had made for him." He held the shiny silver ring up. "This is it. I don't know how..." He looked up again, scanning the tin tiles. "But this is it. It has his maker's mark on it."

Andrea glanced at Taka.

"No, no, no," Taka said, shaking his head.

A young man with a food-stained apron folded over and tied at his waist pushed through the swinging kitchen doors and came to stand next to Louie. Early twenties, square jaw, dark eyes lively in his expressive face, his hair shaved close to his head. Andrea looked to Louie, her brows raised, but he didn't acknowledge the man who could be his son, they shared so much resemblance.

"I think someone has a question for you," Andrea said, tipping her chin at the employee.

Louie looked towards the kitchen and frowned. "Who?"

"Tell him Aaron needs to clear a few things up," the young man said.

Her blood already rising to the challenge, Andrea couldn't stop herself from grinning. "He says his name is Aaron."

ELLE ANDREWS PATT

Elle Andrews Patt received an Honorable Mention from Writers of The Future for **Prelude To A Murder Conviction**. She has won multiple Royal Palm Literary Awards for Published Short Fiction, Novella, and Unpublished Novel from the Florida Writers Association since her first win in 2013. She was invited to join the Alvarium Experiment during its 2014 inception and has published award-winning **Manteo, Someday Loyal,** and **Regarding Mr. Bulkington**, as well as Prometheus Saga 2 western, **Remuda,** with them. Her work has appeared in online magazines such as *Saw Palm*, *The Rag,* and *DarkFuse* as well as several anthologies. She is represented by the Donald Maass Literary Agency.

Elle writes literary and speculative fiction, mucks stalls, and works as a freelance digital marketer. In the past, she has made her living as a vet tech, pizza maker, and horse breeding farm manager among many other ventures. She currently lives with her family in Tennessee

Visit Elle at **www.elleandrewspatt.com** to read award-winning **"Becky's Story"** for free and for links to her other work and publishing news.

Facebook: @ElleAndrewsPattFiction

Twitter: @LAndrewsPatt

Instagram: elleandrewspatt

Made in the USA
San Bernardino, CA
03 May 2020